Praise for Lois Richer
and her novels

"Small town flavor...add(s) spice to the
fun in this heartwarming love story."
—*Romantic Times BOOKreviews* on
Faithfully Yours

"Three elderly ladies provide a charming
bit of comic relief in this lively,
entertaining conclusion to Lois Richer's
FAITH, HOPE & CHARITY trio."
—*Romantic Times BOOKreviews* on
Sweet Charity

LOIS RICHER

Faithfully Yours

Sweet Charity

Steeple
Hill®

Published by Steeple Hill Books™

STEEPLE HILL BOOKS

Steeple
Hill®

ISBN-13: 978-0-373-65272-3
ISBN-10:   0-373-65272-0

FAITHFULLY YOURS AND SWEET CHARITY

FAITHFULLY YOURS
Copyright © 1997 by Lois M. Richer

SWEET CHARITY
Copyright © 1998 by Lois M. Richer

Printed in U.S.A.

CONTENTS

Books by Lois Richer

Love Inspired

Love Inspired Suspense

  *Faith, Hope & Charity
**Brides of the Seasons
  ‡If Wishes Were Weddings
  †Blessings in Disguise
††Finders, Inc.

LOIS RICHER

Sneaking a flashlight under the blankets, hiding in a thicket of Caragana bushes where no one could see, pushing books into socks to take to camp—those are just some of the things Lois Richer freely admits to in her pursuit of the written word.

"I'm a book-aholic. I can't do without stories," she confesses. "It's always been that way."

FAITHFULLY YOURS

But the Lord said unto Samuel, Look not on his countenance, or on the height of his stature; because I have refused him: for *the Lord seeth* not as man seeth; for man looketh on the outward appearance, but the Lord looketh on the heart.

—*1 Samuel* 16:7

To my husband, Barry, on our fifteenth wedding anniversary, with much love and appreciation for your unwavering support.

Chapter One

"That man will turn my hair gray," Gillian Langford sputtered, twisting the emerald engagement band around the ring finger on her right hand in frustration.

"Not yet, I hope," Mary Teale teased, her eyes flashing. "This is only your third year teaching—your first at JFK Elementary."

"And it may be my last in the fair town of Mossbank, North Dakota," Gillian retorted. "I'm not kidding! Mr. Nivens is so strict, I've forgotten half of the six thousand rules he's made in the past five weeks." There was a sudden silence in the staff room, and Gillian turned around in her chair to see why, her heart sinking as she did.

"That fact is very evident, Miss Langford." Her nemesis stood behind her, his face hardened into the usual stern lines. "I would like to speak to you privately, please. In my office."

"Now?" Gillian heard the squeak of surprise in her voice and wished she had been able to control it. He didn't need to know how badly her feet were aching.

"If you please?"

She forced herself to follow his tall form and noted the

short, precise cut of his hair above his stiff white shirt collar. Jeremy Nivens was at all times perfectly groomed with never a hair out of place or a spot on his tie. Gillian hated that. She felt like a grubby child when she stood next to all that neatness.

"Be seated, Miss Langford." He sat stiffly behind his massive desk, his back ramrod straight, arms resting on the desktop. "I wanted to discuss this afternoon's unfortunate incident with you."

Gillian frowned. What in the world was old Jerry talking about now, she fumed, and then corrected herself for using the term bestowed on him by the other teachers. Actually, Jeremy Nivens wasn't all that old, her aunt Hope had assured her. But you couldn't tell it from his unyielding demeanor.

Gillian had noticed other aspects about him, too. He was certainly good-looking with that tall, lean, wide-shouldered body under a perfectly tailored suit. He had the long, straight, haughty nose of an aristocrat with the same high cheekbones and patrician features.

As she stared across at him, Gillian almost grinned. This situation reminded her of her own schooldays and the times she had been reprimanded by the principal. Only this time it was more serious; her job was at stake. Mr. Nivens's chilly blue-gray gaze was focused directly on her. Again.

"I'm sorry, I don't quite follow," she said softly, rubbing her shoeless foot against the carpet on his office floor. "Did something unusual happen today?"

"I'm speaking about that disgraceful display on the playground this afternoon." His icy stare wiped the smile off her face. "My science students were totally unable to concentrate on their work, with you and your students racing about, shrieking like wild animals."

"It was phys ed," she told him shortly. "They're supposed to run around. Goodness knows, they needed a breath of fresh air after the stuffiness of this school.'' She had referred to the current heat wave, but it was obvious from the grim tightening of his face that the principal had taken her reference personally.

"Rules and regulations do not make a school stuffy, Miss Langford. They make it an orderly place where children can learn more easily.'' As he spoke, Mr. Nivens flicked a speck of dust off his gleaming oak desk and straightened the already-neat sheaf of papers on top into a military-precise line. ''Which is why the children can't run in the hall, use profanity or chew gum on the school premises. If everyone follows the rules and conforms to what's expected of them, the school year will progress smoothly. For all of us.''

His eyes narrowed. ''Which is why I suggest you get rid of the blue and yellow chalk and use the *regulation* white in your classroom. Colors are only to be used for special occasions. Now, about your, er, outfit.''

Gillian glanced down at herself worriedly. So far in one month's teaching at JFK a button on her blouse had come undone in his presence, he'd reprimanded her for wearing sandals and not wearing hose in the classroom, and he'd given her a lecture on the advisability of keeping her hair tied back, after one of her students had inadvertently caught his watch in it. What now?

''My suit?'' Gillian stared down at herself.

She'd chosen her current outfit partially because of the dull brown color that couldn't be easily marked, and partly because it had a lack of buttons, zippers or other fasteners. And she definitely had panty hose on, Gillian grimaced. She'd been sweltering in them all afternoon. His glare was frigid and she bristled under the indignity of it all.

''What's the matter with my clothes this time, Mr. Nivens?'' she demanded, a blaze of indignation lighting up her clear green eyes. All her life her parents had told her to make allowances for people who had beliefs different from her own, but Gillian figured she'd given Jeremy Nivens about as much room as he was going to get.

"Well," he began solemnly, folding his fingers tepee style on top of the desk. Gillian caught a faint tinge of pink on his cheekbones. "I'm sure it's a wonderful suit for some things but it does not, er, lend itself to gymnastics." His eyes followed the smooth, fitted lines of the knit cotton as it hugged her well-shaped form and emphasized her obvious assets. "Your skirt, for instance. It's far too short."

"It's below my knees," she sputtered angrily.

"Perhaps. But when you bend over to get the ball, it has certain, er, disadvantages. Both front and back." Jeremy averted his eyes from her angry, red face. "And I can hardly imagine those shoes are meant for football."

It was the last straw in a long, tiring day and Gillian felt her usual calm demeanor explode. She bent over and retrieved her shoes, barely noticing the way her neckline gaped slightly in the front. She stood, thrusting her long curls behind her ears, and glared at the man behind the desk.

"Why you rude, obnoxious man! I wore these stupid heels because you said we had to be dressed in a businesslike fashion at all times. And I bought this suit because thus far in my employment there has not been one item of my clothing in my wardrobe that you deem suitable for the business of teaching. Well, tough!" Gillian practically bellowed the word.

"From now on I wear what I want, when I want, the way I want. If you have some complaint, I'll be pleased to take it up with the Human Rights people. Your only business is with my job, and I do that very well."

"Miss Langford, if you would kindly be seated…"

"No, I won't. I've tried to go along with your silly little regulations and your unceasing demands for weeks now. I've taught in other schools and never had anyone question my taste in clothes. And I'm not taking it from you anymore. You're making my life miserable, and you're doing it on purpose. You think I'll quit, don't you?'' She stared at him as the thought dawned. ''You think that if you keep at me, I'll give up and leave. We'll, I'm not going,'' she told him firmly.

''Miss Langford, I am not trying to force your resignation. I merely wanted to advise you that the entire grade-six class was ogling your, er, posterior this afternoon!''

Jeremy Nivens's generally unmoving face was full of fury. His dark eyebrows drew together as he glared down at her, mouth pursed in a straight, disapproving line. He had surged to his feet and now stood towering over her, even though Gillian stood five feet eight inches in her stocking feet.

''I was trying to spare you some embarrassment,'' he offered a moment later, in his normal hard tones.

''You know what? Don't bother! From now on I'm going to wear exactly what I've always worn to teach my classes. I'm sorry you don't approve of slacks but I like them. And shorts. And jeans. And when the occasion demands, I will wear them.''

''Business attire is the only appropriate apparel in this school,'' he began his lecture again. Gillian walked to the door in her stocking feet and pulled it open, ignoring the icy coolness of his words.

''I work with twenty-eight first-graders. I have to be comfortable, to be able to get down on their level when I need to. I certainly don't need to dress up for some high-powered, executive-type office. If you want to institute a school uniform, fine. But until then, don't try to force me to conform to your strictures.'' Her green eyes glittered with frustration as she thrust the last stab home.

''You know, Mr. Nivens, you could have closed the blinds if the view was so disturbing,'' Gillian told him savagely. She tossed him one more angry glance over her shoulder and then strode from the office, high heels dangling from one finger as she left the school, muttering dire epithets all the way home. As she walked, she reviewed her stormy relationship with Jeremy Nivens.

"Of all the nerve," she grumbled. "For two cents I'd go back to Boston and St. Anne's without a qualm."

But she knew it was all talk. She couldn't go back; not now. Since Michael's death she hadn't been able to face living alone in the city, remembering their special haunts, driving past the places they'd gone together, attending the same church they'd attended together and where they had planned to say their vows. The pain of his death was too new, too fresh there. She'd had to get away, and Aunt Hope had been the answer to her prayers. In a lot of ways.

"Hello, dear. Did you have a nice day at school?"

Gillian had been so preoccupied with herself she hadn't noticed the slim woman busily raking leaves on the front lawn. She studied her tall, blond aunt curiously, noting her ageless, blue eyes that still sparkled and the lean, athletic build Hope worked so hard to retain.

"Nice," she griped angrily. "No, it was rotten. That Carruthers child is a klutz. She spilled the glue all over me. Again. And the Stephens's youngest son is deaf—I'm sure of it." Gillian flopped down on the top step with disgust. "If that weren't enough, that contemptible man nattered at me about my clothes again—said I shouldn't wear these shoes for phys ed. Imbecile! As if I didn't know that."

"Well then, dear, why *did* you wear them?" Hope's voice was quietly curious.

"Because he's ordered us to wear business dress at all times," Gillian bellowed and then grinned wryly. "Sorry, Auntie. I'm taking it out on you, and it's not your fault. But don't worry. I told him that from now on I'll wear what I blasted well please." She spread her arms wide and stared up at the bright sun. "You'd think I looked like a bag lady or something, the way he talks to me."

Her aunt smiled thoughtfully as she stared at the tattered shreds of her niece's panty hose. "Well, those stockings would certainly qualify, my dear." She chuckled.

"Don't you start now," Gillian ordered. "I've had enough for one day. Petty little man." She glared at the cement walkway as if it was to blame for her problems.

"My dear, there are bound to be adjustments with a new principal. You may just have to bite your tongue and accept the changes. Not all change is bad, you know. The possibilities that are ahead of you are endless. Open your eyes."

"I don't want to. They're too tired." Gillian faked a snore. "Thank heavens it's Friday. I intend to relax tonight." She sprang to her feet and leaped up the three stairs. Gillian was almost through the door before she remembered her manners and turned back. "Is that OK with you, Hope, or have you something special planned?"

Her aunt swept the rest of the crackling red and gold leaves into the huge black bag and neatly tied the top. Gillian noticed that her aunt's pale aquamarine pantsuit was as pristine as it had been this morning; her shiny blond hair swaying gently in its neat bob as she lifted the bag and deposited it at the curb.

"Gillian," her aunt chided her softly. "You don't have to keep asking me that. I want this to be your home, too. Please don't feel pressured to involve yourself in my activities. Feel free to go out with people your own age, dear."

"Then you are going out," Gillian muttered, dropping her shoes in the hall and curling comfortably on her aunt's pale floral sofa. "What has bustling Mossbank scheduled for the inmates tonight?"

Hope favored her with a look that spoke volumes about her niece's attitude, but she answered, anyway.

"The church has a fowl supper on tonight. I offered to help in the kitchen." As she spoke, she lifted a huge roaster from the oven. Immediately the house was filled with the succulent aroma of roasting bird and tangy sage dressing.

"I always thought it was a 'fall' supper. Doesn't matter, I'm starved," Gillian breathed, closing her eyes. "Maybe I should go with you. I could help wash up afterward. Who all goes?"

"Almost everyone," her aunt chuckled. "It's an annual event. If I were you I'd get there early." Her astute eyes watched as Gillian twisted the glowing band around her finger. "Please don't think I'm trying to boss you or anything, dear."

Gillian felt her body tighten at the sad but serious look in her aunt's eyes.

"You know you can say anything to me, Hope. I won't mind." Gillian examined her aunt's serious countenance. "What is it?"

"Don't you think it's time to put Michael's ring away, Gilly? He's gone and he's not coming back," she said in a soft but firm tone. "You have to move on."

"I'm not sure I can." Gillian stared at the floor, her mind flooded with memories. "We would have been married by now," she whispered, tears welling in her eyes.

"Oh, darling." Her aunt rushed over and hugged her. "I'm so sorry. I know it hurts. But, dear—" she brushed Gillian's burnished curls off her forehead and pressed a kiss there "—Michael loved life. He wanted to experience everything. Now that he's with God, I don't think he would want you to stop living. There are marvelous things in store for you. You have to accept the changes and move on...go out and find what God has planned specially for you."

"I already know my future," Gillian whispered at last, pressing herself away and straightening the hated brown suit.

"I'm going to teach, Auntie. I'm going to focus my energies on my students and their needs." She smiled sadly at her aunt's worried look. "You and I have a lot in common, you know. We've both lost the men we loved—you in the Viet Nam war and me because of some stupid drunk driver.

"I'm sure I couldn't do better than follow your example. Teaching will be enough for me. It has to be." Gillian choked back a sob and smiled brightly.

"Sweetheart," her aunt began slowly. "Don't use me as a role model for your life." Her eyes were shadowed, and Gillian saw her aunt's face grow sad. "I have had opportunities to marry that I sometimes wish I had taken." She shook her blond head and focused on her niece. "Be very sure of what you ask out of life. You may just get it."

"Right now," Gillian said, grimacing. "I'd settle for Mr. Jeremy Nivens moving to another country. At the very least, another school." She made a face. When Hope chuckled, Gillian jumped up and plucked at the repulsive brown fabric disparagingly. "I'll just go change and we can go to the fall or *'fowl'* supper."

Which was probably how she ended up pouring tea for Jeremy Nivens that evening, she decided later.

"Miss Langford," he murmured, his gray-blue eyes measuring her in the red-checked shirt she wore tucked into her denim skirt. "You look very, er, country tonight."

Gillian knew he was staring at the spot of gravy on her shirt, and she would have liked to tell him how it got there, but instead, she swallowed her acid reply with difficulty. After all, this was the church.

"It's comfortable," she told him shortly. "Do you take cream or sugar?" She held out the tray, knowing perfectly well that he took neither. When he waved it away she turned to leave.

"The meal was excellent." His voice was a low murmur

that she barely caught. "Is there anything I can do to help out? As a member here, I'd like to do my bit."

"I didn't know you went to this church," Gillian blurted out, staring at him aghast. School was bad enough. A person should have the sanctity of their church respected, she fumed.

"It is somewhat less formal than the English one I've attended for years, but I find it compatible with my beliefs. Besides, my great-aunt goes here." He nodded his head at a woman Gillian identified as Faith Rempel.

Although Gillian certainly knew of Faith from her aunt's vivid description of one of the two ladies she called her dearest friends, she herself had never actually met the woman formally.

"Oh, yes," she murmured. "Mrs. Rempel. She's *your* aunt?" It was strange to think of such a happy-looking woman as the old grouch's relation. Gillian watched in interest as a grin creased the principal's stern countenance.

"Apparently my aunt, your aunt and another lady have been great pals for years. I believe the other lady is Mrs. Flowerday. They seem to get along quite well. It must be nice having friends you've known for a long time." His voice was full of something—yearning?

Gillian stared at him. He'd sounded wistful, just for a moment. "It must? Why?"

"Oh, I suppose because they make allowances for you, afford you a few shortcomings." He smiled softly, glancing across at his aunt once more.

"Why, Mr. Nivens," Gillian sputtered, staring at him in shock. "I didn't know you had any."

He looked startled at that; sort of stunned that she would dare to tease him. A faint red crept up his neck, past the stiff collar, to suffuse his cheeks.

"There are those," he muttered snidely, glaring at her, "who say that I have more than my fair share."

It was Gillian's turn to blush, and she did, but thankfully the effect was lost in Pastor Dave's loud cheerful voice. "Just the two folks I was most hoping to corral at this shindig."

Gillian winced at the stomp of the cowboy boots that missed her bare toes by a scant inch and the thick beefy arm that swung round her shoulder. Pastor Dave was a cowboy wannabe and he strove constantly to perfect his image as a long, tall Texan, even when he remained a short, tubby Dakota preacher.

"What can we do to help you out, Pastor?" Gillian queried in a falsely bright voice. "Another piece of pumpkin pie or a fresh cup of coffee?"

"No sirree, Bob. I've eaten a hog's share tonight." The short man chuckled appreciatively, patting his basketball stomach happily. "No, I was hoping you and your friend here would consent to helpin' a busy preacher out with the youth group."

"I'm afraid I haven't had much opportunity to work with young people," she heard Jeremy Nivens begin nervously. "And with the Sunday school class you've given me, I'm not sure I'll have enough free time for anything else."

Gillian peered around Dave's barrel chest to stare at her boss's shaking head.

"I'm afraid I'm in the same boat, Pastor," she murmured, thankful that she wouldn't have to work with old, stuffed-shirt Nivens. Their contact at school was quite enough for her. She didn't need more proximity to know that the two of them would never work well together, especially not in the loose, unrestricted world of teenagers.

"Nonsense," Pastor Dave chortled. "Why, you folks just being here tonight is a good sign that you have Friday evenings free. And I know the young folk would appreciate having you whippersnappers direct their meetin's more than they would old Brother Dave." He whacked Jeremy on the back and patted Gillian's shoulder kindly before moving away. "I'll be calling y'all about an organizational meeting next week," he said, grinning happily. "See ya there."

Gillian stared aghast at the tall, lean man in front of her. It couldn't be. No way. She wasn't going to be conned into this. Not with General Jeremy Nivens.

"I don't think that man listens to what anyone says," Mr. Nivens muttered in frustration. "He bulldozed me into taking the Sunday school boys class, but I can't take on a bunch of hormone-crazy teens, too."

"Well, you don't have to act as if they're juvenile delinquents or something," Gillian said, bristling indignantly. "They're just kids who don't have a whole lot to amuse themselves with in a town this size."

"Hah!" He glared at her, his gray eyes sparkling. "They should be able to make their own fun. Why, these children have every advantage—a lovely countryside, acres of land and rivers and hills. They should be happy to be free of the inner-city ghettos that lots of children are enduring where they don't get enough to eat and—"

"Please," Gillian muttered, holding up one hand. "Spare me the sermon. It sounds just like something my grannie used to say." She shifted to one side as the family behind her moved away from the table, children gaily jumping from bench to bench.

"'When I was a child,'" she said in a scratchy voice meant to copy her grandmother's thready tones. "'We never had the advantages you young things have today. Why I walked three miles to and from school every single day, even when it was forty-below. In bare feet. Without a coat.'"

Mr. Nivens's eyebrows shot up almost to his hairline as he listened to her. When at last he moved, it was to brush off the crumbs from his pant leg and remove a blob of cream

Gillian had slopped on the toe of his shoe when Pastor Dave had grabbed her.

"You're being ridiculous," he murmured, stepping around her carefully. "No one could walk through forty-below without shoes or a coat and survive." He started up the basement stairs after tossing one frowning look at her bright curling tendrils of hair where they lay loose against her neck.

Gillian snapped the tray down on the table and motioned to the folk holding out their cups.

"Help yourself," she advised, with a frown on her face. "I've got something to say to Mr. Nivens."

"Go for it, Missy," Ned Brown advised, grinning like a Cheshire Cat. "That feller needs a bit of loosenin' up. Seems to me you're just the girl to do it."

As she raced up the stairs, Gillian decided Ned was right. She had a whole year of Mr. Jeremy Nivens to get through. She might as well start off as she meant to go on.

He was striding across the parking lot when she emerged—huge, measured strides that made her race to catch up. Fortunately, she wore her most comfortable sandals and could easily run to catch up.

"Just a minute, Mr. Nivens," she called breathlessly. "I have something I want to say."

He stopped and turned to stare at her, the wind ruffling his dark brown hair out of its usual orderly state. One lock of mussed hair tumbled down across his straight forehead, making him seem more human, more approachable, Gillian decided.

"I was making a joke," she said finally, aware that his searching gray-blue eyes had noted her flushed face and untucked shirt. "It was supposed to be funny."

"Oh." He continued to peer at her through the gloom, and Gillian moistened her lips. It was the kind of stare that made her nervous, and she shifted from one foot to the other uneasily. "Was that everything, Miss Langford?"

"My name is Gillian," she told him shortly, frustrated by the cool, distant frigidity his arrogant demeanor projected. "Or Gilly if you prefer."

"It sounds like a name for a little girl," he told her solemnly, his dour look suggesting that she take the information to heart. "At any rate, I barely know you. We are co-workers in a strictly professional capacity. I hardly think we should be on a first-name basis."

"Look, *Mr.* Nivens," she exhorted. "I'm trying to be friendly. That's the way people in Mossbank are, friendly and on a first-name basis. No one at school uses titles except in front of the children." She drew a breath of cool, evening air and counted to ten. "If you don't want to help with the youth group, fine. But don't pretend it's because they're too uncivilized for you to be around." Her eyes moved over his three-piece suit with derision.

"I doubt you and they would have anything in common, anyway," she muttered. "You're far too old for them."

His stern, rigid face cracked a mirthless smile.

"Not so old," he said sternly. "I was a teenager once, also, Miss Langford."

"Really?" Gillian stared at him disbelievingly.

"I'm sure of it." His eyes sparkled at some inner joke as he watched her.

"Well, anyway—" she shrugged "—if you don't want to work with them, just say so."

"I thought I had," he murmured so softly she barely caught the words. He studied her face. "Are you going to fall in with Pastor Dave's suggestions?" he demanded.

"I think I might," she mused, deliberately ignoring that inner voice that quietly but firmly whispered *NO*. "They really need some direction, and there doesn't seem to be anyone else.'' All around them the rustle of wind through the drying leaves and the giggles of children romping in the playground carried in the night air. The musky odor of cranberries decaying in the nearby woods wafted pungently toward them on a light breeze.

"But you're not that much younger than I am," he objected.

"In some ways," she said through gritted teeth. "You and I are light-years apart."

"I suppose that's true," he admitted at last. He turned to leave. "Good night, Miss Lang— Gillian."

As he walked away into the dusky night, Gillian stood with her mouth hanging open. For the first time in over a month, he'd called her by her first name. How strange! Perhaps the man really wasn't as stuffy as she'd thought. Maybe, just maybe, he'd unbend with time.

Then she frowned.

He hadn't outright refused to attend the organizational meeting, had he? Did that mean he intended to show up and offer his staid opinions?

"No way," she muttered angrily. "I don't care how much they need helpers. Mr. Jeremy Nivens is not going to work in the youth group, not if I have anything to say about it."

As she turned to go back inside, Gillian tried to ignore the sight of Jeremy almost lost in the shadows up ahead, children racing along beside him, chattering eagerly as he ignored them.

She had not misread the situation. He wasn't the youth leader type. Not at all.

Was he?

Chapter Two

"Why are there two whole shelves of dog food and only one teensy section with tea?" Charity Flowerday muttered, as she hobbled up and down the aisles of Mossbank's largest grocery store, searching for the ingredients she needed for lunch with her friends. Although why she should have to search for anything was a mystery. She'd lived in this small farming community for almost seventy years. She should know where every single item was kept, she chuckled to herself.

"Ah, tea." She ran her finger along the shelf and plucked a package into her cart. "Now, dessert."

It was impossible to ignore the young tow-headed boy in the junk-food aisle across from frozen foods. He looked much the way her own son had thirty years ago: freckle-faced, grubby, with a tear in both knees of his filthy jeans and his shirttail hanging out.

"School not started yet?" she asked in her usual friendly fashion. It wasn't that she didn't know. Why, her friend Hope's niece had been teaching at the local elementary school for almost a month now, and she was well acquainted with the schedule.

"Buyin' somethin' fer my mom," he muttered, turning his face away and hunching over to peer at the varieties of potato chips currently available. It was obvious that he wasn't interested in carrying on a conversation. Charity shrugged before turning away to squint at the ice cream labels behind the frosted glass doors.

"Hmm, all pretty high in fat and cholesterol," she murmured to herself. Heaven knew women of her age couldn't afford either one, she thought grimly. "Arthur," she called loudly, hoping the proprietor would hear her above the roar of the semi truck unloading outside.

When Art Johnson didn't immediately appear, she shuffled over to the counter to wait for him. The grubby little boy was there ahead of her clutching a fistful of penny candy.

"Hello again, young man. I don't think I've seen you around before. Has your family just moved to Mossbank?" Any newcomer to their fair town was a source of interest for Charity, and she couldn't help the bristle of curiosity that ran through her. "What's your name?"

"Roddy. Roddy Green."

"Well, nice to meet you, Roddy. My name is Mrs. Flowerday. I live at the end of Maple Street in that red brick house. Perhaps you've noticed it?"

"Nope."

Evidently young Mr. Green didn't care to know, either, thought Charity with a tiny smile. Kids nowadays were so different. They didn't bother with all the folderol of petty politeness and such. They just got down to the basics.

"Where's the old guy that runs this place?" the boy demanded sullenly, tapping his fingers on the counter. "I haven't got all day."

"Oh, Mr. Johnson often has to stay at the back while they

unload the truck,'' she explained to him with a smile. ''He counts the pieces as they take them off to be sure he receives everything he should. I'm certain he will be here in a moment.''

''I'm here right now, Charity. Sorry to have kept you waiting. What can I do for you?''

Arthur Johnson smiled at her the same way he had for the past thirty-five years, and Charity smiled back. He had always been a friendly man who took pleasure in meeting the needs of his customers. When he looked at her like that, his face jovial, his balding head burnished in the autumn sun shining through the window, Charity felt her heart give a quick little patter. He was still such a handsome man.

''I was here first,'' Roddy piped up belligerently. He smacked the candy on the counter. ''How much?''

Charity noticed Art's eyebrows rise at the obvious discourtesy, but she shook her head slightly.

''Yes, he was here first, Art,'' Charity murmured.

''All right, then. Twenty-nine cents, please, young man.''

As Charity watched the child's hand slip into his pocket for the change, she noticed his other hand snitch a chocolate bar from the stand in front of him and slip it into his other pocket. She motioned her head downward as Art glanced at her, but this time it was he who shook his head.

''Thanks, son. Now you'd better get back to school.''

'''Bye Art the fart,'' the boy chanted, racing out the door and down the street. They could hear his bellows of laughter ricochet back and forth along the narrow avenue.

''Of all the nerve! Arthur Johnson, you know very well that child stole a chocolate bar from you,'' Charity accused, casting the grocer a black look. ''Why did you let the little hoodlum get away with it? Didn't you see it clearly enough?''

''Oh, I saw it, Charity. My eyes are still pretty good, and that mirror really helps,'' Art chuckled. ''But this isn't the first time I chose to do nothing about it. Not right now. Anyway, that chocolate bar will eat away at his conscience all afternoon. He's not getting away with anything." He pressed her shoulder gently as if to soothe away her indignation. "Now, dear lady, what can I do for my best customer?"

Charity preened a little at the complimentary tone, straightening her shoulders as she blinked up at him girlishly.

"Well, Arthur, I'm having guests for lunch today, and I want to serve ice cream. This may be one of the last really warm days we have this fall, you know."

"I see." Art led the way over to the freezers and tugged out a small round tub. "I have your favorite right back here, Charity. Double chocolate fudge pecan." He beamed down at her.

"Why, I can't believe you remembered. It's ages since I had this. It won't do for Hope, though," Charity said, grimacing. "She's always watching her fat content, and this is bound to send it over the moon." A tinge of frustration edged her words as she shoved the container back into the freezer. "Maybe we'd better have sherbet instead. A nice savory lemon."

"Charity, Hope Langford is so scrawny she could do with a little fattening up. Besides, you know you love chocolate. And this is the light variety with one-third less fat. It's really quite delicious." Art glanced at his hands self-consciously. "I tried it myself last week."

"You ate chocolate ice cream, with *your* cholesterol level?" Charity frowned severely. "You need a woman to look after you, Arthur."

They spent twenty minutes discussing their various health ailments before Charity strolled out the door carrying the container of chocolate ice cream and grinning from ear to ear.

Two and a half hours later Charity was welcoming her two friends to her cosy home and a scrumptious lunch.

"Isn't it lovely out today." That was her friend Faith Rempel who simply never had a bad day. "I can't imagine more perfect weather for walking."

"I thought Jeremy didn't like you walking all over town," Hope Langford questioned. "Has he changed his mind?" Hope's voice was soft and shy, much like the woman herself. At fifty-six, she was the youngest in their group and much concerned over her friend's propensity to accidents. She had, at first, greeted the arrival of Faith's nephew, Jeremy Nivens, with relief.

"Oh, Jeremy's far too busy with school just now. He's trying so hard to make a good impression with this first principalship. The dear boy hasn't been hovering nearly as much this week." Faith brushed the permed lock of gray hair off her forehead absently as she stared at the other two. "I haven't seen him for three days," she told them cheerfully. "Or was it four? Let's see now..."

Charity laughed gaily.

"Oh, Faith," she murmured, leading them out to her small patio and the gaily set table. "Don't tell me you've forgotten what day it is again? I declare that memory of yours is—"

"Just fine," cut in Hope quietly. She frowned at Charity. "I think she does wonderfully well. And if we're talking about Jeremy, I don't think Gillian is particularly impressed with him. She says he's very old-fashioned."

They sat around the table, munching on the low-fat ham sandwiches and crunchy green salad as they discussed the newest educators at the local elementary school.

"Well," Charity murmured. "You must admit your niece is very advanced in some of her ideas. Why, just the other day I heard Gillian complaining about the textbooks. Said they were too passé to be any good!" Her white eyebrows rose with indignation. "We've had those textbooks for years, as you well know, Hope Langford."

Hope hid her smile behind her napkin. Her voice, when she finally spoke, was the same soft tones they had come to expect from her. "Yes, I know the age of some of those books very well. I myself tried to have them replaced just before I retired from teaching. Unfortunately, some folk in the community felt they were adequate, so the money was not forthcoming." Her blue eyes sparkled with mirth at Charity as she smoothed a hand over her blond, chin-length bob. As usual, there wasn't a hair out of place.

"I can't imagine why anyone thinks the children of the nineties still need to focus so completely on President Kennedy's administration," Hope murmured. "Several things have happened since the early sixties, Charity."

"Oh, piffle." Faith stared at them vacantly for several moments, her brow furrowed. Her English accent became more pronounced as she spoke. "I've forgotten whatever it was we were going to discuss today."

"It's all right, dear," Hope whispered, squeezing the other woman's hand gently. "We were going to discuss our Christmas project. Isn't that right, Charity?" She glanced across the table warningly, her thin body rigid in her chair.

"Yes, indeed," Charity murmured gaily. "But not before we've had my special dessert." She rose to stand behind Faith's chair, her tiny frame hidden by the larger woman. "And of course, we'll have tea. You pour, dear." She squeezed the rounded shoulders affectionately.

It was difficult to scoop out the ice cream with her arthritic hands, so Charity took the carton and dishes to Hope for help. They both watched as Faith's faded green eyes lit up with excitement as she tasted her first spoonful.

"Nuts," she crowed. "This ice cream has nuts." She sighed with pleasure. "I do love nuts," she murmured happily.

As they basked in the warm, afternoon sun, sipping tea,

chatting desultorily and ignoring the dirty dishes sitting nearby, Charity held her hands out for them to see.

"I'm afraid I won't be able to quilt this year, girls," she murmured, staring at her gnarled fingers and twisted knuckles. "I just can't manage the needle anymore."

They were aghast.

"But, Charity," Faith exploded. "You've always made a special Christmas quilt every year for as long as I've known you. It's a tradition in Mossbank." Her eyes were huge and filling rapidly with tears. "You can't just give up."

"Well, this year I am choosing something else for my Christmas project." Charity's brown eyes sparkled with a secret.

Hope cleared her voice, curiosity widening her china blue eyes. "What?" she enquired softly.

"I've been praying about it, and this morning I got an answer. I'm going to take on a different kind of project—a person. A little boy named Roddy Green. I watched him steal a chocolate bar at the grocery store this morning when he should have been in school." Charity shifted her feet to rest on a nearby rock, exposing her puffy, swollen ankles. "And I decided he could use a friend," she murmured quietly. "Art told me a little about the boy, and I think we could both benefit from the relationship."

"I don't like that word," Faith told them both, absently pulling a weed from the huge pot of yellow begonias that sat nearby. "It's what Jeremy always talks about when I ask if he has a special girlfriend he's interested in."

"What word is that, dear?" Hope asked mildly confused.

"*Relationship.* My Donald and I never had a relationship, not once in thirty-five years. We had love and friendship and care and concern and sometimes arguments, but we never had anything as cold as a relationship." Faith spat the word out with disgust.

"Young people today do have a different way of looking at things," Hope agreed. Her blond brows drew together as she asked curiously, "And does Jeremy have a relationship with someone?"

Charity watched Hope twist her fingers together as she lounged in her chair. It was that unusual activity that gave the younger woman away, she decided. Hope never fidgeted. Charity wondered what her friend was up to.

"No," Faith answered the question sadly. "Jeremy says he's far too involved in his career to bother with females right now. He really wants to make a success of this school year." Her face drooped as she told them about her great-nephew's visit two or three nights before. "He was most uncomplimentary about my natural garden. Said it resembled a weed patch more than a flower garden. He even pulled up a few of my special species."

"He would." Hope's tones were dry. "He's got his nose buried so far into his policy-and-procedure manuals he can't see real people in front of him. Jeremy Nivens needs to realize that life is about more than school and books."

"He doesn't like me to have the fireplace going, either," Faith told them solemnly. "He said I'm liable to kill myself with it."

"It's gas," Hope cried. "It shuts itself off. What in the world is he so concerned about?"

Faith shrugged her shoulders tiredly, a wan smile curving her full lips.

"Jeremy worries about me, my dears. He's much like his father was, always fussing about things."

"Well," Hope drawled, staring thoughtfully up at the deep blue sky, "I think he needs something else to engage his mind. Something slightly more challenging."

"What are you up to?" Charity demanded finally. "Don't bother to deny it, I can see that glint sparkling in your eyes."

"Oh, tell me, too." Faith clapped her hands in glee. "I love it when you have a plan, Hope. It's always so wonderfully organized, just like you."

Hope smiled a peculiarly smug grin as her eyes moved from one to the other.

"You have to promise not to say a word," she said seriously. "Not a whisper to anyone. If this gets around, he'll never forgive me."

"Who?" Charity demanded irritably.

"Jeremy," Hope told them proudly. "I've decided to make Jeremy my Christmas project. I'm going to find him a wife so he'll be too busy to bother Faith anymore."

Her two friends sat in their lawn chairs, mouths gaping as they absorbed her news. The birds happily chirped around them as a neighbor's lawn mower hummed industriously.

"You mean," Charity asked, "you're going to throw him and Gillian together? I don't think—"

"Of course not," Hope said, cutting her off. "Gillian is a free spirit. She needs a man who can understand that, and not try to fence her in with a lot of silly restrictions. Besides, Jeremy's too old for her."

"Oh, piffle. Jeremy's not that much older than your Gillian," Faith chided, her eyes sparkling at the thought of her great-nephew married.

"In his approach to life in this century, Jeremy rivals Moses," Hope muttered dourly. "I was actually thinking of Letitia Chamberlain. She's a quiet little thing, and she'd do whatever he told her to."

"Well," Charity murmured, staring off into space, "I suppose if you've made up your mind, there's no point in me trying to change it. I do think it's too bad not to continue with your knitting though, Hope. Those mittens you donate are really needed in the cities. Why, I heard the mayor of

Minot on the news the other day. He said they would need at least a hundred pairs in the schools this year!''

Hope smiled. "Oh, I'll still be knitting," she murmured. "And while I am, I can think of new plans for Jeremy." Charity watched the glint of mischievousness sparkle in her friend's eyes and wondered what she was up to.

"It isn't fair," Faith wailed sadly. "You have both chosen your projects, and I don't have one. What shall I choose? I'm not very good at matchmaking but maybe I could try for Gillian."

Charity met Hope's wary glance with her own.

"No!" They both said it together.

"What we mean, dear, is that you're such a good cook and you always do those wonderful dainty trays for the Christmas hampers. Maybe you should do that again." Charity nodded as Hope's soft voice soothed their friend.

"Of course I will continue with *that,*" Faith told them firmly. "But I want a special project. Something really different." Her green eyes narrowed as she pondered the subject. Finally she stood to her feet.

"After all, I do have a bit of time yet. It is only the first week of October, isn't it? I shall think and pray about it. Perhaps the good Lord has some special work that I can do." Faith ambled out the front door, completely forgetting her purse and sweater as she strolled along, mumbling to herself.

"We should have thought of something for her to do, before we announced our ideas," Charity muttered, gathering up their teacups and setting them on the tray. "It's not fair to leave her like that."

Hope carried the dishes back into the house and set about washing them carefully in the old-fashioned sink. She had most of the work done before Charity hobbled in.

"Faith is a strong, competent woman," she stated firmly. "She's not senile, just a little confused sometimes. I think it

will be good for her to think about a Christmas project rather
than Jeremy's odious meddling, for a while." Hope shook her
head with disgust. "That man would drive a saint up the
wall."

"He's certainly been hovering around Faith since he
came," Charity agreed. "I heard him telling her not to use
the oven unless he was there. You know how she loves to
bake. I can't imagine that she'll listen to him."

"It might be best if she did," Hope muttered finally. "I
hate to say it, but her memory is getting worse. I've been
checking up on her myself lately, just to make sure she gets
home safely."

"Funny," Charity mused absently, rubbing liniment on the
aching joints of her hands. "Arthur mentioned something
about seeing her home the other night. Said he found her in
the park, gathering leaves for her collection. In the dark."

"Well, I think we'll just have to be especially careful to
keep track of her with Jeremy around," Hope said with a
frown. "I don't like the way he keeps telling her not to do
this or that, fussing if she goes for a long walk. She's not in
prison, for heaven's sake."

"Yes, I'll watch her, too," Charity agreed, sinking into her
easy chair. "Now about this project of yours? Do you really
think you can find someone suitable for him? He's rather, er,
old-fashioned, dear."

Hope grinned smugly.

"I know. That's why I've decided to hook him up with
Flossie Gerbrandt. She's exactly the same."

"Flossie?" Charity shuddered. "I hate that name. Can't
understand why Clara called her that. Always reminds me of
a rabbit, for some reason." Her brow furrowed in thought. "I
hope you know what you're doing, Hope. I just can't picture
Flossie in her support hose and caftans going to church with
the elegantly turned-out likes of him." She coughed discreetly

behind her hand. "Anyway," she murmured repressively. "The Lord has his own plans for Jeremy Nivens. He doesn't need you to meddle."

"I'm just going to give the man a helping hand," Hope told her, stacking the plates in the cupboard. "Nothing wrong with that, is there?"

Hope sipped her tea pensively, staring at the embroidered Lord's Prayer on the wall. She was lost in thought until Charity's voice called her back to the present.

"Pardon?" she asked softly, enraptured by the picture her mind had drawn.

"I just wondered when you were going to get to work on your new project?"

"Soon, dear. Very soon." Hope returned her gaze to the figure of Jesus holding a sheep in his strong arms. "The sooner the better—for Faith, for Jeremy and for Gillian."

Chapter Three

Gillian stared at the cut on the boy's knee.

"Jed, I told you to stay with the rest of us. How did you do this, anyway?" She dabbed at the injury carefully, noting the dirt imbedded in the cut.

"I had to go pee" she was told in no uncertain terms. "When I was doing up my pants, I tripped on somethin'. It made me fall."

Gillian grinned. No responsibility for Jed. If something had cut him, it certainly wasn't his fault. She grimaced. There was no doubt in her mind that Mr. Nivens would believe that the cut was all her fault.

"Come, children," she called, ushering them ahead of her onto the path through the woods. "We have to get back to the school now. It's almost time for the bell. Quietly, Rowena."

Who are you kidding? she asked herself sourly. Quiet? First-graders? Not likely. As they stumbled and pushed and shoved their way back into the classroom, she glanced round surreptitiously. Her heart fell as she noticed the man in the blue pin-striped suit heading directly for her.

"Come along, children. Let's get your things together now. Don't forget to collect as many leaves as you can this weekend." She handed out knapsacks and lunch bags, just managing to grasp Jed's arm before he headed out the room as the bell rang. "Just a minute, Jed. We'll have to see to that knee."

"Miss Langford? What is the meaning of this bedlam?" Mr. Nivens's voice was raised to counter the excitement coming from the rest of the children now pouring into the hall.

She ignored him as she drew Jed over to the sink and began dabbing antiseptic from the first aid kit onto the child's knee. She held one bony little shoulder firmly as the boy wriggled.

"Ow!" His bellow was loud and angry.

"Has this child injured himself on school property, during school hours, Miss Langford?"

Old Jerry was in a cranky mood, she decided glumly. There was no way he would let her off easily for this one.

"We went on a nature hike, and Jed cut his knee," she told him, still gripping the child's wriggling shoulder. "If you could assist me with this, I'd appreciate it. I have to cleanse the area."

"He should be seen by a doctor," Jeremy Nivens began firmly, but he knelt beside the boy and peered at the affected area. "At least it won't require stitches," he muttered, taking the cotton from her hands and briskly wiping the grit and particles of soil away.

"That hurts, ya know," Jed shrieked. His face was red with anger.

"Nonsense. A great big boy like you wouldn't feel a little nick like this. You have to be strong when these things happen—stiff upper lip and all that." His finger slapped a Band-Aid across the knee with surety, and he pulled Jed's pant leg swiftly down.

"Huh?" Jed sat staring at the older man in perplexity.

Gillian bent down and stared into Jed's puzzled face. "He means that you were very brave for handling that so well, Jed. Here's your knapsack now. You'd better run and get that bus."

As the boy scurried from the room, he cast a suspicious look at Jeremy's suited figure. "My lip's not stiff," he told the older man seriously. "My leg is, though."

"Have a good weekend," Gillian called and waved briskly, watching the most daring member of her class dodge the other children in his rush to get to the bus.

"Miss Langford, you and I need to have a discussion."

She turned back wearily to face her towering boss's stern face. He had that glint in his eye, she noticed. The one that always spelled trouble. For her.

"Have a seat, Mr. Nivens. I'll just clean up a bit as we talk." She avoided his eyes as her hands busily picked up the shuffle of papers on her desk, brushing the bits of twigs and crushed leaves into the garbage.

"I would prefer to speak in my office. In a more formal setting." He was still standing, Gillian noted.

"Oh, why bother to walk all the way down there?" she murmured airily. "We're both here now. Why don't you just tell me what's on your mind?" Smoothly, without a pause in action, Gillian slipped the books into order on her shelves, removing a bubble gum paper from Jonah's reader. When he didn't speak, she finally glanced up and found his remote stare fixed firmly on her. "Well?"

"Miss Langford, do you ever read the notifications I leave in your mailbox?"

He brushed a hand gingerly over the edge of the table, checking for stickiness before reclining against it. It was the most relaxed she had ever seen him, and the sight was very appealing. As she watched, Jeremy brushed a hand through his hair, destroying the immaculately arranged strands. "Miss Langford?"

She jerked her gaze away from the silky softness of his hair and focused on his frowning face.

"Of course I read them," she muttered finally. Her thought winged back over the past few weeks, trying to recall which particular missive he could be referring to. If the truth were known, she barely glanced at his memos lately. She had been centering every bit of time and attention on her students.

Jeremy crossed his arms over his chest.

"Then I'm sure you noticed that I asked teachers to be particularly aware of permission notes and the necessity of having parents sign if their child was to be taken off the school property," he said smugly. "May I have the notes?"

"But we only walked through the land right next door," she told him wide-eyed. "Surely we don't need a permission slip for a little nature walk."

"I take it that you didn't bother to procure the signatures then," he bit out, shaking his head angrily. "Miss Langford, you cannot keep ignoring the rules that are part of the function of this school."

"Oh, but surely for a little nature walk…"

"Your *little walk* may have engendered a lawsuit," he rasped, standing straight and tall before her.

"What?" Gillian stared at him, half-amused. "Why would anyone sue the school?"

"What if Jed's cut becomes infected and requires further treatment? What if one of the children had been badly hurt? What if you were injured and they were without a leader?" His eyes were icy as they glared at her.

Gillian shook her head. "We didn't go to Siberia," she said softly, peering up at him in confusion. "We walked not fifty feet beyond the school property. Any one of them could have made it back safely, without trouble."

"Deidre Hall couldn't," he said angrily, standing directly in front of her. "What about her?"

Gillian thought about the young girl in the wheelchair whom she'd pushed through the undergrowth. She shrugged. "All right, Deidre needed my help. And I was there. Nothing happened. No big deal."

"Not this time, no." His jacket was unbuttoned, and Gillian could see the missing button on his vest as his hands planted themselves firmly on his hips. For some reason that lost button gave her encouragement; maybe Jeremy Nivens was human after all.

"Fine," she murmured softly, staring up into his stern face. "I admit I should have checked with you first. I'm sorry I didn't advise you of my plans or get the childrens' parents to sign permission slips. I'll ensure that it doesn't happen again." Gillian smiled placatingly. "Is that all right?"

"I don't think it is. You have perverse ideas on teaching that seem to dictate constantly removing the children from the classroom. I cannot condone that. The classroom is where they should be doing their learning, not in the woods."

Gillian tried to control the surge of rage that flooded through her at his words. How dare he criticize her efforts! She was a good teacher, darned good. And she focused her attention on teaching children to learn in whatever situation they found themselves.

"My students," she began angrily, "are learning to be aware of the things around them, whether or not they are in the classroom. Today they experienced all five of the sensory perceptions of fall. They saw things in a different way than they would have looking out the window at the woods."

"Five senses?" He jumped on her statement immediately, his voice full of dismay. "What did they eat?"

"We peeled the outer shell off acorns and tried to crunch

the centers. They tasted the flavor of the woods," she told him proudly.

If it was possible, Jeremy Nivens's body grew even tauter as he stood glaring down at her. His hands clenched at his sides, and his jaw tightened.

"They'll probably all get sick," he muttered angrily. His voice was cold and hard. "Why can't you learn to just follow the rules?" he demanded angrily.

"Why can't you learn to live with a few less rules and a lot more feeling in your life?" she flung at him. "This isn't a prison. It's a school—a place of learning and experimentation meant to prepare the children for the future. If you constantly deny them the right to find things out for themselves, how will they solve the problems of their world? You can't keep them under lock and key."

He stood there fuming, his anger palpable between them. Gillian could feel the tension crackling in the air and tried not to wince when his hard, bitter, exasperated tones stabbed at her.

"In the future you *will* okay all field trips with me, whether the students go fifty feet or fifty miles. Do you understand, Miss Langford?"

Gillian stifled the urged to bend over at the waist and salaam to him. He would find nothing funny in such an action, she knew.

"Yes, Mr. Nivens," she murmured softly. "I understand completely." Her voice held a nasty undertone that she did not attempt to disguise. "Would you also like to sit in on my classes and make sure I'm not teaching my students political activism or the making of pipe bombs?"

He turned to leave, stopping by the door for a moment. His eyes glittered with something strange as he smiled dryly at her. "Thank you, Miss Langford," he murmured slyly. "I may yet find it necessary to do that."

She could have kicked herself for offering, and spent the next hour mentally booting herself around the room for falling into his little trap. "Odious manipulator," she mumbled, checking her daybook for the plans she had made. "As if I'd let him in here to check up on me. No way." Of course there was really nothing she could do to stop him, Gillian knew. And if he decided she wasn't doing her job, he could call for a review on her work.

Why did Michael have to die? she asked God for the zillionth time. If he were alive, they would be married, and she would be in her happy, carefree position at St. Anne's, blissfully oblivious to the presence of Mr. Jeremy Nivens and his immense book of rules.

But there was nothing to be gained by going down that road. She would just have to learn to accept it and get on with living. The past was no place to dwell, and time *was* flying by.

Gillian laid out the work she had planned for the next day and checked to see there were enough copies of the Thanksgiving turkey she planned to begin in art class next week. At least she had the children, she consoled herself. She would never have Michael's child, but she had twenty-eight needy ones in her classroom every day, and she intended to see to it that they got the best education she could offer.

Gillian was about two blocks from her aunt's house and dreaming of relaxing for the weekend when she saw the smoke. Thick, billowing, dark gray clouds of smoke rolling out the window of a house. Gillian raced across the street and dashed inside the open front door. This was Faith Rempel's home, she was pretty sure. And if she remembered her aunt's description correctly, Mrs. Rempel lived alone.

Gillian found the woman in her kitchen, slumped over a counter, the smoking remains of a pan with something resembling cherries bubbling blackly on the stove. She snatched a dish towel and grabbed the pan, dumping the entire contents into the sink and pouring water over it. Steam and smoke combined to cover her in a cloud of acrid odors.

"Mrs. Rempel? I'm Hope's niece. Are you all right?" Gillian checked the elderly woman's pulse and was relieved to find it seemed strong and healthy. When the green eyes opened, they stared at Gillian blankly. "Come on, Mrs. Rempel. We'll have to get you out of this smoke."

"Yes, thank you, dear. That would be lovely. I'm afraid my cherries jubilee didn't quite turn out. Such a pity." Faith Rempel's English accent was pronounced as she rose from the table with alacrity and waved her apron back and forth briskly, whooshing the air as she walked.

"Cherries jubilee?" Gillian couldn't believe her ears. Who made cherries jubilee at four-thirty on a Friday afternoon, for goodness sake? And wasn't the sauce supposed to be set on fire when the dish was served, not hours before?

She left Mrs. Rempel sitting on a patio chair outside and checked for further damage in the kitchen before opening all the windows and doors. Thankfully the light, afternoon breeze soon whisked the smelly fumes and billows of blue-black smoke away.

"I've brought you a glass of water, Mrs. Rempel. Are you sure you're all right?" The puffy lines in the woman's face had been there before, Gillian decided, checking her patient once more.

"Of course, dear. I'm perfectly fine." Faith's green eyes stared into hers. "Do I know you?" she asked curiously.

She grinned. "I'm Hope's niece, Gillian. I'm here teaching school."

"Oh, yes," Mrs. Rempel smiled brightly. "You're Jeremy's new girlfriend. You two make the sweetest couple." She stood suddenly and moved briskly to the back door. "I'll have to clean this mess up before he gets here. Jeremy hates a mess.''

"I'll help you,'' Gillian offered, remembering that this woman, according to her aunt, had slight lapses in memory. That would account for her erroneous linking of their names. How strange that such a lovely woman should be old sour-puss's aunt.

"Does he come every day?'' she asked curiously. It seemed odd to think of her boss checking up on his aunt. More likely he came for a free meal so he wouldn't have to dirty his own kitchen, she decided, still fuming at his biting remarks.

"Almost every evening. We have dinner together. I was hoping to surprise him with a new dessert. Piffle,'' she grunted, glaring at the charred remains of the cherries. "Should have turned the heat down sooner.''

Gillian grinned. So Jeremy Nivens came for a free dinner every night. Somehow she had known human kindness wasn't the reason for Jerry's visits. She wondered what he'd think of his aunt's messy kitchen right now.

"You know,'' she told Faith, smiling as she wiped down the counters and stove. "In our family we had a standing joke whenever Mom burned something. We always said she thought we must be little gods because she was serving us burnt offerings.''

Faith giggled appreciatively.

"Underneath all this smoke, something sure smells good,'' Gillian told her seriously. She opened the oven door and sniffed appreciatively. "What is that?''

The older woman blushed, her salt-and-pepper head bending forward shyly.

"Oh, just a little rouladin. Jeremy loves beef, you know. I imagine you'll be cooking it often after you're married, dear.'' She scurried about, putting the last of the now-dry dishes away. "I just need to get a salad together and check the potatoes."

"Uh, Mrs. Rempel, Jeremy and I aren't getting…"

"Oh, silly me. Of course you aren't announcing it right away. I can understand that. You both being so new to the community and all," Faith twittered happily as she rinsed the lettuce and set it carefully in a colander to dry. She grasped Gillian's hand in her own and glanced at her finger. "Oh, you haven't found a ring yet?"

"No, we haven't," Gillian searched for the right words, but she needn't have bothered. Jeremy Nivens's aunt was lost in a world of her own, green eyes sparkling with happiness as she stared at her own rings.

"It seems just last week when Donald and I became engaged. He insisted that I choose my own ring, said it was going to have to last a good long time and he didn't want me wearing something I didn't like. It has lasted, too." She didn't say it, but Gillian could almost hear her thinking that the rings had outlasted the husband.

"He gave me that cabinet over there," Faith pointed to the corner china cabinet in the next room. "For our anniversary it was." Her green eyes grew cloudy. "I forget which one, but I remember Donald saying it was my special place for my little china dolls. He sent them to me from overseas during the war."

"Auntie Fay? Are you all right?"

The anxious tones of her authoritative boss jerked Gillian from her happy daydream of the past. It was strange to hear that note of concern in his voice, but moments later she decided she must have imagined it as he glared across the room at them.

"What are you doing here?" he demanded, staring at Gillian. "Oh, never mind right now. Auntie Fay, the neighbors phoned me to say that there was smoke coming from the house. Are you all right?''

"Oh, I'm just fine, thank you, dear. A wee bit early for dinner, aren't you?'' Faith blinked up at him innocently as her hands tore the lettuce apart and placed it in a crystal bowl. "I'm afraid I haven't got the table set yet.''

"There's no rush,'' he told her softly, his gray eyes gentle. "As you say, I am early. I'll talk to *her* while I wait.'' His head nodded at Gillian, who felt an immediate prickling of anger.

"Yes, I suppose you two lovebirds do have some catching up to do. Go ahead out on the balcony and relax. I remember young love. Why, your fiancée and I were just talking about it.'' Her benign smile left Gillian smiling back, until Jeremy's rough voice roused her.

"Yes,'' he agreed, frowning severely as he grasped Gillian's arm in his firm fingers and tugged her from the room. "I think Miss Langford and I definitely need to have a discussion.''

Obediently Gillian preceded him out the back door and sank onto one of the wicker chairs Faith had placed under the awning. She slipped off her new, black patent shoes and wiggled her feet in the fresh air as she summoned enough nerve up to glance at his forbidding face.

"Would you mind very much telling what in the dickens is going on in this nuthouse now? I mean since you are my fiancée and everything!''

His scathing tone rasped over her nerves, but there was no way he was intimidating her, Gillian decided. Once today was enough. She glared back at him, daring him to holler at her again.

"Well? Exactly when did we become engaged, Miss Langford?''

Gillian couldn't help it, the grin popped to her mouth, split-

ting it wide with mirth. "Since I'm your fiancée and everything," she murmured slyly, "don't you think it's about time
you started calling me Gillian?" Laughter burst out of her at
the stupefied stare on his face. "Well? Jeremy?" It was the
first time she'd seen him dumbfounded, and it was very refreshing. "Honey?" She shook his arm teasingly.

A second later the grin was gone from her mouth as he
tugged her into his arms and kissed her on the mouth. It
wasn't a passionate kiss, or even a very practiced one. In fact,
Gillian suspected it had more to do with anger than anything.

Still and all, it shook her. She liked the feel of his firm lips
against hers, she decided dazedly. And his arms were strong,
but gentle, around her.

"Wh-what are you doing?" she stammered at last, staring
up into his glittery blue eyes. They had a wariness about them
that added to the unreality of the situation.

"Kissing my fiancée. Surely that's allowed?"

Gillian stared at the transformation taking place in front of
her. For once, the stern, haughty face had been replaced with
a handsome, smiling countenance that drew her like a magnet.
It was disconcerting to find that he affected her so. Clearly
he wasn't nearly so bothered by that kiss. His entire demeanor
was calm, cool and collected. Carefully she extricated herself
from his embrace and stepped back.

"Not this early in the relationship," she murmured, peering
up at him from between her lashes. When he said nothing,
she pressed on. "Your aunt is a little confused," she told him
quietly. "I don't know where she got the idea that we are a
couple. Maybe it's due to the fire."

His face blanched.

"Then there really was a fire." He smacked his hand on
his pant leg. "Darn. I was afraid of that." His eyes had
dimmed to cool gray again. "What happened?"

"She was flambéing cherries jubilee, and I think they

caught on fire, which in turn started the pot holder smoking. She had everything well under control when I arrived,'' Gillian lied. ''I merely opened the doors and windows to let the smoke out. No damage done.''

''No damage done?'' Jeremy stared at her as if she'd grown two heads. ''Miss Langford, really! My aunt almost burns her house down. While she's inside, incidentally. She decides to cook cherries jubilee in the middle of the afternoon, and then, out of the blue, decides you're my fiancée.'' His eyes narrowed as he stared at her calmly nodding head. ''I don't think you are a very good influence on my aunt.'' He shook his dark head vehemently. ''Not at all.''

''Oh, I don't know,'' Gillian said, chuckling at his stern look. ''I got her uppity nephew engaged to me without even trying. I must be doing something right.''

The whole town was loony, Jeremy decided, staring at the vibrant young woman in front of him. Absently he noted the way her freckles drifted across her nose and cheeks.

It was her eyes that really got to him, though. They were like jade daggers, stabbing at him in angry little jabs as she bristled up in her chair.

''Oh, for goodness sake,'' she complained at last. ''Can't you tell that your aunt's a little confused? Cut her some slack, would you?''

Jeremy stared. ''I beg your pardon?'' he murmured, trying to figure out what she was talking about. ''Cut some slacks?''

Gillian Langford sighed, pleating her trousers between her fingers as she stared back at him.

''How old are you, Mr. Nivens?''

''Thirty.'' Jeremy was too shocked to stop his immediate response. ''Why?''

''Don't take this personally,'' she told him with a teasing little grin that reinforced how beautiful Gillian Langford really was, "but you act like you're from another planet. Where have you been for the past thirty years?"

"England," he murmured at last. "At least for twenty-eight of them. I was raised in Oxford and attended school there. I was headmaster at a school nearby until this summer, when I returned to the States." His brow creased. "Why?"

Gillian's narrow shoulders shrugged. "Doesn't matter," she murmured, tugging her mane of reddish gold off her face. "Anyway, the point is, your aunt is a little mixed-up. For some reason she's decided that you and I are engaged."

He laughed harshly.

"My aunt is a lot more than slightly confused. She is forgetful, absentminded, preoccupied and inattentive when she is cooking. That's why I'm trying to persuade her to sell this house and go into a nursing home."

"What?"

Jeremy winced at the shrill shriek of her voice. He would have pointed out that the whole affair was none of her business, but he didn't have time. Miss Langford advanced upon him like a Mack truck, letting nothing stop her surge of fury until she stood directly in front of his chair, green eyes glittering.

"You can't! No way. She loves this house and the memories that are hidden away in every nook and corner. You can't expect her to just give it all up. What about getting someone to live in?"

Jeremy snorted. She might be beautiful, this new teacher on his staff, but she wasn't in the least practical.

"In Mossbank? Population five thousand, and that's a high estimate?" He shook his head. "I don't think so."

"But a nursing home? She doesn't need it. She's perfectly self-reliant." Her lips had carried an angry tilt to them. "She just forgets things once in a while."

"I know," he nodded. "Like the fireplace going or the

stove or the kettle. One day it will cause a fire. Like today?''
He peered at her with one eyebrow raised inquiringly. ''What
aren't you telling me that she forgot today?''

''Nothing,'' Gillian answered stoically. ''She just let the
liqueur get a little too hot when she was flambéing the cherries
jubilee. It was out before I got here. I told you that.''

''Yes,'' he nodded slowly. ''I heard exactly what you said.
It's what you didn't say that has me worried.'' He studied the
flaming sparks that reflected off her hair in the late-afternoon
sun. ''And it's knowing that my aunt is a loose cannon, waiting to go off, that is forcing me to consider a facility that can
care for her.''

''But you can't!'' Gillian was aghast that he would consider
such a drastic action. ''She loves the freedom of cooking and
cleaning in her own home. I can't believe that she's in danger.
Not really.'' She glared at him through the fringe of bangs
that fell across her forehead. ''Anyway, Mrs. Flowerday and
my aunt Hope will be watching out for her. And I certainly
will. Among the three of us, she'll be well cared for.''

Jeremy was shaking his head.

''But you can't be here all the time, and neither can I. There
will be those occasions when she will decide to cook some
elaborate dish at five in the morning and no one will be able
to stop her. Next time she may well set herself on fire.'' His
face glanced down at Gillian sadly. ''I don't like it any more
than you, but I simply will not take the risk of her hurting
herself.''

''I don't think you have the right to make such a decision,''
Gillian sputtered angrily. ''You've only just arrived on the
scene. Faith has been managing alone for years now. You
can't just waltz in here and uproot her from everything that's
familiar. It will only confuse her more.''

''Oh, I won't do it right away. I'll talk to her, give her time
to get used to the idea first.'' He stared out across Faith's

ramshackle garden with its wild assortment of plants. "Look at her garden," he muttered, thrusting out one hand. "She's forgotten all about it."

"She hasn't forgotten it," Gillian denied, glaring at him. "She probably hasn't had time to get to it. Especially when she's fixing your meals all the time. That must be quite a burden for her." Her eyes sparkled angrily at him. "Can't you learn to cook, Mr. Nivens?"

Jeremy felt his eyes open wide, startled at the anger in her tones.

"Surely you don't think I come over for dinner just to get a free meal?" he said, furious at her categorization of his motives. "There are any number of restaurants in the town. I can certainly afford to eat regularly at most of them."

"Then why are you here?" Gillian Langford looked down her nose at him disdainfully, daring him to deny her conclusions.

"To make sure Aunt Faith eats at least one decent meal a day. If she thinks I'm coming, she makes a full meal. And eats it." He met her stare head-on. "Otherwise she would make do on tea and toast, and that's not very healthy."

Jeremy watched the dull flush of red suffuse her pronounced cheekbones, making the light sprinkling of freckles across her nose stand out. The reddish strands in her shining hair glittered. Lord, Gillian Langford was a beautiful woman.

He wondered why she wasn't married and how she'd come to live in Mossbank. His eyes swept down to the beautiful ring she always wore on her right hand. He'd noticed it before; many times. It looked like an engagement ring, but even he knew they were worn on the left hand. And no young man came by to claim her after school.

Which no doubt meant that the lady wasn't interested in men. Good! He didn't want to have to deal with overeager suitors hanging around the school, and he felt fairly certain than any suitor of Gillian Langford would be eager.

He glanced up and found her gaze fixed on him: dark, turbulent shadows clouding the green clarity of her eyes.

"My aunt must be about ready by now," he murmured. "Perhaps we had better go in." As he followed her into the house, Jeremy was forced to admit that today her choice of clothing was both suitable for school and extremely attractive.

She wore the long, slim slacks comfortably on her leggy frame, a matching teal silk shirt hanging loosely to her hips. The color was very flattering to her. A short, knitted black vest made the outfit complete and rendered it less casual looking. With her hair on the top of her head, Gillian looked coolly professional, and the picture irked him immeasurably. Why, he wasn't sure.

"Well, I'd better be getting home to Hope's," Gillian told the older woman cheerfully. "She's sure to have dinner ready."

"Yes, Hope is a good cook," Faith enthused. Her forehead pleated in a frown. "Although she does have a tight fist with the butter. Now, dear," she turned to Jeremy. "You are eating with Gillian tonight, aren't you? I would have made more if I'd known you were coming, but when I thought there would be just Art and me..." Her voice trailed away as she gestured to the smiling man seated on the other side of the kitchen table.

Jeremy stared at her in perplexity, wondering what was going on now. A sharp jab in the ribs brought him back to reality immediately, and he glared down at Gillian in frustration.

"Well, the truth is, Auntie Fay," he began, and then swallowed the rest of the sentence as Gillian cut him off.

"Of course he can eat with us. Hope is sure to have plenty.

And if he doesn't like her cooking, I'm sure Jeremy can get something for himself.''

Her eyes opened innocently to stare at him, and Jeremy smiled at the idea of cooking anything in his poorly stocked apartment. ''You know me, Auntie Fay,'' he murmured, just under his breath. His eyes met Gillian's startled ones, and he grinned. ''I'll do anything for a free meal.''

He could see that she felt embarrassed at her previous assumptions about his motives for going to his aunt's, and he would have chortled with delight at the sight of it if the others hadn't been there.

''I just hope Hope isn't serving tofu,'' Gillian whispered in his ear, her shoulder pressing against his chest for just a moment. ''My aunt is really into eating healthy, you know.''

Jeremy felt his stomach lurch strangely. Tofu? As in that curdled white stuff?

''Well, I hope you and your girl have a real nice evening,'' Art said, smiling benignly. ''Faith was telling me about your engagement. Congratulations to you both.''

''But there is nothing to—'' Jeremy gave up trying to explain as the willow wisp of a girl next to him tugged his arm none too gently.

''Thank you very much,'' he heard her say with a laugh. ''I hope the two of you enjoy your dinner. Come on, *honey*,'' Gillian said, wrapping her arm through his.

Before his wits returned, Jeremy found himself standing on the sidewalk in front of his aunt's house next to the beautiful woman who taught first grade in his school. She had removed her arm and he was thankful for that. It wouldn't do for the rest of the town to hear of their bogus engagement. Anyway, even that slight touch bothered him. A lot.

He felt the poke in his side and chanced a look down. She stood there, grinning from ear to ear.

"Well," she charged. "Aren't you going to offer me a ride to Hope's?"

Without conscious thought he opened the passenger side door and waited for her to slip inside his shiny black Mustang convertible. Her hand slid longingly over the leather-covered dashboard as he watched her snuggle into the fawn-colored bucket seat.

"Is that why you wanted to be engaged to me?" he asked solemnly, shifting gears before pulling away from the curb. "So you could ride in my new car?" He glanced at her and surprised a calculating look in her green eyes.

"Oh, that's just one of the many reasons," she murmured softly, sliding her shoes off and squishing her toes in the plush beige carpeting. "I'll tell you the rest of them over dinner."

As he negotiated the streets to her aunt's house, Jeremy frowned. Gillian Langford had arranged this, this misunderstanding, he felt sure. And it was because she had some ulterior motive.

Why then did he feel anticipation instead of fear at finding out just what the gorgeous redhead had in mind? he asked himself.

Chapter Four

"Where did you get this car?" Gillian demanded, breaking the tense silence that hung between them. She brushed her hand over the cool, smooth leather. "It's fabulous. And it doesn't seem like the type of car you'd drive at all," she blurted out. "I mean…" Her voice trailed away in dismay.

Jeremy chuckled. "What did you think I'd drive? Some staid, old family sedan, I'd wager." He laughed out loud at the abashed look on her expressive face. "Don't ever lie," he advised. "You can't hide your true feelings worth a plugged nickel."

She bristled immediately, which was exactly what Jeremy had expected.

"I make it a habit never to lie about anything," she told him pertly. "I learned that in the Sunday school right there." Gillian pointed to the old church as they passed it.

"Did you grow up here?" he asked, suddenly curious about her childhood.

"No." She shook her head. "But I came to visit Hope quite a lot when my parents wanted their own holiday. It was great fun for me, coming from Boston to the freedom of this little town." Gillian pointed to the lovely park with its huge trees and carragana hedge. "We used to pretend there were little caves in that hedge," she told him. "We could hide or have tea parties or lunch and never worry anybody."

"It sounds like you had a happy childhood," he murmured softly.

"Oh, I did," she enthused, grinning as the memories surfaced from long ago. "Whenever I visited Hope's, I was the queen of the castle. She'd let me stay up as long as I wanted. Or at least as long as I could without nodding off." Her thoughts drifted to the times she and Hope had slept outside under the stars.

"I believe children need a regular bedtime." Jeremy's quiet voice interrupted her musings. "It's important for their health and their growth that a regular schedule is maintained."

"Oh, for goodness sake," Gillian snapped, glaring at him angrily. "There you go again with those silly rules. Why do you always do that?" She watched him blink in confusion.

"Do what?" he asked, frowning. "I never did anything. I merely said…"

"I know what you said. It's what you always say. For every situation in life you need a rule." She scowled at him with disgust. "Don't you ever just relax and enjoy the world around you without worrying if it's the right thing to do?"

"It's not a matter of relaxing," he muttered at last, gliding to a stop in front of Hope's compact two-story. "It's a matter of planning things out to get the optimal benefit out of life."

"But I did get the optimal benefit," she argued, sliding out of the seat as his hand went under her elbow. "If I'd been sleeping in my bed, Hope and I wouldn't have been able to discuss the constellations or where God lives, or how the angels come to earth. Those things were just as important to me as a few extra minutes of sleep."

She stared into his handsome face seriously. "My mom

always told us that life is made up of little shining moments like stones in a necklace. They're what make the everyday routine things bearable, because we can take out those stones and remember them with pleasure during the bad times." She beckoned him up the stairs. "Come on in. Hope will have started something."

But unfortunately Hope hadn't. There was a note tacked to the phone informing Gillian that her aunt had gone shopping with Charity Flowerday.

"I'm sorry," she murmured, frowning up at Jeremy, who towered over her, now that she had removed her shoes. "I guess we'll have to find something for ourselves. Do you like tacos?"

His face was a study in contradictions. Gillian would have teased him about it except that he looked so unsure of himself.

"I—I don't know." His eyes met hers, and she was surprised to see uncertainty in their depths. "What is a taco?"

"Well," Gillian began, matter-of-factly arranging the ingredients she would need on the countertop and trying to ignore the spark of electricity she felt fluttering down her sensitive skin whenever Jeremy Nivens came near. "There are two kinds—soft and hard. I like the hard ones, although they're messy to eat."

He watched her defrost a package of meat in the microwave and then dump it into a frying pan. His forehead furrowed.

"Ground beef," he murmured.

"Hamburger, yes. With seasoning and spices. You put it into the shell and add vegetables and cheese to it." She watched his long patrician nose twitch as he caught a hint of the savory cooking odors.

"I'm not sure if I can eat such food," he told her seriously. "It smells as if it's spicy and my stomach is rather queasy about those things."

Gillian grinned at him, enjoying the look of uncertainty on

his handsome face. For once Mr. Jeremy Nivens was not in control. She was going to enjoy this.

As the meat cooked, she shredded lettuce and minced tomatoes. She put Jeremy to work grating cheese. As they toiled side by side, she chattered a mile a minute, hoping to put him at his ease.

"I love tacos. Especially with hot sauce. It just makes your mouth come alive. Michael used to…" Her voice trailed away as she realized what she'd said.

"Michael was your fiancé?" Jeremy's matter-of-fact voice inquired, eyes intent on the cheese as he carefully rubbed the slab of cheddar against her aunt's grater.

Gillian realized that she had been talking about Michael naturally for once, and although the pain was still there, it had diminished to the point where she could talk about him with fondness.

"Yes. He died in a car crash. Anyway, he used to tease me for being a wimp." Her mouth curved in remembrance. "He would load on the hot sauce until my eyes watered and I was coughing like crazy. Michael never even needed a drink of water. You know—" her eyes flashed to him and then looked away in embarrassment at the scrutiny she found there "—the Thai people clench their teeth together and then spread their mouth wide so they can suck air into their mouths, not blow it out. They claim it's the best way to cool your palate."

Jeremy was silent, steadily building the tower of cheese curls on the plate she'd given him. When he finally spoke, it was in a soft, careful voice that was totally unlike his usually brusque tone.

"It must have been very difficult for you," he offered. "Was that why you decided to move here?" His blue-gray eyes met hers steadily, his face set in its usual stern lines.

"Partially." She set the table quickly and scooped the browned meat into a bowl. "I just couldn't stay in Boston anymore. It reminded me too much of him and of what I'd lost.'' Carefully she removed the warmed tacos from the oven and placed them on the table beside the tomatoes and lettuce. A huge pitcher of lemonade and two large glasses completed the job.

''Ok, everything's ready,'' she grinned at him. As he gingerly set the cheese on the table, Gillian lifted a bottle from the fridge. ''Now, for your first taste of tacos. Don't forget the sauce.''

She murmured a short grace for both of them and then showed him how to assemble the items and bite off the end carefully so that the whole thing didn't crumble in his hand.

''It is rather good,'' he murmured, a surprised look on his face. ''And not really hot at all.''

''That's because you haven't used this yet.'' Carefully she spooned a small teaspoonful onto his taco. ''Now try.''

He gasped, and Gillian giggled as his eyes grew round with surprise. Seconds later he was glugging down a huge glass of lemonade.

''Good heavens,'' he whispered. ''That was like fire.'' His eyes were huge as he watched her slather on the sauce and then chew the mouthful with alacrity. ''How can you do that?''

''Practice.'' Gillian giggled. ''Plus the fact that this is extra mild.'' He raised one eyebrow skeptically. ''Don't worry. You'll get used to it.''

Jeremy finished his first taco and started gingerly on a second, carefully avoiding her jar of sauce.

''You reminded me of a visit I once made to my aunt here,'' he told her as they sat companionably sipping the icy lemonade. ''She invited me to stay while my parents attended some teaching sessions at the college. They were anthropologists, you see, and in order to maintain their grant status, they had to return to the States every so often for a report.''

''Was that why you went to boarding school?'' she inquired quietly. ''Because they were so busy?''

He smiled, but his gaze was far away. Gillian wondered idly what kind of a childhood he'd had.

''Not exactly. They spent a lot of time on a dig in Egypt and then Israel. They wanted to make sure my schooling was uninterrupted.'' He smoothed the tablecloth idly, his voice low. ''Anyway, every summer I came to spend several weeks with Auntie Fay. It was like a whole different world for me. The food, the clothes. Even the children were different.''

Jeremy glanced up at her and grimaced.

''I'm afraid I didn't blend in very well, and I must have been an awful nuisance to have around. My aunt took me to the county fair and let me ride on the Ferris wheel until I was sick. I think I must have tasted every flavor and color of cotton candy and sugar cone there was, but it was the candy apple that finally did me in.'' His face had a wistful quality about it that tugged on her heart.

''I've never forgotten the pleasure she gave me in those days. Or the way she would tuck me in at night and kiss me.'' Jeremy glanced at her apologetically. ''There aren't many people who will kiss anyone good-night in boarding school,'' he muttered quietly, his eyes downcast.

''But what about during the summers,'' Gillian demanded angrily. ''Surely you lived with your parents then?''

She couldn't believe it when he shook his head, his sharp gray glance telling her that he thought she should know better than to ask such a silly question. Her tender heart ached at the words.

''Gillian, an archaeological dig is no place for a child. There are valuable artifacts lying about and open pits around which it would be dangerous for a child to play. Not that there was much to play with, anyway. Besides, it was far too hot, as I found out the one summer I insisted on visiting them. I spent most of my time cataloguing their finds. A layer of sand covered everything.''

Gillian stacked the dishes into her aunt's dishwasher with a snap to her wrist that boded ill for the stoneware.

''I happen to feel that real, live children are more valuable than any old artifact from the past.'' She watched as he meticulously wrapped the leftovers and placed them neatly in the fridge. ''It doesn't sound like much of a life for a child,'' she added finally.

He looked surprised.

''Actually it was a very good life. I was able to spend much of the summer studying for the next term. My grades were very good, and I finished my O levels a year ahead of schedule.''

Gillian set the coffee to perk and waved him into the living room. She wanted to tell him that his rigid life-style had robbed him of the carefree play of a child, but who was she to judge. She could only sympathize with the little boy who had spent his time working on the Dewey decimal system for artifacts.

She had just poured them each a cup of the fragrant, steaming coffee when Hope's doorbell rang. It was Pastor Dave, in his usual jovial mood.

''I knew you two would be here,'' he said happily, his booted feet thumping heavily across the floor. ''Heard about your good news, too. Congratulations.'' His round shiny face beamed down at them both.

Gillian could feel the tide of red suffusing her cheeks, as she realized from his sparkling glance that he'd heard about their supposed engagement from Faith.

''Well, thanks anyway, Pastor,'' she murmured, glancing at Jeremy's gaping mouth. ''But we're not engaged. Mr. Nivens and I are merely colleagues.''

''Oh, I remember. Faith did say you and your beau were

trying to keep things quiet. I'll respect your privacy, Gilly, girl. Don't you worry. At least for a while.'' He winked and patted her shoulder, then whooshed down onto the sofa.

Gillian gritted her teeth and willed him to listen.

''You don't understand, Pastor. Jeremy and I aren't engaged. Not at all.'' She glanced at her supposed intended for confirmation and saw a glimmer of mirth deep in his eyes. He couldn't be enjoying this, could he?

''Oh, you've had a little tiff, I suppose. Everybody has them, sweetie. You just have to work through your problems. And at least you're doing that now before you're married.'' Dave patted her hand consolingly. ''That's a good sign that you two are adults, willing to compromise and accommodate the other's point of view. Now about the youth group,'' he winked at them both as they sat on either side of him, mouths hanging open in consternation.

''I just know you and your honey here will make good team leaders for the kids. I've arranged for them to go to Tyndale's farm on Friday night and play Capture the Flag, and I thought you two might like to come along and watch.'' He beamed down on them happily. ''Next week you're on your own.''

As the hefty minister lunged to his feet, Gillian glared at Jeremy. Do something, she telegraphed, and breathed a sigh of relief as he, also, stood up.

''I don't think Gillian, er, that is, Miss Langford and I, well, we don't exactly know just how to, well, deal with...''

He stopped abruptly when the reverend slapped him soundly on the back and bubbled with laughter.

''Course you don't, son,'' Dave chortled happily. ''But you're smart young folk with lots of schoolin'. I have every faith that God will lead you in your dealings with these young people. Anyway, it will be good practice for when your own come, eh!'' He chuckled with glee at their surprised faces.

''Meet you at the church in half an hour,'' his jovial voice chided them. "Don't be late." He surged through the room toward the front door, sniggering to himself as he went. "Well, well. A wedding. Haven't done one of those in a while."

Gillian sank onto the sofa, her knees buckling under the strain as she stared up at her intended. "Could you please stop this freight train?" she asked helplessly. "I think I want to get off."

She heard his hiss of disgust as Jeremy moved in front of her. The silver in his eyes glittered at her like steel, and his mouth was pursed in a hard, straight line of blame.

"Well, it's just a bit late for that, Miss Langford," he accused. "Especially now that the whole town thinks we're about to be married, *honey!*"

"Look," she began, anger poking at the way he was hinting that this was all her fault. "I was only trying to spare your aunt. She was just a little confused, and I didn't want to make it worse."

He shoved his hands in his pockets and glared furiously at her, his mouth grim.

"Well, you've made it much worse," he complained bitterly. "Now we've got the minister planning our wedding."

Gillian felt the chill of those cold gray eyes move over her with disgust as he said, "I don't want to get married. And especially not to a woman who is so obviously the opposite of everything I could want in my wife." His hands clenched and unclenched at his sides. "If I wanted one, that is. Which I don't."

Gillian felt tears of anger press against her eyelids, but there was no way she was giving in. Not with *him* standing there watching.

"Believe me," she enunciated clearly, determined that he would hear every word. "If I ever chose to be engaged again, which I won't, it certainly wouldn't be to some old-fashioned, stuffed shirt from the middle ages.''

He glared at her for so long Gillian thought his eyebrows would be completely lost in his dark mussed-up hair. His words when they came, were soft and menacing.

''Better to be old-fashioned than an airhead with no sense of responsibility. Good night!''

''Good night!''

He turned without a second look and stomped his way to the front door, collecting his suit jacket on the way. Gillian was smugly amused to see that somehow during the evening his tie had loosened and several shirt buttons had come undone. Jeremy Nivens also had taco sauce on his pristine vest, she noticed with satisfaction. Some of the superiority disappeared as she glanced in Hope's mirror and noted the state of her own disheveled appearance.

''Just a minute,'' she cried as he strode down the steps. At her words he stopped dead in his place and waited for her to catch up.

''What are we going to do about the youth group? Pastor Dave is expecting us to take over next week. We're supposed to be there tonight.''

When he looked at her, Gillian flinched at the anger emanating from his frosty gaze.

''Just another situation you've entangled us in, Miss Langford.'' His face was carved in those hard, bitter lines that had been missing for a while tonight.

''Well,'' she murmured quietly, ''are you going to tell him that you can't do it?'' She waited expectantly for his answer.

''No,'' he bellowed, sending her reeling in shock. ''I let him go away believing I would help, and I will. I'll set up a six-week Bible study for them.''

Gillian stared at him, frowning.

''A Bible study,'' she murmured quizzically. ''They usually do something fun on weekends. The Bible studies are on Wednesday evenings.'' She peered up at him curiously.

''Very well, then.'' Jeremy jumped over the side of the car and vaulted into the seat with a move Gillian had only seen in the movies. It was proof positive that there was a lot more to the man than she had suspected, when he could make a move like that so easily.

''You plan their events,'' he muttered angrily. ''I'll plan the food.'' He drove away without a single grinding of gears while she stood there staring after him. Jeremy Nivens was going to provide the food? As she walked back into the house, Gillian grimaced. What would the youth of Mossbank have to eat at their weekly get-togethers? she asked herself. Toast and jam? Or his American version of tea and crumpets? She dismissed the thought as uncharitable and not worthy of her and raced upstairs to change into her jeans and sneakers. If she was going to do this, and it looked like she was, she couldn't afford to be late for the first night.

To say that the youth group meeting that evening was a success would have been an overstatement of the facts. Two boys got into a disagreement after one of them twisted his ankle racing around in the bush behind the house, searching for the flag.

Several of the girls had declined to join in the roughhousing, opting instead to jump on their host's trampoline. Unfortunately, the combined weight of five bouncing teenagers had sent one of them toppling over the side where she'd hung suspended while Gillian and Jeremy tried to disentangle her sweater from the hook it had caught on.

That would have been enough, but Pastor Dave insisted on announcing their ''engagement'' to the assembled throng and then forcing each one to promise that they would keep it under their hats. The youngsters clustered around them excitedly.

The girls wanted to see her ring while the boys stood back with Jeremy and muttered "Good luck."

She was up to her neck in alligators, Gillian admitted when one of the girls spotted the emerald on her right hand and demanded to know if that was her engagement ring. Strangely enough, it didn't hurt nearly as much as she'd thought, to tell them about Michael.

"It was," she murmured softly, perching on the log some-one had placed around the fire pit. "But Michael died shortly before we were to be married. I wear the ring to remind my-self of the happy times we shared."

"That must have hurt pretty badly," Rosa Almirez whispered, placing her hand on Gillian's arm.

"Yes, it did. More than you could imagine."

"How did you get over him?" Janet Sivers asked.

"Well, at first I tried to get away from all the things that reminded me of him and the plans that we had." A movement beyond the circle of girls caught her attention, and she noted Jeremy and the boys moving closer to the fire. "I was really mad at God for letting him die, and I thought He'd done it to spite me. I decided I'd move to Mossbank and teach here."

"I'll bet you thought you'd never find anyone else to love," Marisa Clairns murmured, her eyes dreamy. "And then Mr. Nivens came along."

"Not exactly," Gillian agreed, her eyes drawn to Jeremy's darker ones. "I decided I would never get married. That I would learn how to live on my own, without anyone else." She saw Jeremy's dark eyes narrow as he glanced down at the group around her.

"I was determined to do things my own way until God began working in me, and now I'm beginning to realize that He only wants what is best for me. I have to remind myself that it's not my will but His that needs doing."

"But don't you feel sort of—" Blair Jenkins shrugged her

elegant shoulders "—like a traitor?" she muttered at last. "I mean, Michael was your own true love. You can't just replace him."

Gillian smiled and patted the girl's soft, blond head. "God gives us special people in our lives to teach us things, Blair. I'm not ever going to forget Michael, and no one can take his place in my heart." The words came out with a force meant to reassure Jeremy of her good intentions. Instead he stood back from the group, looking down on her.

But his face was a closed book, and she refused to beg him to understand. Her private feelings about her fiancé were none of his business. She was only telling the girls in the hope that it would help them deal with their own futures.

"Well then, how can you marry Mr. Nivens?" Desiree demanded, her highly made up face accenting the ring that pierced her eyebrow and glinted in the moonlight. "You're saying that you don't love him."

Gillian chuckled, pleased by the girl's astute mind, but just a little worried about the direction the conversation was taking. "No, sweetie. I'm saying that people have different places in our lives. You have brothers and sisters, don't you, Desiree?" She watched the young girl nod uncertainly. "And do you love one of them way more than all the others or is there enough room in your heart for all of them to fit comfortably—maybe even one more if it comes along?"

"Well, right now I'm not feeling a lot of love toward Zane," Desiree admitted, motioning to her older brother who was standing near Jeremy. "He read my diary, without my permission I might add, and I'd like to smack him upside the head." The other girls all giggled in appreciation, darting looks of condemnation at the red-faced youth. "But I get what you mean. Sort of like there's always room for one more."

"Yeah. Like love means different strokes for different

folks,'' Blair added smugly. "And there are all kinds of love.''

"That's exactly right,'' Pastor Dave said, smiling benignly. "And that's what we want to talk about tonight—God's love for each one of us.''

The kids gathered round their pastor, sitting close together on the logs and listening with interest as he outlined God's special enduring love for each one of them. Gillian stayed where she was, relieved to have the focus off her for now.

"You see, guys,'' the pastor continued, "it's like there is no beginning and no end to the love God has for us. And it is always the same, not changing like Desiree said her feelings did when her brother wronged her. God's love is always there, always holding us up, always waiting for us. All we have to do is accept it.''

As she listened, Gillian felt herself allowing some more of the pain and anger and frustration of Michael's death to slowly drain away. She would never understand why he had to die, she realized. But that wasn't important.

What was important was that God had not abandoned her, left her to face life on her own. He would be with her through the good and bad times. She just had to trust in that. And believe that some good would come out of it.

"God can't love us all the same,'' the pastor continued. "You and I have different life experiences, different needs for Him in our lives. What you need from God is different from what I need. That doesn't matter.'' He grinned a beaming smile that included the whole group. "'Cause God already knows that, and He's just waiting for me to ask Him for help.''

As she glanced around at the teenagers, their faces upturned as they listened to their pastor, Gillian said a silent prayer of thanks for the new life she'd been given. *I don't know much about teenagers, God,* she murmured under her breath. *But if*

*You'll help me out, I'll do my best. Even if I have to work
with cranky old Jeremy Nivens.*

She watched, smiling, as the teens jostled for position in
the lineup for chips, pop and hot dogs. They were a good
group, and they needed some direction. Maybe this was one
area she could do some good and help herself out of the dol-
drums while she did.

It was worth a try, wasn't it?

"It was a lovely meal, Hope. A perfect end to our day of
shopping in Minot. And I've never had poached chicken *au
naturel* before." Charity glanced at the leftover colorless,
odorless, tasteless meat that Hope had prepared, and with a
roll of her eyes, decided to change the subject quickly. "How
is your Christmas project going?"

Hope poured out two cups of decaf and carried them across
to the table. Her mind was busy arranging Flossie's encounter
with Jeremy. It wouldn't do to be too overt…subtlety, that
was the key. She sipped her coffee absently as she considered
the upcoming banquet. Maybe she could arrange to have the
two seated together.

"Hope?"

"Yes?" She stared at Charity's frowning face with perplexity. "Is something wrong?" she asked.

"Only the fact that I've asked you the same question three
times without response." Charity looked askance at the fourth
teaspoonful of sugar Hope had laced her coffee with. "And
when did you start eating white sugar?"

Neither of them had a chance to say more, due to the
pounding on Hope's front door.

"It's me, dear," Faith's happy voice chanted. "And Arthur. Don't worry, we've let ourselves in." She breezed into
the kitchen, breathless and ruffled, with the red-faced grocer
trailing close behind.

Charity shoved a chair toward him. "Sit down, Arthur, for heaven's sake. You look like you're about to have a heart attack." She watched his chest heave up and down for a few moments before demanding, "Did you run from the store?"

Arthur shook his bald head negatively as he wheezed and gasped for air. It was Faith's bright chipper voice that filled them in.

"Of course not," she protested, laughing as she flopped into the one vacant chair. "We raced each other here from my house. Arthur came for dinner." She raked her hand through her tumble of gray curls and grinned mischievously at the two women. "And he's got the most wonderful news."

Her bright green eyes sparkled as she patted Arthur's rough hand. "Go ahead, dear. Tell them."

Poor Arthur looked confused, glancing from Faith to Hope to Charity. His mouth was moving but there was no sound coming from it, and Faith was clearly losing patience with him.

"Oh, never mind," she said at last, her hands fluttering madly. "I'll do it myself." She took a deep breath and with a beam of satisfaction told her friends the good news. "Arthur says my Jeremy and your Gillian are engaged. Isn't it wonderful!"

Her two closest friends stared at her as if she'd just told them she was going to marry Arthur Johnson herself. Their mouths hung open in amazement and disbelief.

"It's impossible," Hope muttered, shaking her head as if to dislodge whatever prevented her from understanding such a thing. "Why, they don't even like each other!"

"Of course they like each other. They were kissing on my patio," Faith said fiercely. She wagged a finger in Hope's face. "People who hate each other don't do that."

"It's impossible," Hope whispered, her eyes wide-open. "You must have imagined it."

"I'm sorry, Hope," Arthur offered, rushing to Faith's defense. "But she's not mistaken. I saw it myself."

"There must be some mistake. Gillian can't stand the man."

"Well—" Arthur shook his head ruefully "—perhaps she's changed her mind, because she sure didn't pull away when he wrapped his arms around her and kissed her back. And in broad daylight." His tired eyes sparkled. "That was some kiss."

Faith nodded, grinning as she sipped Hope's overly sweetened coffee. Suddenly her expression changed and she stared at the other two women before turning to Art.

"Maybe we shouldn't have told them," she murmured softly, peering into his strong, steady gaze. "After all, Pastor Dave did say it was a secret."

Hope shrieked in the most unladylike fashion they had ever heard from her. "The pastor knows?" She sank dazedly into the kitchen chair with a weak groan.

Charity shuffled over to fan her friend for several moments, but there was no change on Hope's shocked face.

"Oh, my good Lord," Hope said over and over.

Charity helped the slender woman to her feet, issuing orders as they moved out of the kitchen.

"Faith, you and Arthur see to those dishes. I'm going to get Hope lying down in bed before she falls down. Then we'll all go home and leave her to sort this out in peace."

As they stumbled up the stairs together, Charity was already busy organizing the future for the little boy she'd met in Art's store and the jobs she had all lined up for him. It would be her first step in her own Christmas goodwill towards men project.

Chapter Five

Gillian slowly drove her aunt's car back into the small town at eleven-thirty that night, savoring the peaceful stillness. Where else in the world could you get such a wonderful feeling of security? she asked herself. The sky was bright and clear, its myriad stars perfectly visible in the black velvet expanse. She saw two figures chasing each other around the merry-go-round in the park, and Gillian found herself unintentionally watching them. It looked like fun—a carefree lighthearted romp that sent puffs of air out of their mouths to condense in the cool night air.

Gillian peered through the windshield. It couldn't be... Jeremy's Aunt Faith and Arthur Johnson? A smile curved her lips. Now there was a couple who knew how to enjoy life. She felt a tiny glow of pleasure cascade through her. It looked like her idea for a special Christmas project had been a good one. The older couple seemed to get along well together, and she had no doubt that Art would see Faith safely home, relieving Jeremy's anxiousness.

Ah, life was good. Well, except for one little problem. That silly pretend engagement. It seemed like the whole town knew about that now and believed the entire fabrication.

Sighing, Gillian slipped her car into gear and headed for Hope's. Maybe after a good night's sleep she would come up with some new idea to put a stop to all this, she told herself wistfully. Maybe.

Hope was sitting in front of the fire, busily crocheting another of the delicate white stars she sold as ornaments at the Christmas bazaar. She looked up as Gillian stepped through the door, setting her work carefully on her lap.

"Hello, dear. You're a bit late." Her tone was mildly reproving, and Gillian stared. It didn't sound like her aunt at all.

"I may be from now on," she told her quietly, sinking into the armchair with relief. "The youth group showed absolutely no inclination to go home tonight. Once they get talking, they can go on and on."

"Was Jeremy there?" her aunt asked softly.

"Jeremy? Why, yes. He's agreed to help with the group, after all. How did you know?"

Hope's pale blue eyes were narrowed in disapproval when she glanced up from her handwork. "Arthur and Faith stopped by this evening," she murmured. "They told Charity and me that you two are now engaged." Gillian felt the probing intentness of her aunt's stare. "I do wish you'd told me yourself, dear. I'm not sure this is the time to go barreling into another relationship with a man you barely know and have said repeatedly you despise."

"It's not that I despise him, Hope. Well, not really. He just..."

"Please don't think I'm trying to interfere in your life, Gilly." Hope cut through her halting explanations. "You know I feel very strongly about women making their own decisions in this life. It's just that it's so sudden. And unexpected.''

Gillian grimaced. ''You can say that again,'' she muttered. She tried to explain, as quickly and briefly as possible, exactly how the situation had erupted from Faith's strange memory.

''She was upset from the fire, and I thought she was just confused, so I went along with it. Then Jeremy rushed in and began demanding answers, and she continued talking as if we were the hottest new pair since Anthony and Cleopatra.''

Gillian paused for breath, the remembrance of that time on the patio causing a tide of red to flush her cheeks. Jeremy had kissed her; in anger, it was true. But still.

''But, Gillian,'' her aunt protested. ''Arthur knows about your engagement. Faith said Pastor Dave told them. Apparently the whole town has been informed.''

Gillian groaned, letting her aching head fall into her hands. She couldn't have managed Faith's delusional afternoon with less aplomb if she had tried. Now everyone would think they were engaged and intended to stay that way.

''It's going to look ridiculous if we announce that our one-day engagement is now off,'' she muttered, rubbing the tender spots on her scalp. ''I should have nipped it in the bud instead of playing along and teasing him, calling him endearments. No wonder she thinks there's something going on.'' She heard her aunt speaking through a fog of dismay.

''Calling him endearments?'' Hope's voice was squeaky with shock.

''Never mind, Auntie. It was a very bad joke and I'm paying for it now.'' She stood, tiredly massaging the throbbing pulse in her temple. ''I'm going to bed. I'm so tired I can hardly stand.''

She moved slowly to the stairs and then stopped.

''Hope?''

''Yes, dear?''

Gillian tried to arrange the curious facts of the evening in her mind. Something didn't seem quite right.

"Does Faith suffer from Alzheimer's?"

"I don't know, Gilly." Hope's voice was soft and pensive. "Her memory has been getting worse for a while now, but it usually involves forgetting where she's left something or not turning something off. This is completely different." She switched off the lamp and followed her niece up the stairs. "Why?"

"Oh, just something I was wondering about. Good night, Hope."

"Good night, dear. You know," Hope said, stopping at the door to her room, tears glistening at the corners of her eyes. "I've been praying for Faith for months now, asking God to heal her," she murmured. "She's been my friend for so many years now, and I can't bear to think of her forgetting all the wonderful times we three have had together. I can't imagine going to visit her one day and Faith not knowing who I am."

Gillian patted her aunt's shoulder. "God gave you Faith when you needed her all those years ago," she consoled her aunt. "I can't imagine that he's going to abandon you now."

Hope brushed away the tears and smiled her wide, cheerful smile as they hugged each other. "Thank you, Gilly. I'm sure you're right. He never gives us more than he knows we can deal with."

But as she lay in bed, the night sounds quiet around her, Gillian replayed the afternoon's events through her mind. She distinctly remembered Faith saying she had made the rouladin because beef was Jeremy's favorite dish.

How was it then that the older woman had claimed, only minutes later, that she and Arthur intended having a quiet meal together? She had even said there wouldn't be enough for Jeremy and almost ordered him to eat with Gillian.

Something about the incident bothered her, and as Gillian

snuggled her head against the pillow, she wondered if Faith Rempel was as confused as everyone believed. Maybe she was just a little bit, well, crazy?

Either way, Gillian was going to have to talk to Jeremy Nivens *again* and try to sort out the whole engagement thing. And the nursing-home issue. Slightly barmy or not, Faith wasn't the type who would do well in the restrictive atmosphere of a nursing home.

Gillian closed her eyes and refused to think about it anymore. The whole thing was too preposterous to believe. She'd come to Mossbank to learn how to survive as a single woman after God had taken her intended husband and left her on her own. She'd had no intention of even dating anyone again, let alone getting engaged. And certainly not to the likes of Jeremy Nivens. Not ever!

As she lay in bed, her Bible open in front of her, Gillian reread the verse she'd underlined that morning. "If your faith is as large as a mustard seed," she mused, pausing on the text. It seemed as if God was asking her to trust in him, to believe that he would manage it all for the best.

"I'll try to believe," she whispered in the private darkness of her room. "But, please God, could you help me sort out these strange encounters he and I keep having? Maybe somehow we could learn to be friends, with Your help."

Gillian had just applied pale pink polish to the last toe on her right foot when the doorbell rang.

"Blast it," she muttered, trying to stand and keep her toes elevated while retaining the puffs of cotton she'd placed between them. The bell rang again. "Come in," she yelled, but there was no response. In a jerky, halting gait she walked on her heels to the door and yanked it open, glaring at the man who stood outside.

"Yes," she demanded rudely, furious that Jeremy had

caught her with her hair in a towel, her toes separated by blobs of white and clothed in her rattiest old sweats.

She watched his eyes widen as they took in the thick, brown crusty layer of clay that covered her face, leaving just her eyes and mouth untouched. His blue-gray eyes widened even more as they moved down over the yellow knit sweatshirt that hung sloppily, exposing one shoulder, and the ragged joggers with the tears in both knees. But they stayed fixed on her elevated, white-cushioned toes the longest.

"Oh," he said.

The silence stretched between them.

"Is that all you came to say?" she asked perversely. "Thanks so much for sharing it with me."

"I guess this is a bad time to call," he muttered, his eyes riveted on her shirt front.

Gillian could have laughed at the ridiculous statement but she bit down on her lip. She moved slightly back on her heels trying to balance herself without falling backward.

"Do you need a doctor?" Jeremy asked.

Gillian stared. Was it possible that Faith's mental problems had been passed through the family to Jeremy? she wondered.

"Er, no, thank you." He looked relieved, she decided.

"It's just that you've cut yourself," he murmured, staring at the spatters of bright red on her sweatpants.

"It's nail polish," she told him, turning away from the door. "Come on in. I've got to sit down. Standing like this for more than two minutes is a real pain."

He followed her in to stand in the middle of the room, watching as she flopped onto the sofa and began to remove the rolls of cotton from between her toes.

"They're dry now," she answered the curious look in his eyes.

"Your toes?"

"The nail polish."

"Oh." He stood there gaping, as if he had never seen a woman with painted toenails before.

It was very disconcerting, Gillian decided, overly conscious now of the tight clay mask on her face, pulling her skin ever more taut as it dried. There was nothing for it, she was going to have to go wash her face.

"Excuse me a moment," she told him hurriedly, her skin a dried and barren wasteland under its cake of hard clay. "I'll be right back. Have a seat." She dashed out of the room without a backward glance.

Jeremy looked around, his eyes carefully observing that it was impossible to follow her orders. Every seat in Miss Langford's living room seemed to be covered with something. Clothes of every vibrant shade lay scattered here and there. He didn't recognize many of them, but something brown, tossed haphazardly on a nearby chair, caught his interest.

He picked up the note on top and read "Sally Ann." He recognized the suit as the one she'd worn in the schoolyard one fateful afternoon. If he recalled correctly, and he did, her skirt had blown up, exposing those long, slender legs and catching his class's attention. He wondered why she was giving the suit away. It was a much more suitable color for teaching than many of the other garments he noticed lying around.

Jeremy's attention caught on the bits of silk and lace he saw sprawled over the little side table. Although he averted his eyes as soon as he realized what they were, he couldn't shake the feeling of voyeurism at the sight of her delicate, lace-trimmed slips. They, too, were in bright peacock shades that he was coming to realize were part and parcel of Gillian Langford's dynamic personality.

"There, now." Gillian surged back into the room, her face clean and shining from the scrubbing it had received. The hard brown gunk was gone, and her lovely skin glowed with vitality. Her hair was free of its towel and lay against her head in tiny damp, wispy red curls that glimmered with golden highlights.

"Oh, dear. I'm so sorry. I was doing a bit of mending, and I'm afraid I've left everything all over."

Jeremy watched as Gillian scooped armloads of clothes up into her arms and whisked up the staircase with them. She showed little outward embarrassment when she picked up the sheerest, silkiest nightgown, but he could see a tinge of pink behind the spattering of freckles on her high cheekbones.

"There, now. Have a seat."

She was puffing slightly from all the stairs, and Jeremy watched her with interest. She sat there, calmly waiting for him to say something as he searched his memory for the reason for this visit.

"I hope you haven't suffered any repercussions from our supposed engagement," she said finally, covering the gap in conversation.

His brain snapped to attention. The engagement; that was it. He wanted to talk to her about their engagement. "I think we have a small matter to discuss," he muttered, and immediately wished he had shut up. She was right, Jeremy decided. He did sound like a stuffed shirt sometimes. But it *was* rather difficult to disengage yourself from an engagement that had really never been.

"That is, er, we should come to some agreement about our intentions. Not mine, but..." his voice trailed away. There just wasn't any delicate way to ask for an unengagement, he decided glumly.

"Oh, I see," she said with a grin, twisting her feet under her. "You want to weasel out of the nuptials. Is that it?"

"I never 'weasled in' as you so elegantly put it," he blustered. "You're the one who told my aunt that we would be married." He stopped because she was vehemently shaking her head.

"No," Gillian corrected him. Her golden-red curls glistened in a shaft of sun that poured through the window. "Your aunt told *me* we were getting married. I thought she might still be confused by the accident and went along with it."

"Well, obviously we can't continue the charade," he told her, picking off the white hairs from his slacks. The more he picked, the more there were.

"What is this, anyway?" he demanded finally, holding a handful of the white fluff out. He missed her answer because his nose twitched just then, and he couldn't suppress the loud sneeze that erupted.

"Cat hair," she told him smugly. "Mrs. Daniels was here and she brings her cats wherever she goes. Gee, I hope she didn't get it on my new black wool. It picks up everything."

Jeremy was beginning to feel like Alice falling down the tunnel. Everything was whirling and changing around him, and it seemed he had no influence over anything. It was not a pleasant feeling for a man who thrived on controlling his own universe, he decided.

"If you don't mind," he began sharply, "I'd like to get back to the matter at hand. The engagement," he prodded, when her eyes stared back at him blankly.

"I don't see that there's much we can do at this point," Gillian said quietly.

He stared at her.

"We're going to look like lunatics," she told him briskly. "If we get engaged one day and break up the next." Her shiny head shook decisively. "No, I think it's far better if we just let it stand for a while. Once the preparations for Christmas begin, no one will notice if you and I are no longer engaged."

Jeremy couldn't help it. Good manners forbade it, and yet for the second time in one afternoon his mouth hung wide open as he stared rather stupidly at her. "Do I understand you correctly, Miss Langford?" he murmured. "You wish the inhabitants of this community to believe that we two are engaged, until such time as the novelty wears off, and then you propose to quietly dispense with the subterfuge?" He shook his head. "That would be lying, Miss Langford, and I do not approve of lying."

"Oh, get over yourself," she muttered rudely.

Jeremy pretended he hadn't heard it. "And what on earth would I do with the engagement ring, once you decided you no longer needed it?" he demanded, glaring at her in his most severe form.

"Oh, great," she chirped, clasping her hands together happily. "You mean you'll go along with it?"

"No, I don't mean that at all." He glared at her. "I'm trying to look at this situation rationally and with some forethought."

It was hopeless, Jeremy decided. The woman hadn't a serious bone in her shapely little body. For some strange reason he suddenly thought of her fiancé, Michael, and wondered what the man who had put up with all this nonsense had been like. He would have given a great deal to ask the man some very pertinent questions right now.

"No, of course I won't go along with it," he muttered. "It's ridiculous. The board would be down my throat."

"Oh, the board!" She kissed her fingers into the air. "Ned's the chairman, and I don't think he'd care one iota what we do in our spare time. And we don't need a ring. I could say that we're having a special one made, or that we haven't decided on one yet or something." Her big iridescent green eyes narrowed, and Jeremy felt his pulse pick up. "Besides, we couldn't disappoint your aunt, now could we? After all, she was so happy about us."

"There is no us!" He felt his temper exploding and poured

every effort into containing it. "Why do you insist on carrying on with this ludicrous situation? We have nothing in common, so I very much doubt that anyone would be surprised at the sudden breakup."

He watched her face, studying the mobile features with interest. She was a curious mix, he decided. Like a coltish young girl galloping through life. And yet he knew that she was no teenager.

"Well then, what about your aunt?" she demanded. "How can you disappoint her like this? She's so excited right now. She thinks you're finally going to settle down and be happy."

Jeremy would have interrupted then, but Gillian, it seemed, wasn't quite finished. He watched as her expression went from tenderness to indignation.

"I can't believe that you would actually send that woman to a nursing home," she grated, green eyes sparkling with indignation. "Faith will be heartbroken when she learns you think she's so incompetent that she has to have full-time care."

"Then I'll just have to deal with that, won't I," Jeremy returned evenly. He should have stopped there, but he felt obliged to answer the condemnation evident on her lovely face. "I love my aunt, you know. And I'm trying to protect her as best I can."

"By locking her up?" Gillian demanded. "You know she'll hate that!"

He sighed, controlling his temper with difficulty. That was something new, Jeremy admitted. Until he'd come to this little town he'd seldom felt anger, let alone had to control it. He'd lived his life on the basis of rationality—every decision he'd made had been carefully weighed as to the best possible outcome and benefit, and Auntie Fay was no different.

"It's my duty to see that she is properly cared for," he reiterated quietly. "Since I cannot be there all the time, I have to find another solution. The nursing home is the best resolution to the problem.''

''There is no problem!'' Gillian's voice was raised in anger, and Jeremy fought his own temper with difficulty. ''Faith is perfectly fine on her own. So she burned something, so what? Lots of women burn a meal or two in their lifetimes.'' Her eyes shot little jade daggers at him. ''You would know that if you had ever cooked anything,'' she muttered snidely.

''It's not just the fire,'' he admitted finally, knowing she wouldn't give up until he'd said it all. Gillian Langford bore a striking resemblance to a bulldog with a large juicy bone when she got herself into this mode. ''Today I found some ice cream she'd forgotten in the back of her car. It had melted into the upholstery and took quite a bit of time and energy to clean up. Faith doesn't even remember buying it.''

''So what?'' Her narrow shoulders shrugged inelegantly. ''I've bought things and forgotten them at the store after I've paid for them. That doesn't prove I should be put away where no one will pay me the least bit of attention. If she goes into a home, Faith will undoubtedly become more confused and forgetful from the stress of all the changes. She needs familiar surroundings.''

Jeremy sighed. He didn't feel perfectly satisfied with this decision himself. It certainly didn't help to have to argue it all out with a woman who couldn't understand the fear that rose in him when he realized that he could have lost the one person in the world whom he most wanted to take care of.

''Look,'' he offered at last, keeping his tones even and calm, ''Auntie Fay isn't the issue here, right now. What I came here to discuss with you is this preposterous engagement. I can't continue to live a lie. We are going to have to tell the truth. If we look ridiculous, so be it.''

He shifted in his chair uneasily, wondering if he wasn't a fool to divest himself of the most beautiful woman in town.

He'd never had much to do with the fairer sex, but even Jeremy knew that Gillian Langford was something special when it came to the female of the species.

"I suggest that we speak to the pastor tomorrow after church." He forced the words out, anyway, unwilling to acknowledge the dull sense of loss he was feeling. "We have to do the right thing," he repeated to himself. "We can't keep living a lie."

Gillian chose that moment to jump up from her chair. "Then we'd better come up with a plan as to exactly how we're going to handle this," she said quickly. "It won't be easy. The whole town knows about us by now. You think of something while I get us a drink." She stared at him until he nodded, then moved to slip past his chair. But her pink toes seemed caught on the tassels of the rug, and she lost her balance.

Jeremy watched wide-eyed as Gillian reached out for something that wasn't there, teetered in midair for nanoseconds and then landed with a flurry on his lap. He reached out protectively to hold her slim shape steady.

It was sheer unfortunate circumstance that the three elderly women happened to walk in the door at that precise moment. He saw Gillian's aunt Hope study them suspiciously through astute blue eyes. She took note of the way his arm was curved around Gillian's waist and the way she dangled rather inelegantly on his lap...as if they had just finished some heavy-duty necking, he considered sourly.

"Oh, piffle!" Faith's high voice twittered in the yawning silence, drawing everyone's attention to her. Gillian took the opportunity to stand, freeing herself from his embrace, her eyes quickly slewing away from his.

"We should have given them another few minutes. Hello, young lovers," Faith trilled gaily.

Gillian met Jeremy's dark, forbidding gaze with her own

and clearly heard the frustration in the words he whispered. "Oh, brother. Now look what you've done!"

Gillian hurried into the small church, checking for early arrivals as she did. D-day! And *D* was for *denial*…as in engagement.

"Hello, dear," Faith Rempel murmured. "Arriving a bit early, are you?"

"Hello, Mrs. Rempel." Gillian felt herself flushing at the glint of knowing in the older woman's eyes. She'd seen the same look yesterday when the three older women had busied themselves, leaving her and Jeremy alone and embarrassed.

Gillian slipped off her heavy, black wool coat and hung it up with more care than was strictly necessary.

"I'm supposed to play the organ today, and I was hoping to get in a few moments' practice before Sunday school."

Faith nodded benignly.

"I know, dear. Jeremy's already here. Go on in. You'll find him behind the piano."

Faith turned away and immediately began chatting with another elderly woman who had just come through the door. Gillian didn't hear a word they were saying; all she could hear was the loud and forceful notes of the doxology resounding around the high ceilings of the sanctuary.

She stepped through the doors, tilting her head to one side as Jeremy switched tunes and began a lilting but complicated rendition of Beethoven's "Hymn to Joy" from the *Ninth Symphony.*

Jeremy Nivens was good, Gillian admitted. Very good. He played the baby grand with firm authority and yet careful attention to detail. The fortes were steady and decisive while the pianissimos were delicate, light touches that communicated a depth of feeling for the songs. And through the entire rippling melody, she heard not one wrong note.

Sucking in a breath for courage, she walked slowly down the aisle, slipped off her shoes and took her position behind the organ, switching it on and setting the worn knobs just the way she wanted. He looked startled to see her there, but merely nodded his dark head at her.

"I was going to try number two hundred next," he murmured, waiting until she found it.

Gillian nodded, relieved to find that she knew the song. In fact, "Count Your Blessings" had always been her mother's favorite song, and she'd heard it repeated in poem form often over the years. The organ was simple to manage, and even though she hadn't played for months, it responded to her every request, matching the piano and Jeremy's notes beat for beat.

"You're very good," she told him when the last chords had died away. "I had no idea you could play."

He grinned back at her, a slight mocking note to his smile. "Probably thought I was too old for music, right?"

Gillian grimaced ruefully at the remark, knowing she'd asked for it with her own uncharitable remarks weeks ago.

"I'm sorry," she offered quietly. "I should never have said a lot of what I did."

"Even if it was the truth?" He took pity on her after a moment and explained that he'd begun taking lessons when he was four.

"I've always loved the piano. At school the other kids used to have to pry me away from it. And of course we always had a school choir. It was good training in the classics, and there's nothing better than an old English church for a cappella singing."

He was flipping through several papers on the piano bench.

"I thought maybe this would do for the offertory," he murmured, handing her a copy of "All Creatures of Our God and King."

The sheet music was arranged for piano and organ and thankfully, Gillian noted, the organ section was fairly straight-forward. "Could we run over it once before everyone ar-rives?" she asked, glancing up to find his dark eyes fixed appreciatively on her navy silk dress. "I'm afraid I haven't played in some time."

He shrugged. "Why not?"

The notes were carefully placed in several keys so that the total effect was one of building adoration for God's wonderful creation, providence and redemption as the harmony re-sounded throughout the joyous anthem.

"You play very well," he said, closing the lid as children began arriving for Sunday school. "I'm afraid that's all I can do for now, though. I've got that class the pastor landed me with, and they'll tear the room apart if I leave them for very long."

Gillian chuckled, straightening her dress as she slipped her feet back into her bright red heels. She picked up the matching leather handbag and walked with him to the Christian edu-cation rooms.

"They had better not," she chuckled, pushing a stray ten-dril off her cheek. "I have the room next door, and my girls are very well behaved."

His eyes widened in disbelief. "Don't tell me you were conned, too?"

"Not exactly conned," Gillian said, looking up at him with a pert grin. "Let's just say there was no opportunity to re-fuse." She tugged open the door to her class and motioned to the rows of seated girls who sat watching them and giggling behind their hands. "See, I told you."

Just then a paper airplane sailed out from the room next door and there was a loud thump. Jeremy raised his left eye-brow at her and frowned. "And I told you," he muttered darkly, "they're wild, untamed animals. See you later." He

was inside with the door closed before Gillian made her response.

"Yes. Later."

Later turned out to be only seconds before the morning
service began and there was no time to do anything more than
place her purse and Bible in a nearby pew and climb onto the
organ bench once more.

The hymns the pastor had chosen were happy lilting ones
that people sang when they wanted to praise God, and Gillian
enjoyed hearing the small congregation join their voices in
tribute to Him. The music included many of the same songs
she had sung for years, and she managed to play them quite
easily.

Jeremy, it seemed, wasn't quite so pleased. He frowned
when Pastor Dave neglected to ask the congregation to stand
for "This Is My Father's World" and "All People That On
Earth Do Dwell." And he was almost scowling when junior
church was canceled and the offertory held back to just before
the sermon. Thankfully, however, his ill humor wasn't directed at her. Their number went smoothly, inspiring the pastor's kind remarks afterward.

As Jeremy sat down beside her in the pew, Gillian felt
prickles of awareness as she heard the minister's next words.
"They make a good team on the instruments, don't they folks.
And I'm sure most everyone knows by now that these two
are engaged, so Jeremy and Gillian will be teaming up together in the future as well."

She closed her eyes at the murmuring and cheerful smiles
directed their way. She ignored Jeremy's ramrod-straight
backbone and the tense way he held himself in the seat. It
was getting worse by the minute, she decided grimly. There
was no way they could back out now without looking totally
insane, but she still intended to give him the opportunity.

Gillian took a deep breath, opened her eyes and focused

them on the minister. There was nothing she could do right now. But somehow, God would show her the next step. For the moment she intended to enjoy the morning message.

"Folks, I want to talk to you today about your neighbor," Pastor Dave began with a wide grin down at them. His eyes twinkled with mirth. "You know, I once had a neighbor who insisted on wearing his hair combed from one side of his head, clean over the bald spot on the top to the other side. He sprayed and patted and combed that mess and when a good wind came along, that hair stood to attention like a private saluting a colonel."

The audience laughed at the mental picture.

"He wore clothes from the sixties and shoes from World War II. I never had too much to do with the fellow. Always figured he was a little weird and if I got too near, some of it might rub off. Some folks might say it already has."

Gillian sat in her seat, nervously aware of the man seated next to her as the crowd laughed at the pastor's joke. From time to time, Jeremy's shoulder brushed hers and she felt a tingle of awareness. When it happened, she would shift slightly and refocus on the minister. It happened that she was shifting quite a lot.

"But you know, dear ones, that one day I really needed a friend to help me out and that fellow was the only person around. I had to swallow my pride and ask his help even though I'd avoided talking to him in the past."

The minister's voice was solemn and quiet in the stillness of the sanctuary. Even the children sat silent, listening.

"Well, it turned out that Duncan was more than willing to help me out of a tight spot. In fact he went beyond help. He went the second mile. And as we talked that day, I began to realize that Duncan was on the verge of suicide. Everyone at the university avoided him or made fun of him, and he felt the stigma deeply." Pastor Dave cleared his husky voice.

"His average was nine on the Stainer Scale of Nine. He couldn't go any higher. He had no less than four prestigious job offers from companies that had responded to his impressive résumé."

Gillian felt Jeremy tense beside her as a baby cried out its discomfort, but as the minister began speaking again, her attention was fixed on the pulpit.

"But on that particular day Duncan was at the bottom of the despair trough. The one job he'd really wanted had been offered to someone far less qualified, simply because Duncan hadn't fit the company image for their top man. He wasn't tall, wasn't handsome, and he was bald."

Gillian noticed several of the members dabbing at their eyes.

"There wasn't much I could say. Duncan knew why he'd been rejected. And he was hurting. Badly. I could have told him it didn't matter, but that would have hurt him more, because to Duncan, it mattered. A lot." Pastor Dave smiled.

"Duncan wanted just one thing from me. He didn't want to be judged and found wanting again. He certainly didn't want pity. And he really wasn't interested in trying to become someone he wasn't." A silence of expectation floated in the room as every eye focused on the minister.

"Good old Duncan just wanted acceptance from me. He'd already made up his mind that if he was rejected once more, he'd kill himself. And I stood between him and that decision."

Pastor Dave looked around at the congregation and smiled at them. "What we're talking about here is acceptance. A little charity. I'm happy to say that I didn't miss it that particular time, but I wonder how often we Christians actually are able to bypass the outward appearance and accept the person inside who is desperately crying out for our attention."

His words went on and on, but Gillian was focused on what

he had said about accepting other people for who they are. Some part of her conscience nagged her about that phrase; poking and prodding until she was forced to acknowledge that she hadn't always accepted people for who they were. Especially lately. Especially the man seated next to her.

But then, there was such a lot about Jeremy Nivens that needed correction. Even now he was sitting there impatiently checking his watch every few minutes, as if that would remind the pastor that the service usually ended about this time.

Gillian came out from her reverie just in time to hear Pastor Dave's final admonitions.

"We have to learn to accept people for who they are, without trying to tamper with their personalities. This week let's all see if we can pass around a little of that unconditional acceptance that Christ gave to us."

Gillian moved to the organ and played the last hymn, her thoughts still whirling madly. When the pastor had moved to the foyer and half of the congregation had left their seats, she looked at Jeremy and, noting his nod, ended on the last verse. He got up from the piano immediately, closing the lid carefully.

"Jeremy," she murmured quietly, knowing she had to make the first move. "I'll go with you to talk to Reverend Dave after everyone has left. We can clear up this misconception about the engagement then."

He raised his dark eyebrows as he stared at her in disbelief. "Are you deranged?" he demanded furiously. His eyes glared down at her like chips of cold, blue-gray ice. "He's just announced the happy event to the entire congregation. Here comes someone now. No doubt a congratulatory word." He frowned in distaste. "It appears that we have little choice but to go along with this for now, Miss, er, Gillian. We'll go for lunch together and discuss the situation then."

Gillian kept her voice low as Lavinia Holt surged toward

them, a red-faced Flossie in tow. "But my aunt is expecting…"

"Oh, bother the aunts," he exploded, grasping her arm in his and urging her forward. "They have done quite enough." He bent his head to her ear in a manner that suggested a lover's intimate conversation but was, in reality, a direct order. "Do not invite that Flossie woman to come with us. I have had quite enough of her company for a very long time."

Lavinia burst upon them then, and it was impossible to question him further, but as Gillian glanced past Jeremy's black-suited shoulder, she caught a curious gleam of smug satisfaction in her aunt's eye.

Now what, she asked herself, *is that all about?*

Chapter Six

The restaurant teemed with families and friends enjoying the delicious brunch arranged so colorfully on big mirrored plates. Gillian wasn't sure how, but Jeremy had managed through sheer power of personality to procure the most secluded table in the house. She allowed him to take her coat before sinking into the chair and glancing around.

Good! There was no one she knew nearby.

"What would you like to have for lunch?" he asked her, frowning as he studied the lineup at the brunch trolley.

"We didn't have to come here," Gillian murmured, glancing around at the highly polished silver and sparkling glasses. "We could have talked just as well in the park." She risked a look at his glowering face and smiled. "You could have *kicked* something there."

Jeremy's eyes opened wide but he was denied a reply as the waitress showed up. They decided on soup and salad.

"And I'd like a slice of apricot cheesecake for dessert," Gillian said, smiling. "It looks too good to resist. Do you want some?" She glanced at her companion.

"No, thanks," he replied. "I'm not one for desserts. I will

have some coffee, though. Decaf, please.'' When the waitress turned to leave, he leaned back in his chair and stared at her. ''Well, Miss Langford, how do you propose to resolve this situation now?''

Gillian felt some of her good humor dissipate while struggling to maintain the smile on her face. If she had hoped for a friendly, uncomplicated lunch, it was obvious that Jeremy had no such intent.

''Why do you insist on calling me that?'' she hissed. ''You know my name, and people are going to think it a little strange if you call your fiancée 'Miss' all the time.''

''Miss Langford, this is not...''

''It's *Gillian*,'' she grated.

''*Gillian*,'' he started again. ''This situation is not of my making, and I assure you that I do not intend to allow it to go on for one second longer than necessary.'' Jeremy rubbed his chin.

It was obvious that he detested saying the words, Gillian decided. ''Don't worry,'' she told him impishly. ''I'm not all that demanding. Flowers once in a while. A meal now and then. Maybe a kiss or two under the moonlight.'' His eyes glittered with some emotion she couldn't quite define and Gillian wondered why she'd added that last, when she had no intention of being kissed by this man again.

''Miss, sorry, Gillian,'' he began, ''I don't think...''

''Kidding,'' she told him hastily. ''I'm kidding.''

''Oh. Too bad,'' he added. Gillian thought she detected the hint of a teasing smile on his lips for just an instant. She didn't know what to make of his reply. It wasn't quite the answer she'd expected.

Silence yawned between them until the waitress brought their soup. It was Gillian's favorite, beef barley, with chunks of colorful vegetables floating in the thick savory broth.

''This is excellent,'' she murmured, breathing in the aroma.

She saw his handsome face glower at her across the table. "What's the matter?"

"Nothing," he told her. "I hadn't realized they'd put in peas, that's all. I ate enough peas at school to cure me of them for a lifetime," he muttered dourly. "In fact, all the food I ate at school was pretty bad. Perhaps that's why I enjoy Aunt Faith's cooking so much." He patted his washboard stomach with a grin. "Everything she makes is a temptation."

"Ah," Gillian grinned. "You don't look as if you need to worry about your weight." She studied his broad shoulders and wide strong chest, then caught herself and stared down into her soup.

"I intend to have a good, long life," he said sincerely. "Which is why I watch what I eat."

He sounded so smug that Gillian couldn't help saying, "Dull, but long."

He flushed at that, glaring at her as she dipped a cracker into her steaming bowl. "My life is not dull. Not at all. I enjoy my work—I like an organized approach." His eyes sparkled with glee at her crinkled nose and just to tease her, he deliberately moved the cup and saucer an inch to the left.

"But don't you find it sort of, well, boring, to have everything so…programmed? I'll bet you even know what you're having for dinner tonight."

He glanced up, startled. "What's wrong with that?"

"Nothing," she agreed. "It's just that there's no opportunity to try something new…to enjoy something completely spontaneous." She saw his dark eyebrow rise mockingly.

"I do believe that I've had enough spontaneity for one week, Miss—Gillian. It's not every day that a man finds himself engaged to a woman he barely knows and then hears the news proclaimed from the pulpit."

Gillian blushed. "Well, okay. I get your point." She pushed the soup bowl away and leaned back in her chair to study him. "But that was sprung on you. You didn't really relish the change, if you understand what I'm saying."

Jeremy shook his dark head. "I'm afraid I don't," he told her truthfully. "We all have hopes and dreams, but we can't stand around, waiting for them to come true. We need to have a plan and then follow it." He glanced up, his eyes glowing blue. "Take you, for instance. You had your future all mapped out and then something changed. I'm quite sure you didn't embrace the change," he muttered. "I'm sorry. I don't want to hurt you by bringing up the past."

"It's okay," she told him quietly. "You're right, I didn't expect Michael to die. And it was very hard to accept. But I'm learning that God has a plan in everything that happens. I might not like it, but I can't be happy until I accept it and learn to move on." She swallowed the lump in her throat and continued.

"It's getting easier to talk about him now, especially with the kids in the youth group. They're so eager to explore life, to find out the boundaries." She blinked up at him. "That's how Michael was. There weren't many things he wouldn't try at least once, just to find out what it was like."

"What kind of things?" he asked as the waitress brought their salads.

Gillian thought for a moment before a memory slipped into her mind. "Like bungee jumping. He did it, you know. Off a bridge." Gillian wiped away a tear. "I was so scared, but Michael thought it was wonderful. Like skydiving."

"It is pretty dangerous," Jeremy told her. She could hear the disapproval in his voice.

"I guess it is. But Michael always said that God would take him home when He, God, was ready. And until then, he intended to live." She glanced down at her emerald ring; the one they'd chosen together. "I don't think he ever expected to go so soon, but since he did, I'm glad that he got to do some of the things he loved.''

Jeremy said nothing, merely staring at her. She felt his scrutiny but refused to look away. She had nothing to hide. When he spoke, his voice was pensive.

"Perhaps, if he'd taken a little more care, he would have had more time with you. I believe that God has natural laws that we humans aren't supposed to break."

Gillian sat a little straighter, studying him with a frown.

"Why do you always speak of God as if He's some kind of glowering judge, waiting to punish us?" she demanded. "I don't believe He's like that at all. I believe God wants us to do what's right, but when we goof up, He's not standing there with a whip, ready to apply the forty lashes."

"If He didn't want us to obey him, He wouldn't have given all the rules," Jeremy countered.

"The rules are guides, Jeremy. No one is perfect. God knows that. And he's prepared to forgive us. After all," she continued softly, "God is all about love. In everything."

Jeremy began saying something and then stopped abruptly, his face registering amazement. "Good grief," he muttered. "She's followed me here." Gillian was about to turn around when he said, "No, don't look. Just pretend we're a newly engaged couple having a perfectly amiable conversation."

Laughter bubbled up inside her. If only he could see the humor in their situation. "We are newly engaged," she said with a chuckle. "And the conversation was amiable. I thought." Then all words left her as Flossie Gerbrandt stood beside her, smiling a fatuous grin of adoration at Jeremy.

"I'm sorry you had to leave so soon the other evening," Flossie exclaimed in a whispery voice. She brushed her hands over her brightly colored skirt. "I was really enjoying your stories about England."

"Yes," Jeremy murmured. "I enjoyed it, also. But I had quite a bit of schoolwork to finish. Perhaps another time."

Flossie's eyes were wide with curiosity as she glanced from Jeremy to Gillian in surprise, obviously wondering why he hadn't been spending his evenings with his fiancée. There was nothing to do but step into the gap he'd created, Gillian told herself. And warn him about next time. With a tickle of delight, she wove her hand into his bigger one and patted it in true lover-like fashion.

"He means we'd both like to have you over for an evening," Gillian put in graciously. "Perhaps over the holidays."

"That would be nice. When are you getting married?"

Gillian watched Jeremy's eyes as he inadvertently swallowed a mouthful of the steaming coffee. It must have gone down the wrong way, because he began coughing.

"Oh, we're not sure yet, Flossie," Gillian said. "Everything's been moving so fast. We're trying to think of the best possible time, and since both of us work, well, you know what it's like."

Gillian smiled, to take the sting out of her words, recognizing the look of adoration that Flossie directed at her fiancé. Jeremy would have to act his part as her adoring fiancé well, if he didn't want to hurt this woman's feelings.

Flossie finally left a few moments later, and Gillian let the silly smile slip from her face. "You're going to have to do better than that if you want people to believe this engagement is the real thing," she lectured, dipping a fork into her cheesecake. "Mmm-hmm, you really should try this. It's delicious."

"The whole thing is preposterous, and we have your aunt to thank for this current situation."

Gillian felt her eyes open wide with amazement. "Hope?" she squeaked, staring at him. "You're blaming Flossie on Hope?"

Jeremy bristled. "Of course I'm blaming her. She set the

whole thing up, after all. It certainly wasn't my idea to have dinner at Flossie's house.''

Gillian shook her head in confusion. "I don't get it," she murmured. "Why would Hope try to pair the two of you up? Flossie is the one who will get hurt. Unless you really care about her…" She raised one eyebrow inquiringly and accepted his lowered eyebrows as a *no*. Gillian tried to ignore the little flutter of relief in her midsection.

"I certainly have not encouraged her. She's a nice enough woman, just so painfully shy that I hesitate to even speak to her. She needs to be included in more fellowship events." Jeremy eyed the cheesecake with an envious glint in his eye, glancing away only when Gillian pushed the plate toward him.

"Go ahead," she offered generously. "Try it. I think you'll like it."

"I can't," he murmured. "They've taken away my fork."

"Here, you can use mine." Before he could change his mind Gillian had sliced off a bit of the delicious dessert and was holding it to his lips. "I haven't had anything contagious in weeks now," she teased.

With a sigh of resignation, he took the small bite in his own mouth, rolling it around to savor the wonderful flavor. Just when she thought he would agree about how good it was, he surprised her.

"Probably eighteen grams of fat in that slice," he muttered, carefully wiping his lips with his napkin. "But delicious none the same. More, please?"

Gillian was surprised by the glint of humor in his eyes and was about to add her own pithy remark, when they heard a little boy speaking to his friend nearby.

"Well, maybe I do gotta be an angel, but I sure aren't playing no harp. I'm gonna play the drums!"

Gillian giggled at the note of pride in the squeaky voice

and turned to see if she could identify the source. As she did, her eyes fell on a small table in the far corner of the room. Faith Rempel sat staring as her companion, Art Johnson, who spoke in obviously worried tones, his forehead creased.

"Oh, look," she said to Jeremy. "There's your aunt with Art. Looks like they're really interested in something. I think they make a wonderful couple."

"'*Couple,*'" Jeremy echoed bitterly, setting his teaspoon against the saucer with more force than was strictly necessary as he glared at the two. "They're not a couple. He's just trying to inveigle himself into my aunt's good graces. He obviously wants something."

"Why would you say that?" Gillian demanded. "He's been a good friend to her lately, taking her for walks and having dinner with her. I think it's wonderful that she has some companionship. You don't have to worry so much about her now. Wouldn't it be wonderful if they fell in love?" Her voice died away dreamily as she stared at the elderly pair across the room.

Seconds later she felt Jeremy's strong fingers close around her arm. "My aunt was married for over thirty years to the same man," he informed her angrily, spots of color dotting his cheekbones. "I hardly think it's likely that she would find someone to fill my uncle's place. Fall in love indeed!" He glared at her.

"I'm sure she did love her husband," Gillian agreed calmly. "But just because she's loved one man, doesn't mean she can't love another. Your uncle is gone and Faith is still here. I think it would be wonderful if she could find someone to share these last years with." She didn't add that she hoped Art's presence would keep Faith out of the nursing home.

"Ha," he crowed triumphantly. "You say you think my aunt should get involved again, but you follow a different set of rules for yourself." His eyes gleamed at her. "Your fiancé died, but you still have your whole life ahead of you. Surely you want to find someone to grow old with?''

Gillian tried. Nobody could say she didn't work extra hard to stifle the response that came bubbling up from her subconscious. But it didn't help. The words spilled out helter-skelter, anyway, destroying the smile on his smug countenance. ''Some might say I've taken that step a little too early,'' Gillian said softly. ''I mean getting engaged so soon after moving here, *and* to my boss.''

He sighed then; a deep, wrenching sigh that admitted the hopelessness of his situation. ''Does anyone win with you?'' he asked with a small laugh. ''Ever?'' But there was a sparkle in his eyes and a determined set to those broad shoulders that told her he wasn't totally dismayed.

She could have been depressed by that look, except that Jeremy Nivens was tall, dark and very good looking. And perhaps the push-pull sense of challenge between them was more exciting than she'd ever admit. And she suddenly realized that she wouldn't mind losing a battle or two to him once in a while if it meant he'd relax that rigidly-controlling stance of his and let her see what went on behind the depths of his blue-grey eyes.

''Come on,'' she invited, gathering up her purse. ''It's almost time for choir practice. They're going to start on the Christmas cantata today.''

''I had intended to finish some paperwork this afternoon,'' he muttered in her ear as he held her coat out. ''I'm not sure I'll have enough time for choir this year.''

''Sure you will,'' Gillian said gaily, threading her arm through his.

''No, I'm sure that I—''

''If you don't,'' Gillian told him quietly, ''Verda will have you building sets for the Sunday school pageant. They're doing a five-act play.''

Reluctantly he steered them toward the church.

"I guess I can just fit in practice time," he muttered, his breath catching at the sound of her merry laugh.

The same thing happened an hour later when Flossie asked Gillian to sing a duet with him. Jeremy felt his whole body come tinglingly alive as her clear contralto tones ran over the sweet pure notes.

It was just another facet that he was learning about Miss Gillian Langford, he admitted. She had a beautiful voice, obviously well trained, as she sustained the last note for eight full counts. He felt his own voice ring true on his notes when the time came for his tenor part in the song.

"Oh, perfect," Flossie breathed when they finished the song in harmony. "You sing wonderfully together. You'll have a real ministry with that after you're married."

Jeremy felt that same old tinge of regret creep up on him. Gillian Langford was a beautiful, talented woman, whom any man would be proud to acknowledge as his soon-to-be bride. But she just wasn't right for him.

He wanted someone less, well, colorful. Someone who wouldn't draw people's attention when she walked through a room. Someone who didn't always try to change the status quo. Someone who followed the rules instead of making up her own. Someone who was content to follow the path *he'd* chosen, instead of veering off into little side journeys that took a completely different turn from the events he wanted to occur in his life.

His eyes moved over her slim, graceful form as she stood talking to several couples in the foyer. Her green eyes flashed, bringing her whole face alive and setting off the glints of reddish gold in her hair.

Jeremy wanted someone less, well…his mind sought for the right word. *Dynamic,* he decided. That was it—a woman who was more calm and stable in her reactions. Those were the assets he was looking for in a woman.

Against his will his eyes were drawn back to her generous smile as she chuckled at some joke an elderly bald-headed man murmured for her ears alone.

No, he told himself. Gillian Langford wasn't at all suitable. Was she?

"I didn't do nuthin'!"

Red-faced and belligerent, seven-year-old Roddy Green glared at his teacher with all the aplomb of a confident politician. It would have been convincing, too, if Gillian hadn't seen him slip a handful of elastic bands into his pocket.

"Roddy, we are supposed to be discussing Thanksgiving, and the pilgrims who had the very first Thanksgiving in our country many years ago…and all the things we have to be thankful for." She fixed him with her sternest look while removing his stash of projectiles.

She would have liked to rub the throbbing spot on the back of her neck, but that would be a sure sign that he'd gotten to her; Roddy could read adult reactions like a book.

"I don't got nuthin' to be thankful for," he muttered angrily, stabbing the toe of his filthy sneaker into the mat.

"I don't have *anything*," Gillian corrected, holding on to his arm when he would have ducked away. "And you have lots to be thankful for. How about your home and your parents and food in your tummy and a warm coat for the winter?"

To her amazement he burst into tears, yanking his arm out of her grip and dashing through the door in a flurry of action. Fortunately Gillian had an aide present in her room on Wednesdays, and mere seconds elapsed before she grabbed her coat and headed out after him.

Roddy was sitting in a little grove of trees just beyond the schoolyard. Technically it was off-limits to the students, but she wasn't about to discuss that now.

"Roddy? What's the matter?" Gingerly she placed her hand on his bony shoulder, leaving it there when he didn't flinch away. Gillian waited while he gulped and sobbed, dashing his sleeve across his face before glaring up at her.

"It's sumpthin' I can't talk about," he told her. "I promised my mom I wouldn't go blabbin'." He sniffed sadly, and new tears welled in his big sorrowful eyes.

"I certainly wouldn't want you to do that," Gillian murmured agreeably, slipping her arm a little farther around him. "But sometimes talking things over with a friend can really help. I'd like to be your friend, Roddy. Would that be okay?"

She waited breathlessly for his answer, sensing somehow that this child needed help. He peered up at her through the hank of dark, unkempt hair that hung over one eye. His look was skeptical, but at least he didn't pull away.

"I know how it is," she commiserated. "Every so often things just get too big for us, and even praying about it seems hard. That's when it's nice to have someone to talk to." She breathed her own prayer for heavenly guidance before tipping his grubby chin up toward her.

"Can't you just tell me a little about what's wrong? I know something is bothering you, because you haven't been doing your work as well as before. And today you weren't even listening during storytime." Gillian glanced around the schoolyard. "I didn't see you playing soccer at recess, either, Roddy, and I know that's your very favorite."

"I…I was tired of playing that baby game. 'Sides, I don't got no ball to play with. The other kids don't like me to play with them. They say I'm dirty."

The words came out on a tiny half sob of pain, and Gillian felt her heart shatter at the cruel words. She didn't have a chance to say anything because suddenly the words were pouring out of him.

"I know I need to get cleaned up, but I haven't got time. I gotta get supper for my brothers and help my ma get them to bed. Then it's my job to wash all the dishes." He said it with a sort of fierce pride. "Since my dad ain't there no more, I'm the man of the family."

He looked fearful, as if he had revealed some secret. Gillian murmured something soothing.

"I'm not s'posed to tell anybody 'bout my dad goin'," he muttered. "I didn't even tell Miz Flowerlady an' she said she's my special friend."

Gillian frowned thoughtfully.

"You mean Mrs. Flowerday?" she asked quietly. When he nodded, she pretended a previous knowledge of the relationship. "Yes, she's a really good person to have as a friend. Besides that, she can bake cookies like you wouldn't believe."

"I know," Roddy agreed, eyes glowing. "I go past her place sometimes, and she gives me some. I'm s'posed to be doin' jobs for her, but I can't. I gotta help my mom till she gets better."

It got sadder and sadder, Gillian decided, swallowing past the huge lump in her throat with difficulty. She straightened her shoulders briskly. Roddy definitely didn't want her pity.

"Well, my goodness," she said. "You are a man to be able to do all that." She stared at her hands, thinking madly. "I guess in the morning, what with your brothers and all, you don't have much time to make a lunch do you?"

He glanced at her sheepishly.

"I forgot to get some more peanut butter," he muttered. Gillian guessed that there probably wasn't any money for it.

"Well, Roddy. The thing is, our class will be having some homework for the next few weeks, and it's going to take some extra time. Maybe on Saturday you could bring your brothers to my place while your mom rests. Then you could have time to do some homework.''

''Oh, no,'' he gasped, staring at her in consternation. ''I couldn't do that. My mom would be really mad!''

''But, Roddy, she would be able to rest much better, don't you think? And I'm going to be at home all day. I'd like to have visitors. You could just bring them over in their stroller for a little while, couldn't you?''

He looked doubtful.

''Well,'' Gillian murmured, hating to push. ''You talk it over with your mom. And I'll make some gingerbread men from my aunt's secret recipe just in case you can come. Okay?''

He took a long time in replying. ''I guess.''

Gillian smiled and got to her feet.

''In the meantime,'' she said nonchalantly, walking back toward the school with him. ''I have a shirt and a pair of overalls that I bought for my nephew for his birthday. I found out that he's too big for both of them. Since I can't take them back, why don't you try them? I'd sure hate to just throw them out.''

''You mean blue jean overalls,'' he breathed, peering up at her with huge, awestruck eyes.

''Yep,'' she grinned. ''The real thing.''

''All right!'' he cheered, racing ahead. Seconds later he was back in front of her. ''Uh, thank you,'' he murmured.

''That's quite all right. I'll get them at noon when I go home for lunch. Okay?''

He nodded, obviously thrilled.

''Now how about if we go back and finish our drawings?''

He cocked his shaggy head to one side. ''Y'know,'' he muttered, holding the door wide for her to go through, ''I don't like drawing pilgrims and turkeys. They're too hard.''

Gillian grinned and led him back inside. *Back to normal,* she thought. *Almost.*

An hour later she was determinedly dragging the principal from his office.

"Come on, Jeremy. We have to hurry. I only have an hour." Gillian tugged open the door of his car and slid inside.

"Er, what, exactly, is this about, Miss—" he stopped as she gave a low growl of warning. "I mean, Gillian."

"It's about a little boy who's carrying the weight of the world on his shoulders," she muttered, leaning over to glance at the speedometer. "Can't you step on it?"

"I'm already doing forty," he told her. "And why are you dragging me downtown, anyway? I'm not involved."

"Oh, yes you are," she told him, grinning. "I want you to go to Frobisher's and get a pair of running shoes while I pick up some overalls at Hanson's Department Store."

"Why do you suddenly need new shoes at lunch hour on a Wednesday?" he asked crankily, peering at his watch. "At this rate, I'll never have time to eat. I'm starving."

"I don't need shoes, Roddy does. Here's the size. I want those new white ones with the black streaks on the side. And a pair of black socks," she added as an afterthought. As soon as Jeremy slid to a stop she was out of the car. "I'll meet you back here as soon as you get them."

"But, but…"

She left him sitting there "butting." There was no time to waste if she was going to pull this off. She also had to get a phone call through to Charity before lunch was over. Jeremy wasn't likely to give her any time off during school hours, she decided grumpily.

Within moments, Gillian had her fingers on a pair of the coveted overalls. She bought a pair a little larger than she thought he would need, just in case her guess was off. Anyway, they'd probably shrink in the wash. If they ever got washed.

A red-and-black-plaid shirt in warm brushed cotton matched very well. On an impulse she tossed in the denim cap that hung nearby. Ten minutes later, with all the tags snipped and in a plain brown bag, Gillian hurried back to the car.

Jeremy was leaning on the front fender, shoe box in hand as he gazed at the colorful display in the local café. Mouth-watering burgers, delicious sandwiches with crunchy pickles and golden steaming pies with rich cherries oozing out filled the windows in glorious Technicolor.

"Did you get them?" Gillian asked breathlessly. Without waiting for his answer, she tugged the shoes from the tissue-filled box. "Have to get rid of this stuff," she muttered and handed him the box and paper. "Here."

"Wait a minute," he grumbled, staring at what she'd given him. "It's not as if he will wear the things for very long, anyway. We'll soon be knee-deep in snow." He peered down at the runners she was shoving into her bag. "Do you know how much they charge for those things?"

"No," she murmured, intent on arranging everything neatly in her brown bag. "And I don't care. Money's not an object right now."

"Since when?" he grumbled. His stomach protested loudly, bringing Gillian's laughing glance back up to meet his glare. "I'm probably going to starve to death, you know. You had no right to give my lunch away to that scruffy child. Auntie Fay made those roast beef sandwiches just the way I like them. She even put in a piece of her special carrot cake. I love that cake." He closed his eyes in remembrance.

"Far too much fat for a man your age," Gillian informed him pertly. She grinned at him happily. "Anyway, he needed it more than you. I suspect he hasn't been eating properly."

She nodded at the café. "Let's go in here and have a nice nutritious low-fat salad. We've got half an hour before we have to go back."

Once they'd placed their orders, Jeremy tilted back in his chair and stared across the table at her.

"Why was it we needed to make this rush trip again?" he asked, frowning as the lunch-crowd volume grew.

"Sssh! I want to keep this between you and me," she hissed, glancing around to make sure no one was listening. When Gillian was satisfied that no one had heard his comments, she leaned toward him, beckoned his head nearer and explained.

"So you see, I've got to get someone over there to check up on the mother. Maybe she needs help. I know I would. Twins are no easy task!"

Jeremy shrugged. "You could always call in Social Services," he said, crunching into a cashew that had lain on the top of his chicken salad. "They have people trained to handle these situations."

Gillian snorted. "We don't even know if there is a 'situation' as you put it. And who do you think Roddy will suspect when those outsiders come rushing in? *Me,* that's who. Besides, his mother asked him not to tell their woes to the whole town. She's probably embarrassed or something."

"And your solution is?" His face was full of skepticism.

"I'm going to get Charity Flowerday on the case. Apparently she's already made some overtures toward Roddy. If anyone can figure out a way to help that family, Mrs. Flowerday can."

Chapter Seven

"Hello, Hope, dear. How are you? Frightful weather, isn't it?" Charity Flowerday bustled through the door and shook off the thick layer of wet snowflakes on her shoulders. "I was hoping to speak to Gillian. Is she home?"

"No. She and Jeremy are working late at school—preparing for the school Christmas pageant, they said." Hope shook her blond head with disdain. "I love this coat of yours," she murmured, stroking one hand over the muskrat hairs. "Do you think other people, outside of Mossbank, I mean, still wear fur coats?"

"I imagine." Charity smiled, slipping her feet from her galoshes. "I loved them myself. There is nothing like the warm cosiness of mink or fox."

"I know," Hope said with a sigh. "Especially when it's forty below and there is a stiff north wind. Of course, you know, most folks have cars nowadays. They drive wherever they're going."

"Well, there is that of course," Charity agreed. She sank into the soft, plushy armchair and sighed at the warmth coming from the fireplace. "But I think the reason furs have gone

out of vogue these days is because there was such a fuss about
animal rights and such.'' She stared into the glowing coals
thoughtfully before resuming her train of thought.

"I don't think anyone in my generation ever thought of
that. I know I didn't. We simply wanted fur because it's so
warm. Now I see these movie stars marching around, carrying
signs and such, making everyone else embarrassed to even
admit they own a fur coat, let alone wear it in public.''

They sat there for several seconds before Hope sighed
again, a deep, heartfelt, tired breath of air that came from the
depths of her very soul.

"Why, Hope, what's the matter?" Charity stared at her
friend curiously, wondering at the tiny frown that pleated
Hope's smooth forehead. "Are you worried about something?"

"Someone," Hope replied in a dull flat voice. "Gillian."

"Gillian? But why, dear? She seems so happy these days.
Why she was full of vim and vinegar when she asked me to
check out little Roddy's situation. And Jeremy was there, too.
Bought a pair of shoes for the lad, I believe.'' Charity beamed
across at her friend, genial benevolence casting her generous
features in a less-harsh light.

"*That's* exactly what I'm afraid of. They're doing far too
many things together. I'm afraid Gillian is growing attached
to him.'' Hope stabbed the needle through her cross-stitch
fabric viciously and tugged it through the other side without
regard for the fine fabric.

"But surely that's good. After all, dear. They are engaged.'' Charity's tired eyes opened wide when Hope jumped
to her feet.

"It's pretend," Hope insisted. "Why are you all acting as
if it's the greatest thing when you know as well as I do that
it's only a temporary misunderstanding?''

"Well," Charity murmured, lifting her half-completed af-

ghan from her bag and knitting furiously. "It doesn't look
like it's temporary anymore. She was kissing him that day,
remember. And they have been spending an awful lot of time
together."

She ticked the occasions off with a click of her needles.
"The youth group, choir, the instruments at church, Roddy,
and now the Christmas program." She shook her head, smiling from ear to ear. "Where there's smoke, there's fire, my
mother always said. Seems to me that there is a lot of smoke
between those two. And I'm glad. They're good for each
other." Charity placidly knit another few rows before sensing
that something was wrong. "Hope?"

"Do you *dare* say that they are falling in love?" The words
came through tightly clenched teeth. "Don't you dare."

"But, Hope," Charity protested, laying aside her handwork. "I think it would be a wonderful thing if they grew to
love each other. Jeremy is a good foil for Gillian's natural
exuberance. And she's a catalyst for change in his life. I think
God has done very well by those two young people."

"It's too soon," Hope protested angrily. "Far too soon
after Michael's death for her to know her own mind. Why,
she hasn't even grieved him properly!"

"Oh, my dear." Charity placed her arm around her friend's
narrow shoulders and squeezed them. "How can you say that?
There is no set period of mourning. And God's timing is always right. If He has brought them together, we should do all
we can to help them on their path."

"And if He hasn't?"

Charity smiled at the doom and gloom in her friend's voice.
"If it isn't God's will that Gillian and Jeremy pursue this
relationship, then He will direct it that way." She patted
Hope's shoulder before resuming her seat. "It's our job to
pray for His direction in their lives, and it's His job to direct."

"I suppose," Hope answered halfheartedly. "But I so

wanted someone special for *Flossie*. That girl deserves a medal for the life she's led with that mother of hers."

"I think," Charity giggled girlishly, flushing a faint pink, "that God is working in that area, too. I noticed Lester Brown talking to her last Sunday. He seemed fairly smitten."

"Oh, pshaw! Lester Brown is ten years older than Flossie," Hope protested. "And a widower, to boot."

"So what?" Charity sniffed airily. "He's a good, kind man who treats Flossie as if she were a queen. And he *doesn't* live with his mother. In my books he's okay."

Hope was about to explain all the reasons why Lester Brown was totally unsuitable for her protégée when the front door flew open and Faith bounded through.

"Oh, my," Charity breathed.

"Lord love us," Hope said.

"Oh, piffle," Faith exclaimed. "Now I've gotten all this snow inside your lovely hall, Hope. Sorry. It's just that I really must sit down for a moment."

With a whoosh, Faith plunked down onto a nearby chair and scrunched her eyes tightly closed. She had on her snowsuit; the one in her favorite shade of pale pink. Thick snow encrusted the heavy mittens lying at her feet in a pool of melting snow.

"Oh, thank goodness," she said, blinking at them several moments later. "For a moment there, everything was spinning round and round. It's much better now." Her bony fingers reached up to touch the area just above her hairline, disturbing the wild disorder of her hair. "Just here, it seems to be a bit tender," she told them.

"Where have you been?" Hope demanded, picking up her mittens and wiping the floor in a swift economical movement.

"What have you been doing?" Charity asked at the same time, peering over her glasses at the disheveled woman. "You look like you fell face first into a snowbank."

"I did!" Faith's eyes glowed brightly in her ruddy face. "And I hit my head on the teeter-totter. I think it's okay now, though. I couldn't have been out for that long."

"Faith Rempel, do you mean to tell me that you were out in all this snow, by yourself, knocked unconscious?" Hope's scandalized tones were squeaky with disbelief.

"You have to go out in the snow to cross-country ski," Faith told them simply. She smiled happily. "It was wonderful—all that fresh white snow. I fairly flew over the trail. Fresh powder. That's what the kids call it." She wore a pleased, proud look on her face as she imparted the information.

"Fresh powder, indeed!" Hope glared at the older woman in frustration. "It's supposed to get quite cold tonight," she grumbled. "What would you have done if you'd been stuck in that snowbank overnight? Hmm?"

"I would have wished my friend Hope was there with some of her yummy hot chocolate." Faith peered up at her hostess wistfully. "Please?"

"Of all the silly, extravagant, overblown ideas! Men!" Gillian's voice rang out, clear and angry. "Hope, I'm home." The three elderly ladies glanced at each other and then winced as the front door slammed shut.

"I can hear that, dear. We're just going to indulge in some of my infamous hot chocolate. Would you like some?"

"Oh. Hello." Gillian stood at the entryway, hands clenched at her sides. Her gaze rested on Faith's bemused face for several moments before she declared in frustration, "Jeremy Nivens is a horse's patoot!" Then, turning, she stomped up the stairs to her room.

"Well." Charity smiled, resuming her knitting at lightning speed. "That certainly clarifies matters."

"What do you mean, Charity?" Hope stared at the tiny

woman's complacent figure. "She's furious. Shouldn't I go and talk to her?"

"Oh, I don't think so, dear." Faith shook her salt-and-pepper head negatively as she eased one arm out of her snowsuit. "When a person gets into that state there's only one thing to do—let them sort it out for themselves."

"What state?" Hope looked disbelievingly from one to the other of her nonchalant friends. "What state?" she demanded again, an edge to her normally soft tone.

"Gillian's in love," Faith murmured with a coy grin. She looked for confirmation to Charity who merely nodded.

"Deeply," she said before her needles resumed their clackety-clack sound in the silent room.

"He's crazy. Totally out to lunch. Bonkers!" Gillian viciously stabbed the carrots on her plate with each angry word. "He thinks he can just order something and it will be done."

"Who, dear?" Hope inquired mildly, as if she didn't know.

"Jeremy pigheaded Nivens, that's who!" Gillian glared at her aunt. "And don't you dare try to smooth it over. This time he's gone too far."

"Gillian," her aunt began, aghast. "I would never take his side over yours. You know that. Now, calm down and tell me what the problem is this time."

"The problem," Gillian said between clenched teeth, "is that Mr. Nivens feels that our JFK Elementary should put on a play for the parents this year. A four-part play that involves all classes, extensive costumes, six massive sets and hours of practicing."

"Well, that sounds lovely, dear. I think the parents will enjoy seeing their children on stage as part of the school body. In my day we could never afford the time out of the classroom for such an elaborate affair but then..."

Gillian cringed as her aunt hit on the main point of contention between herself and the principal. Her ire surged up once again as she cut Hope off in mid-sentence.

"That," she grated, "was exactly my point when I looked over what he intended. It's almost Thanksgiving, Hope. There is hardly enough time to prepare a class recitation, let alone a four-part play."

"But, surely if you scheduled practices for after school and Saturdays, you could fit it all in?" Hope crunched thoughtfully on her carrots. "I mean, obviously the parents will help. And I don't mind sewing some costumes."

"Ha! After school and on Saturdays, you say. Wonderful! Fine idea! Except that Pastor Dave was by today to inform me that Jeremy thinks it would be a great idea for the kids of the youth group to go skiing a week from Saturday."

"Oh, how wonderful. I'm sure they'll enjoy that." Hope brightened considerably at the news, failing to notice the red suffusing Gillian's already-flushed face.

"Yes, it's *fantastic*. Except that I had already promised my Sunday school class that we would go to the city and do some Christmas shopping that day. Now what are we supposed to do—change our plans for *him?"*

The gall of the man, Gillian fumed. She wasn't about to tell her aunt how Jeremy had practically ordered her to go along with his play idea—right in front of the other teachers! Engagement or not, he had no right to pull rank in such a despicable manner.

The youth group thing was merely icing on the cake. Proof positive that they could never, ever work together. They were supposed to function as a team with the kids—in tandem, planning each outing jointly. But now, apparently, he'd gone ahead and booked the ski hill and even rented skis without even consulting her. It was…infuriating, she decided at last. But it was also just like something Mr. Jeremy Nivens would do. Why, she had a good mind to— The doorbell rang just then, cutting off her nasty thoughts.

"I'll get it, Hope. You finish your meal." Gillian pulled the door open with a wide, plastic smile that quickly cracked when she saw the tall, lean man standing outside. "What do you want?" she demanded, furious that he would confront her here, in her own home. Was there no refuge?

"I hope I'm not disrupting your meal," he said politely, stepping through the door without waiting to be asked.

"Yes, you are," Gillian said curtly, snapping the door closed. "But then, what's new? You have a tendency to proceed like a bull moose."

"Is something the matter, Gillian?" he murmured softly, his innocent eyes peering down at her. She couldn't fault the note of concern in his low voice. "It's not still the play, is it? I tried to explain how easy it would be, but you stormed out before I could say anything."

Gillian flopped down into the armchair and glared at him.

"What is there to say?" she demanded sharply. "You *advised* us that we would be doing the play. Don't kid yourself that there was any free choice involved."

She watched as he sat down opposite her on the sofa. He sat perched on the edge of the cushions as if ready to take flight at any moment. The smooth note of concern had evaporated from his voice and a frown had narrowed his eyes.

"Okay," he muttered. "What's the problem this time? What have I done wrong now?"

Gillian stared at him, outraged that he'd even ask such a thing.

"You know blessed well," she spat out, her newly manicured fingernails digging into her palms.

"No," Jeremy said wearily, raking one hand through his usually neat hair. "Actually I don't. But I have a feeling you're going to tell me."

And Gillian did. Clearly, concisely and without sparing her words.

"It's a good thing we're not actually engaged," she finished, holding her tears back with difficulty. "I'd call the whole thing off, if my intended husband pushed and bullied people the way you do."

"I didn't know about your plans, Gillian. You never mentioned that your class was planning an outing. And you could have. The Sunday school superintendent specifically asked everyone about their Christmas plans last week."

"It wasn't planned then," she told him sourly. "And that still doesn't absolve you of planning youth group activities *without* me."

He sighed a deep sigh; long, drawn out and full of frustration. It whistled loudly through the silent room. Belatedly, Gillian wondered where her aunt had gotten to.

"I didn't *plan* anything," he protested angrily. "As usual with regard to us, the pastor is a little off the mark. The ski hill merely called back with the rates and advised me that they had a cancelation and that I could book it now and cancel later if the time wasn't suitable. I thought it was a good idea to book it just in case.

"If you're that much against skiing, we can cancel right now." His chin jutted out in that hard, determined line that bespoke his disgust with the whole sequence of events.

"What I'm against is people trying to order me around. I am not some subservient species, Jeremy Nivens. I do have a brain, and I can think for myself." Gillian crossed her arms over her chest and glared at him.

"Oh, for goodness sake," he muttered, surging to his feet. "This is ridiculous. I thought perhaps we might have a civil conversation for once, but I see that's impossible. Again." He brushed past her to snatch up his coat. "We'll have to find some other time, when you're not so irrational, to plan future youth meetings."

Gillian grabbed his arm as he strode toward the door. "That's what you're here for? To plan youth group meetings?" Gillian stared at him, wondering if all her faculties were working. "Very well, then," she said briskly. "Let's begin." She swept back into the living room and tugged out a pad of paper and pen. She'd show him who was irrational, Gillian decided grimly.

"Now, then. This Saturday we have that scavenger hunt, right? And next Friday? Or were you going to cancel that and have it Saturday instead?" She sat perched on the edge of the sofa, pencil at the ready.

"Will you stop acting like some eager-beaver secretary?" he murmured. "We agreed we would be partners in this. If you don't want to go skiing on Saturday, why not say so?"

"It is not that I don't want to go skiing," Gillian enunciated clearly. "I quite like skiing. The point is that I have made other commitments. Don't you ever do anything with your Sunday school class?"

He stared at her.

"That bunch of hooligans? I don't think so. I had to ask Mr. Johnson to help me out on Sundays just to keep them all in line. You saw what they're like."

Gillian stared at him as a new idea popped to life. It might work, and it would offer a perfect way out of the present impasse.

"Why not invite them to go skiing?" she asked softly. "They're too young for youth group, and yet they are desperately searching for their own niche in the church. Maybe an excursion of their own is just what they need."

"It certainly isn't what I need," Jeremy groaned. "How in the world would I get them there, together and in one piece?

Without going insane, I mean?'' He gave her a sour look that told her he was not enamored of the prospect.

"I've already chartered a bus,'' Gillian told him excitedly. "It's only half-full because I hadn't gotten around to telling the girls they could invite a friend on this shopping excursion. Your aunt is coming with us. If Mr. Johnson came with your boys, it would be great.'' She grinned at the thought of the preteens' pleasure in leaving their elders behind.

"I don't know,'' Jeremy muttered thoughtfully, studying his toes. "Downhill skiing can be dangerous for someone who doesn't know the rules.'' He rubbed his chin. "I have taught others, of course, and I was once a member of the ski patrol.''

Gillian knew what was coming and blurted it out, just to prove she had a head on her shoulders. "You'd need permission slips from the parents, of course,'' she said smugly. "My girls have already handed them in. And they'll have to cover the cost of their equipment and food.''

He raised one eyebrow. "I'm happy to see you've taken such precautions,'' he told her. One long finger rubbed at the cord pulsing in his neck. "That still leaves Friday night and the youth group, though. What will we do about that?''

Gillian grinned. Here it was; opportunity just waiting for her. "Snowmobiling,'' she crowed. "The Reids invited us to use their farm whenever we wanted. They have two machines and I've counted six others that I think would be available. Mrs. Reid even said she would be happy to make hot chocolate afterward.''

Gillian waited for Jeremy's response. It was halfhearted at best.

"I don't know much about snowmobiling,'' he murmured, staring at her curiously.

"But I do,'' Gillian told him gleefully. "I've ridden one hundreds of times. I learned when our family moved to Canada for two years. The Canadian prairies are one of the best places in the world to ride a snowmobile.''

"Isn't it rather, er, dangerous?'' he asked quietly. "I've heard stories of people being killed.''

Gillian nodded solemnly. "If you go too fast, it is dangerous,'' she agreed. "But maybe Mr. Reid would mark out a trail. I know they have a huge meadow that is completely unfenced. Aunt Hope and I used to go berry picking there. We could simply follow the trail.''

Jeremy looked less than thrilled with the idea, but he offered no concrete resistance to her plans. They discussed several other things before he got up to leave.

"I hope this has resolved some of the tension between us,'' he said, pulling on his overcoat once more. Blue twinkles sparkled in his everchanging eyes. "Although I don't know how you could accuse me of being unwilling to cooperate,'' he muttered, shoving the buttons through their buttonholes willy-nilly. "You arranged everything for the snowmobiling. I had nothing to say about it.''

"Well,'' Gillian murmured, feeling pleased that they were back on speaking terms, at least. "We each have our strengths, I guess. Mind you—'' she handed him his gloves "—I'm still furious about that silly play you've chosen for the school. For the next few weeks we'll be doing nothing but practicing.''

Jeremy shook his head, chuckling as he stepped out the door.

"Please don't start that again. It's already past eleven, and I'm on supervision bright and early tomorrow morning. Besides—'' he grinned at her across the sparkling snow "—it won't be that bad. You'll see.''

Gillian watched him walk down the path. He was almost out the gate before he turned back.

"By the way,'' he called. "How's the Green situation?''

"Charity is on the case,'' she called back.

* * *

"Hello," Charity Flowerday beamed up at the emaciated woman who had answered the door. "I'm looking for Roddy. Is this where he lives?"

"Why, yes," the woman whispered, pausing to cough raggedly into a handkerchief. "I'm his mother. But he's at school." A piercing cry rang through the air. "Oh, dear. I have to go."

She whirled away so quickly, she didn't notice Charity squeeze inside through the door. By quickly divesting herself of her coat and galoshes, Charity just managed to follow the woman into the kitchen. On the floor sat two identical two-year-olds, one banging on the other one's pot.

"Oh, what lovely babies," Charity exclaimed, reaching down to touch one tousled brown head. "What are their names?"

"Oh, you startled me!" Mrs. Green put a hand to her chest. "I didn't realize you'd followed me."

"And I'm sorry I did that," Charity said. "It was very rude of me, of course. But I wanted to talk to you about Roddy, and I knew you didn't want to stand chatting at the door. Especially with these two big enough to get into everything." She waited silently until the woman had finished yet another bout of coughing.

"My dear Mrs. Green," she murmured, resting her hand on the woman's thin arm. "You sound as if you're ill." She peered assessingly at the wan complexion and the tired eyes.

"I'm very tired," the other woman admitted. "I'll just get the twins down for their nap and then I'll rest." Slowly she removed two half-full bottles from the old refrigerator in the corner. "Come on Charlie, Patrick. Time for a nap."

The boys stood quickly enough, eyeing Charity as they toddled over to their mother.

"No bed," muttered one of the tykes, grabbing the bottle

out of his mother's hand, ready to toss it across the room.

Swifter than an eagle, Charity slid the object out of his grasp and returned it to his mother. She held out her own hand.

"Come along, my boy. When mother says it's nap time, we have to obey. Mother needs a nap, too. She's very tired. Here we go, now." She nodded encouragingly at Mrs. Green and was relieved to find the woman understood her signal. Seconds later the boys were in bed, happily sucking down their milk.

"Now, why don't we sit in here. That's right, you just put your feet up on the sofa and rest. I sometimes chatter on, so you'll be sure to tell me, won't you." Charity smiled, noticing the droop of the woman's eyes.

"Something about Roddy, you said." Mrs. Green yawned delicately, trying to hold her eyelids up with apparent difficulty.

"Oh, Roddy. Such a lovely boy. Comes to see me, you know." Charity babbled away, her eagle eye noticing just when Mrs. Green nodded off. "Just loves my cookies, he does." She kept up the monotonous babble until she was sure the other woman was asleep. Then, tiptoeing out of the living room, she gently closed the door to the kitchen and opened her purse.

"Such a wonderful thing, these cell phones," she murmured, punching in a number on the keypad with little difficulty. "My Melanie always did think of the most wonderful Mother's Day gifts. Of course, it probably comes from working in the nursing home. So practical." She spared a thought for Faith's possible admittance into that home and winced as the woman's voice came on the line.

"Hello, Faith? This is Charity. Charity Flowerday. Yes, dear, that's the one. Now listen carefully. I have a job for you."

* * *

Three hours later Gillian found all three of the women sitting around the Green kitchen table enjoying a cup of coffee.

"But where's Mrs. Green?" she asked curiously, shushing when Hope told her to. "I need to talk to her about Roddy's costume for the Christmas play," she whispered.

"Don't you be bothering that sickly woman with the likes of that," Charity muttered, folding the last basket of laundry Faith had lugged in from her car. "She's worn to a frazzle with those two."

"Those two" sat on a blanket on the gleaming floor, Faith between them, munching on a cookie.

"I think you should check those squares," Charity murmured just loudly enough for Faith to hear. The older woman got to her feet and looked into the oven. "They look lovely, Faith, dear."

"Everything looks real nice," Roddy murmured, staring around his home with interest. His finger slipped over the bright red vinyl on the kitchen chairs. "Where'd these come from?"

"Why, Roddy Green," Charity pretended surprise. "These are your very own kitchen chairs. I just washed them and used a bit of sealing glue on them."

Roddy didn't look convinced, especially when he saw the bit of leftover vinyl sitting on the counter, but his attention was caught by the wonderful spicy odor wafting through the house. He sniffed several times and then licked his lips.

"Gingerbread," he cried, causing everyone to hiss "Shhhhh".

"Roddy, I think the twins want to play outside now. I brought over a little sleigh for you to use. I think they'll both fit into it." Hope watched in admiration as the seven-year-old slid the two toddlers into their snowsuits without difficulty. "My, you are good at that," she said.

Flushed at the kind words, but happily chewing on his own cookie, Roddy ushered the twins out the door. With a shriek of laughter they plunged face-first into the snowbank and rolled in it excitedly.

As soon as the children had left, Charity stood to her feet. "Now, ladies, this woman needs help. Her husband is off looking for work in the city, and she's been left alone with hardly any money and three young 'uns, to boot. We've done all the cooking and cleaning we can for now, but she's got to get to a doctor or these children will be orphans."

"I'm not that sick," a weak voice from the doorway murmured. "I can still care for my family."

"Of course you can," Charity murmured. "But first, Hope here is going to take you down to see Doctor Dan to get something for that cough. Don't worry—" she held up one hand, forestalling the protests they all knew were coming "—we'll watch the children till you get back."

It took a round of introductions and a few moments of heavy-duty persuasion, but finally Anita, as she had told them to call her, pulled on her worn wool coat and headed for the door. Her face brightened considerably when her hand found the loose change in her pocket. She'd forgotten all about it, she murmured. Maybe she could afford some medicine, after all.

Once they'd left, Charity turned to Gillian.

"That girl needs a warm winter coat—maybe nothing fancy, but something warm. And some gloves and boots. Can you handle that?"

Gillian nodded, a little stunned by the overwhelming need of Roddy's family. "Yes, I think so. I have several bags of clothes in my room that I was going to give away. She's more than welcome. I'll go get them right now.'' She scurried out of the kitchen.

"Faith, you get on the phone to Jeremy," Charity said. "I want him to look at this furnace. Something's not working right. This house is too cold for those young children." She pulled a pan of golden Santas and stars and Christmas trees a little nearer and began decorating each with colored icing. "Then, of course, we've got to get some groceries here. I couldn't haul over near enough."

"Arthur would help," Faith squealed happily. "He'd bring over whatever you needed."

"Of course," Charity said, beaming. "While you talk to your nephew, I'll make a list."

Gillian heard the two of them chuckling merrily as she tugged on her boots and buttoned up her jacket. The meager confines of Roddy's home had shocked her. They didn't even have the bare necessities in this house. And that coat of Anita's!

As she pulled on her warm leather gloves, she thought again about those red, worn fingers that Anita had tried to hide in her tattered gloves. And a picture of the lovely new navy coat she'd just purchased for herself floated guiltily through her mind.

She didn't need it, Gillian reflected. Not really. Her white melton was barely two years old, and there wasn't a mark on it since she'd had it cleaned. She thought of the matching red leather gloves and the red woolen scarf she'd purchased especially to go with the new coat. Anita had the kind of blond fairness that would suit the dark color, she thought. And the red would give her pale skin some color.

When you do it unto the least of my brothers, you do it unto me.

It was a verse she had read in her private Bible study that

very morning. Had God meant her to help out Anita with her new coat? Surely her white one would do just as well?

A little voice whispered inside her head as she plodded through the snow-clogged streets, *Would you have Jesus wear the white or the navy coat?*

She scurried onward, knowing what she had to do. It wasn't that much of a sacrifice, Gillian told herself, snuggling against the fur collar of her jacket. She would still be dry and warm in her other coat. She jumped as a car horn sounded behind her.

"Where are you going?" Jeremy asked, his dark head catching snowflakes as he leaned out the window. "I thought everyone was at the Green house."

Gillian stepped over the snowbank and slipped into the seat beside him. "They are," she told him, rubbing her hands in the warm air coming from the heater. "I'm on my way to Hope's to pick up a few things for Anita, that's Mrs. Green, while she sees the doctor. Apparently that's why Roddy's been so unkempt." In a few short sentences, she relayed the whole sad story. "Faith was trying to reach you when I left. Something about checking the furnace."

"I don't know anything about furnaces," he told her grimly. "Why don't they just get a repairman? And if it's dangerous, I certainly don't want my aunt involved!" He glared at her as if the whole situation were her fault.

"Look," she said, exasperated by his attitude. "This is a family that needs help. Christmas is supposed to be a time for giving. Can't you spare a few moments to give a little to someone else for a change?"

Jeremy swallowed his retort as he noticed the flash of ire in her sparkling green eyes. All right, he had sounded uncharitable. But blast it, anyway, it had been a day to forget, and he had no wish to add anything else.

"Okay. We'll go to Hope's and you can get what you

need,'' he said acquiescing. ''Then I'll drive you back and take a look at this monstrosity. But I'm warning you, I don't know anything about furnaces or repairing them. Absolutely nothing.''

Jeremy watched as she jumped out of the car once they reached her aunt's. She moved like lightning, he decided. No wasted effort; no pretense. Just get the job done. He liked that about her. He followed her inside.

But as she slipped off her jacket and bent over to unlace her boots, Jeremy decided there were certainly other assets about his pretend fiancée that he had overlooked. Her hair, for one thing. It burst out of her cap like fairy dust suddenly set free. He mocked his poetic thoughts even as he watched the light sparkle off the soft curls that stood out around her head from the static electricity.

''There,'' she said, straightening as she tugged her royal blue sweater over her hips. She waved him in. ''I'm going to be a few minutes so make yourself at home.''

And sure enough, a few moments later she was trying to manhandle a huge black garbage bag down the stairs.

''Here,'' he offered, meeting her halfway and taking the weight in his arms easily. Jeremy set it down in the middle of the living room and straightened to find her directly in front of him, mere inches away. His breath caught in his throat at her luminous beauty, and he reached out to touch one glistening curl that had strayed across her eyes.

Gillian stood perfectly still, allowing him to move the strand as she stared back at him. Her eyes were wide-open, innocent. Her lips rosy and shiny as she gently swiped her tongue across them.

It happened so quickly that Jeremy decided later he couldn't have stopped himself even if he'd wanted to. His hand curved around her chin as he leaned forward and pressed his lips against her full mouth. He moved his mouth against her gossamer-soft one and felt Gillian's shiver of response.

She didn't move away. She didn't even open her eyes to chastise him. Instead, her head tilted just a little to allow him greater access. Jeremy took that as a yes and wrapped his other arm around her slim waist as he deepened the kiss. She stiffened for just a second, and then her arms were draped around his shoulders and, hallelujah, she was kissing him back.

When Jeremy finally pulled back he found Gillian's clear, wide gaze fixed on him.

"Why did you do that?" she murmured, her fingers pressing against the lapel of his jacket.

"Because you're very beautiful and I wanted to." He smiled, feeling more lighthearted than he had in years. "Didn't you want me to?"

As Jeremy stood silent, Gillian blushed a deep, startling rose. She lowered her gaze, long golden lashes hiding her eyes from him.

"Actually, I did," she whispered in a voice so soft he barely heard it.

"Good," he muttered, tugging her against him once more. "Because I'm going to do it again."

Gillian's strong arms slipped around his neck as she pulled his head a little nearer. "Good," she echoed breathlessly.

Less tentative, more demanding on Jeremy's part, this kiss asked more questions, which he noticed she willingly answered. It could have gone on and on, but the telephone rang, abruptly breaking their silent communication.

Jeremy let his arms fall away and stepped back as she moved toward the phone. His eyes intently followed her, noting the swift rise of that wonderful color to her cheeks and the way her eyes glanced at him and then skittered away when she saw him watching her. Jeremy smiled to himself and sank onto the nearby sofa.

Gillian wasn't any less affected by this new intimacy than he was. Good, because he fully intended that there would be more. He had this ridiculous insatiable craving to touch those lips once more; to trace the planes of her beautiful face and nibble on her earlobe. It was crazy. It was wonderful.

It wasn't like him at all.

"That was Hope." Gillian stood by the phone, twiddling the cord between her fingers. "She wants us to bring some of her raspberry jam over." Not once did she look at him.

Jeremy stood and walked over beside her rigid form. When he placed his hand on her shoulder, Gillian lifted wide, startled eyes to stare at him.

"I'll say I'm sorry, if you want," he told her, allowing the smile to tug at the corners of his mouth. "But I'd be lying. I'm not sorry I kissed you." He grinned. "And sometime, at a more convenient time, I fully intend to do it again."

His heart sank as Gillian just stared at him, as wide-eyed as a doe. Then, just when he was sure all hope was gone, her eyes began to glow with that inner light.

"And I fully intend to kiss you back," she told him, smiling. "But right now we've got to get back to the Greens'." And leaning over, she teetered on her tiptoes as her lips grazed his cheek. "Later."

It was a promise, Jeremy decided. One that he'd hold her to, hopefully *sooner*.

"What is all this stuff?" With a grunt of relief, Jeremy stuffed the last bag into his back seat and tilted the driver's seat back in its usual position. "We should have called a mover."

"Mostly it's clothes I bought to get you off my back," Gillian told him pertly. "You did spend the first few weeks of September telling me how inappropriately I dressed, remember? I blew a big chunk of my wages buying black, navy and neutral-colored clothes.''

He snorted. ''I never said any such thing. I merely suggested—''

Gillian held up one hand. ''You know what…'' she told him, frowning fiercely, ''don't go there. We'll only end up arguing some more, and I think we've gotten beyond that these past months.''

He nodded, edging closer to her.

''Far beyond that,'' he agreed, slipping one arm around her waist.

He watched, not totally amused, as Gillian ducked away from him and climbed into the car, eyes brimming with laughter.

''We have work to do. Remember? The Greens,'' she chided, watching him frown.

Jeremy shifted gears easily and moved the car slowly away from the curb, enjoying the rub of her shoulder against his in the small confines of the sports car. Gillian sat with a huge box on her lap.

He kept careful watch as she handed it to Mrs. Green and noted the glow on her lovely face.

''Oh, but it looks new,'' Anita protested, lifting the expensive wool coat from the tissue.

''It is.'' Gillian said.

''But you can't give away your new coat,'' the woman protested folding it back into the box with a sigh of regret.

''Well, if you don't want it, I guess I'll have to find someone else,'' Gillian told her, smiling. ''I certainly can't wear it. There's something about the fabric that bothers my skin, must be allergies. I break out in a rash,'' she told them.

Of conscience, Jeremy felt like adding, for he had seen her remove the tags from the coat and gloves at Hope's and knew full well she could have returned both to the exclusive shop she'd gotten them from. He'd also seen her press her cheek against the soft cashmere and sniff the new leather.

But now, as he watched her give away the lovely clothes and saw the smile of joy cross her face when Anita tried them on, he felt a pang of something deep inside.

Yes, Gillian Langford was a sight to behold. She might wear bright, colorful clothes, and she certainly was hotheaded. And no one could argue that wherever she went, heads didn't turn to notice the stunning auburn hair. But today he had seen something completely different; something that had him realizing he really knew very little about the beautiful woman everyone thought he would marry.

Today he had seen deep inside, to the generosity and kind spirit that was just as bright and just as glorious as her outward beauty. And suddenly he wanted her to turn that loving, caring smile she was bestowing on those children on him. He wanted to be the recipient of one of those dazzling grins and return one of her spontaneous hugs.

So when she sat down next to him at the dinner table with the aunts, Arthur Johnson, Anita and her children gathered around to say grace over the savory stew and fresh biscuits, Jeremy reached under the crisp, white tablecloth and clasped her hand in his. And when she glanced at him in startled surprise, he bent his head near hers, eyes twinkling, and whispered for her ears only, "After all, we are engaged! Remember?"

Chapter Eight

"All right, children!" Gillian tried to keep the Christmas spirit in her voice, but it was difficult to do when the surrounding din had nearly reached ten on the Richter scale. "Choir, I want you to try that last number once more."

Obediently, the kindergarten and first-graders lined up, albeit helter-skelter. She looked around for her pianist, but Jeremy was busy trying to get the members of the cast into costume and ready to go on stage. Puffing her bangs out of her eyes in resignation, Gillian straightened the last little girl into line and then sat down at the piano herself. Although she had never even seen this music before, she decided to give it her best shot. Someone had to!

"All right, children, here we go. One, two, three, four. 'City side....'" And indeed, off they went. Off-key, off tempo and in no particular order.

Half an hour later Gillian sank onto the staff-room sofa, thrust her feet up onto a nearby chair and blissfully sipped at her coffee. She needed this. It had been a Friday to end all Fridays.

Around the room the other teachers were packing up to go

home for the weekend, but Gillian ignored them as she closed her eyes and dreamed of Christmas holidays; of mornings spent lounging lazily in bed; quiet solemn afternoons of uninterrupted reading. They opened in startled awareness, when she felt the cool press of masculine lips against hers.

"Jeremy," she gasped, straightening in such a rush, some of the cooled coffee slopped over the mug and onto her white corduroy pants. "You can't do that in public!"

"It isn't public," he told her, grinning as he waved a hand around the empty staff room. "Everyone has gone home. Long, long ago."

"Oh." She yawned. "I'm dead."

"It has been a trying week," he admitted, lifting the mug from her hands and sipping from it. For some reason, the gesture sent tingles of awareness through Gillian's body that heightened when he sank down beside her and placed his arm along the sofa back behind her.

"By the way," he told her, playing with a curl escaped from her neat chignon. "That last song you were doing with the choir?"

"I know," she groaned, tilting her head back and feeling his hand rub her scalp. "Don't remind me. It was awful."

He laughed. "Yes, it was. Part of the reason it was so awful is because you were doing it in a different key. I transposed it into five flats. It's easier and the kids can hold pitch better." He chuckled at her groan of dismay. "And the other problem was that you had the wrong boy singing the solo."

"No wonder he didn't know the words," she exclaimed, glaring at him. "You might have said something." The words died as he leaned closer and brought his lips to within inches of hers.

"I thought I just did," Jeremy murmured before moving closer.

Gillian wanted that kiss; had waited days for it. And nothing and no one was going to stop her from enjoying it. Long moments later she laid her head on his shoulder and murmured, "This is nice. I could just go to sleep."

"I don't know why not," Jeremy murmured, brushing a gentle hand across her hair as he stood to his feet. "As long as you've got the snacks ready for tonight, your time is your own."

Gillian narrowed her eyes and peered up at him.

"What snacks?" she asked warily, rising from the sofa as a tiny feather of dismay wafted through her mind. "What's going on tonight?"

"Snowmobiling. Have you forgotten?" He tugged her by the arm over to the coat stand. "Go home and rest. You'll need it."

Gillian felt all the old anger begin to rise anew. "But why is it my responsibility to arrange the food?" she demanded. "You are supposed to be part of this 'team.' It wouldn't hurt you to help out once in a while." She saw the tightening around his mouth, felt the sizzle of electricity in the room as his eyes darkened and his brow furrowed.

"Just a blasted minute here," he muttered. "You distinctly told me that our hosts would provide the hot chocolate. I'm sure you said that you would look after the snacks. In fact, I could almost swear to it."

Gillian bristled. "There is no swearing on school property," she told him self-righteously. "And don't go all grim and nasty just because you imagined something that never happened. I got the snacks last time, you get them this time." She snatched up her coat and thrust her arms into it angrily.

"I can't. I've got a parent coming in this afternoon," he told her, glancing at his watch. "In about five minutes, actually. I'll barely make it to the church on time as it is."

"Well, my time is important, too," she told him, frowning.

"I know that," he sighed with long-suffering forbearance,

irritating Gillian to no end. "But just this once could you help me out and pick up something for them? Donuts, chips and dip—they'll inhale anything."

"For your information," she flung, knowing it was sheer tiredness that was making her so cranky, but feeling justified anyway, "I *have* helped you out. On numerous occasions. With no thanks for my efforts. It's about time you did some of the work you're so eager to dish out. The rest of us are tired of being your peons." She snatched her coat up and angrily marched out the door without a backward glance.

But halfway down the hall Gillian remembered that he expected her to supply the food. "And pick up the donuts or whatever yourself," she called grumpily. "I'm going home to soak in the tub."

Let his high-and-mighty bossiness fill those bottomless pits called children for once, she told her nagging, reprimanding conscience. *It surely is about time he took on some of that job.*

Still, as she lay in Hope's big tub with the soft subtle fragrance of rose-scented bath oil drifting around her, she couldn't help but wonder what kind of food Jeremy would bring.

"As long as it isn't egg salad sandwiches," she muttered, frowning as she dipped her head under the water.

There was a surplus of youth and a shortage of cars that evening, and it wasn't easy to find a ride to the farm. Even now Gillian was sure the good reverend wondered why Jeremy wasn't driving his fiancée to the event.

"He's probably going to be late," she told Pastor Dave. "Tonight Jeremy is supplying the food."

"Oh, boy," a teenager groaned from the back seat. "I hope you know what you're doing, Gillian. He doesn't like normal junk food, you know. He always says there's too much fat in chips and too much sugar in pop."

"Yeah," Marissa's voice chimed in. She giggled. "I never noticed that he applied the same theory to pie, though. Mrs. Rempel told my mom that whenever she makes pies, Jeremy pigs out. I watched him at the church supper at Thanksgiving and it's true! He had *three* pieces."

Gillian smiled, recalling the night in question with mirth. Jeremy had been scandalized that there was only one kind of salad available. And he'd rudely labeled the gravy as "artery-clogging fat." But when he'd passed the pie table, his eyes had glistened with avaricious glee.

The kids from town sat twittering in the back, whispers whizzing back and forth between them. Gillian grinned, knowing all that exuberance would soon be outside in the fresh air. They were a good bunch of kids; full of mischief, but caring.

Jeremy was already there when Pastor Dave's car rolled down the lane into the farmyard. He stood in the middle of the path, talking to several of the men who had brought snowmobiles for the kids to use. As everyone tumbled out of the car, Gillian took her time, studying the situation as she strove to think of something to overcome the angry words of earlier.

When she looked up, however, Jeremy's eyes met hers. To her surprise they were glowing with excitement. He grinned and motioned her over.

"Mr. Reid has made a trail for us. It follows through the woods, goes through a couple of fields and ends up back here. And there are more than enough snowmobiles for everyone to share." He rubbed his hands with glee. "It's all worked out very well."

As if he had some part in that, Gillian grumbled to herself as she nodded and shook hands with the men who had so graciously loaned their machines.

"Thank you very much. We really appreciate this. And the kids will be very careful with them, won't you?" Gillian glanced around at the group of grinning faces, glistening with good health, and listened as they called their thanks to the men.

Mr. Reid, Pastor Dave and the other men organized everyone on a machine, some in pairs, some singly. One by one, they were shown the controls, told the dangers and warned to stay on the track. It was only as they came to the last one that Gillian noticed she and Jeremy had been paired. Apparently this was not to his liking for his face had grown pale.

"I think I remember most of it," she told a smiling Mr. Reid. "It's been a long time, but some things you don't forget easily."

Gillian snapped on her helmet and turned, only to find Jeremy's huge eyes staring at the black leather seat with something remarkably like fear. She held out his helmet, and when he didn't immediately take it, slid it on his head herself. "I'll drive first since I've been on one of these before. You just hang on to me."

It wasn't what she wanted. In fact, the less contact she could have with this disturbing man, the better. But the rest of the group was sitting, waiting. It was obvious they didn't sense Jeremy's fear, and something, some regret for the way she'd spoken this afternoon, made Gillian want to keep it that way.

"You lead, Tim," she called out to the oldest Reid boy. "You already know the way. The rest of us will follow, but not too closely. Jeremy and I'll follow behind everyone else to make sure no one is left stranded. Okay?"

They all nodded their agreement.

"No stopping on the trail, Gillian," someone called out teasingly. The other kids chimed in, making their catcalls loud and embarrassing.

Gillian slid down her visor and pulled up her gloves, hoping that no one would notice the red stain she felt flooding her cheeks. A stop on the way was the farthest thing from her mind right now. When she waved her hand, Tim started off down the track, the others following at an evenly spaced distance.

"Climb on," she told Jeremy quietly. "We'd better get going."

"Perhaps it would be best if I stayed here. Just in case someone is needed..."

Gillian flipped up her visor and glared up at him, hoping anger would do the trick. "Are you crazy?" she demanded inelegantly. "I'm not taking that bunch into the bush on my own. If anybody stays, it's me. Now either you get on, or you go by yourself."

He did, but it took several moments for him to adjust himself to the feel and slope of the seat, and by that time the rest of the group had long since moved out of sight. Gillian took her place in front of him and gunned the engine twice before taking off. He slammed into her from behind as they flopped over a mound of snow, and seconds later she felt his hands around her waist.

The evening was a lovely, clear, crisp one with thousands of stars twinkling brightly overhead. Gillian breathed in the fresh air with relish, bounding along in the cold, but snug in her warm ski suit. Jeremy had righted himself somewhat. However, his hands still clung to her tightly, sending tingles of awareness all through her body. She had to expend considerable effort to concentrate properly on her driving.

You haven't thought about Michael for days.

The thought came from out of the vast blue-black of the sky above, and it sent Gillian reeling. She had come to this small town to grieve and to dwell on her loss and the past; to live a future full of regret. And yet, a few short months later she felt more alive than she had in a long time. Why, even tonight the wind seemed sharper, the air fresher, the pain less bitter.

How is this possible, Lord? she questioned. *Didn't I really love Michael, after all? Was it only infatuation, to be forgotten so quickly?*

She thought of the strange new feelings that rose up within her whenever the man behind her came near. Somehow her day brightened perceptibly with his presence. It didn't matter that they didn't always agree. And she had long since forgiven him for the slights she had first felt. But what about now? What about when Jeremy touched her, kissed her, as he'd done earlier today. Was that love?

Gillian was jolted out of her reverie by the tapping on her shoulder. She slowed down and glanced behind, tilting up her visor as she did. "What's the matter?" she asked curiously. "Are you too cold?"

He shook his head.

"You don't like it, do you?"

"No, that's not it. It's just that, uh, I was wondering if, that is—" He stopped for a moment and then it all came tumbling out in a rush. "Do you think I could learn to drive this thing?"

Relief swept over her. He wasn't going to be a party pooper, after all. "Of course." Gillian pushed herself upward and swung one leg over to step into the snow. Immediately she sank in the white, fluffy snow to well above her knees. "Whoops." She giggled, grabbing his outstretched hand. "I forgot about this part."

Jeremy slid up into the driver's place and with his help, Gillian finally clambered back up onto the running board, huffing and puffing at the exertion made more difficult by the thick layers of clothing. Quickly she explained the controls and then urged him to try them out.

"We're losing sight of the others," she murmured, watching the last machine round the bend. "If we're not behind them, they'll tease us endlessly."

Jeremy grinned, snapping his helmet back into position and gunning the engine. "Yes, ma'am." He saluted.

Seconds later Gillian felt her head jerk backward as he hit the accelerator a little too fast. They whizzed down the trail and around the bend and came upon Reva and Ned Brown.

"You're too close," Gillian yelled, but evidently Jeremy had already figured that out as he jerked abruptly off the trail, over a small mogul and smacked down on the other side with a thud that sent them both through the air to land on the ground behind the now-quietly purring snowmobile.

Gillian lay there staring at the stars, wondering if they were in the sky or her head. She felt winded and dazed as she tried to remember why she had ever suggested this. There were voices now; lots of them. Someone tugged off her helmet, and she could make out a number of children from the youth group gathered around.

"Are you okay? Anything broken?" Hands whipped up and down her legs and arms, checking briskly for injuries.

"Jeremy," she gasped, sucking oxygen into her starved lungs.

"Is fine. How about you?" He was sitting beside her, grinning as if he had just completed the Grand Prix for snowmobiles.

"Okay, I think. Ooooooh!" She rubbed a spot on her left hip gently, feeling the tenderness with each movement she made. "I'm going to have a bruise there, though."

"What happened, anyway?" Reva asked, staring down at Jeremy. "Didn't you hear Gillian tell us not to go too fast? You were really moving."

Gillian looked at Jeremy and noticed that he'd removed his helmet. His dark hair stood out wildly around his pale face and there was the beginnings of a bruise on his temple. But he was grinning from ear to ear.

"I just never expected it to respond so easily," he murmured. "It was great. I can hardly wait to try again."

Gillian groaned as she got to her feet with his help.

"I can," she muttered. "I can wait quite a while."

"Before you go roaring off again, I think you'd better check your machine, Jeremy," one of the older boys snickered. "You might have to dig it out of that snowbank you hit first."

Jeremy whirled around in dismay, glancing first right, then left, looking for damage. The entire group burst out laughing when his relieved gaze finally landed on the softly purring red machine sitting quietly by the trail.

"You guys," he said. "You had me worried there for a moment. I thought I'd really done some damage."

"Only to me," Gillian grumbled, moving to take her place on the back of the snowmobile. "Come on, guys, let's move. This is when I could really use some hot chocolate."

One or two of the girls teased her about her aging status, but within a few minutes they were back on the trail, moving at a sedate pace.

"No more bronco riding," she warned Jeremy. "If you intend on doing that again, you do it alone."

He grinned at her, holding up his right hand. "I promise."

They wound through the forest, filling the silence with the roar of engines. Jeremy flicked the lights off for a moment. It was very dark, eerie, but for the shafts of bright moonlight that lit up a glade here and there. Every so often Gillian felt the tingle of fresh snow on her neck as an evergreen bough sifted down some of the light powdery covering that balanced on its branches.

And then they were out of the woods and into the open meadow covered by a blanket of snow. Mile after mile they crossed, sometimes weaving away from the path, but always returning to it again. Up ahead, some of the group was stopped, and Jeremy slowed to find out the problem.

Twelve teenagers lay flat on their backs in the snow, waving arms and legs rhythmically.

"Come on," Tim and Reva called. "It's great."

Jeremy studied them curiously before glancing back at Gillian.

"What, exactly, are they doing? Or shouldn't I ask?"

"They're making snow angels, of course. I can't believe you haven't done that before." When he shook his head, she sighed and pointed. "Watch the snow when they get up."

They sat silent as Tim pulled Reva out of the snow. And sure enough, there in the smooth, puffy whiteness was indeed the outline of an angel. Quick as a wink, Gillian turned and shoved as hard as she could, tumbling Jeremy into the snow.

"Hey," he protested, but it was too late. Gillian had already flopped down beside him and was tugging on his arm.

"Like this," she instructed.

They had almost finished when a pelter of snowballs caught them square in the face. Scrambling to their feet, they completely destroyed the imprint as they balled-up some snow and fired at the group now surrounding them.

"You're outnumbered," someone shouted as a huge ball of soft snow hit Gillian smack on the mouth. "Give in!"

"Never," she shouted back, chucking snowballs even faster. It was only seconds later that she noticed Jeremy was no longer there. Turning, she saw him sprawled in the snow while several boys laughingly washed his face.

"Hey," she yelled, tossing several missiles at them. It was a mistake. Within moments her attackers had doubled their effort and she could only flounder through the deep snow toward her machine when they gave pursuit.

"Your turn," the girls chorused, mock-threateningly. It was

only through the cleverest bargaining, fierce warnings and promising things she could never deliver that Gillian escaped the same fate.

At last, tired and laughing, the entire group mounted their snowmobiles and headed off for the Reids' home. When they trooped into the house, Gillian's nose twitched at the delicious odors emanating from the kitchen. What in the world had Jeremy come up with for supper? she wondered.

"Pizza," several boys hollered, smacking their lips in delight. "All right!" They high-fived one another in eager anticipation. Even the girls were casting mouthwatering glances toward the kitchen.

"Why, you're just in time," Mrs. Reid said, smiling. "Mrs. Rempel and Mr. Johnson just now dropped off these things. They're still hot."

As the kids jostled one another for a slice of pizza and a cup of hot chocolate, Gillian nudged Jeremy in the ribs.

"That's cheating and you know it," she teased. "You were supposed to bring something *you* made for this group of ravenous wolves. I'm going to have to speak to Faith about this."

He grinned, tweaking her nose.

"Don't you dare," he whispered. "You already know how much I cook and how well. Besides—" he watched the pizza disappear with worried eyes "—I'm starved."

"Hey, Jeremy," one of the teens called out. "You're not eating any, are you?"

Jeremy stared at the girl, his forehead furrowed. "Why not?" he demanded.

"Far too much fat in this stuff," she chirped, and proceeded to stuff the rest of the piece into her mouth.

"So, I'll take a walk later or something," he muttered, snatching up one of the most heavily loaded slices.

Giggles burst out of the girls, and the guys openly guffawed him.

"Opt for the 'or something,' Gillian," they teased. "Just don't get on a snowmobile with him."

And to Jeremy's obvious embarrassment, the youth group, in garbled bits of conversation, told the Reids all about his snowmobile prowess, or lack thereof. That prompted a discussion on being grateful. Since it was only a week after Thanksgiving, they all had a great time talking about things to be thankful for. Everyone joined in on the subject; no one was left out. Mr. Reid then gave a short devotional about showing thanks as well as saying it.

And suddenly the evening was over.

Gillian felt proud of their group. The kids had handled the machines and themselves with respect in spite of the naysayers at church who had repeatedly reminded her of her foolishness in thinking of such a thing for the youth group.

And one of those very people was present right now, she noted, arching one eyebrow at Jeremy. In fact, he had been the loudest of them. How was it that suddenly he couldn't seem to stay away from the machines?

Gillian watched curiously as he finished a short discussion with Mr. Reid, half ran over to the bright red racing unit that Tim Reid had been driving and jumped on. Seconds later he went whizzing past her, obviously intent on making for the open field.

Gillian watched as he zigged and zagged across the snow. A number of the youth were going home by snowmobile, and she waved and called goodbye to them, smiling at their remarks about the maniac on the red snow machine. When at last he got off, Jeremy's face was flushed with the cold. But nothing could dim the glow in those blue eyes.

As everyone filed back to the cars, Gillian felt a hand tugging on her arm. She turned in surprise to see Jeremy's solemn figure behind her.

"I'll give you a ride back, Gillian," he offered quietly.

"It's all right," Gillian said just as quietly. "I came with the pastor. I can go back with him."

"He's not coming back out here," Jeremy told her. His hand moved to her back, urging her toward the cars. "I'm taking everyone who rode with him, as well as my own crew. Come on. I need to talk to you, anyway."

Gillian went because she assumed they would say whatever needed to be said on the way back. She hadn't counted on the wealth of giggling passengers crowded into the car.

"I don't think there's enough room," she told him, eyeing the mass of wriggling bodies.

"Sure there is," he told her blithely. "We might have to squeeze at bit, but we'll manage."

Gillian ended up squished next to Jeremy's lean body, sharing a corner of his seat, with her legs tucked in the space between the seats. His arm across the back of the seat allowed her more room. It also send shivers of awareness over her.

"Are you okay?" he murmured in her ear, reaching to twist the key.

"I think so. Changing gears might be a little difficult for you, though," she said, wondering if he would return his arm to its place behind her after moving it to the gearshift by the steering wheel.

"Well, if *you* shifted, it would be easier," Jeremy agreed.

Gillian straightened.

"Me? I can't drive a stick shift," she told him, panic-stricken at the thought. "I'll wreck your transmission."

"No, you won't," he said confidently. "And even if you did, it's still under warranty. Want to try it?" His eyes sparkled down at her. "Come on, Gillian. You're always telling me to take a new risk."

She tried to absorb what he was telling her and ignore the tingles of awareness where his arm brushed her shoulder.

They putted off down the road as Gillian tried to figure out the intricacies of the five-speed manual transmission wondering why anyone would buy a car that didn't shift itself down or up or whatever.

The teens laughed outright at her tentative attempts, and when the car stalled in the middle of the farmyard, they only laughed the harder.

"You gotta shift with more authority," one boy offered knowledgeably from the back seat. "Act as if you know what you're doing."

"But I haven't a clue what I'm doing," she told them as the gears ground once more. "And it's obvious that I am no authority on this particular subject. Why don't they make just one gear?"

Jeremy chuckled in her left ear.

"Come on, Gillian," the two teens in the front seat chorused. "Try to remember. You can do it."

As Jeremy pressed the clutch down, Gillian tried once more to find second. Without notable success.

"Here," Jeremy murmured in her ear. "Like this." His hand covered hers, and the gearshift slid smoothly into place, and the car raced ahead. "It's not really that difficult."

Gillian shifted away from him a little, wishing suddenly that he'd purchased a bigger car. It was embarrassing to be squished up against him, but at least all the others were equally crowded.

"Sorry," he murmured, as his arm brushed against her once more. "I guess I should have told Pastor Dave that we would need his car to get back to town."

"Where did he go, anyway?" she asked curiously. "I didn't even see him leave."

Jeremy shook his head.

"Nor I, but Mr. Reid told me there's someone out here that he's been asked to visit. He was going on from the Reids and he wasn't sure how late he'd be." He helped her shift into a higher gear and then leaned back comfortably. "I told him that we'd agreed we could both handle the youth group from here on in."

"You mean you guys are gonna be the leaders?" Desiree asked from her perch in the back seat. "Cool."

"All right!" Two boys high-fived each other, grinning. "Say hello to the good times."

Gillian grimaced at Jeremy before twisting her head around.

"What are some of the things you'd like to do?" she asked the group as they huddled together over the front seats. And immediately wished she hadn't, as all sorts of totally ridiculous suggestions flowed from the excited teens.

"And for sure we could have a bridal shower for you, Gillian," one of the girls suggested. "It would be so much fun. Just think of the decorations, Emily. And my mom makes a really good punch. It's even red and we could make little heart ice cubes."

Gillian felt her heart sink to her shoes. This ridiculous, pretend engagement was beginning to get to her. And she certainly wasn't sitting in as the bride for the whole church to shower. Even Jeremy's mixed-up old aunt couldn't ask that much of her.

"I don't think there's any need to plan that far ahead," she heard Jeremy stammer, and she grinned at the nervousness in his voice. "Let's just take one youth group meeting at a time."

"I vote we have a cookie bake before Christmas," Gina chirped. "That way we could make up little trays of baking for the seniors in our church and the community who don't have anyone to make them home-baked treats."

Gillian jerked her head around and found Jeremy's face just inches from her own, his glittering blue-gray eyes staring into hers. His mouth was a heartbeat away from hers, and she could smell the chocolate on his breath as he sighed a deep, hearty sigh of resignation.

"Auntie Fay," he muttered, helping her shift into third.

Gillian nodded her head and left her hand where it was, nestled under his. She relaxed against the curve of the leather seat and allowed his body to support her.

"Absolutely," she whispered. "It's all her fault, anyway."

Their eyes finally broke apart when one of the teens began singing a familiar chorus. Thankfully everyone joined in, and no one noticed the surreptitious looks Gillian and Jeremy cast each other. Looks that Gillian would have liked to ponder a little longer, if she'd been alone.

Chapter Nine

It was growing late by the time they dropped the last passenger off at home. Gillian had long since claimed the passenger seat in the front, a move that did have some merit. For instance, the thick curving leather bucket was much more comfortable than her former position squished between Jeremy and the wriggling teens.

Of course, she did miss Jeremy's arm around her shoulder. But on the other hand, she was no longer so terribly tense—waiting and wondering if and when he would touch her.

"You know, it will soon be Christmas," she murmured, staring out at some of the houses people had begun to decorate. "It's my very favorite time of the year."

"It's not mine," Jeremy snorted. "All that consumerism and hype about giving. If people thought about that a little more during the year, we'd all be happier. And why is there so much emphasis on parties? Some people hate parties."

Gillian gritted her teeth and swallowed down the response that begged for release. He probably hadn't had many good memories of Christmas to resurrect from his childhood, she reminded herself.

"I'll bet you're one of those people who never do your shopping until the twenty-fourth," she joked. "And then you get all cranky and upset when everything is picked over." It was an intriguing thought and she dwelt on it for several long moments. Until his voice broke through her reverie.

"I don't shop at Christmas," he informed her coldly. "If I decide to give anyone a gift, I simply write out a cheque."

Gillian stared in disbelief. "Nothing?" she asked on a whisper.

"Not one single thing," he confirmed vehemently.

She was startled and rather dismayed, but not for anything would she let him see her feelings.

"This does not bode well for our future together," Gillian advised him finally, smiling rather sadly. "I absolutely insist on my fiancé giving me a gift rather than a cheque. Money is so impersonal."

There was silence for a few moments. Christmas carols played softly in the background on his CD. Gillian was lost in her own plans for Christmas until she heard his voice.

"What did Michael give you last year?" he inquired quietly. Gillian jerked her head around to stare at him, but could read nothing on that implacable face. "I'm sorry," he murmured. "If it will hurt you to speak about him, just forget it."

"No," she told him in amazement. "It doesn't hurt. Not really. Not anymore. And it's rather nice to remember the past sometimes." She turned to smile at him. "Michael gave me a gold locket. We had our pictures taken in one of those booths, and he cut them out and put them inside."

"Was it later that you were engaged?" His tone was mild and Gillian could find nothing that gave away his true feelings although she scrutinized him closely.

"Yes. Michael asked me to marry him on my birthday in March. We'd gone out for dinner, you see." The memories were flooding over her now, warming her with a love from the past.

"Michael had frozen my ring in an ice cube. After I said yes, he proposed a toast." She chuckled. "I was complaining about there being something in my drink. He got really red and flustered when I asked him to call the waiter over for a fresh one."

Jeremy smiled. It was the kind of silly romantic gesture he would expect of someone Gillian Langford would get engaged to. And it was totally unlike anything he himself would ever do. If he wanted to get married, that is.

But his plans didn't call for marriage. Not yet. He had given himself three years at JFK Elementary. Three years to make good and move on. He had planned it for so long; a move to something bigger and better; more satisfying.

For as long as he could remember, Jeremy's focus had been straightforward and deliberate. He fully intended to become headmaster of a very prestigious boys' academy in England before he turned forty. That meant proving himself as an educator in the States, and JFK was merely a stepping stone along the way. He had no intention of becoming encumbered with a wife until he was thirty-five, and then she would be exactly the opposite of the woman seated next to him.

He grinned to himself as he thought how silly it would be to imagine that Gillian Langford would be content to stay home and be a mother. She was a dynamic, charismatic woman who thrived on other people and the challenge of her work. He'd seen that very clearly these past few weeks.

"Did you want children? You and Michael, I mean," he blurted out, trying to picture her with her own tow-headed little ones.

Her glistening autumn-colored head whirled around; green eyes wide with shock. "Uh, pardon?"

Jeremy wished that he had somehow rephrased that, but it

was too late to worry about it now. Besides, he really wanted to know. To see if his idea fit the picture.

"I just wondered if you had planned on children," he repeated, more softly now.

"We never really talked about it," Gillian told him seriously. She was still peering at him through the gloom of the car interior. "I suppose I'd always thought in terms of a boy and a girl, but probably not right away. We were both just getting settled in our careers, and Michael's law practice was building up nicely."

Silence reigned for a few taut moments. Jeremy could see her fiddling with the end of her scarf. Suddenly her head tilted up, her green eyes meeting his with a question.

"Why did you ask that?" she murmured.

Jeremy couldn't help it; he flushed to the roots of his hair. It was an innocent enough question. After all, he'd been probing the depths of her former relationship, why shouldn't she question him?

"Would you like to have children?" Jeremy heard the hesitancy in her soft voice as she posed the question.

"Six," he stated clearly. "Not too far apart. And I don't care if they're boys or girls." He waited for her reaction.

"Why six?" she asked quizzically. "Is there something magic about that number?"

"So they won't be alone," he muttered, wishing he'd never brought the subject of children up. He lifted his chin. "I'd like to have a houseful of family. And a wife that stayed home with them," he told her sharply. "I don't much care for day cares and baby-sitters."

"Well," Gillian sputtered. "With six children, it probably wouldn't pay for her to go out to work anyhow." She sat quietly for a few moments, obviously considering his words. "I don't think you'd like that at all," she said finally. "It's a pipe dream that you've carried because you were an only child.''

"On the contrary, Gillian," he told her, angrily gripping the steering wheel in frustration, "I've thought about it long and hard, and I can assure you that is exactly what I want. At thirty-five, I'll be fairly well set in my career and ready to take on a wife.''

"You mean you've even got the year picked out when you'll get married?" She sounded stunned.

"A person owes it to himself and his future family to have these things organized and planned for a satisfying future." He heard the defensiveness in his own hardening voice.

"But think for a moment, will you?" Gillian protested. "Just think about this rosy, idyllic picture for a good long moment. Six children—running around, leaving their toys everywhere, arguing. Laundry, clothes, bicycles on the driveway, activities to chauffeur them to.''

"I've considered all that," he told her coldly, wishing she would just stop talking. But Miss Gillian Langford was shaking her head in dismay.

"I don't think you've thought about it at all. Not realistically, anyway," she stated clearly. "You're a neatness freak. You like everything organized right down to a T. You want everyone to follow your specific set of rules and do things your way.''

"And?" He deliberately fixed her with his coldest look. It didn't faze her in the least, of course. She just kept right on jabbing at him with his words, destroying his dream.

"Look, Jeremy. Kids need more than other kids around to play with. They need to feel loved and cared for and free to be kids." She shook her head. "Think about the kids at school for a moment. Some organization is good, and it's necessary when you are dealing with that many children. But sometimes they need to just sit alone and dream…to spread out their toys and build that space station of the future.''

''Discipline is the key,'' he reiterated acidly. ''If they know the rules and learn to follow them, their lives will be much happier.''

Gillian shook her head at him again, more vehemently this time. ''Don't you see?'' she argued. ''There is more to it than that. In the Old Testament, there was a strict and stringent code of rules that took a whole sect of the population just to study them! Nobody could keep them all, there were so many. But God changed that. He made the regulations dealing with the body less important and the state of the heart far more significant.''

She reached across the car and placed her hand on his arm. Jeremy felt the tingle of awareness at her touch ripple all the way up his arm.

''Don't you see?'' she burst out, impassioned. ''What all of us need are not more rules. We need love—unconditional acceptance that tells us that no matter what we do, someone will always love us. Just because they do, and not because we did or didn't keep ninety-five percent of the rules this week.''

''You're always denigrating responsibility and the role of personal accountability for one's actions,'' he countered. ''But that is exactly what is wrong with society today. No one is responsible for anything. If the rules are too difficult, change them or throw them out.''

He might have known she wouldn't give up, Jeremy thought in frustration. She never could let his opinion go without challenging it.

''Not at all,'' Gillian protested grimly. ''I'm merely saying that there is more to raising children than a whole ream of rules they have to follow. What you are proposing sounds more like a military academy than a caring, loving home.''

"And what you're proposing is a laissez-faire approach that has everyone running around wildly amok, here and there, doing his own thing. If you think about it rationally for a moment, you'll realize that—"

She interrupted him. Again!

"You always claim rationality when someone doesn't agree with you," Gillian charged angrily. "I am quite rational, thank you very much. And I'm also human enough to know that all people, but especially children, need love to nurture them through the hard knocks of life." Her emerald eyes glared at him, flashes of light from the dashboard reflecting in pinpoint stabs. "Haven't you ever done something just for the sheer pleasure of it?"

"Actually, I—"

She cut him off again. "Yes, you have," she grinned, eyes sparkling now as her hands flew through the air emphasizing her point. "Tonight. On the snowmobile. You let go and really had fun: You raced that machine around Mr. Reid's yard like a kid with a new toy." She studied his burning cheeks, wondering at his reaction.

"You're thinking of buying one, aren't you?" she crowed.

"Well, what if I am?" Jeremy sputtered, angry at her easy perception of him. He'd made it a practice over the years to hide his emotions. How did this woman manage to read him so easily? "There's nothing wrong with me owning a snowmobile, is there?" he challenged belligerently. "I am an adult—solvent, and in my right mind."

"I'm not so sure about that last part," she said, laughing out loud at his dark look. "You did fall tonight. Maybe you hit your head."

"Now, just one minute," Jeremy began. That was as far as he got.

"I just want to know one thing," Gillian asked pointedly.

"What?"

They were parked in front of her aunt's house, and Jeremy could afford the time it took to study her jubilant face. It did not reassure him. He leaned back in his seat and gathered his composure about him like a cloak. "Well?"

"When you were dashing around on that machine at the Reids'," she began, unable to hide her pleasure at his discomfort.

"I was not dashing," Jeremy protested. To no avail.

"When you were *dashing around,*" she repeated, grinning from ear to ear like a teasing Cheshire cat. "Did you think about the noise you were making? Noise that most likely bothered the neighbors or the Reids' cattle?"

The woman was watching him closely, and Jeremy strove to keep his face devoid of emotion, even though his mind was reeling with the possible consequences of his hasty actions.

"Did you pause to consider the damage you might be doing to that crop of winter wheat that had sprouted under the snow?" Gillian had the nerve to laugh at his aghast look. "And, last of all, did you happen to think about the rest of us, standing around in the cold, waiting for you to finish your joyride?"

"I, um, I didn't realize…" Jeremy didn't quite know what to say. It was ridiculous to think that a man in his position had behaved so childishly, without forethought for his actions.

"The answer is no." Gillian snorted in amusement. "And that was because you just let go, for once in your life, and enjoyed the moment." She licked her finger and stroked a number one in the air gleefully.

"I was just—"

"Being a kid," she cheered. "I know. Wasn't it great to let go of all the old *shoulds* and *should nots* and just have some fun?"

Jeremy felt her fingers thread through his and squeeze

gently as if she were trying to reassure him that such exploits
were perfectly natural.

"That's why kids are kids and parents are adults," she told
him, frowning slightly. "The kid has to have the freedom to
try new things, yes. And the parent has to set up the boundaries, reasonable boundaries, to make sure that no one gets
hurt. But no one has the right to take away the freedom of
childhood."

Jeremy eyed her dubiously. Some of what she said made
sense, there was no doubt. But there was still the matter of
responsibility; he had no intention of abandoning his opinion
on that!

He was about to remind her of it when Hope's front door
flew open and the older woman scurried down the walk toward his car. She had no coat covering her thin shoulders.
Instead she trailed it along behind, yanking on a soft knitted
hat as she moved. Her face was pinched and white. Jeremy
pressed the button to unroll Gillian's window and called out
a greeting.

"Is anything the matter, Miss Langford?"

"You have to go to Faith's immediately," Hope gasped,
sliding adroitly into the seat behind Gillian's. "Arthur just
phoned. She's fallen. Off the roof."

"The roof," Jeremy gasped, slamming into first. "What in
the world was she doing on the roof?"

"I don't know," Hope whispered miserably. "Arthur just
said he had found her lying in the snow."

"Oh, my God!" It was a prayer that Gillian silently en-
dorsed as he drove the short distance to his aunt's home. They
found Arthur kneeling on the front lawn, cradling Faith's head
in his lap.

"She's alive," he called out to them excitedly.

"Of course I'm alive, you silly man," Faith said, rising
awkwardly to her feet. She was a bit shaky, but her hand was

firmly enmeshed in Arthur's, and her smile of adoration was for him alone.

"Auntie Fay, what in the world were you doing on the roof?" Jeremy demanded, searching the tired, faded eyes. "You might have been killed!"

"Oh, piffle," the older woman protested, walking slowly across the lawn and up the steps to her front door. "I won't be going for a long time yet, Jeremy. The Lord has too much for me to do." She pushed open the door after brushing Arthur's cheek with her cold lips. "Come along in, my dears," she said merrily. "It's so nice to have company. I'll make tea."

"No, Auntie, you won't." Jeremy angrily brushed Arthur's hand off his aunt's shoulder and ushered her into the nearest easy chair. "I want you to sit down there until I check you over. You've had a nasty fall and you should rest." His hands moved carefully over her arms and legs, and finding no damage, he got to his feet and stood glaring down at her.

"I'll make her a hot drink," Hope murmured, scurrying from the room.

From the corner of his eyes, he could see Gillian sink down onto the sofa. He knew the feeling; he felt like his rubbery legs wouldn't hold him for much longer, either. His frown deepened as Arthur seated himself near Faith and enfolded her hand in his, despite Jeremy's scathing glance.

"I still want to know what in the world you were doing on the roof," her nephew demanded from his position across the room. It was the only seat left, and he had to take it. Fear and shock still raced through him at the thought of his beloved aunt lying helpless in the snow while he'd been out. Joyriding like a pubescent teenager!

"Putting up the Christmas lights, of course, dear," she told him placidly. "I do it every year. Blue ones, thousands of them. Of course, I don't actually put them up."

Jeremy sighed in relief at that news and immediately sucked in his breath in dismay when she continued.

"Actually I just take out the burned-out bulbs and put in new ones." She smiled happily at him. "Next week I'll put up the manger scene. You remember that. Your uncle made it years ago. It was the Christmas you came to visit us."

Immediately he was lost in the memory of that long-ago time when he'd flown across the Atlantic by himself so that he could spend Christmas with his own family. He'd been ten, he recalled, and they'd made him feel like he was their son. Uncle Donald had already started the crèche. By the time Jeremy arrived, there was only the rough-hewn manger to build and the donkeys to paint. He'd done it lovingly, with great care, because it mattered to Auntie Fay.

"Here you go, dear. Drink this up now and you'll feel better soon." Hope handed mugs to everyone.

"What is it?" Faith demanded, peering into the cup. "I won't drink some silly herbal remedy, you know."

"It's peppermint tea," Hope told her, a smile playing around her thin lips. "Yours, not mine."

"Oh, good. I love peppermint tea." Faith sipped daintily from the steaming cup, her eyes cloudy with some far-off dream.

"Does your head hurt?" Hope asked softly, searching the older woman's face for some sign of injury.

"Of course not," Faith giggled. "I landed in the snowbank, silly. Just had the wind knocked out of me. It was actually rather fun. For a few moments I was flying, just like the birds."

"Do you finally see why she has to go into a home?" Jeremy hissed from his position behind Gillian. He felt all the old anger and frustration at the situation rise up inside. Why did it have to be his aunt who was senile? Dear old Auntie Fay who wouldn't hurt a flea?

''No, I don't!'' Gillian scowled back at him. ''She's perfectly fine. Arthur was here and he looked after her. Nothing has changed.''

''Everything has changed! She could have been killed.'' His face whitened at the thought of life without Auntie Fay.

''You could have been killed when you took that trail too fast tonight,'' Gillian flung at him. Her eyes were like chips of jade. ''You weren't. Neither was she. Relax.'' Her finger poked him painfully in the chest. ''And *you* do those bulbs next time.''

He couldn't believe she would compare the two. One had no bearing on the other. ''But don't you see, if she had been properly supervised, Auntie Fay would never have even gone up the ladder, let alone fallen.''

Gillian rolled her eyes. ''And if you hadn't gone snow-mobiling, you wouldn't have tipped into the snow. Life is full of risks. Would you rather have not taken the risk, and missed the enjoyment of the ride?''

Jeremy felt all the old familiar frustrations he had always experienced with this woman rise up and clutch him around the neck. The thought of Auntie Fay lying there in the snow, dead or dying, sent his heart into his mouth.

''I have to keep her safe,'' he said huskily. ''I can't let something like this happen again. She can't die. Not now.''

''She'll die in a nursing home,'' Gillian whispered fiercely. ''Even if you keep her body preserved and intact, her soul will wither up and die if she's forbidden the enjoyment she finds in life. It would be like a prison. How can you do that to her?''

''How can I not?'' he retorted angrily.

A burst of merry laughter across the room drew their gazes to the happy group seated in front of the fireplace. The flames crackled merrily, their warmth filling the room, Jeremy noticed. He wondered if that would be the next thing he'd have to deal with: a house fire. Firm resolve strengthened his back-bone as he made a mental note to call the gas company and have the thing disconnected.

"What are you two whispering about?" Faith asked, her face wreathed in a happy smile.

Jeremy would have answered her then; would have laid it all out plain and clear right there in front of everyone. But as usual, Gillian interrupted him.

"We were just discussing the trip into the city tomorrow," she said quietly. "I think I'd better get home so I can get some sleep to prepare for twelve hours with a bunch of pre-teen girls. Good night, Faith. Have pleasant dreams."

"I always do dear," Faith said back, her gentle face glowing with joy. "And I'll be over bright and early tomorrow morning to accompany you. I'm looking forward to it." She rubbed her hands together with glee.

"Oh, but *you* can't go, Auntie Fay. Not after that fall. Why you'll overtax yourself and…"

"We're both going," Arthur informed him with a scowl. Jeremy was frustrated at being interrupted again. "We have to take those lads skiing, remember." He winked at Jeremy. "Besides, Faith says she feels fine." Arthur smiled at Hope and Gillian. "We'll both see you tomorrow morning."

"Yes, I'll pop on home now, too," Hope murmured, picking up her coat.

Good manners dictated that Jeremy leave then, also, since he had been the one to drive Hope and Gillian over. On the ride back, no one said a word. But the air was tense with things left unsaid, and Jeremy knew from the down-turned line of her lips that he hadn't heard the last of any of it from Gillian.

That was okay. He had a few last things to say on the subject himself. And he would have launched into it when Hope left them alone a few minutes later except that Gillian's usually brilliant vivacity was suddenly dimmed, and she moved sluggishly to take off her coat; her beautiful face drawn and weary.

Somehow, when she looked at him with those expressive eyes, her vibrant curls cascading around her shoulders, the words wouldn't come. And they still didn't when Gillian leaned toward him tiredly.

"Could you just hold me for a moment, Jeremy?" she murmured, wrapping her arms around his waist as she leaned her head on his shoulder. "I need a hug very badly just now."

"What's the problem?" he asked quietly, unsure of how to deal with this new situation.

"It's just that when I saw her lying there in the snow, for a minute, just one minute, it reminded me of Michael and I didn't know how I was going to deal with death again. It hurts, Jeremy. It hurts."

"I know," he murmured, brushing his hand over her bright hair. "It always hurts to lose someone special. That's why I want to take care of Auntie Fay."

But even as he said the words, he knew how ridiculous they were. Everyone died sometime. Faith wouldn't live forever any more than he would. They would all breathe their last and move on to meet their maker. So why not enjoy some of what life offered right now?

And so he stood there, his arms around Gillian's slim figure, his chin resting on her silky hair, and held on to his pretend fiancée. And as he breathed in the light floral sweetness of her perfume, he wondered if he wasn't missing something in his categorization of the vivacious Miss Langford—some tiny missing piece that was essential to knowing the real woman under all that effervescent exterior. Something that had to do with the little girl hiding inside; the one who needed a hug from him when she remembered the bad things in life.

Chapter Ten

"'It came upon a midnight clear.'"

The voices rang out through the narrow confines of the bus as thirty voices joined in yet another Christmas carol. Gillian grinned with relief. So far their little group of preteens from the Sunday school had been as well behaved as any of the kids in the youth group they'd supervised.

The girls were thrilled that they were going to go shopping on their own, and the boys had good-naturedly decreed that they *might* consider taking the female of the species skiing next time.

If there was a next time, Gillian thought, a whisper of sadness hanging in her mind as she remembered Jeremy's decree of the night before.

She glanced toward the front of the bus where Faith sat beside a bedraggled-looking little girl. They were busy talking a mile a minute, and Gillian could only imagine what about. She had half an idea that the only way little Suzy Briggs had been able to come was because Faith had found her odd jobs to do around her house for the past two weeks. Gillian knew that Suzy intended to spend every dime she'd earned on gifts for her large and needy family.

Privately Gillian thought it would be nice for the girl to spend a little on herself. Her fair hair badly needed a professional cut; it hung in shinglelike layers on her small head, straight as a stick and most unbecoming. The other girls all wore jeans and sweaters under their ski jackets but Suzy had on an old pair of baggy black trousers that were far too big for her and a short-sleeved wrinkled blouse in the ugliest shade of pea green imaginable.

"I think we'd better discuss the rules now," Jeremy murmured in her ear. "We're about five miles from the mall."

Gillian nodded and cleared her throat. She refused to look at him, afraid he'd see the condemnation in her eyes. It hurt to look at Faith and know what he had planned for her.

Memories of the night before and Jeremy's arms around her drifted across her mind. It felt so right; so good. And yet it wasn't. She could never condone his plans for his aunt. And even though she had succumbed to need last night, and leaned against Jeremy, drawing his strength into herself, Gillian had no intention of doing that again.

Why ask for more heartache? she told herself. Jeremy's ideas for the future and her own were so far apart, nothing could close the chasm.

She loved him; she knew that now. It was a love that had grown up in spite of her desire to mourn Michael. She had intended to avoid love, and instead it had sneaked up behind and conked her on the head.

But it was a futile love. They were worlds apart. She wanted children, all right, Gillian assured herself. But she wanted them to be healthy, happy individuals, not little robots that performed all the correct responses but took no joy in life.

And she wanted to live her future, not spend it being afraid of the next cataclysmic event. Most of all, she wanted a husband who would love her for herself. Jeremy wasn't the man for that. He had this preconceived stereotypical idea that she was some bubble-headed creature who couldn't be trusted to distinguish left from right.

"Gillian?" She turned to find his blue-gray eyes peering down at her. "We're almost there," he reminded.

"Yes, I know. Girls," she called out abruptly and waited for their heads to turn toward her. "We'll be arriving shortly. I just wanted to go over a few of the rules of this expedition. Number one—everyone stays in the mall. Nobody leaves without my consent. Number two—we all meet for lunch in the food court at noon. Number three—we all stick together in groups of two or three. I don't want anyone wandering off to do their own thing. Clear?"

When they all hollered their agreement, it struck Gillian as funny. Here she was, the person who had been trying to get Jeremy to ease up on his multitude of rules and now she was here, doing exactly the same thing. Evidently he noticed it, too.

"You see," he said with a grin, brushing a long strand of hair out of her eyes. "Rules are good."

"*Some* rules," she asserted. "Others are just excuses to impose your will on someone else. Come on, ladies," she called, grabbing her purse and leading the way. "On Dancer, on Prancer."

"We'll meet you back at this door with the bus at five," Jeremy called over the hubbub of noise as the girls jostled for position while Suzy helped Faith down the stairs. "Have fun."

"We will," they chimed in boisterous unison.

And they did.

It was a whirlwind of activity inside the mall and the girls quickly disappeared into the throng of shoppers, pairing off in groups of two and three. Faith was tugging at Suzy's arm.

"Come on, girl," she scolded, "we've got to get a move on if we're going to use that free coupon I have for Alfred's."

Gillian scurried along behind them, curious to see what was at Alfred's. It turned out to be a hair salon. And, wonder of wonders, they had an opening immediately for Suzy to use Faith's coupon.

"You go ahead, honey. Let them do their job. You'll be surprised at the difference it makes. I'm going to have a cup of coffee while I wait." Faith spent a few moments consulting with Alfred. "He says an hour. I'll be back then. All right?"

Poor Suzy nodded in a dazed fashion as the stylist with bleached white hair tinted purple on the ends escorted her back to the sink. She seemed fascinated by the curious assortment of colors on the back of his head and barely nodded when Gillian told her she'd stay with Faith.

"Nothing weird, Alfred, remember?" Faith's voice rang through the salon causing several heads to turn. But Alfred was unabashed. He grinned from multiringed ear to ear and tripped forward in his strange high-heeled shoes to pat Jeremy's aunt on the shoulder.

"You know me, Faith," he said in a normal tone that was totally unlike the high squeaky voice he'd used earlier. "You can count on me." He stepped back when Faith tried to slip a bill into his pocket.

"No way, Faith. I got my Christmas gift when you helped finance this place last year. The little girl's cut is on the house."

"Thank you, dear," Faith murmured, kissing his cheek. "You always were the sweetest child in my Sunday school class."

Alfred looked decidedly pained at that, Gillian thought,

amused. But he bore it in good form, waving goodbye with his black-nailed pinkie.

"Now, Gillian, dear," Faith murmured as they walked away from the salon. The older woman slipped her arm into hers and beamed. "I have a couple of stops to make before we have that coffee."

In fact, they made ten stops in all. Gillian watched as Faith purchased a pair of jeans similar to what the girls on the bus had worn. They were in a size far too small to be Faith's, although the sweater that went along with them was in her favorite pale pink.

Then there were the toy stores, where they loaded up on a remote-controlled car, a video game, a road race set and two rather heavy construction machines. The ladies' store sold her an ivory sweater that was far too large for Faith and the jewelery store had a wonderful pair of earrings and matching necklace that Faith declared "just perfect." There were also several books, two nut trays, a pair of slippers and a man's sweater in a brilliant peacock blue.

"That's for Jeremy," Faith confided, grinning. "He wears so many dark colors, I think he might enjoy a change."

"Yes, I'm sure he would," Gillian agreed dubiously, glancing warily at the bright yellow slash across the sweater's front panel. She wondered if she had imagined the sparkle of delight in Faith's eyes when she paid for it.

"You know these are going to be too heavy to lug around all afternoon," Gillian said, hoisting the metal vehicles a little higher in her arms.

"Oh, my dear, how thoughtless of me. I've let you carry everything! We need a locker. Now let me think." Faith glanced around several times as if getting her bearings. "Over here, I believe. Ah, I was right." She grinned, delighted with her good memory.

Once the articles were safely stored, they hurried back to

the salon to find a beautiful young woman waiting for them. Suzy's pale hair had been expertly trimmed close to the head in the back and sides. A straight fall the color of spun gold lay just above her ears.

"Oh, Suzy," Gillian breathed excitedly. "You look beautiful. Why, your eyes are just gorgeous!"

"Of course they are," Faith agreed. "Those great big baby browns were just hiding, waiting to be discovered." She scurried over to Alfred who was busily snipping another patron's hair. Gillian didn't hear what Faith said, but whatever it was, Alfred let out a shout of laughter and hugged the older woman tightly.

"Have a wonderful Christmas," he called out as they left. His voice was back to its strange pitch, she noticed absently.

"*Now* I need coffee," Faith declared.

Gillian heartily agreed and they treated Suzy to a milk shake. It was then that she noticed Suzy's beautifully manicured nails. Gone were the torn and dirty ends. They were perfectly filed and buffed to a gleaming natural shine. And the girl had just the tiniest bit of pale pink lipstick on, too.

Gillian shook her head in amazement. Dear sweet Faith, plain and ordinary as she was, had seen the hidden beauty in this girl as no one else had. It was obvious in the way Suzy now walked and talked, that her self-esteem had been greatly enhanced.

"Now, dear," Faith began, laying her hand on Gillian's arm. "Suzy and I have several things to do. And they're secret. We don't want anyone to know. So you just go ahead and do your own shopping. We'll meet you back here with the others for lunch."

Secretly relieved, Gillian argued only a little and finally left them in front of a shoe store contemplating runners for Suzy's brother. She'd been hoping to do some shopping herself and it looked like this was her opportunity.

Gillian swept through the mall quickly, choosing a gift for each member on her list with care. She was scurrying back to meet the others when she saw it.

A snowmobile helmet.

It was black with red flames on the side and the words "So Race Me" applied across the back. The visor was electrically heated, she was told, to prevent cloudy vision.

Gillian instantly decided that she would never find anything more suitable and purchased it without a second thought. Even if Jeremy never wore it, and she really hoped he would, he would be reminded of the one time in his adult life that he had let loose and just had fun. Her purchase meant a quick trip back to the locker area, and so she was late meeting the girls.

A quick look around the food court set her nerves jangling. No Faith. She counted the girls and noted with relief that they were all present. Where had the woman gone?

"Suzy," she asked, standing behind her. The girls stopped talking as they noticed the concern in her voice. "Where is Faith?"

"She said she wanted to get some of those specialty coffee beans," Suzy told her, glancing around. "She was right over...I don't see her, Gillian!"

Gillian felt the apprehension and disquiet that had plagued her all morning build to new heights as she surveyed the milling crowd.

"Please, Lord," she begged silently.

"There she is," Suzy called out with a gasp of relief. "Over there."

As she spotted her friend, Gillian felt some of the tension in her shoulders and neck ebb away. She looked toward Faith, assessing her from Jeremy's viewpoint and wondered how the other woman was doing. What she saw made her smile with delight. The tousled-headed senior was eyeing the Mexican stall next door with a decidedly greedy look.

"I'm starved," Jeremy's aunt announced cheerily.

Her words proved to be the perfect tension breaker. As they all laughed appreciatively, Gillian stuffed the nagging worry to the back of her mind. Of course it had been a good idea to invite Faith. The girls loved her, and she made no pretence about the obvious affection she felt for each of them. She sat munching on Mexi fries and admiring each girl's taste and choice.

"Well, girls," Gillian interrupted finally, glancing at her watch. "I think we'd better get back at it. There are only four and a half hours until the mall closes!"

Amidst the burst of laughter, Suzy moved to Gillian's side.

"I'll keep my eye on her this afternoon," she offered softly, her pretty mouth spread wide in a smile.

"Oh, Suzy, that's very sweet of you to offer," Gillian murmured, patting the girl's hand. "But you don't have to. You go off with the other girls and have a good time."

"I know I don't have to," Suzy answered. "I want to. And Mrs. Rempel has the best time of anyone I know."

"She does, doesn't she?" Gillian agreed, nodding. "How about this then—you get to shop with Faith until three. We'll all meet back here for a break, and then it will be my turn. Share and share alike, you know."

The rest of the girls agreed to return at three, and Gillian went off to do another round of shopping, this time for her parents. Her father was easy. Anything pertinent to golfing suited him just fine. But her mother was another story altogether, and Gillian was deep in a study of delicate crystal cherubs when she glanced at her watch and noticed the time.

Three-ten!

She was late and at the far end of the mall. With as much haste as possible she rushed through the crowd of shoppers, bumping and excusing as she went. The food court was jammed with other people taking a break, and she couldn't spot the girls anywhere. Fear rose, clutching at her throat as she scanned the table in a systematic pattern, praying for help.

How could you take a bunch of girls and an old woman into this crowded mall and then let them go off while you calmly spent your time shopping, a little voice inside her head nagged. *You're supposed to be the one in charge; well, then, take charge! Find those girls!*

"Miss Langford?" Gillian wheeled around, puffing out a sigh of relief as she saw three of her group standing near.

"Where are you seated?" she asked breathlessly. "I couldn't spot you guys in this crowd."

"Uh, well, the thing is, Miss Langford." The tallest one shuffled and looked down at her shoes. Gillian felt her nerves tauten as she saw the dismal looks on their faces.

"What's the matter?" she demanded. Something inside her wound even tighter as she saw how white their faces were. "Where are the others?"

Only by extreme control could Gillian keep herself from shrieking at them. She searched the masses once more but there was no one she knew standing by.

"Mrs. Rempel is lost. Suzy's looking for her. She took the others to help."

Waves of foreboding washed over Gillian as she struggled to remain calm.

"But how could she be lost? Suzy was going to stay with her, she said."

Stop condemning the girl, she commanded herself. *Suzy wasn't in charge, you were.*

"Suzy said Mrs. Rempel wanted to rest for a moment. Suzy left her on a bench outside a music store. You know, those areas where husbands can sit and wait for their wives." Jessica waited for Gillian's nod of understanding. "Well, Suzy got held up at the cash register, and when she came out Mrs. Rempel was gone. We've been looking for her for fifteen minutes. If anyone finds her, they'll take her back to the food court and wait for the others. Is that okay?''

The young girl's uncertainty in the face of this disaster touched Gillian and she patted the narrow shoulder gently.

"Not just 'okay,' Jessica. Very well done. You girls have been a wonderful help. I know you all care about Mrs. Rempel, so let's concentrate on finding her, all right?''

They all nodded enthusiastically and paired off to search anew. Gillian strode through the mall, frantically winding up one aisle and down the other. She'd left one of the girls in the meeting place, and the security people had made an announcement, but a half hour later Faith had not shown up.

When the girls returned at four, tired and worried, and still without Faith, Gillian knew she would have to call Jeremy. The police would have to be alerted, and they would need to make another search before the mall closed.

"We need to pray, Miss Langford. Mrs. Rempel said she always prays when she's mixed-up or confused.''

Gillian smiled. "You're absolutely right, Suzy, and I should have done that already. Let's pray now.''

She shepherded the girls into a little circle, and they all bowed their heads.

"Please, Lord,'' Gillian murmured. "We're in trouble here and we don't know what to do. But we know that You know where Faith is and that You are there protecting her. Help us to believe and show us the right way. For we ask in Your name. Amen.'' When she glanced up she saw many of the girls wiping tears from their eyes.

"Okay, ladies. This is what we're going to do.'' She outlined her idea of starting at one end and proceeding through to the other. "Two of you will stand guard at the elevators and escalators. The rest of you go through quickly but thoroughly. Ask the sales people for help.''

"What are *you* going to do?" one of them asked her softly.

Gillian tried not to look as worried as she felt.

"I'm going to call her nephew and Mr. Johnson at the ski hill."

There was a low whistle.

"He's going to be furious. And Mr. Nivens gets really hot when he's angry." It was the understatement of the year, but Gillian refused to dwell on it.

"Can't be helped," she muttered, slinging her jacket over one arm. "We have to find Faith. That's the most important thing right now. Ready, girls?" They nodded and raced off to do her bidding.

It took forever to get the attendant to agree to call Jeremy to the phone. And eons passed before his low deep voice rumbled across the line.

"Gillian?"

"How did you know it was me?" she asked surprised.

"I just knew. Something's wrong, isn't it?" He sounded wary and just a little unsure.

Gillian took a deep breath, breathed a prayer and blurted it all out.

"It's Faith. We can't find her."

"What do you mean you can't find her? Surely you didn't let her go wandering around alone in her condition. Of all the hare-brained, stupid…"

"You can holler at me later," she said, cutting him off. "Right now we need help. The girls and I have been searching for almost an hour and we can't find her anywhere. She was sitting on a bench, resting. And then she was gone."

"What? Grown women don't just vanish."

He sounded ready to lecture her again, and Gillian brushed

a tear from her eye as distressing images of Faith in trouble ran through her mind.

Please God, don't let her be in trouble.

"I don't have time for this," she told him briskly. "I need to help the girls look. Are you coming or not?"

"Of course I'm coming."

She breathed a sigh of relief and explained their arrangements if someone found the older woman.

"If you check the food court first, you'll know whether or not she's been found."

"Fine. I'll see you shortly." He sounded as worried as she was, and Gillian could only empathize with his anxiety. She knew how much he loved his aunt.

"Jeremy?"

"Yes?" His voice was brusque, and Gillian shivered, thinking of the terrible things that could happen to a woman on the street, alone.

"Please hurry," she whispered softly, clenching her hand into a fist. "I'm so scared." Tears flowed down her cheeks as she pictured dear, lovable Faith alone in the city.

"I'm coming. I'll find her," he assured her grimly. "Just hold on."

He arrived twenty minutes later, disheveled and gray with worry. Gillian rushed up to him and, oblivious to Arthur Johnson or the boys clustered round, wrapped her arms around Jeremy and hung on, needing the solid assurance of his strength. Although the girls had been back and forth several times, no one had found the elderly woman.

"It's all right," he muttered, brushing his hand over her hair awkwardly. "She's fine. I'm sure she just wandered off somewhere to relax for a few minutes. Or got involved in looking at something. We'll find her." His thumb brushed the tears from her cheeks, and then he gently set her away from him. "Now, tell me what you've already done."

Swallowing her sobs of worry and frustration, Gillian explained the systematic search of the mall that the girls had conducted.

"They're going from one end to the other again now," she told him. "So far nothing."

He thought for a moment and then beckoned the boys nearer. For once Gillian was glad of his rational, organized mind as he brought calm to the situation.

"Okay guys, here's the plan. We're going to start at the opposite end from the girls. Anybody finds my aunt, they bring her right back here. Okay?" They nodded. "Good. Away you go. Check in every fifteen minutes." He glanced at Gillian. "Is the mall Security in on this?"

"Yes, I alerted them a while ago. They've got several men looking for her with the girls. So far nothing."

Arthur stepped forward.

"I'm going to do some looking for Faith on my own," he told them. "I'll talk to some of the people here—see if anyone noticed her." He patted Gillian's arm. "Don't worry, girl. She's fine. God is watching over her. She's just forgotten the time."

With a smile and a wave he walked off toward an elderly man who sat snoring nearby.

"Miss Langford?" Gillian turned to find the security guard she'd contacted earlier striding toward her. "Any news?"

"No. No one's seen her. This is Mrs. Rempel's nephew, Jeremy Nivens. Jeremy, this is Peter Brown, the head of Security."

"Mr. Nivens, I'm glad to see you here. Miss Langford has been trying to do it all. She could use a little help." He turned to Gillian. "I've checked with Metro. Those hoodlums you reported seeing earlier today are in custody, so they aren't involved in this. That's a good sign. I have to admit I was worried about kidnapping for a while there."

"Kidnapping," Jeremy bellowed. "Why would someone want to kidnap my aunt?"

Mr. Brown explained briefly about the latest group of troublemakers who had recently been haunting the mall.

"Needless to say, we're happy that Miss Langford and her charges had no contact with the men."

"But she might have run into them later," Jeremy exploded, staring at Gillian in dismay. "I can't believe you would let her go off *shopping* under such circumstances. She was probably nervous and confused and needed watching." He glared at her accusingly.

Gillian felt the heat of her own anger rise up. She'd known he would find a way to blame her. Good grief, she blamed herself.

"Faith wasn't nervous or confused," she said, rebutting his erroneous conclusions. "She said she was hungry. We sat down together and ate lunch."

"Ah. So then you just let her wander off by herself. Good thinking."

"No, we did not *let* her wander off by herself. Although she is a grown woman and fully capable of deciding that for herself." Gillian bristled at the sarcasm in his voice.

"Auntie Fay wouldn't even be making these choices if she was in a nursing home. Someone *competent* would be caring for her."

The blue in Jeremy's eyes had frozen into a hard glittering glacier of reproach and Gillian wondered how she had ever thought she could rely on him when he had just made such an abrupt about-face. He didn't care about her, not really. She was just a convenience; there to blame everything on when he needed a scapegoat.

"I am competent," Gillian said between clenched teeth. "We were taking turns shopping with her. Suzy said Faith wanted to sit down for a moment. She agreed to wait there while Suzy paid for their purchases. When she returned, Faith was gone.''

"My aunt should never have been left alone." Jeremy's low voice was full of scorn. "Someone with a more serious outlook on life would have recognized the precariousness of her situation."

Gillian whooshed out her anger on a sigh of frustration as she glared at the tall grim-faced man.

"Someone like you, you mean? Someone who wants to keep that wonderful woman jailed in a cell for old people. Someone who won't let her enjoy anything in her life without a watchdog there to make sure she won't take too much pleasure, have too much fun."

"If this is your idea of fun, Gillian, I'm afraid I have to agree. I would never have subjected my aunt to these crowds and confusion. Once again, your irresponsibility has landed someone else in trouble." His face was cold and hard with disdain as he frowned down at her.

Gillian felt all the pleasure and wonder she had known in his arms, the joy when his lips melted on hers, suddenly drain away. She should have known, she told herself. She should have known it couldn't last. He had an image of her that could not, no, would not be swayed. It really didn't matter what happened between them now. Jeremy had just proven his total distrust of her whole theory on enjoying life. And it hurt. A lot.

"We'd better get looking," she told him softly. "There's no point in standing here arguing anymore. You just can't, or won't, accept that your aunt is a thinking, feeling human being, who is fully capable of making her own choices in life."

"Someone made a choice here," he expostulated. His mouth curved bitterly. "The wrong one."

"You can't keep her fenced in, Jeremy." Gillian tried one last time to force him to see. "You'll only hurt her if you try.'' With that she walked away, joining three of the girls who were starting the search once more.

For over an hour they combed through the throngs of people, moving here and there when they thought they spotted Faith, only to turn away disappointed when an unfamiliar face peered back. Several times Gillian sent one of the girls to check the food area, but there was no good news.

"Let's just check outside, along the parking area. Perhaps someone has seen her or knows where she might have gone.'' They had only gone a few steps toward the exit doors when Glenda pointed.

"Look,'' she gasped excitedly. "Mr. Johnson's found her.''

And sure enough, there was Faith, beaming happily, her arm curved into Arthur's as they strolled across the mall.

"Don't ply her with a bunch of questions just yet, girls,'' Gillian advised them quietly. "She might be a little confused. And we'll want to get her to Jeremy right away.''

"Hi, Faith. All done your shopping now?'' Suzy's voice bordered on tremulous when Faith greeted the other members of the search party now seated at an empty table.

"My dear, I simply gave up. I decided to get a breath of fresh air. That's when I heard the church bells.'' She had a vague, faraway look in her eyes, but other than that, the older woman seemed perfectly fine.

Gillian breathed a sigh of relief as she whispered a prayer of thanksgiving. "I'm going to have Jeremy paged,'' she told Arthur. "Could you stay with her?''

The older man's faded eyes twinkled merrily. "I intend to keep her by my side for the rest of our lives,'' he confided.

Gillian whispered a word to the hovering guard and watched him hasten across to his office. Moments later the announcement boomed around the mall.

"I'm so happy for you, Arthur. You're exactly what Faith

needs," she told him grinning. "But you might have an argument from Jeremy on that." Her face fell. "He wants to put her in a nursing home."

Arthur's face shone with an inner light, and Gillian noticed the gentle way he enfolded Faith's hand in his.

"Nothing is stronger than love," he told her softly, nodding his head toward the young man who was rushing down the aisle toward them. "Not even him. You just have to have faith." He grinned. "And Faith!"

Gillian watched as Jeremy hugged his aunt with relief. She listened to his questions and Faith's soft answers.

"Oh, piffle," she exclaimed in vexation. "I'm so sorry I worried everyone. I heard the bells, you see. And I wanted to explore the church a little closer. Oh, Jeremy, the choir they have there! It's like a group of angels." She closed her eyes in remembrance and drew a deep breath. "I could listen for hours."

"You did." Gillian laughed and ignored Jeremy's glaring eyes. "But I'm glad you enjoyed this excursion as much as the girls did. And I'm sure the guys had a wonderful time skiing, too."

"I did," John Vernon informed them. "But I was sure glad we had to leave early. My legs are tired!" The other boys concurred with varying degrees of grimacing, and Gillian smiled at them all.

"Well, I think it's time for supper. How about the rest of you?"

"Pizza," Suzy chirped. "But not here. We need some fresh scenery." Everyone except Jeremy, Faith and Arthur burst out laughing at her assessment of their worrisome afternoon. The older couple were too busy gazing into each other's eyes to hear the discussion, but Jeremy made his feelings known.

"I think we'd better wait to eat until we get home," he decreed. "It is a bit of a drive and I'm sure my aunt is tired."

"Why don't we ask *Faith* what she'd prefer to do?" Gillian murmured into the dismayed silence of the children. "We can't guess about her feelings. We should ask her."

"Thank you, dear," Faith murmured, glancing from Arthur to Jeremy. "As it happens, I'm starving. Those faritas we had at lunch were good, but there wasn't much to them. Pizza sounds wonderful."

"Fajitas, Mrs. Rempel. They're called fajitas. But I thought you had a taco salad?" Suzy peered at her friend in concern, obviously wondering about her memory.

"Oh, I did. And then I had the faritas. And Mexi fries." Faith beamed at the young girl. "Such small portions they give," she complained, rubbing her stomach.

Chapter Eleven

"I'm sure I don't know what I'm going to do about this quilt project for Faith and Arthur's wedding," Charity Flowerday complained to Anita as they sat together beside the quilt frame assembled in Charity's front room. "Every other year I've made a quilt for someone as a special project. But this year my hands are too stiff to do more than a few stitches here and there."

"Why, I'll help you, of course," Anita murmured, her eyes brightening as she stared down at the colorful blocks. "I love to quilt. And the boys do sleep for a while each afternoon."

"Thank you, dear. That would be a great help." Charity patted the slender white hand gently and smiled vaguely. "It's not just the quilt that's bothering me, of course. I had so hoped and prayed that Faith would be happy this Christmas."

"But I hear Mrs. Rempel is getting married on Christmas Eve. I'm sure she couldn't be happier. She just glows."

"Harrumph! That's the problem right there. She and Art want to get married, and it would be a wonderful match, but that silly old Jeremy is putting a spike into the works. I declare, if I were a little stronger, and that man a little smaller,

I'd put him over my knee." She nodded toward her best china teapot sitting on the table.

"Pour the tea, would you, Anita? I just want to soak in a little more of this lovely warmth, and then I'll put the heating pad away."

"Are your hands very bad?" Anita asked, her forehead furrowed with concern.

"Yes, today they certainly are. This time of year is usually good for me. Once that cold weather sets in, the arthritis seems to settle down. But with all this warm, cold, warm, cold, they ache constantly." She grimaced. "Now I'm not going to bore you with all the ugly details of getting old. You're far too young and pretty for that."

They sat sipping the strong, fragrant tea and munching on the shortbread Anita had baked only that morning.

"Did I tell you that Sean's coming home next week?" Anita asked, her face a happy reflection of the good news. "He's managed to save quite a lot while he's been in that camp up north. There was nothing to spend it on." She frowned as she replaced her cup on the saucer. "Of course, the work is over now, so we'll have to make it last. There's not much work for him around here."

"Anita! That's wonderful news. I know how lonesome you and the boys have been and what a big load you've been carrying on those small shoulders. We'll just have to pray that the Lord will provide something around here for him." Charity's face grew thoughtful. "And it wouldn't hurt to throw in a word or two for those two," she murmured, jerking her head toward the window where Jeremy and Gillian stood outside arguing.

"They'll be there all day if one of us doesn't let them in," Anita said lightly. "I've never seen two more opposite people. They argue over everything."

"Yes, it's sad, isn't it? I remember a time when the two of

them had begun to get along quite well. Faith's plans only seem to have helped draw the battle lines." She shook her head sadly. "I never really understood how they came to be engaged, but now that they are, I do wish they could find some common ground."

"They have," Anita chuckled, rising from her seat on the sofa. "Their common ground today just happens to be in the street outside your door. I'll go get them, shall I?"

Without waiting for a response, the slim, elegant figure disappeared toward the front of the house. Charity clicked off the heating pad and sat staring at it bemusedly.

"I just have to find a way, Lord. Anita and her family are coming along fine now, and it's time I focused on Faith. She deserves happiness, Lord, and I know Art will make her very happy." She sipped her tea absently, staring down at her swollen ankles. "It's just that Jeremy's putting so much pressure on her right now. It must be so distressing. Could you just give me a sign, some little signal that this will all work out?"

"Excuse me, Mrs. Flowerday." Jeremy Nivens's low rumbly voice filled the tiny room.

"Of course, dear. Please come in, won't you? Anita, do we have any more tea?"

"Um, we don't really want any...."

"I'd love a cup," Gillian's bright voice broke in. "I've been slaving over this ridiculous concert for ages. My feet are killing me."

"Of course they are. Do sit down, Gillian, dear. How is the school pageant going?"

"Wonderfully!"

"Awfully!"

"Well, there seems to be some disparity of opinion here," Charity chuckled. "Which is it?" She could feel the spark of tension as her two guests glared at each other.

"It *was* going all right," Gillian began. "The kids were starting to learn their songs and the glee club has come along really well."

"And thank you so much for making those cummerbunds and ties," Jeremy told Anita, accepting the tea from her with a smile. "When we get them all dressed in white shirts and dark slacks, they'll look wonderful."

"I enjoyed sewing them," Anita murmured. "It was nice to be able to repay you for all you've done."

"The choir bit sounds lovely," Charity murmured, glancing from one to the other. "We've haven't had a children's choir here for ages. Why were you arguing?"

"Because Gillian claims she can't get all the children to learn their parts in a week, and that's all we've got left." Jeremy scowled across at his fiancée and Charity smothered the grin that twitched at her lips as Gillian glared back.

"And?"

"He wants to do *The Nutcracker Suite*," Gillian wailed on a note of pure frustration.

"Do you mean the ballet?" Charity gasped, dumbfounded by his aspirations.

"Yep. Costumes and all. I just can't do it all and cover my lesson plans, too. There's too much work." Gillian's face was flushed with anger. "*He—*" she stabbed a finger in Jeremy's direction "—thinks I'm whining and not trying hard enough, but I just can't do any more. I promised to help Faith with the wedding, and that takes a lot of time, too."

"A wedding that shouldn't even be taking place," Jeremy grumbled. He glared at Charity. "What's the rush, anyway? It's not as if they're two young lovers. They've known each other for years."

"Which is why they don't want to waste any more time," Gillian hurled at him. Charity watched her green eyes blazing with indignation. "You've thrown up every barrier you can

to their happiness. Shame on you. Why can't you be happy
for her?''

"Because she's wrong!" He slammed the teacup down on
the table in a manner that had Charity worrying about her
Royal Doulton china.

"She's not wrong. She's deliriously happy!"

"She's delirious, all right," Jeremy agreed with grim concern. "Yesterday I found her out on the front lawn golfing!"

"What's wrong with that?" Charity asked, hiding her dismay behind a facade of well-being.

"At twenty-five below? In three feet of snow? I'd say it's
enough to have her committed."

"You wouldn't." Gillian's face had paled to an alabaster
white that frightened Charity. "She was trying out an idea I
had for youth group next week—snow golf. She's not crazy."

"Well before any of this goes any further I'm taking her
to that old fellow, what's his name?" Jeremy thought for a
moment. "Doctor Green, I think it is. I want her to have a
complete physical and then I'm going to speak to the man
myself, just to make sure." He glared at Gillian defensively.

"You're just looking for a label so you can classify someone else's perfectly natural idiosyncracies on that chart of
yours." But Charity could see the despair behind Gillian's
brave facade.

Charity glanced from one to the other of the opponents and
decided the Lord had given her a sign. This was going to be
her Christmas project, no doubt about it. If she could keep
these two from killing each other before Faith's wedding, she
would have done everyone a favor.

"Jeremy, you wouldn't really have her committed, would
you?" Gillian's voice was full of fear and foreboding.

"I've already seen the woman at the nursing home," Jeremy muttered, a tide of red coloring his cheeks. "Melanie
something or other. She says that they have a bed open right

now and that with Alzheimer's patients it's best for them to have constant care.'' His voice lowered. ''I've come to suspect that's what's wrong with her.''

His face grew red under Charity's dire look. ''I don't want to do it, but she's going to need professional care. A lot of it. I know I can't manage it on my own. Not without quitting my job. The woman at the nursing home said such arrangements rarely work out best for the patient anyways.''

''My Melanie?'' Charity blazed angrily. ''My daughter told you that?'' She glared at him balefully. ''I'm sure she didn't know exactly whom you were planning on getting into that bed, did she?''

Charity could see she was right. She struggled to her feet with difficulty. Moving slowly across the room, she came to stand in front of her best friend's nephew and fixed him with her most severe look as her cane rapped him twice against the ankle.

''Now you listen to me young man, and you listen well. I am most distressed to hear such talk. Faith Rempel has been my dearest friend for more years than I can remember, and I will not have you destroying the happiness she's finally managed to find. After all these years she deserves to be with Arthur.''

''But she's my aunt,'' Jeremy protested, surging to his feet.

''Sit down and don't speak again until I invite you to,'' Charity hissed through clenched teeth. He sat. ''Faith *is* your aunt, although what she did to deserve such a miserable nephew, I can't imagine. Do you mean to sit there and tell me that you actually thought you might have your dear 'Auntie Fay' committed to a nursing home against her will, without her consent? This is your idea of love?''

''I wasn't really going to go through with that,'' he muttered, his face flushed as he stared at his hands.

Charity breathed a sigh of relief and sat down on the chair Anita had pushed close for her to use.

"I certainly hope not," she muttered. Her hand gripped the cane as she stared at him. "Judge Conroy is a friend of hers and I don't think you'd get it passed, but even the attempt would wound poor Faith so deeply." She poked her cane against his leg. "Don't you read your Bible, boy?"

"Yes, of course I do," he answered, his dark eyes glaring at her belligerently. "Every day."

"Well I suggest that tomorrow morning you start reading Paul's first letter to the Corinthians, chapter thirteen. If this so-called love that you feel for your aunt can't allow her the freedom to be who she is, what good is it?" She reached for her worn, large-print edition on a nearby table and flipped the onionskin pages with familiarity.

"Paul says that love is *patient,* love is *kind.* Love is never *selfish.* Love doesn't demand its own way." She glanced up, checking to see if he was paying attention to what she had said.

"If you *love* someone you will be loyal to him or her no matter what the cost. You will always believe in her, always expect the best of her, and always stand your ground in defending her. That's God's version of love, Jeremy. Is that the kind of love you feel toward Faith? Or is the kind of love you have the kind that demands its own way—the kind that sets you up as God...all knowing?"

She pushed herself upward and motioned toward the door. "I want you to go for a drive and think long and hard on that. You've always had Faith in your corner, cheering you on. And I don't think that's going to change just because she gets married. But can't you allow her this little bit of happiness?"

"It's not that I don't want her to be happy," he said sadly. "It's just that I'm concerned about her. She's getting more forgetful each day. I couldn't bear it if..." He let the words die away, unspoken.

"I know you mean well, son. I know you think you know what's best for her. But look deep into your heart and ask yourself if you're really giving Arthur a fair chance? And if you still feel justified, then you're going to have to accept that they don't agree with you and move on with your own life."

Charity grasped his arm with her arthritic hands and exerted enough pressure that he would look at her. "If you can't be happy for her, then at least get out of her way so that she can live her life the way she wants. You can still be there whenever she needs you, son."

Charity watched as he surged to his feet, her heart sinking as she realized he'd heard none of what she'd said.

"It's obvious that you don't understand the consequences of what you're asking me to do," he almost snarled. "I have only my aunt's best interests at heart. And I will be the one who has to pick up the pieces of this debacle."

"Really?" Charity appraised him with a shrewd glance. "Then there's obviously nothing I or anyone else can say to change your mind. We will just have to agree to differ on this subject! Good day."

She returned to her chair, silently issuing a few pertinent prayers to heaven to guide this obstinate young man. When she heard the front door close, she lifted her head to stare at her two remaining guests.

"That is one very determined young man."

Gillian laughed, albeit a little hysterically. "That's the understatement of the year," she muttered. "You should see him at school."

"I don't have to now. I've heard many reports of his work with the students. I haven't seen such dedication to imparting knowledge since your aunt retired." Charity fixed the young woman in her sights. "You love him, don't you?"

She watched the flush of red on Gillian's fair skin and secretly smiled to herself. *Ah, thank you, Lord, maybe there's hope here yet.* "That's no doubt why you agreed to marry the man."

"But I didn't! It was all a mistake, you see," Gillian explained breathlessly. "Faith got confused and called me his future wife. I thought it would be a good idea to play along—you know, not upset her." She grimaced. "Everything snowballed after that. Every time we decided to clear things up, something else happened. After the pastor announced it in church one Sunday morning, we decided to let it go for a while."

Charity shook her head tiredly. Youth, she reminisced. How very tiring it was.

"You see, we thought we could 'break up' just before Christmas. Everyone would be so busy with their Christmas plans that they wouldn't even notice, and when they did it would all be in the past. I never wanted to hurt anyone."

"Yes, dear. I understand all that. I think I've known there was something wrong between you for some time. But do you love him?"

"I didn't want to." Gillian stared at her hands, twisting them around and around. "He's not at all the type of man I want to marry." Her big green eyes stared at Charity, willing her to understand.

"In fact, I came here mourning Michael. I never thought, not even for a moment, that I could be interested in anyone again." Gillian brushed a tear from her eye and Charity reached out to pat her shoulder. "He's so…rigid," Gillian wailed. "You saw what he was like. It's either his way or not at all."

They sat together, the three of them, in Charity's tiny living room, remembering Jeremy's words.

"It's true," the older woman said. "Faith is a tad forgetful.

And she does tend to get so involved in the moment that everything else leaves her head. But I don't believe, I will not believe, that she is a danger to herself or anyone else.''

"After they are married, Mr. Johnson would be nearby to watch out for her," Anita offered thoughtfully. "That should relieve some of Mr. Nivens's worries."

Charity shook her head. "I'm not at all convinced that worry about her safety is really what's at the bottom of this, Anita. No," she said, nibbling on her fingernail thoughtfully. "I think there's a much deeper reason why Jeremy is so opposed to this."

"He's opposed to everything," Gillian put in grumpily. "You should see the extent of this *Nutcracker* production. It's overwhelming for a little place like Mossbank. What's all the fuss for?"

"In a way, I can understand that part of it," Charity murmured. "This is his first year here, his first teaching year in America. He wants to make good; show that he's up to it."

"You mean he wants to make his mark," Anita said doubtfully. "But why?"

"I think it's to do with his future plans." Gillian's forehead was creased in a frown. "Something he said once makes me think that he's not planning on staying in Mossbank for the rest of his life. I just can't quite recall..." She fell silent, lost in thought.

"Well, you and Hope would know more about this than I," Charity said, bringing them back to the issue at hand. "But surely if he's trying to score Brownie points, as we used to call it, he's hoping that it will influence his future somewhere else. Maybe someplace with a drama school?" She glanced at Gillian for confirmation.

"No, I don't think it's that," Gillian said slowly. "His interest is in the music, not the drama. Anyway, *The Nutcracker* doesn't have any words, remember?"

"Are they really going to do a ballet?" Anita asked. Her mouth curved downward. "Roddy will kick up the biggest fuss if he has to wear a tutu."

"No, no." Gillian burst out laughing. Charity noticed the difference a smile made to that beautiful face. "There's only one little girl who actually dances; the rest just play their parts normally. Jeremy was actually quite clever when he wrote the scenes. It's quite modern."

"And the children don't mind doing it?" Charity watched carefully.

"Actually," the young teacher admitted, her eyes downcast. "They're rather enjoying it. It's just those of us who have to assemble the sets and costumes and prompt and direct who are pulling out our hair."

"The other teachers are complaining, too?" Charity tried to hold the disapproval from her voice.

"There has almost been a mutiny," Gillian admitted, bright spots of red coloring her cheeks. "We're all bogged down with the after-hours practices and workshops, etcetera. We're drowning."

"You should have asked for help," Charity chided gently. "This is a small community. We're used to pitching in. Now let's see..." She tapped her cheek thoughtfully. "I can think of several people who would help with sets. And Anita here is more than capable of directing the costume making."

"Actually, I have a trunkful of costumes that might be suitable," the woman murmured shyly. "I used to work with little theater when we lived in the East. Would you like to look?"

Charity watched as the two huddled over a list of what Gillian anticipated they would need. She was satisfied that the immediate problems would be handled, but her concern was for the young man and woman who were at loggerheads with each other.

"Thank you, Mrs. Flowerday. You're a lifesaver. Jeremy

will be furious when he finds out I've enlisted all this help. He wanted it to be a surprise for the parents."

"Parents don't care about the surprise part," Charity murmured. "They just want to see their own child on stage. Don't you worry about Jeremy Nivens. I'll deal with him." She faced Gillian head-on and spoke her mind.

"Right now I'm more concerned with you and this wall you've built up between you. You've never really answered my question, but I believe you are in love with Jeremy." She waited until Gillian nodded her head. "Then it's up to you to put a stop to this mutiny, as you call it. You're going to have to try working together…find a way to make your goals mesh. That's the first step."

"Oh, but that's impossible," Gillian cried. "We're exact opposites. Whatever I say, he hates, and he's always after me for breaking some rule he's devised. He has thousands of them," she confided in a whisper.

Charity shook her head firmly. "He is your boss. And he is a co-worker. He deserves your respect and your cooperation. And you love him, don't you?"

"I don't know how it came about but, yes, I do. He's so legalistic, though. And he's always…"

Charity cut the diatribe short with a smile. "My mother, God bless her, used to have a saying when we children were fighting. 'It's not what he did, it's what you do that counts.' That's the real meaning of Corinthians, don't you think?"

"You mean I should just go along with whatever he wants, meekly accepting his way?" Gillian's face was the picture of dubiousness.

"No, I'm saying that you need to find a way to get along. The New Testament church was full of people going their own way, and the writers were continually exhorting the people to ignore the petty stuff and act in a manner pleasing to God. I think God would be pleased if you could make your workplace a happy, cohesive arena where others could see God at work.''

"Keep it to myself? I have tried, you know."

"I know, dear. But the boiling point can be averted if you move away from the source of the heat or adapt to the conditions. You have to choose to understand what makes him like that…what's underneath all this need to control."

"Perhaps you're right. I've been trying to fix Jeremy for so long that I've lost my perspective about where he fits into God's plan for my life." Charity watched as the lovely face stared off into the distance. "Perhaps I need to get away and think about that."

"I know it sounds easy," Charity told her. "And I doubt that it will be, but God is teaching something here. It's up to all of us to understand what it is He wants us to learn." Charity felt the tiredness surge up in her suddenly, draining her of the strength needed to lift herself from the chair. Fervently she wished her guests would go home, but she would not ask them to leave. She let her eyes close for a moment as she whispered a prayer.

"Oh, dear. That's the boys. Thank goodness they've finally awakened." Anita grinned. "I was afraid I was going to be up all night. Roddy will be home soon from the boys' club. I'd better get going."

"I need to move, too," Gillian said. "I've gotten so comfortable here, I almost forgot I'm supposed to meet Hope for dinner downtown." She grinned at Charity's surprised look. "She's agreed to try the fried chicken place."

Charity gaped. "My dear, if you can work that miracle, you can do anything God sets before you." She accepted the soft kiss with a smile and shooed them both away, patting the smooth cheeks of Anita's sons as they toddled out the door.

"We'll start on the quilt tomorrow, Charity," Anita called

from the sidewalk. "It will go quite quickly. You just wait and see."

As she walked back inside to begin her own dinner preparations, Charity decided that everything went quickly these days. Too quickly.

Slow me down, Lord, she breathed, stirring the pot of soup Anita had made earlier. *Slow me down and show me how to use what little wisdom I've accumulated to help these hurting lives.*

Jeremy's words came back then, his fear evident on the craggy lines of his white face. *And Lord,* she added in an afterthought, *please keep Faith safe and under your umbrella of care.*

And having covered every base she could think of, Charity sank down into her favorite chair, propped up her aching feet and sipped at her soup as she watched the dismal state of the world's affairs unfold on the television.

Just one other thing, Lord, she murmured as she prepared for bed a little later. *I just wanted to give a big "Thank You" that I'm not young anymore! It's far too wearing.*

Chapter Twelve

"Quiet everyone!" Gillian glanced at the rosy faces spread out before her and wondered yet again at the wisdom of doing this. "Mrs. Rempel is going to help us make snowflake Christmas cards this afternoon, so I want you all to listen very carefully, okay?"

The children nodded their heads in unison just like little robots, their eyes wide with wonder at the gray-haired woman standing at the front of the class.

Faith took her cue right on target and began her story in a hushed voice. "When I was a very tiny girl, I lived in a country called England, far across the sea."

Bethany thrust up her hand. "Is that why you talk funny?"

"Yes, dear, I expect it is." Faith smiled, losing none of her animation. "One year my father was injured at work, and for a while we had just enough money to buy our food. It was a cold dreary winter—not as cold as here, because it rained quite a lot, but still very cool." She shivered and Gillian watched the children's eyes grow wide.

"We had to spend a lot of our money on coal to heat our

home, and there was nothing left over to buy Christmas presents.''

"You mean there wouldn't be anything under the tree?" The boy sounded amazed at such a thing.

"We couldn't even get a tree," Faith told him sadly. "But my mother and father still wanted us to have a happy time at Christmas so they decided we should all make something to decorate our home. Then, on Christmas morning we would bring them all out and that would be our gifts to each other."

"No Nintendo?" Timothy Wentworth asked softly. Faith shook her head.

"No candy canes?" Melanie whispered.

"None."

"No Christmas oranges?"

"No," Faith smiled. "But we had lots of mother's wonderful baking. There were always gingerbread men to decorate and stars and angels. I liked to decorate the Christmas tree cookies best. I'd put one of those little silver candy balls on each branch."

"Is that what you made for your Christmas decoration?" Chad asked, as impatient as usual.

"No." Faith waited until they were all watching her and then frowned. "I didn't have anything to make. Christmas was coming closer and closer, and I couldn't think of one single thing that would be a good decoration."

"You could always string popcorn," one tiny voice volunteered. "My granny says she *always* did that."

"Or make paper chains," another offered. "You just need glue and paper."

"I suppose I could have, but my sisters were smaller and they needed to make something simple like that. Besides, I wanted to have something really spectacular to show to my family. I loved them very much and I wanted to show it, you see."

The children nodded with understanding.

"Couldn't you get a job?" Tiffany asked. "My brother shovels snow and he gets five whole dollars for it."

"Ohh!" The other kids were flabbergasted by such a huge sum.

"I don't think there was anyone in my village who could have paid five dollars for me to shovel," Faith told them softly. "So I prayed. Every night before I went to bed, I would get down on my knees and tell God that I wanted something really special for my family."

"I done that," Jonah Andrews grumbled. "I didn't do no good, though. We didn't get nothin' from God." The child who had every toy imaginable looked dismally disappointed, as if he'd expected manna to fall from the heavens, Gillian decided.

"Oh, no, dear, that's not true. We always get an answer from God. But sometimes we don't want to hear what He says and sometimes we don't like what He brings." Faith's face was shining with joy, and Gillian found herself amazed at the assurance she saw there.

How could Faith, with all the difficulties in her life, still have so much trust that God would work everything out? Gillian scorned her own untrusting attitude.

"Is that all?" Buddy Hirsch complained. "I'm hungry."

"You're always hungry," Roddy scoffed. "I bet Mrs. Rempel's gonna tell us about how they had to starve and not have any turkey dinner at all, aren't you?" he demanded, peering up at the older woman.

"I can't tell you anything if you're all talking," Faith said softly, her eyes twinkling. The children settled down immediately. "Now, I told you that I was praying every night for God to hear me, right?" A flurry of little heads nodded.

"Well, on the day before Christmas I still didn't hear God's answer. I'd waited and listened. I obeyed my mother and helped my dad. I did everything I could so that I'd be able to hear the answer, and still it didn't come. I was really disappointed because now it was too late, and I didn't have a gift for my family.''

The childrens' eyes were huge as she whispered the last words. Gillian could see their mouths in round oh's of anticipation and wished suddenly that Jeremy were here to see how wonderfully his aunt related to her kids. It would be everyone's loss if Faith were locked away in some senior citizen's home, unable to share her wisdom with these little ones.

''Anyway, I was walking home, shuffling my feet through the snow. You know how you do when you're mad? Well, I was mad, really mad. I stopped in front of a store to look at the wonderful dolls in the window and I got even madder. Why couldn't my sisters and I have those dolls, I yelled at God. We deserved them, and we'd never had anything like them before.''

Gillian watched twenty-four pairs of eyes widen when Faith told them she had yelled at God. She could relate, she thought wryly. Goodness knew, she'd been yelling at God an awful lot herself lately. Especially in matters to do with Jeremy Nivens.

Why couldn't the man just admit that he was attracted to her? Just for once, why couldn't he let go of his stern facade of control and let her in past the barriers he always erected? They had something special; she knew they did. Why wouldn't he acknowledge that there was something growing between them?

''Well, as I stood there, fuming and fussing, an elderly lady spoke from behind me. She was very tiny and she had on an elegant fur coat and a wonderful hat with an ostrich feather. And on her hands she wore the finest leather gloves.''

Faith pantomimed the motions, patting her head and pretending to pull on a pair of long gloves.

"'What's the matter little girl?' she asked me in a soft voice. I glared up at her and told her I was mad." Faith's eyes surveyed her captive audience. Her voice dropped to a whisper. "'Why...why are you so angry at God? He's given you a wonderful family, a warm home and enough to eat. What's wrong with that?'"

Gillian noticed several children nodding. They were from families that were almost destitute after paying off huge loans for the land they farmed. Faith was continuing.

"Well, I just told her, 'I want Christmas presents for my family. I want to be like all the other people who give gifts under the tree. I want to give them something special." She shook her gray head. "That lady just stared at me. She never said a word for a very long time and then she said, 'Come with me, dear.' So I did. I followed her. All the way home."

Gillian caught Jasmine's eye before she could start on her recitation about following people you don't know. She put her finger to her lips and was gratified to see the little girl nod.

"That lady lived in a great big huge house up on the top of a hill. And when we went in and sat in front of a big warm fire, another lady brought cookies and tea. I ate as many as I could and then I sat back in my chair and listened when the lady began talking."

The children leaned forward, knowing they were getting to the good part.

"'Your name is Faith, isn't it?' she whispered in a funny soft voice. I nodded. 'And what do you want most this Christmas, Faith?' she asked me. So I told her. 'I want to be rich like you. I want to have a big house and lots of money... enough to buy presents for everyone. I want to be like other kids.'" Faith paused for a moment.

"She smiled a very funny smile and then patted me on the head. 'Do you know about God?' she asked me. I told her that I'd known about God for a long time. 'Well then,' she said. 'Can you tell me two things in the world that God created that are the same?'" Faith smiled down at them, waiting for someone to answer.

There was silence for the longest time as her charges thought through the puzzle, trying to figure it out.

"I know," Roddy bellowed, thrusting his arm up toward the ceiling. "Twins!"

Everyone agreed that God made twins the same, but Faith was shaking her head.

"Close," she told them with a smile. "Twins look an awful lot alike and they sometimes dress the same, but if you look really closely, there's always some little difference. Either they have a different look to their face or they like different things, or maybe one has a mole the other doesn't have. If you try really hard you can tell them apart."

The children appeared to be considering that.

"Well, this old lady told me that God even makes snowflakes different. Did you know there are no two snowflakes the same? Each one is just a little different from all the others. Why is that, do you suppose?" She waited a moment.

"I told the lady that I didn't know, and she said, 'God likes people and snowflakes to be themselves. He doesn't want us to try and look like or act like someone else. He wants us to be our very own special selves, just the way He made us.'" There was a light tinkling laugh.

"Well, I thought that was pretty good, so I asked her why God didn't make us all rich like her. And do you know what she said?" Every head shook as every eye fastened on Faith expectantly.

"She said, 'Oh, no, child. You don't want to be like me, all alone in this big old house with my family all dead and gone. God gave you a very special family, a unique one, all your own. Just like the snowflakes. Now you have to learn how to use all the wonderful things God gave especially to you. God doesn't want another one of me, he wants a one-of-a-kind person like you.'"

Faith's face became sad. "I felt sad for her. She had no one to share with. I had my sisters and my parents but she had no one. So I decided to give her a gift, as well as my family, by bringing everyone together. On Christmas Day we all went to her house and sang songs and sat around the fire. She asked my father if we could stay and have dinner with her, and it was the most wonderful dinner I've ever eaten."

"Was it turkey?" Roddy asked.

"No." Faith shook her head. "It was something completely different—her own special way of celebrating."

"So whenever it gets near Christmas, I like to think of that lady, and I like to look at snowflakes and see how different they are. That reminds me that God made me just the way I am."

"I didn't never see no snowflake by itself before," Roddy muttered, clearly deep in thought. "How d'ya do that?"

"That's what I'm going to show you," Faith said happily. She slipped across to the window, slid it open and carefully pulled in a huge sheet of black bristol board.

"I put this in the freezer last night, and this morning when it started to snow, I set it outside. Now the snowflakes won't melt for a minute or two and you can see how different each one is."

The children crowded around, eager to experience this hands-on information. As they oohed and aahed over the melting flakes, Gillian wondered if Faith wasn't hinting just a little at her and Jeremy's ongoing argument.

There could be no doubt that the man was different; as far removed from Michael as anyone could be. But that didn't mean she loved him any less. Perhaps God was telling her to make some adjustments.

As she and Faith worked side by side, folding and unfolding white paper that the children cut into snowflakes of every size and description, Gillian was struck again by how gently God worked. Such a great truth and yet Faith had applied it so easily. She decided to think about it again later, when she had more time.

"Jeremy?" Gillian watched as those muscular shoulders covered by a thin cotton T-shirt stretched as he set down the paintbrush he'd been wielding across the massive set several parents had constructed only that morning. "Could I speak to you for a moment? Please?"

"Yes?" His voice was not in the least welcoming, and Gillian tried to recall the verse she'd read only this morning: "Thou wilt keep him in perfect peace whose mind is stayed on Thee."

"I'm trying, Lord," she whispered. "I'm trying." She straightened her backbone and concentrated on her next words.

"I wondered if you would consider handling the youth group alone this weekend." The words came out in a rush as she waited for his explosion.

"Why? Is something wrong?" He resumed his even strokes, back and forth across the plywood.

"Not exactly. I just need to go back to Boston. Just for a day or two. To get my bearings. It's personal." She finished at last, embarrassed at having said so much.

Jeremy slowly put down his brush, dusted his hands on his paint-spattered overalls and straightened. His face was a mask of tightly controlled tension as he glared down at her.

"You're choosing *now*, when we're this close—" he held his thumb and forefinger millimeters apart "—to putting on this play?"

"I think things are pretty well in hand, thanks to the parents," she murmured reasonably. "Aren't they?"

"Perhaps at school. But what about the youth group? What are they doing tomorrow night, anyway?" He looked grim and forbidding, and Gillian's heart ached with pain.

If only he could relax a little; let someone take on a bit of the responsibility for a while. She knew it wasn't likely. He'd insisted on painting the backdrops himself, even though several very qualified drama students from the high school had offered.

"Gillian?" He was frowning down at her.

"Oh, sorry," she muttered, embarrassed at having been caught daydreaming.

"Why do you always do that?" he demanded angrily. His eyes were cold and hard.

"Do what?" Gillian asked blankly, staring at him.

"Apologize in that little-girl voice as if I'm some type of ogre." He thrust his hands into his pocket angrily.

"Oh, sorry," she said automatically and then slapped her hand over her mouth in dismay as he rolled his eyes. "I wasn't really apologizing," she tried to explain. "More like coming back down to earth."

"*Sorry* is the accepted English word for an apology," he advised her through clenched teeth. "It does not mean daydreaming."

The tide rose in her, red and hot, in answer to his nasty tone and griping words. *Don't play this game,* a little voice whispered inside her mind, and Gillian swallowed down the angry response.

"I was asking if you thought you could handle the youth group," she reminded him carefully. "They're supposed to go skating, if you recall. And then one of the parents offered to build a fire in the park and bring hot dogs for everyone to roast."

"Hah! As if anyone could feed enough to that bunch of devouring animals." He shook his head with stern disapproval. "I just read an article that says there's far too much fat in the diets of North Americans. Especially teenagers."

Gillian smiled. She had to. The gauntlet had been thrown down so often in the past few moments, she should have been red-hot. If not for the Lord's help. And her vow to try to understand this man.

"Yes, I suppose it must seem that way to you," she nodded, considering his words. "What was your favorite food in England?"

His eyes opened wide as he stared at her, but finally a glint of humor broke through to tug at the corner of his mouth.

"Roast beef, mashed potatoes, gravy and apple pie," he admitted at last.

Gillian's eyebrows rose. "And you have the nerve to talk about our diet." She chuckled. "It's rather like the pot calling the kettle black."

"I suppose," he admitted at last. His eyes narrowed. "I don't understand the need to slather everything with ketchup, though. How do they even taste the flavor of the food?"

Gillian slipped the brush out of his hand and added a few strokes to the curve of draperies painted around the window.

"I think that's the whole purpose," she said with a chuckle. "They don't taste anything *but* the ketchup!"

He removed the brush before studying her work critically.

"I prefer to do this myself," he murmured, wiping away her work and carefully painting in a new drapery.

Gillian watched as he worked, sadness welling up inside her at his refusal to allow anyone past the shell he had created.

"You can't do it all, Jeremy," she whispered, wishing she understood this complex man. "Sooner or later you're going to have to take what other people offer. We all need each other."

She stepped back, her heel grazing the unsteady platform behind. His hand grasped her arm, holding her steady as she regained her balance. Gillian was amazed to find herself mere inches from his quizzical gaze.

"You're very much like my aunt in some ways," he murmured, holding her gaze with his own. She felt his eyes graze across her face and felt her cheeks color at the intricate inspection he was giving her. "You always want everything to move along smoothly and happily, everyone getting along famously."

"What's wrong with that?" she demanded softly, refusing to step away from his challenge.

"It's unrealistic. Life isn't always like that, Gillian. Take you and me. You always want to look on the bright side and ignore the problems."

"And you only ever see the problems," she quipped back. "The pessimist and the optimist."

"You live in a fairy-tale world where you made Michael into Prince Charming and you were the fairy princess." He shook his head, a grim smile curving his lips as his fingers slid up her arm to twiddle absently with the bouncing curls on her shoulder. "Life is hard. There are a lot of bad things that happen. It's much easier to deal with them if you've done some preparation."

"Michael used to say 'Seize the day,'" she retorted. "He taught me not to spend my life in worry and fear for what might happen tomorrow. I want to live today to the full. Can't you let go of your inhibitions and enjoy what God has given?"

"You can't make me into Michael," he muttered, as his arms moved across her back to pull her against him. His lips grazed her forehead and moved down purposefully toward her mouth. "I am me—a different person with a different life experience."

"You don't always have to run him down," Gillian whispered, breathless with waiting as his lips moved nearer hers. "He was a wonderful man."

"I'm sure he was. And I'm equally sure I'm not nearly as wonderful. But one thing I will admit…your Michael certainly knew how to find a beautiful woman." His eyes blazed into hers. "I hope you won't be sorry, but I am going to seize the moment and kiss you."

And with that, his mouth touched hers softly, gently, drawing a response Gillian could not have stopped. In fact, she amazed herself with her own fervor as her hands just naturally moved up to his shoulders and she let her fingers rove through his crisp dark hair.

His lips were strong and sure as they kissed her, not unlike Jeremy himself. But even as he kissed her so masterfully, there was an uncertainty, a question behind his touch, a mistrust. It was as if he were afraid she would reject him now.

With the tiniest movement, Gillian answered that, holding him closer and answering with her own soft lips, drawing in a tiny gasp when his mouth moved to her neck and touched the pulse that hammered there.

It didn't last long enough.

"We shouldn't be doing this," he murmured huskily, pressing her gently away. "This is a public building. Anyone might walk in."

Gillian slowly lifted her hands away from his wide shoulders, her mind whirling with the information that was traveling to her brain. He'd kissed her. And what a kiss!

"Why not?" she managed at last. "We are supposed to be engaged." Her eyes took in the splotches of red on his cheekbones as he stepped backward and turned to focus once more on his painting.

Long and empty, the silence dragged out between them until Jeremy finally laid down his brush and turned and faced her. His voice, when it came, was soft but strong and she could hear the bitter tones underneath.

"But we both know that's a facade, don't we, Gillian?" he asked her. "I think you've made it quite clear that you're looking for someone to take your former fiancé's place. We both know that's not me." His eyes were clear and focused as they stared back at her and Gillian felt the air sizzle with electricity.

"I am who I am, Gillian. I'm not a knight in shining armor and I can't pretend to be. I hold strong opinions and I'm not afraid to say what I think. I've never been the romantic type, never even considered freezing rings in ice cubes. And I don't believe in making grand, airy gestures like all the best heroes."

He reached up and pressed back a curl that was bouncing tantalizingly near her mouth. His eyes were icy steel now and they penetrated through the foggy haze of her mind, bringing her to startled awareness. He was serious, she realized. Deadly serious.

"But when I love someone, Gillian, it will be with all of me. I won't renege on my promise, but neither will I do silly things to prove myself. I will always protect those people that I love. That's part of who I am."

"I know," she whispered sadly. "I've seen how much you care for Faith. But, Jeremy, sometimes your protection hurts the very people you say you love. Can't you just let them be?"

She stared at him for several moments before turning away, the light of hope dying inside her. His cool, implacable face never changed its look. He would insist on pushing the business with Faith, she knew. He felt it was his duty.

Help me through this, she prayed silently as she made her way out to Hope's smoothly purring car. *Let me find the answers to unlock his heart, because I love him, Lord. And I think he could love me. If he'd let himself.*

Chapter Thirteen

Jeremy breathed a sigh of relief and slowly eased his shaky legs forward. "I'll kill her for this," he told himself, easing one skate in front of the other. "If I don't die first."

It was an emotional outburst, he realized. Something he hadn't been prone to until Gillian's advent into his life. He struggled to keep his balance as a group of his ruffians swooped past, almost toppling him in their haste to move on.

"Hey, Jeremy, you gotta slide. Like this," David Crest moved slowly beside him, gliding his feet in a smooth, firm motion that did send the boy sailing over the glistening ice with athletic prowess. "No, don't walk," he ordered. "Slide."

Jeremy tried it and to his surprise found that the smooth motions propelled him forward at a rate he could almost control.

"Way to go, teach," David cheered.

That was right before he forgot to concentrate and landed on his keister. Hard.

"Whoof, that was some landing. You okay?" David's curious face peered down at him.

"Bruised," Jeremy returned acidly. "And probably damaged for life, but fine." He hoisted himself to his feet with all the elegance of a lumbering elephant and dusted off his new jeans. "It's very hard," he told the boy grimly.

"Yeah," David laughed. "Ice usually is."

"I didn't mean that. I meant learning how to skate. I don't think I'm coordinated enough for this." Jeremy glanced bitterly at the frolicking youth around him and gingerly set one foot in front of the other as he headed for the gate. "I've had enough."

"No way," David yelled and swooped up behind him, pressing gently from behind. "Now just relax and let yourself glide," he ordered, laughing. "I'll do all the work until you figure out your balance."

Before he killed her, he'd kiss her senseless, Jeremy decided, unable to do anything but let the wind whistle past his ears as his young instructor propelled him across the ice at the speed of light. It was Gillian Langford's fault that he was out here, endangering life and limb with a bunch of ungrateful kids. Bad enough that he had agreed to help with this youth group, but now she'd left him alone with them.

That was what usually happened, he reflected grimly. People generally left him and expected that he would manage. And he usually did. But it sure wasn't easy. But sometimes he found himself wishing he had a little help. Fortunately he'd had a lot of practice at going it alone in life, he told himself sternly, tamping down thoughts of his would-be fiancée and how much he missed her.

A picture of Gillian's happy, laughing face thrust itself into his mind, and he wondered how she would manage to make this cold, hard ice a positive experience. Or shed humor on the fact that he was being shoved around the ice like a sack of potatoes. She'd have a field day with that!

Somehow, thank God, he and David managed to avoid the other skaters as they moved around the edge of the oval rink.

But all the same, Jeremy found himself clutching the boards with relief whenever he got near enough. Which wasn't half as often as he wanted.

"She's really going to pay for this," he griped as David whizzed him over a little nearer to the opening in the boards.

"Who?"

"Gillian," Jeremy spat out grimly. With extreme attention to detail, he stepped carefully toward the edge, lifting one foot in front of the other and promptly landed on his rear with one skate bent uncomfortably under his other leg.

"I told you, slide don't walk. Why is Gillian gonna get it?" David demanded, hauling him to his feet and nodding as Jeremy began to slip and slide across the ice like an acrobat. "She already knows how to skate. I saw her teaching the girls a double toe loop the other day."

"She's good at everything, isn't she?" Jeremy sighed. He brushed a hand across his snow-covered pants. "And I feel like an idiot. I'm going in," he said defeatedly.

David followed behind like a little puppy intent on trailing its master. "Just relax for a minute or two and then try again," he suggested. "It's not really that difficult, and it doesn't take a whole lot of skill, you know. Just practice."

"I hate skating," Jeremy told him childishly and then wished he'd kept his mouth shut. Why was it that everything the woman did managed to make him look like an incompetent, old-fashioned idiot?

"Gillian would show you how, if she was here," David told him seriously. "She's really good at teaching people things. And she never makes fun of you. I like that about her." He tugged a candy bar from his pocket and shucked the paper off in one wrist motion. "Want some?"

Jeremy shook his head and the boy popped the entire bar into his mouth. Seconds later he was talking again. "Like the other day when I was telling her about this friend of mine.

Well, she's not a close friend. Not yet. But she could be. Maybe. Someday."

Jeremy prayed fervently that this wasn't going to end up in a counseling session. He had no practical experience to offer the boy when it came to women. He didn't understand them himself and he certainly didn't want to try to explain them to someone else; especially not a teenager.

So he kept silent. Which didn't seem to faze David in the least.

"You see, Myra's pretty cool, for a girl. Or she could be. But she's always snapping her gum when she talks. That gets to me." He glugged down half a bottle of soda and continued. "She's smart and funny but I get tired of always hearing the same jokes over and over." He stopped, obviously waiting for him to comment, Jeremy decided, and mentally added another point to the list of items he'd bombard Gillian with when she returned.

"D'ya think I should tell her about the stuff she does that bugs me?"

David sounded dreadfully unsure and Jeremy searched his mind for an answer. There wasn't one. "Uh, well, I guess if you want to be around her and something she's doing is bothering you, you should explain that and ask her to stop." There, that sounded okay, he decided.

"She's got this laugh, you see," David muttered, staring at his feet. "I mean she's really a good friend and everything. She even helped me do a physics assignment that was totally Greek to me. But that laugh." He shook his head dismally.

Jeremy felt inspiration strike and turned toward the boy excitedly. "Maybe you should tell me what it is that you like about her," he said helpfully. *Thank you, God. I would never have thought of that.*

David's forehead drew together in perplexity. "I dunno. Lots of stuff. What do you like about Gillian? Besides that she's a babe."

"A what?" Jeremy stared at him aghast.

"A babe, a dish. You know—" he grinned "—easy on the eyes." He made a motion with his hands that Jeremy understood to mean Gillian's well-formed figure.

"Yes, Gillian is very lovely," he conceded absently, thinking about the vivacious, beautiful woman he was supposedly engaged to. Thinking about the way he felt every time he set eyes on her.

"Yeah, but she's no ditz," David agreed thoughtfully. "You gotta admit she's smart, too. An' she hasn't always had it so easy. My sister heard her telling one of the girls that when she was little she was pretty sick. Her parents got her to take up sports to build up her strength."

"Oh." Jeremy considered the information in a new light. For some reason he'd always thought Gillian had lived life on a bed of roses. Now it seemed that she, too, had experienced her share of problems.

"So what else do you like about her?" David pressed. "Like don't you think it's cool how she always thinks up cool things for us to do? She doesn't care if I dress differently or wear my hair like this. At least I don't think so. She never mentioned it."

Jeremy remembered Gillian's generous gift to Roddy's mother. And he recalled the way she'd gotten on her hands and knees to clean the bathroom at old Mr. Gentry's house last week when the youth group had raised money for a missionary by cleaning homes for seniors. It did seem as if his fiancée was less interested in outward appearances than getting to the heart of the matter.

"And man, can she cook. If I ever get married, I'm picking a lady who can make pies like Gillian does. Those apple pies we had at her aunt's house for the progressive supper were great!"

Jeremy would have liked to point out that he hadn't been able to taste that particular pie because David had consumed half a pie all by himself, but in the end he decided not to. After all, he was supposed to be the leader here.

"Well, anyhow, what do you think? Should I tell Myra that I don't like certain things like the way she laughs an' stuff or should I just forget it?"

There was no room for prevarication here, Jeremy realized grimly. The kid was asking the worst possible person for advice about interpersonal relationships, and Jeremy had an idea that his own experiences wouldn't exactly help David.

"The thing is, if I tell her she wears too much makeup and her skirts are too short, she's gonna get mad. And I don't really want her to be mad at me. I like her. A lot. So whadya think, Jeremy?"

Fervently, ardently, Jeremy begged God to send Gillian to get him out of this situation. He pleaded with everything he owned, but three minutes later David still sat beside him, waiting for the pearl of wisdom to leave Jeremy's lips and give him direction.

"Well, as I see it," Jeremy began, feeling his way through the maze of the feminine psyche with no clue as to his destination, "people don't generally like to hear other people talk about their faults. I mean, I don't." That's for sure, he muttered silently. "So, if you really want this girl for a friend—" he glanced at the boy for confirmation and watched the dark head nod firmly "—then I think you're going to have to accept that she is the way she is and learn to get along with that."

"You mean deal with it," David considered, scratching his head.

"Well, yes. Either that or find another friend. One who meets your specifications." That sounded pretty good. Jeremy congratulated himself.

"And you don't think I should tell her about the gum or the makeup or other stuff?" David looked doubtful, so Jeremy hastened to clarify his position.

"Well, *if*, someday, she should *ask* if you think she's wearing too much makeup, I suppose you could tell her, kindly, what you think. I guess that's what Pastor Dave meant in his sermon on Sunday about accepting the unlovely. Don't you think?" He peered at David searchingly, hoping he wasn't being sacrilegious or something.

"I guess. My mom says kinda the same thing when my sister and I have an argument and I'm trying to tell her what my sister has done. She always waits till I'm finished and then she gives me this look and says, 'It's not what *she did*, it's what *you do* that counts.' Like I'm only responsible for me."

As the rest of the group joined them and they made their way to the park for the wiener roast, Jeremy felt the impact of David's words impinging on his skull in a never-ending tune. *It's not what she did that counts. It's what you do.*

Over and over they rolled through his brain for the rest of the evening, even when he was alone at home, with the lights turned low. They reminded him of his judgmental attitude toward Gillian. He'd argued with her about everything, and yet she had still managed to put another person's need in front of their bickering.

He thought of his aunt and the fear that gripped him when he considered the future without her. What would happen when he moved on, went back to England? Who would ensure that she stayed safe and protected if he didn't look after that now, before things got out of hand? Alzheimer's, Doctor Green had said. Progressively getting worse.

"Is it so wrong, Lord?" he prayed, pouring out his fear and worry. "Is it so terrible to want to keep her away from the dangers of life? Am I wrong to impose my will in this matter?"

The answer came seconds later in the shrill peal of the telephone. "Jeremy?" Arthur's voice sounded strained.

"You'd better come over here right away. Faith has been mugged. She needs to see a doctor."

Cold, overwhelming dread flooded his mind as Jeremy hung up and reached for his jacket. His eyes fell on the brochures that lay on the hall table describing the conditions in Sunset Retirement Home just outside of Mossbank.

He thought of his aunt, lying hurt and bleeding in the cold winter air, and rage filled him. A black, primal rage that threatened to overwhelm him. "I wasn't wrong," he said angrily, snatching up the forms and stuffing them into one pocket. "She shouldn't be left alone. It's too dangerous."

And as he sped through the icy streets, Gillian's sad green eyes stared back at him from the dark night sky. "It's not what you did or said that matters," he told her angrily. "It's what I do now that counts. It's my responsibility to protect my aunt and I'm going to do it."

"Gilly, dear, are you sure you have to go back so quickly? Couldn't you spend a few more hours with us?" Her mother's worried gaze studied her daughter's pale face with a knowing perception. "It's Jeremy, isn't it? He's the one God has sent you."

"Yes, I think so Mom," Gillian whispered tearfully. "But I can't imagine how He's going to work this one out. Especially now that Faith's been hurt. I know Jeremy will feel that it's his duty to get her into a home somewhere, away from everyone." She stopped packing long enough to stare up at her mother. "He's going to stop her wedding, Mom. I can feel it."

"Then go back and straighten it out, Gilly. God will give you the words and the ways to do what He wants. Just keep praying."

Three hours later, Gillian wearily clambered into her aunt's car and demanded, "How is she?"

Hope's face was white and strained as she faced her niece. "She's not well, Gillian. The doctor found a tumor when they did the scan. Apparently Doctor Green missed it when Jeremy took her in for a check-up. They're operating tomorrow."

"So soon?" Gillian gasped at the news, gripping the door handle with fingers suddenly gone weak. "What about the wedding?"

"Faith says she's not letting Arthur get away, tumor or no. She insists that she's going through with it. And the doctors aren't saying no." Hope's lips turned upward in the vestige of a smile. "She's tough, Gilly. And she has God on her side. She's convinced He has something very special planned."

"Can I see her?" Gillian asked quietly. "Can she talk for a while?"

"We'll go straight there. She was asking about you this morning."

To look at her, Faith was no different from any other day, save for the fact that she had several stitches along the hairline.

"I finally get to have a beauty mark," she giggled, hugging Gillian close. "I've missed you, dear. And so has Jeremy. He's been mooning around like a lost lamb without you." Her bright eyes twinkled merrily. "Well, piffle! Why don't you two go and say hello properly, while I discuss something with Hope?"

As Jeremy's hand moved under her arm, Gillian felt herself being propelled from the room. She went because she could see the stark fear in his eyes and feel the tenseness in his body.

"Come on, Jeremy," she whispered, guiding him to a soft-cushioned chair in the waiting area down the hall. "Sit down. You must be exhausted."

"I shouldn't have waited," he told her baldly. "Dr. Green said he wanted to have more tests done. I should have checked her in weeks ago. None of this would have happened if I'd done that." He glared at her furiously. "You kept insisting she'd be all right. And I knew better. It's my fault she's in there."

"Jeremy, Faith trusts in God. And I believe this is all part of His plan for her life. If she hadn't been mugged by those boys, the doctors would not likely have found the tumor until it was too late."

"It may be too late now," he told her grimly.

"I don't believe that, and you don't, either," she said sternly. "Faith is healthy and happy. She's had some wonderful times since you've been here and she's enjoyed every day that God has given her. He's not going to let her down now, when she needs Him the most. He loves her."

"So do I," she heard him whisper. "And I don't want her to die."

Gillian's reaction was immediate. She wrapped her arms around him and hugged him close against her body, trying desperately to infuse this man she loved with some of her own faith.

"She was always there," he whispered brokenly. "She always knew how much it hurt not to have a regular home and a normal family. To me she was my family, and when I'm with her everything seems like it will be okay." He looked at her, his face an agony of remorse. "I love her."

"I know," she whispered back. "I know."

Gillian sat there with him for a long time, content to hold him, offering what comfort she could. And he held her, too, his arms a strong secure brace around her. When at last she drew away, she was prepared to tell him of her love, of the longing she had to share her love with him for as long as God gave them.

"Jeremy, when I left here, I went to Boston and I thought of what you said about me trying to make you into Michael. It's true, in a way. I did think that I could replace him...sort of show God that he hadn't taken away everything.'' She drew in a deep breath and continued, watching his back for some sign that he was listening.

"But what I discovered was that Michael is a part of my past. I loved him, yes. But he's gone, and the love I have now is a different kind of love.'' He stood there, still and unmoving.

"What I'm trying to say is that in spite of all the aunts and all their manipulations, I've fallen in love with you. I know we've argued and disagreed about just about everything over the past few months. I know that we started off on the wrong foot. But somehow, through all of that, God has shown me that what I've been feeling for you is far different from what I felt for Michael.'' She had to get up, try to see his face. "You were right when you said I was living in a fairyland. I was. I wanted a prince to come and carry me away from the pain of losing someone. I wanted to pretend that I was forever doomed.'' Gillian smiled at her own foolishness. "The star-crossed lover, if you like.''

"And now?'' His words were low, hushed, waiting.

"Now I've come to realize that through all of our butting of heads, I've been forced to deal with reality and accept that you are not Michael. But that through God's workings, you have made your own special place in my heart. I'm trying to say I love you, Jeremy. I have for a long time.''

The silence was agonizing, and Gillian could have screamed with tension. Instead, she stood silent, waiting for his well-thought-out reply. His answer was nothing like she'd expected.

"I suppose it's natural that you would think that,'' he told her baldly. "You see me as some kind of flawed character who needs your taming influence to fit into this fantasy dream you've created.'' He smiled half-heartedly.

"You had a wonderful home, a happy family. You're beautiful, talented. You have a way with people that draws them in toward you and makes them feel wanted; needed. And that's good. But I am not your next fixer-upper project, Gillian.'' He shook his head sadly. "I'm not your next Roddy Green.''

"I'm so sorry," she whispered, shocked at his admission. "I never meant…''

"Don't apologize. I don't think you're even aware of it. But nonetheless, it's the way you see me," he said tiredly, shrugging off the hand she laid on his shoulder. "I admit it. I'm attracted to you. You're a very beautiful woman; what man wouldn't want to possess all that beauty? To say to the world, this is my wife. But you're not in love with me, not the real me.'' He shook his head. "You don't even know who I am. You've imagined a fantasy man that isn't anywhere near reality.''

"But I know you've changed…'' she began, trying to make him see that she wasn't dreaming anymore.

"No," he told her firmly. "I haven't changed one whit. I'm the same person I always was; the same man who lives his life by the rules that you despise so thoroughly.

"I am who I am, Gillian. In spite of all your daydreams and illusions. You can't make me change into something I'll never be, even if I wanted you to.'' He sighed. "I'll confess, I could easily allow myself to say what you want to hear. What we both *wish* could be true. But I know that someday you'd see me for who I really am and maybe even despise me.'' He paused. "I don't want either of us to be hurt that way.''

"But I don't want to change you," she sputtered, standing where she was, mouth hanging open as she listened to his impassioned words.

"Yes, you do.'' His smile was dull and self-deprecating. "You don't love me, Gillian. Not the real me. In time I believe you'll agree that what I've said is true. In time,'' he added in a husky tone, "you may even thank me.''

The words were quietly spoken, but underneath that cold harshness, Gillian could hear a note of…pain?

"In spite of your best attempts, I have to stick to my beliefs. You see, this is my aunt, my family we're discussing here. All right, you've encouraged this stupid idea of hers. Fine. I'm not going to oppose it any longer. If Aunt Faith wants to marry Arthur Johnson, she's free to do so. But don't expect me to be happy about it. I won't. Because it's not best for her. It's all wrong. Just like this ridiculous fiasco engagement you concocted to save your image."

Jeremy wheeled away, but felt her hand on his arm. He looked down. Perfectly shaped oval nails were buffed to a natural shine on delicate hands that could have graced a cosmetic ad.

"I'm sorry you hate me so much, Jeremy," he heard her murmur and felt a pang of remorse as he saw the diamond droplets that glimmered below her lashes. "I never realized that I was hurting you so badly. But for the record, I never considered you a challenge or a project. And I certainly don't want to change you. I just want to love you."

She sniffed delicately, and his heart softened again. But he couldn't allow himself to be moved by her tears. Not this time.

"I know you don't like my clothes. You've told me that often enough." She sniffed. "I know you think there are rules for every occasion and that I break all of them. I'm sorry about that. Really sorry. I can't help how I look, and even that seems to annoy you."

Her voice lowered as her huge emerald eyes met his. They were wide and guileless, and Jeremy felt he could drown in their depths. With every shred of willpower he had left, he restrained himself from taking her into his arms.

"I think you're a wonderful caring nephew and that Faith is so lucky to have you in her life. We all are. The way you've moved in and taken over with the youth group is a real pleasure to watch. And the school, even if I do say so, is far better run than any school I've taught in."

She lowered her voice, and he leaned in to hear her better. "I think I argued with you so much because you shook me out of my rut, made my perfect life very uncomfortable. You made me see things in a new way."

He heard the true regret in her voice and wondered at the wobble of emotion that he could discern beneath that calm facade.

"But most of all, I want to apologize for embroiling you in this silly engagement. I really did have the best of motives when I went along with Faith's error, but it's gone on too long, and I can see that it's time for me to set things right."

"I didn't mean—"

"I'm sorry, Jeremy." She cut him off. "Truly sorry. I promise I won't embarrass you again." Jeremy watched as her face drew near to his and her soft lips brushed over his cheek. "Maybe someday you'll believe that I truly didn't mean to hurt you."

He stood there, transfixed, as she walked away down the hospital corridor. He saw Reverend Dave come bursting through the door and heard his hearty greeting. Gillian's was softer but the words carried to him clearly over the shining floor tiles.

"I'm not a bride-to-be, Pastor. I never was. I made the whole thing up, and it's time I owned up to it. Could I talk to you? Privately?"

Jeremy watched dumbfounded as the two walked back out the door. Instead of relief that the whole debacle was finally over he felt...what? Sadness? A sense of loss?

He shook his head in frustration. It didn't make sense. He should be feeling relieved that he and Gillian would finally be freed from this ridiculous pretense.

Shouldn't he?

Chapter Fourteen

"All right children, this is your big night. I want each of you to do your very best. Watch carefully when Mr. Nivens gives you directions. Pay attention. Is everyone ready?"

Some looked painfully ill and others looked like overwound tops that just had to spin or they would burst. Gillian smiled gently at all of them and directed them out of her room and onto the stage. Jeremy had chosen her class to be the toys in his new revised *Nutcracker* and she was beginning to see how apt his choice had been.

Each student wore a costume. There were tin soldiers and fairy princesses. Firemen with trucks and animals galore. The music for the entire play had been adapted from the original score, and she could hear Jeremy's fine fingers in the light, bright recorded notes.

"All right, children," she whispered. "Let's begin. Everyone at attention."

They plodded onto the stage and waited stiffly for the curtain to lift, but once it had they fell into their parts naturally, keeping still as mice when Fritz and Clara and all the birthday guests celebrated.

As she watched from behind the curtain, Gillian felt a sense of pride fill her. The scenery was spectacular; Jeremy had arranged to catch all the essence of an old resplendent country house. A huge Christmas tree sparkled and glittered in the corner, lending a truly festive air to the proceedings.

At last the Sugar Plum Fairy danced across the stage, pirouetting and prancing as if born to it. When it was time for Gillian's toys to move, they twisted and turned and marched as briskly as they'd been taught without one faltering step. Their faces shone with enthusiasm, and if anyone heard the ping of the sword hitting the metal table leg, they didn't let on.

"It's going okay, isn't it?" Jeremy's voice was hushed and faintly questioning in her ear, and Gillian smiled.

"It's going perfectly," she acknowledged, smiling up at him. "You've done a wonderful job with all of it. The parents are just beaming."

He stood there, staring down at her for the longest time. And then his arms reached out and he tugged her into his embrace, his mouth hard and urgent on hers as he kissed with all the pent-up fury of a storm just unleashed.

And Gillian kissed him back, uncaring that several of the lighting students stood nearby snickering at them from the sidelines. When he finally let go, his eyes were warm and caressing.

"Thank you," he whispered.

"You're welcome." She smiled back.

He studied her quizzically for several moments before stepping away. "I have to go," he murmured and turned around, striding back into the curtains without a backward glance.

"I know," she murmured, more to herself than anyone. "But I can wait."

It was an exhausting evening for the teachers. And everyone breathed a sigh of relief as the children in the last item on the program filed onto the stage. It was time for the carols with a different groups of singers. First the glee club, which included the entire school body, filed out to fill up the stage and overflowed onto the risers in front. They gave a rousing rendition of "Frosty" and then "I Saw Mommy Kissing Santa Claus." Next were the choral singers clad in their festive red cummerbunds and bow ties.

As she seated her students in the back of the gymnasium, Gillian noted their proud stance and careful scrutiny of their leader. They kept their eyes focused on Jeremy, who stood before them in his black suit, hand upheld, ready to give the signal to begin.

Their voices rose in two of the older English carols so often heard in the vaulted cathedrals of Britain. Her own students were silent as every eye focused on the two soloists, whose clear, pure voices rose over the crowd.

And then, the pièce de résistance. The select chorus. These were Jeremy's hand-picked singers. Children who had displayed a natural ability with music. Their voices blended, falling and rising in a harmony of praise and thanksgiving for the miracle of the Christmas birth.

After the thundering applause had died away, Jeremy stepped forward to the microphone.

"Ladies and gentlemen, JFK Elementary would like to present their final number. 'O Holy Night.'"

Gillian stared. She thought they'd scrapped the idea weeks ago. Why was he now attempting this? It was complicated, not only for the singers who had a huge range of notes to cover, but also for the pantomimers who would play Mary, Joseph, shepherds and wise men.

Lord, please give us a hand here, she prayed silently. *And be with Jeremy no matter what happens.*

* * *

"It was fantastic! I've never seen such a masterpiece. Those kids deserve a medal."

Gillian grinned at the praise flowing from ecstatic parents around her. *Thank you, Lord,* she breathed, as one after another parent shook the principal's hand.

"Don't know how you did it, Mr. Nivens," one father exclaimed. "Never thought Josiah could sit still for that long."

Jeremy's face shone with the praise. "Truthfully, neither did I. I guess practice makes perfect, right Josiah?" The little boy grinned, displaying a huge gap between his teeth.

"It was a wonderful start to the Christmas holidays," Hope congratulated her later. "You must be very pleased."

"Yes, I am," Gillian agreed, stretching her toes against the fur-lined warmth of her boots. "It feels wonderful to know that he pulled it off."

A light tapping on her car window grabbed Gillian's attention, and she rolled down the glass to see Jeremy standing outside.

"I need to talk to you about this," he said clearly, holding out the envelope with her resignation inside. "I'm going to be here for a while longer, but maybe I could pick you up in a hour and we could go for coffee."

Gillian smiled. "I'm sorry but I think I've just about had it for tonight," she told him softly. "With the cookie bake planned for tomorrow and Faith's wedding the next day, I think I need to go home and relax."

He frowned. "I'd forgotten about that. Cookies, eh? How long will it take?"

"I suspect all day," Gillian grinned. "You know that bunch. They eat as much as they can. But I'm sure we'll have a few minutes to talk then, if you still want to."

He leaned his head down directly in front of hers and smiled grimly. "Oh, I'll still want to," he told her. "But I suppose it can wait."

"Why don't you relax, too," she encouraged. "Rest on your laurels. That was a fantastic closing number."

"It was good, wasn't it," he agreed. "The kids really got into it. I'll bet you were surprised that we pulled it off."

"No," she shook her head, the words coming easily. "I think you can do whatever you set your mind to. I was wrong to question that. And tonight was just the beginning for you."

"Well, we'll see." He leaned in toward her, and then glancing up at Hope, obviously thought better. He pulled his head away and straightened, staring at them both with a strange look on his face. "Good night."

"Good night."

As they drove away, Hope glanced at her niece curiously. "Why didn't you go with him? I know you still love him. You don't have to leave right away. Why not hear him out?"

Gillian leaned her head back on the headrest and closed her eyes. No one, not even Hope knew how badly she wanted to be with Jeremy tonight. But she wanted more than he could give her. She wanted it to be his shoulder she leaned on, his arms holding her closely.

"I can't, Hope. He needs time to deal with Faith's marriage, and I need to distance myself from him. He sees me as a manipulating, domineering foe. I don't want to horn in on his limelight. Besides—" she curved her gloved hand into a fist at her side "—what's the point? I'm leaving Mossbank."

The normally immaculate home of Hope Langford was bursting at the seams with laughter, cookie dough and teenagers, who were all busily engaged in preparing little care boxes for the seniors in Mossbank and the surrounding area.

Gillian had found little time to stop for even a sip of coffee let alone a discussion with Jeremy. It wasn't that he hadn't tried to speak to her. He had. Numerous times. And each time he approached she busied herself with yet another project

which had resulted in more varieties of cookies than anyone
had seen outside the local bakery.

"Don't you think we have about enough?" Myra asked
doubtfully, casting a worried glance at the cookie sheets cooling over every available surface.

"Yes," Gillian agreed, puffing her bangs off her heated
face. "This is the last batch. I purposely left the ginger snaps
till last so I could bake them slowly."

It was a lie. She hadn't even intended on baking so many
cookies until *he* had shown up with several boys in tow. His
eyes had a strange somber look to them that she couldn't
understand, but Gillian had no desire to get into it now. Not
with more than twenty teens hanging around, listening in.

"I really would like to speak to you," Jeremy murmured
from behind her shoulder. "Privately."

Gillian jumped, burning her hand against the hot pan as she
jerked her head around to stare at him. "Ohh," she groaned
between clenched teeth.

Without saying a word, Jeremy grasped her arm in his and
led her to the sink. Seconds later her hand was beneath the
tap and the cool relief of water removed some of the sting.

He held it there until she was sure it would freeze and only
allowed her to pull away when the red area lightened to a
pinkish glow.

"Sit down and relax for a moment," he ordered. "I can
handle the rest of this."

"But I…"

"You've done enough. Relax."

So although she would have preferred to get away in private and have a good bawl, she sat there and sipped the hot
sweet black coffee he had poured for her.

And dreamed of what could have been. As she watched
Jeremy move between the groups, she fantasized that this was
their home and these some of their children. The tall, skinny

boy who was laughing up at Jeremy looked a lot like him; he'd probably resemble any son Jeremy had. But it wouldn't be her son.

It was a long time before Gillian realized that the kitchen, indeed the entire house had quietened down to its usual relative silence. She gazed around at the messy kitchen, watching Jeremy scrubbing the cookie sheets. He looked perfectly at home, she decided, stifling the laugh that rose as she caught sight of the frilly white embroidered apron he wore.

"Where did everyone go?" she asked at last in a voice no one would have recognized as hers. "Why is it suddenly so quiet?"

He glanced at her over his shoulder.

"They've gone home for lunch, although I've no idea how they can eat another bite. At two o'clock those who can are coming back and we're going to deliver the cookies." His sharp gray eyes took note of her pale face and then moved to study the red patch of skin covering her hand. "How do you feel?"

"I'm fine," she told him, ignoring the whirl of her stomach as she stood to her feet. "I can do that."

He lifted the cloth beyond her reach and grinned. "Don't be silly. You've been baking for hours. The least I can do is clean up a little. We're supposed to be partners in this, remember?"

The words rang hollowly in her ears, and Gillian had to swallow down the pain. They would never be partners. She'd spoiled all that.

With a few economic moves, she had loaded the dishwasher with mixing bowls, spatulas and spoons that had littered her aunt's pristine counters. As she started the pot wash cycle, she felt his hand on her arm.

"Gillian?" His voice was low and husky and she couldn't help the shiver of awareness that moved through her.

"Yes?" She swiped the counter one last time in a businesslike fashion, drained the sink and hung up the cloth.

"Will you please stop dashing about and sit down for a moment. I want to ask you something."

Dread filled her. He was going to tell her how sorry he was. That he didn't love her. Never would.

She jutted her chin out defiantly as she sat in the nearest chair. Jeremy sat down beside her, studying his hands where they lay on the tabletop. His jeans...*jeans?* She did a double-take and then mocked herself.

They were perfectly pressed jeans with a knife edge crease down the front. She wondered idly if they had a brand name tag on the back pocket.

"What is it?" she whispered at last when the tension threatened to overwhelm her.

"Why did you resign?" His face was a mass of confusion as he stared at her. "I know you like living here, and I've seen you with your class. You're a natural at teaching. Why would you suddenly want to leave, when you said you intended to stay?" His eyes were a soft gray-blue, probing and searching her face for answers.

"I think it's better if I go now. Before things get any worse," she told him quietly. "I don't want to cause any more problems for you. You did a wonderful presentation at Christmas. That should help you when you decide to apply for a better position."

"But why now?" he demanded.

"It's a good time. People will assume I'm leaving because our engagement broke off. No one will blame you. You can go ahead, do your job as you planned without my interference." She refused to look at him. "It's for the best."

"Gillian?" His finger tipped her chin upward and she had to meet his gaze. He was frowning at her, as if he couldn't figure it all out. "I know I've led you to believe differently, but I really don't care what people think about this supposed engagement," he assured her quietly. "If I've learned one thing while I've been in Mossbank, it's that people will talk regardless of what you do, so you might as well try to please yourself."

There was silence in the tiny kitchen as Gillian digested this piece of information.

"Besides, I don't want you to go. I'll have to hire a substitute until the board can find another teacher. The children will be upset at losing you. It causes an awful lot of problems," he complained loudly.

"There's not really any problem," Gillian told him steadily. "Flossie Gerbrandt has agreed to cover for me until they can find someone else. She's a very good teacher and she'll be thrilled to be working with you."

"I don't want Flossie Gerbrandt," he thundered, his eyes dark with fury. "The woman follows me around constantly as it is, asking all manner of ridiculous questions."

"She's got a crush on you," Gillian told him gently. When his eyes opened wide, she nodded. "Flossie is very shy and has trouble getting a conversation started. But if you give her a chance, I'm sure you'll find you both have a lot in common."

"Hah," he grunted. "Like what?"

"Classical music, for one thing. Flossie plays the cello and she's very good." Gillian made herself say the words even though she detested it. "And she's been to England, too. You could talk about that."

"I don't want to talk about classical music or England," he barked. His eyes narrowed. "What will happen to the youth group? I can't manage it alone."

"Jeremy, you have a wonderful way with these kids once you let yourself loosen up. Why, only this morning David was telling me about the excellent advice you gave him. They respect and admire you. You'll do fine.''

"What advice?" he demanded, frowning. "I don't have any advice to give teenagers. I don't know anything about them.''

"Something about not pointing out his girlfriend's bubble gum," she murmured, trying to remember exactly what David had said. "I don't remember exactly."

Jeremy did. All of a sudden the conversation sounded in his mind, crystal clear. He heard himself telling David to either accept the flaws or find someone else.

What a farce it was! Here he was driving away the one person who made him feel things he'd never felt, because he couldn't accept who she was.

"Gillian, I wanted to tell you that..."

"I'm sorry," she interrupted. "I've just got to get going. I promised Faith that I'd finish her headpiece. The wedding is tomorrow, you know." She studied him for a moment. "Are you sure you won't walk her down the aisle? You are her only family."

Jeremy wished fervently that he'd never withheld himself from his aunt's wedding plans. He dearly wanted to make her happy, and since she seemed intent on going through with this wedding, he knew it was pointless to keep arguing. He owed her that much. And a lot more.

"Well, I'm sorry that you can't give in on this one issue," Gillian told him sadly. She glanced away from his searching eyes. "But I do have to go. Faith needs all the support she can get right now, and I can't let her down." She smiled in a way that made Jeremy's heart race and the blood pound in his ears. "But don't worry, I'll see you again before I leave."

"When will that be?" he asked, thoroughly out of sorts with the whole conversation. Was he never to be allowed to finish a sentence with this woman?

Gillian swept through the kitchen to the front hall, snatching up her coat and shrugging into it before he could help her. It irked him. He'd wanted to touch those bright, curling strands once more.

He'd wanted to touch *her.*

"I'm going to spend Christmas with Hope. I don't want her to be alone. But the next day I'm heading back to Boston. It's time I got on with my life. See you!" And with a wave and a halfhearted smile that tugged at his heart strings, she walked out the door.

"Wonderful," he muttered, flopping down onto the sofa. "She doesn't want Hope to be alone. Art doesn't want my aunt to be alone. Why am I the only one who'll be alone?"

"Because you want it that way."

His head whirled around in surprise. Hope Langford stood in the doorway, a frown marring the clear beauty of her face.

"I beg your pardon?" He couldn't believe she'd interrupted his private conversation. Even if it was with himself.

"You should—from a lot of people. But I'm not sure I'm one of them," Hope muttered as she hung up her coat and removed her snow boots. When she came into the room, her clear blue eyes chastised him roundly.

"You do realize that you're making everyone thoroughly miserable, don't you?"

"Me?" He stared. "What have I done?"

"You've hurt my niece, for one thing." There was a cold fury in the voice.

"But I've been trying to persuade her to stay. She won't listen. She's determined to go, so that our ridiculous 'engagement' will be terminated. She thinks people will blame her and feel sorry for me. As if I want that." Jeremy clenched his fist in anger. "I want her to stay."

"Gillian is in love with you. How do you think it feels for

her to know you don't want anything to do with her—that you dislike so much about her?''

"I don't dislike her at all. I love her!'' His mouth fell open in amazement. He hadn't realized the truth of the statement until just now.

"Is that why you let this supposed engagement go on so long? Is that why you called her selfish and inconsiderate and bullied her for weeks on end? Because you love her?'' Hope's voice bit into his with disdain. "Some love.''

"Yes, it is,'' he agreed in stupefied wonder.

"Are you going to try and order her around the way you've ordered Faith? You've made my niece's life a misery, Mr. Nivens. She can't even enjoy Faith's wedding, although she's worked like a trooper to make it happen. Gillian's so worried that you'll do something to spoil your aunt's happiness that she's not eating, not sleeping. Your 'love' is tearing her apart.''

Jeremy winced at the scathing reprimand.

"I do love my aunt, Miss Langford. And I have no intention of spoiling her day. I wish her and Art every happiness.''

"You do?''

"Of course. I was merely concerned for her safety. But since they found the tumor, well,'' he swallowed down the fear and continued, needing to tell someone. "I've realized that she might only have a little while left. I want it to be a happy time.'' He barely caught the next words.

"It's benign.''

"What?'' He stared at her, afraid to believe.

"She got a phone call this morning while I was there. It was benign. Nothing to worry about. The doctor said she's fine.''

"Oh, my God!'' Jeremy breathed a silent prayer of thanks, sinking back onto the sofa. "I can't believe it.''

"Neither could she. But she's afraid if you find out, you'll try to stop the wedding.'' Hope's words were blunt, but Jeremy welcomed them. They cut to the heart of the matter, and he had no time to dawdle now.

''I'm not going to stop it,'' he told her grinning. ''I'm going to be part of it.''

Hope's face lit up like a Christmas tree, and she threw herself into his arms, pressing a soft kiss to his cheek. ''Thank you, Jeremy. Thank you so much.''

He grinned. ''Don't thank me,'' he told her softly. ''It's going to be my pleasure.'' He smiled slowly, setting her back on her feet. ''But do you really think you should go around kissing the man who is engaged to your niece? Even if we are going to be related?''

Hope stared at him as her hands automatically straightened her tidy hair.

''But it's all a sham. A pretense. You're not really going to marry Gillian.'' Her eyes widened. Her voice dropped to a whisper. ''Are you?''

For once, Jeremy felt as if the whole world was his. With a peculiar little smile, he hoisted himself from the sofa and walked slowly over to the door, yanking on his jacket as he went, mindless of the way he unevenly buttoned it.

''Yes,'' he whispered. ''I think I am.'' He pulled open the door and stepped outside, completely unmoved by the icy wind or the whirling snowflakes. ''She just doesn't know it yet.''

As he swept out the door and down the walk, Hope rushed over to close the door, pausing a moment to watch him hurry away in his compact sports car with an unusual grinding of gears.

''My, oh my,'' she murmured, pressing the solid oak door into place. ''Will wonders never cease?''

She was still standing there a few moments later when the doorbell rang. Half fearfully, afraid he'd come to his senses, she opened the door a crack and peered outside. A group of fifteen or twenty teenagers stood outside, grinning like a pack of wolves.

"Is Jeremy here?" one of them asked. "We're supposed to deliver the cookies this afternoon and he and Gillian were going to drive us."

Hope smiled, a wonderful heartfelt smile that lifted her stern lips and brought a glow to her eyes. "I think," she told them happily, "that we will have to make alternate arrangements. I'm afraid Jeremy and Gillian are going to be tied up."

"Property settlement," Janice Cheevers nodded knowingly. "Always happens when there's a breakup. Too bad. They were a neat couple."

"Yeah," a tall, lanky boy muttered as he brushed past Hope. "I dunno why they don't just kiss and make up. Isn't love supposed to forgive all?"

"With God's help," Hope murmured, closing her eyes in a soft prayer. "With God's help."

Chapter Fifteen

The small church was packed to capacity for Faith Rempel's wedding. Gillian had seen no one that she couldn't identify from the small community, and every single face beamed with good wishes for the elderly couple.

The Christmas decorations were glittering in the candlelight of hundreds of glowing tapers decorating the platform. She herself had arranged the silky flowers in graceful baskets which would be changed tomorrow to hold the fresh arrangements for the Christmas Eve service tomorrow night. Everything was ready.

Except for Jeremy.

No matter how hard she searched, Gillian couldn't find his face anywhere in the happy group of well-wishers. Well, why would he be there? she asked herself firmly. He'd rejected his great-aunt's decision adamantly. He wouldn't change just because she had begged him to.

Minnie Klemp pressed the loud key on the organ and everyone surged to their feet. Gillian watched as her aunt stepped down the aisle first. Hope looked magnificent in her emerald silk suit, gliding slowly down the aisle as she cradled her creamy white Persian roses gracefully across one arm. She took her place beside Harry Conroy, the local judge and Art's longtime golf buddy.

Next came Charity, carefully following the carpeted path in her odd-gaited, delicate mincing steps, covered from head to toe in bright holly-berry red. Her roses were also white and she carried them proudly, her arthritic fingers grasping them tenderly. Her partner, Frank Bellows, slipped his arm through hers in support, and Charity smiled up at him gratefully. Gillian grinned. If she wasn't mistaken, the undertaker had a special glint in his eye when he looked at Charity Flowerday.

Then all heads focused on the back as Faith came through the door. Her wedding dress was an elegant ivory lace that lent a glow of radiance to her jubilant face. No one could say this radiant woman was too old for a bridal gown, Gillian thought fiercely. Jeremy's aunt looked blissfully exultant in the timeless silk gown.

Faith carried a bouquet of crimson red roses interspersed with deep green foliage. They were tied with a pale glossy ribbon and she held them with one hand. Her other was looped through Jeremy's!

Gillian gasped. He'd come. He'd actually relented and come to the wedding. Not only that, he was participating and from the look on his face, enjoying it.

She could only stare in disbelief as they walked slowly up the aisle. When they passed her, Jeremy's eyes rested on her for a moment and Gillian felt the same old thud-thud her heart always gave when he was around. The glint of blue in his soft gray eyes made her knees weak with love. How could she go on, knowing their own pretended engagement would never result in such a wonderful finale?

They stopped in front of her as Faith loosened one of her bright roses from the bouquet and reached past Jeremy to hand to it to her. Gillian took it with a lump in her throat, barely catching Faith's whispered words.

"For my soon-to-be great-niece."

Gillian forced herself to ignore the shaft of pain at the thought Faith's words engendered. She couldn't dwell on those words or she would burst into tears. Instead she forced herself to concentrate on the pair, young and old, moving regally down the aisle.

When the minister asked, "Who gives this woman to be married?" Gillian heard Jeremy's response in stunned disbelief. And then he handed his aunt over to her husband-to-be with careful elegance, pressing a kiss against her smooth, paper-thin cheek. A second later he was standing beside Gillian, holding her hand in his.

The entire ceremony passed by in a daze for Gillian as she kept glancing at her and Jeremy's entwined fingers. Opal Everet sang 'Oh Perfect Love,' Pastor Dave pronounced them husband and wife, and Arthur Johnson kissed his new bride with a gusto that brought appreciative laughs from the audience.

But other than that, Gillian heard nothing. The soloist launched into her second number, but the words held no meaning, no special significance for her. In fact, Gillian was so out of it, Jeremy had to tug on her hand to get her to stand when Mr. and Mrs. Arthur Johnson were presented to the congregation.

Gillian followed as the happy couple walked back out of the church and found her path through the church vestibule blocked.

"I have to talk to you, Gillian," Jeremy whispered urgently. "I've been trying to do that since yesterday. It's important." His eyes gleamed with some hidden fire, and Gillian could feel the tension emanating from his tall, lean body.

She didn't understand what he wanted. They had said everything there was to say. But something told her that whatever he wanted to say needed to be discussed away from the maddening crowd; without the interested gaze of the townspeople looking on.

"This is Faith and Arthur's day," she murmured, slipping past him and into the crowd. "Whatever we need to say to each other can wait. I don't want to spoil their day with another argument."

His fingers wrapped around her arm like tentacles, and he pulled her back into the protection of the pew, turning so that he shielded her from the rest of the wedding guests who were leaving the church.

"Okay," he agreed smiling. "If you insist, we'll wait. But, I need to do this now," he murmured, before his mouth came down on hers in a soft demanding kiss that left her breathless but wanting more. "And you'd better be warned. I'm going to need to do that a lot more in the future. Come on." He grasped her fingers, his eyes glittering with something she couldn't decipher. "Let's go help Auntie Fay celebrate."

And they did!

They tossed confetti on the couple until the colored circles covered their graying hair and grinning faces. They toasted them repeatedly at the reception and tinkled their glasses over and over, calling for the groom to kiss his bride. And before the couple left in their car, Jeremy tied a bunch of old cans to the bumper of Art's Jeep while Gillian whispered a few last words to Faith.

"I'm so happy for you and Arthur, Faith. You really belong together." Gillian tried to mask the jealousy she felt at the beaming smile of pure happiness Faith gave her.

"Yes, Gillian, we do. I'm so glad that God gave me another chance at love. And I have to tell you that I think He's doing the same thing for you." Faith patted her hand tenderly, the new band of gold sparkling on her finger. "I know Jeremy loves you. And I know you love him. You may have convinced each other that you're only pretending to be engaged, but I think that's what you both really want."

"Oh, Faith," Gillian murmured, brushing a tear from the corner of her eye. "I know you're confused about this but Jeremy and I were never really engaged. You just imagined that."

Faith grinned. It was a smug, self-satisfied grin that tilted the edges of her mouth and left her green eyes sparkling like a cat's. "Did I?" she mused. "How strange."

There was a peculiar quality to those lovely eyes that had Gillian questioning her own sanity for a moment until Faith began speaking again.

"My dear Gillian," she said kindly. "I could never be confused about something so important. I deliberately threw the two of you together as part of my Christmas project. I knew that once you two learned to accept each other for who you are and stopped trying to change the other, you'd be happy together."

Faith wrapped her arm in Arthur's and pressed her cheek against his shoulder lovingly. She smiled at Gillian who was backing away from the car.

"Don't disappoint us, dear," the old woman whispered, just before the car drove off.

"Disappoint them?" Gillian whispered to herself in perplexity. "Now what in the world had the old girl meant by that? Christmas project, indeed!"

Gillian watched them go with confusion. What did any of it mean? Faith's cryptic remarks? Jeremy kissing her? What had that kiss meant? Why was he there? What had suddenly changed between them?

Her heart was full of excitement and anticipation and wonder but she tamped it down ruthlessly. Just because she had given up on her desire to stay single didn't mean that Jeremy had also had a change of heart recently.

But after all, God *did* work in mysterious ways. Didn't He?

As the newlyweds drove off to the jangle of cans, Jeremy grasped Gillian by the shoulders and turned her to face him.

"Can you walk in those things?" he asked, referring to her frivolous new shoes with their dangerously high heels. "Never mind," he muttered finally, glancing around. "I know the perfect place."

In one smooth motion he scooped her up into his arms and carried her across the street to the church. Gillian was too stunned to do anything but stare at his sudden impetuosity. Especially with half the town watching, knowing grins covering their faces.

The old church was deserted; everyone was still gathered at the hall celebrating. The tapers had long since gone out, but the Christmas tree was still lit and someone had turned on the light above the pulpit, sending a beam of white light down over the mass of bright red poinsettias. Their fragrance filled the burnished wooden building, reminding Gillian of the season. When Jeremy simply set her down on the pew and then sat beside her, staring at her through the gloom, she decided to start the ball rolling.

"We should be at the hall," she murmured finally. "The others will be wondering where we've gone to." Jeremy still said nothing, gazing down at her. Gillian fidgeted in her seat, straightening her skirt nervously.

"I owe you an apology," he murmured. "I was wrong."

"Wrong," she repeated, her brow furrowing as she peered up at him. "Why?"

"Because I tried to change you. Tried to make you and all the others into something they aren't. Something none of you were ever intended to be." He grimaced, wrapping his fingers around hers. "That's better," he murmured softly.

"Jeremy," Gillian pleaded, staring into the warmth of his soft gray eyes. "Will you please tell me what you're talking about? Why did you suddenly decide to come to the wedding?"

His eyes glittered with satisfaction. "Because I wanted to know what it would be like when you and I get married."

"What?" Gillian stared at him, her eyes wide with disbelief. "But we agreed. We've called off that silly engagement. It was just pretend, anyway."

"If you want to call it off, you go ahead. I'm not. I like being engaged to you, my darling Miss Langford. But I think I'd like being married better."

None of it made any sense to Gillian. What was he saying, for Pete's sake?

"I know this doesn't conform to the usual procedure for such occasions," he told her softly, tugging her closer beside him. His fingers slid smoothly over hers as he cradled her hands in his. "But for once, I'm going to make my own rules."

He brushed the tendril of silky hair off her forehead and pressed a kiss there. And another on the side of her neck where her pulse beat furiously. Then his hands cupped her chin and his eyes stared straight into hers, melting and drawing her into their rich shining depths.

"I love you, Miss Gillian Langford. I love you so much, I get nervous when I don't see you for even a few moments. And I'm miserable and unhappy when you're not there to brighten the day. I love the way you dedicate yourself to helping others whether they want it or not, and I'm sorry I tried to stop you from doing what you do best—simply being Gillian, the woman that God created."

Gillian felt her skin growing warm under his caressing touch, steadily, incessantly hotter until she felt like a glowing ember that basked in the radiance of a brightly burning fire.

"I don't know what to say," she whispered.

He shook his head in amusement. "Don't tell me you're lost for words." He chuckled. "It's a miracle."

"No." She shook her head dazedly. "But this is."

"Yes," he agreed, nodding. "A Christmas miracle from God. He taught me that in Him there is only one rule. Love. And when we love someone, that love takes care of all the other rules."

His finger traced the outline of his face as he spoke. "I've lived so long with the idea that God was a stern judge who kept a detailed tally of every little mistake we made that I lost sight of the real meaning of His love for us." Jeremy brushed his mouth across her hand before continuing.

"He doesn't care if we sit or stand to sing the hymns. He doesn't care if we have the offertory before or after the special music. He doesn't even care if junior church gets canceled and the babies bawl all through the sermon. Most especially He doesn't care if Faith forgets a few things now and then. He loves her as she is."

His face was close to hers now, his breath a whisper against the sensitive skin of her face. Gillian bemusedly slid one hand lightly over the dear hard lines of his beloved face and waited patiently for him to finish.

"I finally realized that what we do isn't as important as what we think," he told her. "It doesn't matter because I can never be good enough or strict enough or wise enough."

His smile was wide and tender. "It isn't the rules or the keeping of them that's important," he murmured. "It's what you've got inside. Forcing people to obey rules will never change that."

She didn't really need to ask anymore, but Gillian knew he was just bursting to tell her. "And what is it that you have inside?" she asked softly, half-afraid to believe.

"Love," he crowed proudly. "For you. Big and wide and

all encompassing." His arms curved round her, pulling her to her feet and against his strong body.

"Big enough to forgive me for all the things I've done?" Her question was timidly quiet.

"My darling Gillian, there is nothing to forgive," he told her sincerely. "I love you just the way you are." His eyes moved over her, memorizing each detail. "God put this love in my heart and His love is never ending."

"But Jeremy, we're nothing alike," she protested mildly, hoping he'd brush away her protests.

He did.

"Thank goodness! I don't want to love someone like me." He grinned. "I know we'll have disagreements. Everyone does. But isn't His love enough to cover them all?"

She would never again see this man as rigid and unbending, Gillian decided. To her he would always be Jeremy: strong and independent, determined to do the right thing no matter what.

"I love you," he murmured in her ear, softly but clearly.

"That's good," she answered, brushing her lips against his chin. "Because I have a fair bit of that particular emotion myself. I thought maybe we could share?"

"No way," he muttered, glaring at her fiercely. "Not this time, Gillian."

Her heart dropped to the floor as she wondered if she'd been wrong once more. "Wh-what do you mean?" she stammered, staring up at him fearfully.

His arms tightened around her once before he let her go. "I mean that you did the proposing last time, Gillian Langford. This time it's my turn and I intend to follow, to the letter, all the correct and proper procedures."

He knelt in front of her, holding her hands in his, blue-gray eyes glowing with emotion. "I would very much like to be engaged to you, darling Miss Langford," he whispered softly.

"For real. With a true commitment and all the expectations for our future that entails." His fingers tightened around hers. "Would you please marry me?"

"Yes," she cried, trying to tug him upward. "Yes, yes, yes."

But Jeremy Nivens had never been a man to be hurried and he wasn't about to start now. Slowly, thoughtfully, he got off his knees and stood before her. His words were soft but full of meaning. "Then would you mind wearing this ring as a token of how much I love and adore and appreciate you?" he murmured. "And as my promise that I'll never try to change you again." He snapped open the small black jeweler's case Gillian glimpsed in his hand.

She gasped at the beauty of it. It sparkled and glittered in the dimness of the old church like a fire that refused to be doused. Two slivers of glittering gold wound round out of the band and up around the high-set diamond, holding it between their grip protectively.

"It's so delicate," she whispered, awestruck as he slipped it onto her finger.

"It only looks that way," he teased, smoothing back a tendril with his finger. "Rather like you. Beautiful and fragile as a flower. But inside…ah, inside, my dear Gillian, you are a pure, clear diamond."

"It's so beautiful. I've never seen such a setting." She held up her hand and admired it in the fading light. "I never expected this," she said tearfully. "I never expected you."

"I chose this especially because it reminded me of something," he told her smiling. "It reminds me that there are two of us, different and individual in our own right. But because of God and the love He's given us, we will be joined as one and held in the palm of God's hand."

Gillian wrapped her arms around her fiancé's neck and

hugged him as hard as she could, reveling in the touch of his tender yet strong mouth on hers.

"Thank you, God," she whispered, letting her eyes wing upward for a moment. "He's so much more than I deserve or dreamed of."

"What are you saying?" Jeremy demanded, tipping his head back to gaze into her starry eyes.

Gillian just beamed, letting the love that filled her heart and soul pour out on a free, unrestricted wave of undulation.

"I'm just thanking the original matchmaker," she whispered, pointing upward.

Jeremy grinned. "Yes, and you can thank Arthur and Aunt Faith later," he murmured, his lips tickling her earlobe. "Without their interference, the Lord would have had a much more difficult task."

As their heads tilted toward each other and they sealed their engagement with a long satisfying kiss, two elderly women watched for a moment longer from their hiding place in the vestibule and then tiptoed noiselessly out into the cold winter night. "I think we can consider our Christmas projects for this year a success," Charity murmured, clutching her friend's arm as they negotiated the slippery streets.

"Aren't they always," Hope agreed smugly. "Especially with a little divine assistance."

They giggled together like young girls, sticking out their tongues to catch the fluffy white snowflakes that drifted slowly down from heaven and dropped silently to earth, covering everything with a soft white blanket of peace.

And just down the street, Faith rested her head against her new husband's shoulder as their car sped away from town for the first night of their married life.

"You know, Arthur," she said happily, squeezing his hand fondly, "I can hardly wait for next Christmas. I have a real inspiration for my project next year!"

Epilogue

"You're going to do what?" Jeremy demanded, staring at his wife in dismay. "But it's almost Christmas. We've got the pageant to plan for and the choir to rehearse. Our new drama club starts in January. You can't quit."

Gillian laughed, pressing a kiss on the tip of his nose.

"Overachieving as usual! Jeremy darling, I intend to help you with all that, and I'll work through into the early spring but then I'm leaving JFK. At least for a little while."

Jeremy sank into his plush principal's chair and tugged her slight form onto his lap, slipping his fingers through the bright coppery strands of her lovely hair.

"I've done it again, haven't I?" he groaned, pressing his lips against her forehead. "I've pushed and bullied and made you fed up with me. Darling, I'm so sorry. I've tried, really tried not to be so…"

She cut him off mid-sentence.

"Jeremy Nivens, will you please let me speak?"

Her gorgeous emerald eyes flashed with temper and something he couldn't quite define. Some hint of excitement that teased and tantalized till he couldn't look away.

"Gillian, darling," he breathed anxiously, his arms tightening around her protectively. "Please don't tell me you're ill."

"I will be," she whispered. "Every morning apparently. For a few months anyway." Her face softened as she lifted one hand to cup his cheek. "I'm pregnant, Jeremy. We're going to have a baby!"

"A baby? But I hadn't planned on that till next year…er, that is, a baby?" He stared at her, struck dumb by the possibilities such a thing engendered.

"Well," Gillian huffed indignantly as a secret grin tugged at the sides of her mouth, "I am sorry that we're ahead of your all-important schedule, but I'm not taking all the blame!"

He kissed her then as the words sank in, holding her tightly and whispering a prayer of thanksgiving. When at last she could move, his wife wiggled around until her glowing eyes stared straight into his.

"There's just one thing I want to make perfectly clear," she told him firmly. "We are not, I repeat, not having six children. That's asking for problems."

Jeremy soothed her with heartfelt endearments as he placed his brown hand on her tummy.

"I'm going to be a father," he mumbled, his eyes a deep dark blue. "Me, a parent."

"Jeremy? Did you hear me? I said I'm not having six children. Two maybe. Even three. But not six. Jeremy?" The last word came out on a sigh of delight as her husband tugged her mouth down to his.

"We'll talk about it," he whispered tenderly. "Negotiate. Discuss both sides of the issue and come to some understanding. After all, we've gotten rather good at it, don't you think?"

"Mmm," she sighed. "I guess love is all about compromise, isn't it?'' She grinned impishly. ''Would I be compromising your male ego if I told you to shut up and kiss me?''

''I think you'd be perfectly justified, my darling Gillian. And I'd be perfectly happy to oblige.''

And he was about to when a new idea suddenly struck.

''You know Faith is going to say she planned the whole thing, don't you?'' he murmured, fingering her engagement ring and the gold band that protected it. ''She's been talking about her 'project' for weeks now.'' His happy grin belied the dourness of his words.

''I'm happy to have her and the others share in it,'' Gillian answered, snuggling a little closer. ''After all, everyone needs a little Faith, Hope and Charity. Right, darling?''

Jeremy agreed wholeheartedly with her astute assessment of the situation.

''Yes, dear.''

And then he kissed her.

* * * * *

Dear Reader,

Thanks for picking up *Faithfully Yours*. In case you didn't know, this book is the first in a series of three that I've entitled FAITH, HOPE & CHARITY. These three lovely ladies came into my imagination of their own accord and stayed around with the agreement that I pay specific attention to what they will and will not tolerate. They have given me much to think about as I pondered the majesty of God's plan for each person on this earth and His love specifically tailored for every individual.

I hope you enjoy Gillian and Jeremy's story and their struggles to search for the loveliness that is sometimes hidden beneath the surface. Can it be that we often miss the best in another because we too readily see only a bad temper or ragged clothes? If we would but look beneath the surface, we would see such beauty in the souls of others.

SWEET CHARITY

There is no fear in love;
but perfect love casts out fear.
—*1 John* 4:18

To my sons Cristopher and Joshua

May you always have an abundance of sweet
charity with an added helping of patience.
You've already got persistence down pat!
Love, Mom

Prologue

Dr. Christopher Davis yanked off his green surgical cap and tossed it onto a nearby chair in his office. "Thanks, Macy," he muttered, taking the cup from the hovering secretary's hand and inhaling the fresh-ground aroma. "Traeger's always did make the best Viennese extradark roast."

"They should," she mumbled. "They charge you an arm and a leg for those beans." She ignored his grin. "You'd better drink it fast. The next one is a toughie."

"You mean the abdominal?" Christopher frowned. "Yes, it's going to be rough."

"Jimmy Jones," Macy reminded him with a frown. "His name is Jimmy."

"Oh, yeah. I forgot." Chris shrugged off the reprimand, knowing she thought him heartless. "I can't help it," he defended himself. "This is the fifth operation this morning. We had to start at five because of the power surge last night. Hey, it's Tuesday, isn't it?"

At Macy's nod he continued, "That means there will be interns watching." His shoulders tightened but he refused to

show his discomfort. ''They usually like watching these abdominal things.''

''They like watching *you* because you explain everything
to them,'' Macy told him, grinning as she thrust a single white
sheet under his nose. ''By the way, your mother has summoned you to dinner tonight. Seven-thirty sharp!'' Macy
rolled her eyes. ''And this fax came in a short while ago. The
cover sheet was marked urgent.'' Quietly she left, closing the
office door softly behind her.

Christopher sank into his leather chair and started reading.

Dear Chris,

   Hey, old buddy! I know we haven't heard from each
other in a while, although I have heard rave reviews
about your work in Boston. Just yesterday I was talking
to our old prof and he said you had resigned. Your timing
is perfect, Chris, because I really need your help. Jessica's in her third trimester now, but she's having numerous difficulties. We've been advised to get to Loma
Linda ASAP.

   I'm hoping you'll agree to fill in for me while we are
away. I know this place is nothing like the big city, but
I'd sure appreciate it if you could take over here for the
next little while. With all your experience, I'm sure you
could handle everything easily. The only thing is, I have
no idea how long we'll be gone.

   Please think about it, would you? And let me know
immediately. Thanks, pal.

Dan

Chris scanned the letter quickly, noting that a Dr. Green
shared the practice. It took several moments of squinting at
the notation below to assemble the patterns into something
resembling English. Dan, he recalled fondly, had the worst

handwriting he'd ever seen. And that was saying something, he mused, even for a GP. Head to one side, he peered at the odd pen scratches once more. He thought it read, ''Jori Jessop is my nurse now and if anyone can keep you in line, it's her. Tall, dark and gorgeous. I think you might even enjoy it here!''

Chris snorted. Yeah, right. He'd known a lot of office nurses in his day and he'd never met one that he was remotely interested in.

Still, he mused, it would be a change. He was tired of these hectic days. He'd finally, at age thirty-six, fulfilled his parents' expectations; attained the status they'd always said he would. In fact, Chris mused, he was on top of his game right now.

And bored out of his mind. Wasn't there supposed to be more to life than working day after day in this cold impersonal hospital; more to life than spending endless days and nights in the operating room? Good grief, he couldn't even remember the patients' names anymore! Life had become one long surgical assembly line.

Which was why he'd asked for a leave of absence six weeks ago. Never mind that he hadn't yet had the opportunity to take it. Maybe now was the perfect time.

''Operating Room Four will be ready for you in fifteen minutes, Doctor.'' Chris's surgical nurse's voice came through the speakerphone.

Life was bound to be pretty slow in—what was it?—Mossbank, North Dakota.

It sounded like just the place to sit and cogitate. Which was probably all there was to do in a farming community that barely appeared on the map.

Clicking on his computer, Chris peered at the letterhead of Dan's office and then faxed a note to his friend via the modem on his desk, grinning all the while.

At least they had faxes in this one-horse town.

* * *

"I know you've had a full day, Dan. But could I talk to you? Just for a moment." Nurse Jordanna Jessop stood waiting for her boss to look up from the chart he was reading.

"Of course, Jori. Come on in." He folded the file and laid it aside. "What's up?"

"I need some advice on something and I don't know who else to ask. It's about my future." Jori kept her eyes focused on her hands and tried to stop twisting them. "The thing is, I've sort of been on hold here, these last few years, and now I think it's time for me to make some decisions."

"You're quitting?" Dr. Dan stared. "But I thought you intended to stay here permanently!"

"No, I'm not leaving. I'm settled here now. That's what I want to talk to you about." She took a deep breath and blurted it all out. "I've decided to have a child."

She peered up at him through her lashes, knowing her friend would be shocked. "I was hoping you could advise me on my options."

"Your, er, options? Jori, are you pregnant?" She could see the sad look in his eyes and hastened to correct him.

"No. Of course not. But I'd like to be. Now, as I see it, I have three choices. I can try to adopt, but the government agency I've been corresponding with didn't seem too hopeful about my chances. Especially since I'm single. Still, I'm not giving up yet. Are you listening?"

"Yes, I'm listening." Dan sounded strange, Jori noted, and decided to make this quick.

"There's also something like a five-year wait if I want to adopt a newborn. And a fast, private adoption is very expensive—and risky."

"Oh, Jordanna, I don't think that's what you want." Dan's voice was full of doubt. "Sometimes birth mothers change their minds. I wouldn't want to see you get hurt."

"Yes, I know. There's also the cost. I'd have to deplete what little I have in my savings to pay for a private adoption. That would leave me with almost nothing if something went wrong with the baby."

"Well, as far as I know, that leaves marriage." Dan grinned happily. "Why don't you try that?"

"With whom? There aren't a lot of available men around here," she said, smoothing the skirt on her white uniform. "And I don't want to move because of my father. Besides—" her full lips turned down "—would you want to date Rodney Little or Gary Norton after you'd seen their medical records?"

"I can't say I'd want to date a man at all," Dan teased. "But I do think there's someone you might be interested in. And fortunately for you he's healthy as a horse. Also tall and good-looking."

"You're not going to trot out that replacement doctor that's coming, are you?" Jori groaned with exasperation. "I told you, I don't want to get involved with some pompous, egocentric surgeon who's doing us all a favor just by agreeing to come to little old Mossbank!" She stood in a huff, frustration making her voice rise. "Never mind! I'll deal with this myself. There's got to be some way I can manage."

"Jori." Dan's voice was soft with sympathy. "Jess and I aren't abandoning you. We'll be back. Just keep the faith, honey. Keep waiting on the Lord."

"The Lord helps those who help themselves." And with that, Jori whirled from the room, chagrin wrinkling her forehead.

"There's got to be a way, Lord," she said to herself. "There's just got to be a way."

Chapter One

"Thank you very much, Mrs. Flowerday. Yes, I'm sure the doctor will be thrilled." Swallowing the burble of laughter that threatened her otherwise solemn facade, Jordanna Jessop carefully lifted the plastic container from the older woman's hands.

"It's the least I can do. We're all so happy to have Dr. Dan's friend here. A doctor needs someone to look after him, keeping such busy hours and all." The warm brown eyes were speculative as she looked at Jori. "He's very handsome, isn't he, dear?"

Mrs. Charity Flowerday shivered delicately. "His eyes are the very same color as the Aegean Sea, I'll wager! And when he stands there in that white coat, well!" She twittered. "It's enough to make your heart speed up, isn't it, dear?"

"I hadn't really noticed," Jori murmured, unwilling to discuss the latest addition to the small town. "It's been so busy, you see."

"Yes, I heard your father went into the home. So sad, dear." She patted Jori's hand affectionately. "And on top of that, I imagine it's hard to get used to a new doctor after working with Dr. Dan for this long. And of course, Dr. Chris is from the city and all. Probably needs a good woman to teach him the ropes." She glanced at Jori speculatively.

"Our Dr. Dan knew about country folks, of course. Such a good man," Charity breathed. "And Jessica is the sweetest woman! I've just been praying as hard as I can for that dear baby." A lone tear trickled down her smooth white cheek until she managed to collect herself, the sweet smile curving her lips once more. "Enough chitchat! I'd better be on my way. I'm baking pies today. The church bake sale, you know. I do wish this weather would cool off. Bye!"

As Charity Flowerday hobbled out the door, Jori turned away, shoulders shaking with repressed laughter. If she was any judge of character, and she was, the doctor would be somewhat less than appreciative of this latest goodwill gesture from the town's busiest busybody.

She didn't like the allusion Charity had just made to Dr. Davis's need for a wife. Oh, well! Charity Flowerday, Faith Johnson and Hope Conroy were known for their ability to pair off any single adult who came to the district. That was fine by Jori—as long as they didn't include her in their she-nanigans!

With her normally unflappable control in place, Jori strode down the hall to the tiny, dull office that presently housed Christopher Davis, M.D. She tapped gently before entering. "Dr. Davis?"

There wasn't any answer. Instead, the good doctor sat studying a file, totally unaware of her presence. For some reason Jori couldn't explain, she was loath to break his concentration.

She studied her temporary boss and the way his golden blond head was bent over the file, hiding his spectacular velvet blue eyes. Her gaze focused on his tanned features, assessing him the way a photographer had taught her to size up a subject. His face was all angles and hard edges, perfectly sculpted with a wide forehead, jutting cheekbones and beautiful lips.

Yep, Jori decided silently, a real lady-killer. Good thing he wasn't her type. Of course, she had known that the moment Dan introduced them.

Big, bossy and boisterous. Jori had cataloged the newcomer right away. Dr. Christopher Davis was not her kind of man. Not at all.

"Yes, Nurse. What is it?" The interloper's deep gravelly voice demanded her immediate attention.

Jori flushed lightly before thrusting out Charity's plastic-boxed gift. "This is for you," she told him, a smirk tipping up the corners of her pert mouth as he groaned loudly.

"Not another praline cheesecake delight," he begged, holding his rib cage in protest. A tiny smile teased the corner of his mouth. Privately, she decided he would be a whole lot more handsome if he made an effort to smile all the time.

"How many is that now? Eight? Ten?" His eyes twinkled across at her.

It really wasn't any wonder the ladies of Mossbank had been in a flap this past week, Jori decided, almost melting under that blaze of perfectly even white smile.

"I don't know. Entirely too many, that's for sure." For some reason his intense scrutiny made her nervous and Jori fiddled with some papers on his desk, bursting into speech when he got to his feet.

"This one will be delicious, though. Charity Flowerday is an excellent cook. It will also be the richest," she warned. Her eyes skittered away from his and then returned for a closer look. "She loves to double the chocolate in everything."

"Hmm, double chocolate," he teased. "A woman after my own heart. How old is she?" His grin made it obvious he'd overheard at least part of the matchmaking schemes currently going on around town.

She ignored that and continued her silent scrutiny. He was taller than she, which was saying something. At five foot ten, few men ever towered over her. Dr. Davis, on the other hand, was about six foot four and all lean muscle. He had the broad strong shoulders women always swooned over, and a wide chest that could accommodate any female's weary head.

"I don't believe anyone can get too much chocolate," he muttered softly. "But this is definitely way too much cheese-cake. Do you think there will be any more?"

"'Fraid so," Jori murmured, shoving aside four other des-serts that had arrived earlier that afternoon to make room for the latest addition. "You should never have said Mrs. Belle's was the best praline cheesecake you had ever tasted. It's like you laid down a challenge around here."

"Too bad you couldn't have said something two days ago," Christopher groused, moving to toss one of the less attractive packages into the trash.

"No!" Jori grabbed the thickly muscled forearm, inter-rupting his attempt at making a basket.

"I wouldn't do that if I were you," she told him seriously, her long fingers tightening as he tried to pull away.

Christopher glanced from her hand on his arm, to her slim body pressed against his desk, to her flushed face.

"Why?" he drawled, obviously curious about her sudden change from quiet, efficient assistant to the disheveled woman who clung to his arm as if her life depended on it.

Jori took the package from him and gently set it on the tabletop once more. "Emery Laser cleans this place every night. His mother is Jasmine Laser." She waited for the light of comprehension, and when it didn't dawn across his frown-ing countenance, Jori read the tiny card attached to the white carton she had just rescued.

"'To Dr. Davis, for your kind assistance.' Signed," she said, pausing for effect, "'Jasmine Laser.'"

"I take it I would be stepping on toes," he moaned, sinking back into his chair, hands tugging the golden strands of his shining hair into tousled disarray.

"To say the least," Jori told him, glad she'd averted disaster. "Chucking that...mess...would make you an even greater subject of discussion—rather unkind discussion."

"I wish to heck Dan had explained just what I was getting into when he asked for my assistance," Chris snorted, searching for a place to spread out his files.

Dan Gordon had been Mossbank's general practitioner for as long as Jori had been the office nurse. Their working relationship had been a brother-sister one tempered by a lot of friendly bantering. It was something she was beginning to miss with Dr. Christopher Davis. Of course, Dan had been born and raised in a small town and was well used to the unspoken rules that governed the community, unlike his famous, big-city counterpart.

"Look at this place," the new doctor crankily demanded, pointing to the cake boxes of various shapes, sizes and colors scattered on almost every available surface.

"Think of it as proof of your good standing in this community," she told him. "It shows how much you're appreciated. You're lucky they've taken a shine to you."

When a groan of dismay was her only answer, Jori grudgingly picked up three of the earliest arrivals and stuffed them into the vaccine refrigerator that stood in the corner.

"They can't stay there forever, you know," she advised, frowning at his lounging figure. "Sooner or later you're going to have to find a solution to this problem." Jori stared at him curiously, her brown eyes frankly questioning his intent. "What did you do with the rest?"

His blue eyes lit up at that.

"They're safely stored in Dan and Jessica's freezer, just waiting for the soon-to-be parents to come home." His golden brows drew together in a frown. "Although I'm not sure a new mother should be eating that stuff." His sudden grin made her catch her breath. "I'm not sure anyone should." He chuckled at his own little joke.

"Well, then—" Jori started to suggest that he simply add to his private stash, but his deep voice interrupted her immediately.

"Forget it. It's full."

"Sorry, can't help you then," she told him, moving toward the door.

"Can't or won't?" he asked crankily. His blue eyes widened with a new thought. "Why don't you take one of them home? Surely you and your boyfriend could manage at least one of the blasted things."

Jori turned to stare at him. "I don't have a boyfriend and if I did, the last thing I'd feed him would be Emma Simms's cheesecake. It's like sand."

He squinted at her curiously. "Someone who looks like you doesn't have a boyfriend?" His perfect lips slashed open in a mocking grin. "No dreams of marriage and babies, Nurse Jessop? I thought all women dreamed of Prince Charming and white picket fences."

"Prince Charming was highly overrated," she told him, grimly noting how close he'd come to the mark. "And for your information, I already have a white picket fence. Someday I intend to have a child to share it with." Jori immediately wished she had been able to shut up about that.

One blond eyebrow lifted haughtily.

"A child but no husband. Interesting. And how do you plan on accomplishing that?" he inquired softly.

Jori tilted her head back, her face heating with color. "It's not really your business anyhow. Those cheesecakes *are*." It was rude but she felt compelled to get his focus off her.

He sighed, blinking at the offensive desserts. "Why couldn't they bring roast beef with mashed potatoes and an apple pie?"

Something in the tone of Chris's mournful voice stopped Jori's swift departure. Turning abruptly, her round brown eyes searched his face. "How did you know?"

"Know what?" he asked. His blue eyes surveyed Jori's confusion with a measured glance before she saw enlightenment dawn and berated herself for once more letting her tongue speak too soon. "You are having that tonight, aren't you, Jori?" He inclined his head, his eyes bright as he considered her sulky expression.

"And if there's no boyfriend, there should be lots to share. Am I right?" Bright and eager, his blue eyes dared her to refuse.

Jori exhaled in defeat. There was no point in denying that she'd planned that particular dinner. He would hear about it through the grapevine anyway, since she always made up a tray for Maddy Hopkins. The same local etiquette that demanded he not choose any patient's cooking over another dictated that she invite him for one meal.

Social responsibility. She hated the phrase. With a sigh of frustration Jori accepted her lot. She had orders to be hospitable to Dan's replacement—at least until he returned. She might as well start tonight.

"Six o'clock," she said without preamble and recited her address. "If you're late I'm not waiting."

Turning, Jori strode from the room, frustrated with the situation. She had counted on a quiet evening at home, alone. Time to get her faculties together before she visited her father tomorrow at Sunset Retirement Home. Time to accept that the

Alzheimer's had almost taken over and James Jessop would never be the same.

There was no way tonight would be quiet, not with Christopher Davis's loud, booming laugh and even bigger personality. He easily overtook a room, filling it with himself. She had seen it numerous times in the past week. Nobody was immune to his charm, it seemed.

Jori sighed. "I am. I will be."

She had no room in her structured life for anybody like him. If and when she did date, it was always with someone like herself; someone who prized the stable security that life in Mossbank offered. Someone, she told herself, who could see themselves living in the small friendly community in twenty years' time.

Her days of elegant dining and fancy dress were a part of the past and she was glad. She wanted the calm peace that life in her hometown always gave. Acceptance, serenity, tranquility and no surprises.

"There's no way I'm having anything to do with him," she muttered, ignoring her co-worker's amused glance from across the room. Jori snatched the next file up and tossed it into his pickup basket. "Christopher Davis is the exact opposite of what I'm looking for in a husband."

It was highly unlikely that she'd ever get married, Jori assured herself for the third time that week. But if she did, she would opt for a mundane, ordinary trustworthy man who lived in the same small town. They would raise their child in a good, solid home to grow up in and they'd be with James whenever he needed them.

And there wouldn't be any of the disastrous upheavals that had marked her life in the past. She would build a haven, Jori resolved. A place to be who she was without pretense. With her lips set in a determined line, she called out the next patient's name.

No, siree. Dr. Christopher Davis bore just a little too much resemblance to those handsome, pushy, overwhelming men in her past. And look how ugly that had turned out.

It was best to concentrate on building a life for herself here in Mossbank and ignore outsiders. This was her home; these were her friends. They'd stood by her when no one else would.

Supermodel Jordanna Jessop was no more. But Jori Jessop owed the people of Mossbank a huge debt of gratitude, and she had no intention of reneging on that debt.

"There goes Jori home," Faith Johnson murmured to her friends as she sipped another mouthful of the iced tea she had just made. "Such a beautiful girl, but so withdrawn."

"I don't think she's withdrawn at all," Charity commented, adding another teaspoon of sugar to her glass. "If I'd had to deal with that awful young man—what was his name?" She stopped to think and then shook her head. "Well, anyway, if I suffered through all that terrible publicity because of a man who said he loved me, I would be quiet, too."

"She is very good in the office," Hope murmured thoughtfully. "I think Dr. Davis likes having her there, too. When she's busy with a patient, he's always looking at her."

"I don't know how she can work with a man who looks like that," Charity fluttered her hand in the warm spring air. "He has the looks of that fellow in the movies, what's his name? Tom Hanks?"

"Tom Hanks has dark hair," Hope muttered.

"I know but the clean-cut, handsomely chiseled look is the same, don't you think?" Charity's eyes gleamed with appreciation. "We need a few more good-looking men in this town."

"Jordanna has such lovely hair, don't you think?" Hope

tried desperately to steer the subject away from men. "So long and glossy. Why, she can even sit on it!"

"My hair used to be near that color," Charity told them. She frowned when Faith laughed. "Well, it did! But it was so long ago, I expect you've forgotten. I was slim and beautiful, too. Once."

"She's having him over for dinner tonight." Faith's soft voice dropped into the conversation.

"How do you know that?" Charity's eyes widened.

"I happened to hear her tell Dr. Davis to be there at six sharp."

"Oh, my," Charity whispered. "That sounds promising."

"It sounds ridiculous," Hope told her firmly. "Jori's merely being kind. There's nothing *romantic* about it." She sounded scandalized. "They are from two different worlds. He's flamboyant, loud and unruly. She's quiet and reserved. Not at all suited."

Faith chuckled. "You've said that before." She grinned. "And you were just as wrong about me and Arthur as you are about those two." Her head cocked sideways. "I think they'd make a lovely couple. I wonder..." Her voice died away.

"Well, anyway, he's not staying," Hope mused thoughtfully. "Dr. Davis is only here until Dr. Dan and Jessica return with their baby."

"If they return," Faith whispered. "I've been praying so hard for that wee one. Arthur, too. I'm just going to have to let go and trust that God will lay his hand on their lives."

The three ladies sat quietly in the sun pondering the predicament of their beloved doctor and his wife until Christopher Davis roared past in a racy black sports car.

"He'd better slow down," Charity muttered. "This isn't Boston." She glanced at the clouds building in the sky. "I think there's a storm brewing, girls,'' she murmured at last. "Perhaps we'd better move inside."

"We should have had our tea at my house." Hope chuckled as she lifted the tray of dishes. "Then you two could have listened in to Jori and Dr. Davis while they have dinner next door."

"What a good idea," Charity agreed blithely. "Why don't you two scurry on over now? It's Arthur's late night at the store and I've got company coming, so you two will be free to eavesdrop all you like."

Faith frowned. "I don't eavesdrop," she murmured. "I just try to help out where I…who's coming for dinner, Charity?" she asked suddenly.

Charity smiled and patted her friend's gray curls.

"Oh, just a friend," she told them softly. "A good friend."

"But I want to know who it is," Faith lamented. "You've refused to see anyone that Hope and I have lined up for you even though they were all nice men. Take Frank now. He's—"

"You take him," Charity blazed in an unusual show of temper. "I don't want to go out to dinner with Frank Bellows! He's the *undertaker,* for goodness' sake! What would we talk about? My choice in coffins?"

"Charity, there's no need to get so upset," Hope said placatingly, her hand cuddling the older woman's arthritic one. "Your blood pressure is quite high enough. And after all, we're only trying to help."

"Well, you can help by letting me invite my own men friends for dinner." Charity smoothed her skirt in a motion that both her friends recognized meant her feelings were hurt. "I don't need a man. I'm perfectly happy just the way I am."

"All right, we won't ask you over to dinner with anyone anymore," Hope soothed. "We'll let her pick her own men friends, won't we, Faith?"

Charity's round face had almost regained its usual sunny gleam when Faith spoke.

"But she never picks any men to be with, Hope. Not ever!" Faith's voice rose with indignation. "She's alone in this house all the time. God didn't mean for us to be isolated and alone on this earth." She glanced from one to the other, her green eyes finally settling on Charity.

"Don't you want to share your days with someone else? Don't you enjoy having someone to talk to?" Faith's wide smiling mouth was turned down as she studied her friend.

"If I want to talk, I have you two," Charity declared. "And you natter on for so long that a body needs a good rest to recuperate. I like my silence. I like to be peaceful and quiet. It's refreshing."

"Piffle," Faith exclaimed. "It's not normal. God has more in store for us than solitude. You're lonely and you know it."

Ever the peacemaker, Hope stood to her feet gathering her belongings. "Come along, Faith, dear. It's going to rain any moment and I don't want to get my new suit spotted. Thanks for tea, Charity. Enjoy your dinner."

"Whoever it's with," Faith grumbled on her way out the door. She raced back in to grab her purse, her face wreathed in smiles. "Hah! You thought I'd forgotten it, didn't you? Well, I'm far too young for Sunset Retirement Home just yet, Charity Flowerday!" And having gotten the last word in, Faith stumbled down the steps and out into the strong westerly wind.

"I'm sorry, dear," Hope murmured as she watched Charity move awkwardly from the chair. "She doesn't mean to hurt you."

"I know." Charity sighed as she watched Faith throw up her arms and catch the first droplets of rain on her tongue. "Maybe she's right. Maybe I have been hiding out here, missing out on life. Maybe it's time I got involved in what's going on around me.''

"What are you going to do?" Hope's blue eyes were full of fear.

"Live," Charity told her matter-of-factly. "Maybe I'll ask Howard to take me out for dinner instead of me cooking." Her brow was furrowed in thought.

"Howard Steele?" Hope gaped. "But he's years younger than you are!"

"I know." Charity preened in the full-length mirror hanging in the hall. "Do you think I should wear my black silk?" She twisted and turned in front of the glass, trying to see herself from all angles.

"Black silk? But…but that's for special occasions," Hope gasped. "Charity, what is going on?"

"I'm freeing myself. I'm going to be more like Faith— open to new experiences." She pushed her waved hair back into a different style. "No, you're right. The black is too old-fashioned. I think I'll go down to Penelope's and see if she has something a little more in style. A nice bright red, maybe."

"You're going to buy a red dress? To wear on a date with Howard Steele?" Hope sounded scandalized. Her face was a picture of dismay as she watched Charity grasp her car keys and purse and walk slowly to the front door.

"Charity," she asked at last, "are you quite all right?"

"I've never felt better in my life." Charity nodded, motioning for Hope to precede her out the door. "A new outfit, a different hairstyle. It's just the change I need."

"But I liked the old you," Hope said with a perplexed frown.

"Don't say that word again," Charity ordered, moving briskly across the lawn. "You are only as old as you feel and today I feel young and hopeful.'' To herself she hummed the line from a chorus they'd learned in church last week.

"'With God All Things Are Possible'?'' Faith looked at Hope. "Why is she singing that?''

"She's going to buy a new dress. And change her hairstyle. She's even going to ask Howard Steele out for dinner.''

"Howard Steele?'' Faith gasped. "But his wife only just divorced him six years ago. And he's younger than Charity. He's got long hair.'' She added the last as if that were the final nail in poor Howard's personality coffin.

"I know.'' Hope started walking briskly down the street, grimacing at the darkened spots of color on her pristine aqua suit as the raindrops plopped onto it in fat round splatters.

"Oh, well,'' Faith murmured, continuing blithely on with her skipping steps. "At least she's getting out of that house. Since Melanie's marriage, she hardly leaves the place.''

"I know,'' Hope agreed. "But it's Howard Steele she's getting out with!''

"It's not what I had in mind, either,'' Faith assured her. "But the Lord works in mysterious ways.''

"Well, this is certainly very mysterious,'' Hope agreed grimly. She mounted the steps to her home, griping at the inclement weather as she smoothed her hair. "I just hope she doesn't regret her hasty decision.''

Chapter Two

"I love this place, Lord," Jori murmured, a grin tilting the full curve of her lips as she viewed her home with satisfaction, enjoying the riot of flowers that always grew in her rock garden. "Even if Dad can't be here anymore."

She refused to let the sadness ruin her evening. Flop, her cocker spaniel, stood wagging his short, stumpy tail inside the wrought iron gate.

"Hi, boy. Did you have a good day chasing squirrels? You look kind of tired."

The dog always knew when she would be home and his routine never varied. After bestowing an enthusiastic swipe across her face with his pink tongue, Flop padded along behind his mistress as she opened the door and entered the comfortable white bungalow.

"Jori, oh, Jori!" Her neighbor, Hope Conroy, was calling from over the white picket fence that separated their lawns.

"Hi, Hope. How are you?"

"I'm fine, dear, just fine. Am I stopping you from your shower?"

Jori was a little surprised to know that Hope was aware of

her usual custom of showering right after work. She smiled to herself as she realized this was a large part of the reason she'd wanted to move back home. Everyone knew everyone else and cared about them; there was no pretense here.

"Well, I've got time before dinner."

"I hear you're having a guest. Dr. Davis, isn't it?"

Jori didn't bother asking how the woman knew. Nothing was ever a secret in Mossbank. And Hope was Charity Flowerday's best friend. Little wonder!

"Well, yes," she admitted. "He says he's hungry for something other than fast food so I thought I'd share my roast."

"I thought so. You always have roast beef on Thursdays," Hope murmured triumphantly.

"I didn't realize I'd fallen into such a pattern," Jori murmured, disgusted that her life had become an open book.

"Don't worry, dear. I used to do it myself. All single women do. Especially the organized ones and you've always been organized, Jori. I remember you used to have your marbles stored by color and size. So efficient. I imagine you do the same with your bedding, don't you?"

Jori winced at the woman's admiring smile, wondering when she'd become so boring.

"Uh, was there something you wanted to say, Hope?" she asked at last, hoping they could finish their discussion before Mrs. Johnson moseyed over. Jori loved the woman dearly but Faith Johnson had a habit of rearranging a conversation until no one knew exactly what they were discussing. And today was not a day for more confusion.

"Did you ask her yet?" Faith's high clear voice floated over the fence. "Is she really going to do it?"

"Do what?" Jori asked quietly, studying the flush of embarrassment covering Hope's pale cheeks.

"Well, Faith overheard, that is, er, she thought she over-

heard…'' Hope stopped and brushed a wisp of hair out of her
eyes. ''Oh, this is so embarrassing. I do dislike gossip.''

''Just tell me, okay, Hope. I'll try to answer you.'' Jori
patted the perfectly manicured hand gently and watched the
even features organize themselves into their usual uncompro-
mising pattern.

''Very well then, I shall.'' The older woman took a deep
breath and then let it all out in one gasp. ''Are you really
thinking about having a baby, Jordanna? On your own, without benefit of a husband?'' Hope sounded shocked and looked
scandalized that she'd even said the words.

''I…I…'' Jori stopped short as Faith came to lean on the
gate that adjoined the two properties.

''See, I told you. Look at her face. She's going to do it,''
Faith chanted, clapping her hands in excitement. ''A new
baby! Imagine!''

''Just a minute,'' Jori protested, trying desperately to get a
word in. ''I never said I was going to…''

''I overheard you talking with Dr. Davis,'' Faith admitted
and then clapped a hand over her mouth. Her eyes were huge.
''He said it was something to do with a test tube.'' She stared
off into the bright green leaves of Jori's maple tree.

Hope shook her silver blond head. ''You can't do it, Jordanna. The good Lord meant for children to have two parents
to care for them. You of all people should understand how
hard it is to have only one parent around when you need
help.''

For the third time in as many hours, Jori had to hold her
tongue so as not to ask these two nosey women to stop discussing her personal life. She drew a deep breath and prayed
for help.

''I'm not going to have a baby,'' she told them clearly,
ignoring the relief that swept across Hope's face. ''I'm thinking of adopting a child—one that has no home, no parents

and no place to go." She bent down to toss Flop's stick across the grass and then straightened.

"I'm twenty-eight, Hope, and I'm not married. I don't think it's likely to happen any time soon, do you? Considering there are so few single men around Mossbank." She loosed the band holding her hair in a braid and threaded her fingers through the long plait.

"Well, I wouldn't exactly say that," Hope murmured flushing coyly. "After all, Faith and I have both been married at a more advanced age than yours."

"God led me back to Mossbank, I believe that. But He hasn't led any men into my path here and I don't intend to go hunting for one," Jori murmured in disgust, grimacing at the thought. "Mossbank is where I belong and where I want to stay. I have everything I need here. If I can help some child who needs a home and a mother, then that's what I'd like to do.

"I'm sorry, but I have to go now. It's almost time for supper. Bye," she called, striding across the lawn and in through her front door.

After her shower, as she pulled on a comfortable pair of ragged blue jeans, Jori told herself her choice of clothing was in deference to the relaxed atmosphere of her home and had nothing to do with the man who was coming for dinner. Her fingers twitched the hem on a frayed and sleeveless chambray shirt as Jori mentally scorned those ladies who worked so hard at dressing up to impress the new doctor.

"Ridiculous," she muttered to herself. "It's not my style at all. Not that I'm interested," she added, glancing down at the decrepit white sandals which left her toes cooling in the summer sun. "I'm quite content with my life alone, except for Dad, of course."

As she combed out her waist-length hair, Jori brooded on her confrontation with Dr. Davis. He was trouble, that was

for sure. And why did he make her think of things long forgotten; things she could never have?

Her eyes slid over the plastic-wrapped gowns in her closet.
She could still fit into the elegant outfits that had been part
of her daily life seven years ago. Not that it mattered. There
was little call for haute couture in Mossbank.

"This is the first time I've had a date because someone is
interested in my cooking," she told Flop, who woofed his
appreciation. "But that's all he's interested in. And don't go
fawning over him, either. You're supposed to remain faithful
to the one who feeds you."

Flop obviously understood as he licked her hand before
picking up his rawhide bone and heading out of the room.
Pushing her hair into a clip, Jori bounded down the stairs,
Flop padding along behind.

Everything was simmering nicely in the oven. A fresh garden salad would make the meal complete. Leaving the relative
cool of her house, Jori slipped off her sandals and walked
barefoot into the lush garden. She squeezed her toes in the
moist black loam that was her pride and joy.

Sweet peas, fragrant and multicolored had begun blooming
and Jori breathed their heady fragrance. Perfect centerpiece,
she decided, snipping a handful. She laid these on the bench
at the edge of her plot and then moved over to gather some
produce. In her pail she carefully placed furled green lettuce
leaves, plump red radishes, three tiny cucumbers, a round on-
ion and a wisp of dill. She was about to straighten up when
a laughing voice startled her.

"I must say, this is a side of you I have never really seen
before," Dr. Davis teased. "Jori Jessop in the dirt."

"You're early," was the best reply Jori could come up with
as she blushed profusely and then prayed he wouldn't comment on it.

Dr. Christopher Davis was dressed in a natty white cotton

sweater and blue cotton slacks that showed off his blond good looks to perfection.

As if he needed help, she grumbled to herself. Chris Davis was probably the most handsome doctor she had ever seen. That bothered her.

"I hope you didn't dress up just for me," he chuckled, his quick eyes noting her mismatched clothing.

"No, I didn't," she replied brusquely. "We don't dress for dinner in Mossbank."

When he merely laughed, Jori moved skittishly toward the house, pausing only to hose off the soil clinging to her feet. She wanted to get away from his overwhelming presence, but he followed her into the kitchen.

"I'm sorry. I didn't mean to embarrass you, Jori." His lustrous white teeth flashed his wolfish smile at her. "You look very nice, in a down-home kind of way."

"Yeah, right," she murmured, wishing the evening was at an end already.

"Can I help?" he asked, moving his tall, solid body next to hers at the sink.

Somehow, Jori didn't think he meant to soil his well-manicured hands with dirty garden produce so she motioned toward her small dinette set.

"You can set the table if you want." Her voice was less than gracious, but Jori couldn't help it. He made her so nervous.

Christopher worked quickly, loading the plates, cups and silverware into his arms in order to make the least number of trips possible. Jori winced as her favorite china place settings jostled against each other, but at least he was out of her way. For now.

"I like your house," he offered, still in his friendly jovial tone. "Looks like a real home."

Startled, Jori gazed up at him, intrigued by his assessment.

He didn't seem the type to value homes. Before she could reply, Flop sauntered in and wriggled over to their visitor, hips swaying in delight.

"Hello, boy," Chris bent over to ruffle the dog's floppy ears gently, avoiding the dog's wet, pink tongue. "You're a real beauty, aren't you." Surprisingly, the loud voice was soft and gentle as the big man dealt with the enthusiastic dog. "What's his name?" Chris asked, tipping his blond head back to stare up at Jori.

"Flop," she replied brusquely, turning back to her salad. Moments later she felt his big hand on her elbow, turning her to face his shocked look.

"You named a purebred cocker spaniel Flop?" Disbelief flooded his perceptive blue gaze.

"Well, actually his title is Ginger Boy Parkland but I call him Flop. It's what he does best." She giggled, enjoying the look of stupefaction her remark brought.

The dog was obviously perceptive for he chose that moment to drop his plump body onto the floor, his chin resting on his front paws as soulful brown eyes studied them. Seconds later a huge sigh woofed out of him.

"See," she told him in a conspiratorial tone. "It's his trademark."

Christopher shook his head in disbelief. It was clear to Jori that in his exalted opinion, people didn't acquire bloodline animals, have them groomed, teach them dog manners and then bestow a name like Flop.

"Where did you get him?" he asked.

Jori mentally put a guard on her lips. "My dad," she told him shortly, whisking flour into the dark brown beef juices. "He was a homecoming present after I finished nursing school."

She tipped the succulent gravy into an oval bowl and set it on the table with a smack. A platter set to one side bore a small roast of beef, golden brown potatoes and finger-length carrots. She placed the bouquet of sweet peas in the center of the table.

"Everything is ready. Please, have a seat." Her slim hand motioned to the chair opposite hers and she watched as Chris sank into it, licking his lips discreetly.

"I'm really going to enjoy this." He grinned. Those twinkling blue eyes glinted at her. "I appreciate you allowing me to join you tonight, Jori. Thank you."

As if I had a choice, Jori acidly considered replying, but the words stayed inside her head. "I'll just say grace and then we can eat," she murmured.

"Father, bless this food for we are truly grateful for all your blessings. Amen." He murmured an amen, too, and seconds later she watched him tuck into their feast.

It was a small roast. She always had trouble shopping for just herself. Everything came in such large packages and Jori usually got sick of leftovers long before they were gone. Hence the send-out dinners for some of her father's friends.

But, surprisingly, the meal was rapidly diminishing before her eyes. The doctor heaped his large plate full, taking some of everything and then tasting each item thoughtfully, rolling it around on his tongue. When he came to the beef, he closed his eyes in satisfaction, chewing slowly, obviously savoring the rich flavor.

It had been years since she'd watched her father relish her cooking in just that manner and Jori grinned to herself as she tucked into her own well-filled plate, able, for the moment, to dislodge the discomfort she always felt in this man's presence.

"This is so good, a man might even be persuaded to propose," Chris mumbled, his face alight with pleasure as he rolled his eyes.

Jori choked on her water and welcomed his resounding

thump on her back to get her breath. Eyes tearing, she stared
into his handsome face.

"Isn't that a little extreme?" she gasped, her eyes wide
with shock. "Just for a meal?" Surely he wasn't...

Her face flushed with embarrassment as she realized he'd
been teasing her and she'd fallen for it. Again. Silently, Jori
called herself a fool for letting him get to her. It was just that
he unnerved her, she told her jangling nerves. She had known
he would be trouble right from the start. Jori tipped her head
back to glare at him as he burst out laughing.

Jori flashed him a look of disgust before resuming her meal.
Fine, she decided. She simply would not converse with the
man if he couldn't behave. With a sniff of disgust, Jori pushed
away her plate; everything tasted the same anyway. He'd
spoiled even this small pleasure with his vibrant presence
across the table. She stared at her water glass, intent on ignoring him. And Jori could have carried off her pretended
disinterest if he hadn't continued the tomfoolery.

Suddenly he was kneeling beside her, holding the sweet
peas under her nose with one broad hand, while the other
clasped hers, his fingers warm and tingling. His voice was
soft with controlled laughter and his eyes were bright with
glee.

"Please, Ms. Jessop. Say you'll marry me. To be able to
eat like this with a cook that looks like you, I'm willing to
take everything else on spec." His clear blue eyes lingered
on her face. "Please say you will."

"What I will do is douse you with the garden hose if you
don't stop this right now," she warned him severely, repress-
ing her laughter with difficulty. Her hand tugged away from
his and reached out for his half-full plate as she avoided his
all-knowing eyes.

"I guess this means you're finished," she murmured
sweetly, turning to put the dinner plate on the floor. Imme-

diately, Flop moved in, slurping up the entire contents in one fell swoop of his pink tongue. Jori turned to gaze innocently at Chris's startled face.

"Ready for dessert?" Her voice was soft as butter.

"I hadn't finished, you know." He wasn't laughing now. "And I'm starved." Dark as velvet, Chris's dark soulful eyes beseeched her for sympathy. "Please, ma'am, could I have some more?"

It was such an exact duplication of a recent television commercial that Jori couldn't help the laughter that bubbled out of her. He looked like a naughty little boy with his clear solemn eyes, rumpled blond hair and company-perfect sweater. His big hand stuck out toward her.

"Truce," he offered, waiting earnestly for her response.

Jori sighed in capitulation and got up to find another plate for him. He was back in his chair, eyes downcast when she returned to the table.

"Here. Help yourself." Her voice was resigned to his silliness.

Dr. Davis accepted the dinner plate eagerly and ladled huge amounts of food onto his dish once more. Jori leaned back in her chair, quietly sipping her coffee as she watched him. Somehow he didn't seem quite as bad as she had first anticipated. She ignored the chiding little voice in the back of her mind. After all, it wasn't *that* terrible, having him for dinner, she argued with herself.

And when the nagging voice murmured, *I told you so,* Jori ignored its taunting. Her eyes were busy absorbing the picture of Christopher Davis, noted surgeon and infamous ladies' man, eating dinner in *her* kitchen. When he finally leaned back in his chair, she was happy to note that very little of the beef remained.

"I have more if you'd like," she murmured, eyeing the

remains of the potatoes in the pot. "If you don't eat it, I'll have to reheat it for at least the next week."

"No, thanks! Much as I'd like to, I won't be able to walk if I eat another bite. It was really great though."

Standing, Jori carried away the serving dishes to the sink, poured his coffee and then sat down to sip at her own. Christopher waited expectantly, peering at her from under those disgustingly long lashes. When it was clear that nothing more was forthcoming, he rushed to the heart of the matter.

"Where's the pie?" he asked, glancing around her small kitchen.

"What pie?" Jori was jostled out of her bemused thoughts by his question and she stared at him, uncomprehending. Pie was the last thing on her mind just then. She blushed, remembering exactly what she had been thinking of—that maybe he would kiss her.

Huge blue eyes reproached her sadly. "You mean you lied? You don't have apple pie for dessert?"

Indignation welled up. His nerve was just too much!

"Look, Dr. Davis. You invited yourself here. I didn't say I had apple pie, you just assumed it." She stared at his strong muscular body tipped back precariously on the oak chair that had been her father's favorite. "And sit properly on that," she ordered imperiously before realizing to whom she was speaking.

She was rattled, Jori admitted silently, as little waves of tension skittered up her spine to her neck. And *he* was doing it to her.

"Yes, ma'am!" His big grin split across his laughing face as Chris straightened his chair before reaching out to pat her small hand with his larger one. "It's okay if you don't, you know," he soothed. "The dinner was really great even without that."

"Well, thank you so much. I'm so happy I could be of service," she muttered through clenched teeth.

His good humor was apparently unbreachable. As he sat waiting, the doctor merely kept smiling at her.

The man had gall, Jori mused. There was no doubt about that. And he knew exactly which buttons to push to get her dander up. Jori sighed.

Just another reason why he wasn't her type. Still, he did live alone and if he had been eating his meals at the town's fast-food places, it was no wonder he craved a plain home-cooked meal. Calling herself a soft touch, Jori relented.

"I don't have any apple pie," she said, capitulating at last. "But if you could manage a piece of chocolate cake, I can accommodate you."

It was a thinly veiled hint at the amount of food he had consumed, but the good doctor ignored her jibe with that gracious good humor. His brilliant blue eyes sparkled at her as he kissed the hand he still held. Jori pulled her hand away and tucked it behind her back.

"I was just saying that I would really enjoy a piece of chocolate cake right now," he teased.

Jori sneaked a look at him over her shoulder as she cut a huge slice of the rich dessert. "What you should be eating is praline cheesecake," she muttered snidely.

He pretended to stick a finger down his throat, blue eyes rolling backward as he faked a gagging sound. Jori burst out laughing. The oh-so-sober, very handsome, very famous doctor looked ridiculous.

She set a huge piece of fluffy chocolate cake with its whipped mocha icing in front of him and watched him gobble it up with gusto.

"How often do you eat?" she demanded curiously, stunned by the amount of food he had put away.

"I didn't have time for breakfast today," he told her,

shamefaced. He had the grace to look embarrassed as a light flush colored his tanned skin.

"And you didn't have lunch because Mrs. Andrews delivered her baby just about then," Jori guessed. "Did you have dinner last night?"

The big man shrugged his massive shoulders. Jori had to voice her concerns, not just for him but for his patients.

"Chris," she chastised him, only realizing as she said it that she had used his first name. "This practice is a very busy one and you can be kept going for days. You have to make time to eat regularly, or you'll find yourself burned out before Dan gets back. Then what will everyone do?" It was a question she didn't want him to answer.

"Are you worried about me or them?" Chris inquired dryly. It was evident he already knew where her allegiance lay.

"I'm concerned for everyone. If you get sick, you'll toddle off to some expensive hospital in the East and they'll treat you immediately. The people in this town haven't got the money to go to fancy city hospitals. If you leave, they will have no one to help them."

Finished with her spiel, Jori got up and began to systematically clear the table, loading the dishwasher carefully. His fingers on her arm startled her, as did the strength with which he forced her to turn toward him. She was surprised to see his genial face tight with suppressed anger. Blue lightning shot out from his sparkling irises.

"I'm not just playing at medicine, you know," he snapped. "I am fully qualified for most anything that a one-horse town like Mossbank can throw at me." He favored her with a dry look, blue eyes gently mocking. "And I'm not going to cave in if I miss a meal or a night's sleep.

"Don't worry, Jori. All your little farmer friends will be well looked after."

Jori's temper surged upward as the week's tensions of working with him rose to the surface. "If you hate small towns, why did you come here? What is it about this town that you dislike so much anyway, Dr. Davis?" These were her friends and he was acting as if they didn't matter.

"What's the matter, Doc?" she derided. "Afraid you won't get the big accolades in a dinky prairie town? Maybe Boston is where you should have stayed, practicing medicine on people you know nothing about, and care about even less."

"Look, *lady*," Chris's voice boomed out, loud and exasperated. "I came here on my own to help out a friend who was going through a tough time. I don't have to answer to you or anybody." He snorted derisively.

"It's not my fault that there's nothing going on around here besides a matchmaking game and some bored housewives who think baking a bunch of cheesecakes is going to solve anything."

So he had heard the talk! His handsome face was flushed and angry and perversely, Jori was glad about that, even if she had been elected as one of the contestants in Faith's marriage pool. The man was too full of himself. It was refreshing to see him have to shift out of that smugly superior and condescending mode. She would be more than happy to take him down a peg or two.

"You have eyes, Doctor, but you see nothing. Those 'bored housewives' are extremely busy right now. Many of them hold down full-time jobs off the farm and then help their husbands when they finish. And when those two jobs are done, there's still the laundry, housework and kids to look after."

She glared at him bitterly. "But they took time out of their schedules to express their welcome by baking *you* a cheesecake. Okay, it got a little out of hand. You're supposed to be so smart," she said with a smirk. "Find a solution.

"There are local fairs to attend, 4-H events, auctions, barbecues, dances, picnics and a ton of other things to see and do around here." She waved her hands to indicate the plethora of possibilities. "I suggest, Doctor, that you get to know your patients, find out what their existence is like, before you pass judgment on their *dull* way of life."

In high dudgeon, Jori flounced around the kitchen smacking dish upon dish as she prepared to do battle for her town. Every nerve in her body was on full alert as she whirled to face him.

"The people here are independent and proud. Some of them refuse to leave the land their fathers and grandfathers farmed. They've had to start side businesses from their homes to generate enough capital to let them plant another crop after the first one got hailed out or the last swaths got snowed on.

"They raise their own kids without any fancy psychologists or pricey day cares and mostly without the drug scenes you find in cities all over North America." She risked a glance at him and discovered he was frowning.

"They go to church on Sundays, care about each other and spend lots of time and energy helping out their neighbors. And they maintain decent values in a society where no one cares that seniors are abandoned, rape and assault are commonplace and abusing kids is not unusual."

Jori knew her face was red and that she was yelling, but she couldn't help it. The man deserved to be told a few home truths. Fury tossed all caution to the wind as she berated him angrily.

"They create their own fun by being a community who care about each other. If someone loses a barn, everyone pitches in to build another. If a child is lost, we all search until she's found. That's the way it is on the prairies. You stick together to survive." She shoved a plastic-wrapped slice of cake at him.

"Here's your cake." Her huge brown eyes defied him to

comment. "I'm sorry, but I have to ask you to leave. There are some things I need to do right now."

Jori stormed to the front door, ignoring the wagging dog at her heels. She wanted the man out of here. Now. Anyone who was so callous about their patients' welfare should not be part of the only medical team available for miles around.

She yanked the door open and stood grimly beside it, waiting for the eminently eligible surgeon to leave her home. She could see two women walking past her house and groaned inwardly. Mrs. Johnson and Mrs. Conroy. She might have known!

Chris's eyes mirrored his stunned disbelief that anyone should talk to him so peremptorily and if she hadn't been so mad, Jori would have grinned at his shock.

"Good night," she challenged, standing tall and stiff.

Slowly Christopher Davis walked toward the door, still holding his chocolate cake. His blue eyes had softened to a periwinkle tone as he gazed down at her. Then his hand stretched out as his thumb rubbed across her bottom lip. Jori's eyes grew round with surprise and she felt the impact of that light touch right down to her toes.

"You are quite a fierce little thing when you get your dander up, aren't you?" he asked. "Chocolate," he mused, still staring at her.

"What?" Her voice was bemused, disoriented.

"You had chocolate on your lips." With that, Dr. Chris Davis turned to walk through the doorway with that uncaring long-legged grace. He stopped just outside, turned around and fixed her with an amused look.

"Thank you very much for the meal," he offered politely. "I enjoyed it and the company." Bending his lanky form low, Chris rubbed the spaniel's head affectionately. "Bye, Flop." Then he stood tall and straight, his electric blue gaze meeting her dark one head-on.

"Good night, Jordanna Lori Jessop. Dan was right, after all. I am going to enjoy working with you," he added with a grin. And bending down, he placed a very soft, very chaste kiss against her flushed cheek.

Jori barely heard his whispered promise before he disappeared into the dark night.

"I think I might even enjoy getting to know this town of yours."

And there, ogling them from the lawn next door, were two of the town's busiest old ladies. Angrily, Jori slammed the door on his retreating figure. As soon as she came back to earth, that was.

Darn his supercilious attitude anyway. She had returned to Mossbank to live quietly, help out where she could and let her battered world-weary spirit heal. Now, with one kiss, Christopher Davis had threatened all that; rocked her moorings until she wondered if her life really was on the right track.

Shaking her head, Jori went back to the kitchen to clean up the dishes. But the sensation of his lips against her cheek wouldn't be dislodged.

When reason returned Jori berated her foolishly overactive senses. She wished the illustrious blond doctor would have never shown his face in a place so obviously unimportant as Mossbank.

Jori was still frowning when she climbed the stairs to bed.

She closed her eyes tightly, trying desperately to dislodge Faith Johnson's wide grinning smile from her mind.

She wouldn't think about any of it. Not now. She breathed in a few cleansing breaths and then opened her eyes to focus on the moonlit ceiling.

"Lord, you know I don't want any upheaval in my life. I'm not very good at relationships. Besides, I like things just the way they are—calm, unemotional. Please don't send me any more curve balls. I'm not a very good catcher.'' Satisfied that God would understand her meaning, Jori closed her eyes and drifted off to sleep with a picture of a baseball diamond and a tall, blond pitcher clad in a white lab coat stuck firmly in her mind.

Chapter Three

"I'm so sorry for the delay. The doctor has been detained. I'm sure he'll be here soon, Mrs. Andrews."

Outside it was a glorious July afternoon but Jori noticed little of the beauty of the day. Instead her mind whirled with dark thoughts of retribution. She strove to speak smoothly in order to calm the impatience that was running rampant in the waiting room, unwilling to let her friends see how bothered she was by the city doctor's absence.

"Yes, Mrs. Johnson. The doctor will be with you as soon as he can." Jori gritted her teeth in annoyance as she dialed the hospital for the fourth time without success.

Dr. Christopher Davis was late. Very late. And no one seemed to know just where he was. She doubted he would worry about it too much, given his conversation after their meal together mere days ago.

Meanwhile, she had to face a barrage of patients who wanted to be free from the stuffy waiting room to pick saskatoons, or bale hay, or go to the river for a cooling swim.

"I'm sorry. I can't reschedule you. We're full up. You can wait for an opening if you'd like." Jori listened calmly to the third query from Faith Johnson. Inside, a wild mixture of feelings began whirling around, as she heard the sound of the back door opening.

"You're so much like your mother, Jordanna. I remember her quite well. She was tall like you and willowy thin. When you smile you resemble her the most." Faith stared at Jori happily. "Ruth was always smiling at something, even at the end. Life was so full of joy for her."

Privately, Jori wondered if her mother would have found anything to smile about in this situation. A doctor's office functioned on schedules and adherence to them. Christopher Davis was throwing all her carefully made plans out the window.

When he finally came sauntering into his office, all blond boyishness and charm, Jori's tightly held restraint flew out the window.

"Where in the world have you been?" she growled, protected by the thin office walls, as she slapped down the files in front of him. "These people have lives that don't revolve around your Boston time schedule, you know."

"What's the matter?" Big pools of azure stared up at her as Chris blinked in surprise.

His question was bordering on the ridiculous and Jori let him know it. Hands on her hips she surveyed his relaxed happy grin and blasted away with both barrels, ignoring the intriguing scent of his spicy aftershave as it tickled her nose.

"'What's the matter?' you ask. Well, I have twelve people waiting to see a doctor who was supposed to be here over an hour ago. The hospital had no idea where you were. You didn't answer either your cell phone or pager. What do *you* think is the matter?" Jori told him disgustedly, his calm manner only infuriating her more.

"Show the first patient in, please, Nurse." He cooly dismissed her without a word, bending to glance at the first on a stack of files that signaled the afternoon's work.

When she didn't move, Chris's tanned face searched her turbulent eyes. His features were composed, controlled; masking whatever was going on inside those innocent baby blues.

"Jori. The patients." His low tone brooked no nonsense. He was pulling rank, and she knew it, but Jori was too angry to argue.

Turning, she marched from his office, snapping the door shut with venom before retrieving Mr. Hunter and Mrs. Johnson from the lounge and showing them into separate rooms.

And so they progressed through the afternoon. Chris asked her for something only when absolutely necessary and Jori answered, polite but cool. By five-thirty, their obvious feud was a hot topic with the only other person in the office, her co-worker, Glenda McKay.

"What is the matter?" the other woman asked, passing Jori in the hall. "I can almost see the steam coming out of your ears."

"You can't exactly soar with the eagles when you work with a big turkey," Jori told her, grimacing as she heard her name barked in that imperious tone once more.

"You're too intense. Maybe he had a good reason," she cajoled.

"Try to get him in for X rays as soon as possible," Chris said as he entered the room. "Also, I want a full blood workup on Mrs., er—" he checked his notes "—Ainsworth."

He was trying to ignore the dark forbidding looks his very attractive nurse had been tossing his way all afternoon. It wasn't easy; he could hardly miss the daggers those big brown eyes were throwing out.

He hadn't meant to fall asleep; not really. But he wasn't used to these maternity all-nighters. Delivering babies was a somewhat new experience for him.

Chris grinned. Who knew what Jori would do with that information, never mind if she found out the rest. He felt as if he were on trial with her already. Dead batteries in the cell phone couldn't be attributed to him, could they?

Of course, Chris reflected as he scribbled a notation on another file, he should have known better than to offend Jori. His patients raved about her constantly—how wonderful, how kind, how sweet, how lovely. He could see for himself just how gorgeous she was. That he had chosen to ignore their thinly veiled hints regarding her single status was obviously his loss.

It was clear that anyone who said anything about Jori Jessop said only good. She was a paragon of virtue, she was a great cook, she could handle emergencies with more aplomb than an army sergeant—the list went on seemingly endlessly.

She was very interesting, too. He had seen that for himself last evening—before Jori had gone from friendly hostess to fiery virago in about thirty seconds, and all without losing that dignified inner sense of self she always projected. Jordanna Jessop was a woman who knew exactly what she wanted out of life, Chris decided. And he was pretty sure she wanted very little from him, at the moment. With a sigh, Chris went to check on yet another patient.

After he administered an injection to one person, checked another's swollen tonsils and conferred with Mrs. Sanderson about her new hip, Chris caught sight of Jori's slim figure hurrying down the hall. A frown marred the smooth tanned skin of his forehead. Why did he have this ridiculous feeling he knew that face?

Chris was positive he'd never met Jordanna Jessop before and yet there was something about her profile that twigged his memory. Maybe it was those dark eyes—thickly fringed pools of sable that hid deep secrets. He knew those eyes. From somewhere.

He wondered for a moment if she didn't look like one of those women who advertised for a makeup company, but quickly decided he must be wrong. He knew very little about the stuff, but he did know that Nurse Jordanna Jessop didn't need anything to enhance her beauty.

She had a healthy glow that lit up her clear creamy skin. Probably due to the pure life she led here in Hicksville, Chris decided sourly, remembering her accusations of days before. Always something going on, she had said.

He was hanged if he knew where the townspeople held these wild shindigs because Chris had heard and seen nothing happening in the small town since he'd arrived. But then, he hadn't been very successful at mixing in with the locals thus far. Maybe he should just ask somebody for help.

Twenty minutes later Chris had learned all he ever wanted to know about the upcoming country fair from a loquacious Mrs. Flowerday. He vaguely remembered the name—something to do with chocolate, he thought.

"Just ask Jori to bring you, dear," the white-haired woman had enthused, patting his hand. "She always comes. Why, Jori's one of our best supporters." She leaned forward to whisper conspiratorially in his ear. "If you can get a bite of her wild blueberry pie, you're in for a real treat. Jori's got a flair for pastry that rivals mine and I'm not bad in that department."

The woman's plump lips had smacked at the thought and Chris's mouth watered at the picture of such bliss. He might even put up with a one-horse country fair for a piece of home-made wild blueberry pie.

"You say it's near here?" He listened as she described the area, understanding not one whit about the Logan or the Neufeld farms. "And she always goes to this fair?"

"Of course. Everyone goes. It's an annual event." Mrs.

Flowerday was staring at him as if she couldn't believe Chris hadn't heard of it.

"Well, maybe, if I'm off that day, I'll ask her," he mumbled at last in response to the older woman's urging. "She doesn't like me very much, though." He grinned at the understatement.

"Nonsense! Jori likes everyone. She's an angel of human kindness. Why, there's not a person in this town who hasn't been blessed by her thoughtfulness!"

Yeah, right, Chris thought. So it was only with him that she gave with one hand and scratched with the other. Well, he'd see how thoughtful Miss Jori Jessop could be, he decided, and winced as Jori snapped the next file into his hand.

But three days later Jori was as unapproachable as ever and Chris still had not asked her to the fair. He needed an in, he decided, jogging past her house early Saturday morning, his first weekend off. A young girl stood just inside Jori's gate with a pail of plump red raspberries in her hand.

"Hi," he called merrily, enjoying the run and the feel of the fresh breeze on his overheated body.

But when the girl looked up at him, her eyes were those of a startled doe and Chris grinned to himself. Aha! Just the thing. Report this thief stealing from her garden and Miss Jessop would undoubtedly be grateful enough to agree to his plan.

Wrong.

Jori Jessop was spitting mad when he showed up at her door later that day and she let him know it in no uncertain terms.

"What in heaven's name were you thinking of?" she demanded, her long slim hands planted on the full curve of her hips. Her eyes were honed chips of onyx. He shuffled his feet

on her well-trimmed lawn, less sure of his good deed now
that he had started this.

"She's twelve years old, for Pete's sake," she griped.
"What did you think she was going to do anyway, shoot
someone with raspberries?"

Her scathing tone was enough to break the thin line of
control Chris maintained. He pulled himself up to his full
height.

"Now just a blasted minute, here. I tried to do a good deed
and all…"

Her face was a picture in astonishment. "A good deed?
How, pray tell?"

"Well, how did I know the girl had permission to be there?
I thought she was stealing."

Jori pushed the weight of hair off her neck and coiled it
around her hand. Chris watched as she closed her big cocoa
eyes and counted silently to ten before speaking again.

"At six-thirty in the morning? Get real!" She sighed long-
sufferingly before enlightening him. "We have a deal. She
picks the berries and I pay her. She comes on her own time,
when her mother can spare her. She desperately wants a computer and this way she can earn some money."

"Jori." Chris drew in a calming breath as he tried to set
her straight. "She wasn't leaving the pail there. She was taking it."

That aggravating woman merely raised her eyes heavenward as she shook her head in frustration. Her eyes scanned
around the yard before she hissed at him.

"Shh…Be quiet. My neighbors have very sound hearing."
She jerked her head toward the house that Chris knew belonged to Judge Conroy and his wife. "I told her to take the
berries. I was giving them to someone. Nobody was supposed
to know about it."

Chris was completely lost. "Let's see if I've got this right," he mused. "You *paid* someone to pick the berries in your garden so that you could *give* them away? Oh, I see. It's all clear now. Thanks." He smiled at her slightly, peering down his long nose in disdain. The woman didn't make an ounce of sense.

Jori evidently recognized his confusion for she told him flatly, "Just forget about it, okay." Her big eyes glared at him. "And the next time you see someone in my yard, keep walking!"

Jordanna Jessop reminded him of a lily, Chris decided inconsequentially. Tall and slim, she looked delicate enough to break in the slightest wind.

Looks, however, were deceiving. Jori could hold her own any day of the week. Just now her pointed fingernail was back and demanding an answer as she glared at him.

"What were you doing at my house, anyway?" she fumed, her wide mouth turned downward. Her narrow feet with their bright red toenails wriggled in the grass.

"I, uh, I was coming to ask a favor," he muttered, hoping she might let him down easily, without the acid.

"A favor? What favor?" Jori's tone was less than encouraging, incredulous even.

"It doesn't matter." He chickened out, backing toward the gate. "I'd better go. Sorry if I spoiled things for the girl." He made it through the gate, barely, before her sweetly baiting voice stopped him.

"I've got a blueberry pie just out of the oven." She waited silently, knowingly, like a fisherman with a trout on the line while Chris swallowed again. He turned just enough to catch the shrewd grin on her face and knew he was hooked.

"Look," she offered quietly. "I'm sorry I was so harsh. If you'll accept a piece of pie and a cup of coffee as an apology, I'll try to explain."

"Well, if you put it that way," Chris demurred, his mouth watering. "*I* certainly don't hold grudges."

Cheerfully, he ambled along behind her, prepared to find out everything about this famous blueberry pie. Silken strands of her chestnut hair caught in the morning breeze and blew across his face.

Chris detected the faintest scent of wildflowers before Jori moved away, her hair trailing behind. His palms itched to grasp a gleaming handful. Tamping down the wish, he walked inside Jori's home once more.

"It's so lovely today." Jori waved toward the kitchen. "Why don't we have our coffee on the patio?"

Minutes later Chris had a huge piece of steaming blueberry pie in front of him as well as a fragrant mug of the dark brew she favored.

"I can't believe you bake, too," he murmured, more to himself. But she heard him.

She grinned, patting a wriggling Flop. "Now about the berries." She changed topics like quicksilver and Chris strained to follow, commanding his eyes to stop staring at the slim tanned column of her neck just visible in the vee of her long dress.

"You know Mrs. Selnes?" When his forehead furrowed in thought, Jori reminded him. "Six kids, three under seven." His face didn't automatically clear so she fed him a little more info. "One of them ate part of a swab last week."

"Yeah, I remember," he agreed sourly. And he did. He wished she would let him forget that unruly mob.

"Well, she has a rather difficult time," Jori told him.

"Ha! That's taking understatement to new limits," he drawled, eyes open wide. "Six kids! That'd give anyone a hard time."

"Yes, well, anyway, Jennifer comes and picks the berries for money to buy a computer. Then I phone Mrs. Selnes and offer my extras. She needs everything she can get her hands on to feed those kids. Her husband is rather useless. I like to help her out. Goodness knows she's grateful enough.'' Jori's clear forehead creased in thought as she stared straight at him.

"The thing is," she continued, unabashed by his scrutiny. "If she knew I had paid to have them picked, she would insist on paying me and I don't want that." Big as saucers, her dark eyes beseeched him. "Just keep it under your hat, okay?"

Chris nodded slowly. "You mean like the dinner you sent out the other night?"

"How do you know about that?" Jori stared in surprise.

"I stopped in to see the old girl the next evening." He grinned. "Believe me the smell of that roast was memorable."

He chuckled in delight at the dark flush staining her creamy skin once more. She looked slim and very beautiful in the sleeveless yellow dress that flowed to her ankles. Jori's innate grace was apparent when she walked and he wondered again why her face was so familiar.

"I'm impressed," she teased, not quite as acidly as before. "A big-city doctor making house calls. Wow!"

"Thank you, Nurse Jessop. I try." He felt as if he'd finally passed an important test.

"So, what's the favor?" she demanded, obviously anxious to change the subject.

"Uh, the favor?" His mind was addled and Chris had a struggle to organize his thoughts. "Oh, the fair. I wondered if you would take me to the fair." It hadn't come out exactly the way he'd intended, but Chris wasn't going to fuss about that.

His deep blue eyes studied her intently as she digested his request. Her eyes were round with surprise and her pink lips formed a perfect *O*.

"You don't mean the Silven Stream Fair?" she blurted out, obviously aghast at the thought.

"Yeah, I think that's the one. It's some kind of a country fair, isn't it, on today and tomorrow?"

She nodded slowly, as the copper glimmers in her hair caught the sun. A fly buzzed near her face but Jori ignored it.

"Yes, it is, but it's hardly the kind of thing you would be interested in," she advised him. "Very small town, local people sort of thing. Not your stuff at all."

Chris knew he had it coming, but her immediate rebuff still stung, and made him even more determined to figure out just what held her here.

"All the more reason I should attend. I can find out more about this area and its people—what makes them tick." He played his ace where he knew it would do the most good. "That is what you advised, isn't it, Jori? Getting to know the community that I care for?"

He watched her sip a mouthful of coffee that she had laced with cream. Her eyes studied him seriously.

"You really want to go?" Skeptical didn't begin to cover her tone.

He nodded easily. Let her think about it for a moment. He was pretty sure she wouldn't be able to help showing off her prairie town. And if that was the only way he would get to know Miss Jori Jessop a little better, so be it. Besides, if it turned out the fair wasn't everything he'd heard it was going to be, at least he'd get another chance to try her blueberry pie.

"That was excellent," he murmured. "Thank you." Chris scraped his plate clean, swallowing the last bite with relish.

Jori sat silent, peering at him with that probing gaze until he decided to ask the question that had bothered him for days.

"Don't I know you from somewhere?" Her lips curved and

Chris read her thoughts with ease. "It's not just a line," he protested, chuckling at her disbelief. "I keep thinking I've met you somewhere, before Mossbank, and yet I'm positive I never have."

"I used to be a model." She burst out giggling at the look of disbelief on his face. "Really. I guess you've probably seen my pictures in some magazines, although I haven't done anything for the last few years."

He studied the fresh oval of her face more clearly and decided that she had the perfect look for a cover girl. He didn't remember specifically, but he was sure now that he had seen her picture somewhere.

"You used to have shorter hair," he muttered, considering the long fall of hair that trailed over her shoulder. Suddenly he stared straight at her, and asked, "Why did you get into modeling?"

Jori didn't try to evade the question. She merely shrugged her shoulders and stated the bare facts.

"My father became ill, he forgot where he was going or what he was doing. Eventually he was diagnosed with Alzheimer's. He needed round-the-clock care. The pay was good, so I took as many assignments as I could to pay for full-time nursing care at home." She glanced up, tears glistening at the corners of her eyes.

"Dad was always less confused when he was at home and so I tried to keep him comfortable there." She stopped for a moment before continuing. Her voice shook. "He got worse in spite of the best nursing I could afford. I was on a shoot, my last one, when they phoned to say he'd hurt himself."

"I'm sorry, Jori. I didn't know." Chris awkwardly stretched out his big hand to cover hers, uncomfortable with her distress.

She smiled through her tears, wiping a hand carelessly across her eyes. "It's all right," she murmured. "He knows the Lord and in his own way he's happy now. Happy and healthy. Even if he's in the nursing home.'' The assurance in her voice tugged at his heartstrings. "Anyway—'' her soft musical voice caught his ear again "—I decided to come home for a while so I could be near him. I finished up my nursing degree, which I had started before Dad got sick, and I've been living contentedly here ever since.''

Chris detected the slight hesitation in her words and knew there was something she wasn't saying. "But…?'' he questioned, waiting quietly for her to finish.

"Why do you say that?'' she demurred, keeping her eyes averted from his. Her slim hands twisted the napkin lying on the picnic table.

"I came back to help my father. Instead I hurt him.'' Jori's voice was bitter with remorse. Darkly glowing, her eyes stared off into space until she took a deep breath and launched into her story.

"After I'd been home for a week, my fiancé came for a visit. He came to show me some pictures of me that had been published in the tabloids. I had never authorized them, and I don't know where they came from.'' Her beautiful face was filled with distress as she half whispered to him.

"Everybody saw them. The whole country was talking about my promiscuous behavior.'' Her face was strained as she steered her eyes away from his. "They were shots, supposedly of me, nude on a beach.'' Her voice was filled with pain. Chris could only imagine having his privacy invaded so intensely. "They were pasteups. You know—'' she motioned "—my head, someone else's body.'' Her eyes were sad.

"I couldn't have gone back to modeling the exclusive lines if I'd wanted to then. My contract specifically said no nudity.'' Jori grimaced at him. "It was a clause I'd insisted on and Gaston's held me to it. They said I'd degraded them.'' The last words came out on a whisper of shame.

"The tabloids made a lot of money from those photos but they practically ruined my life. I couldn't get work. Everywhere I went people stared at me with a funny little smile. It was awful. So I stayed holed up in Mossbank where everyone was as kind as could be. Someone finally admitted that the pictures were tampered photos that had been released without my permission. I sued and the magazine paid but legal costs ate it." Her chest lifted with the weight of her sigh.

"I found justice, but it was too late. My fiancé decided he'd had enough when I decided to stay here. Trace didn't want a small-town hick for a wife. He was my manager and had always encouraged my modeling, especially when the money started to really come in. Trace liked the high life—traveling, the whole thing." Jori thrust out her chin defiantly, her words bitter and hard.

"He announced our breakup in a national magazine that paid him for the story and then he moved on with a friend of mine. Maybe you've heard of her—Sabrina LeClair?"

Chris nodded, remembering the name from some party or another, he thought. But his mind was busy with Jori's story. He could guess the rest. She had stayed here, safe and secure in her little town, away from the prying eyes of the world. And her trust in people had never returned.

Suddenly, she straightened. He watched as a mask fell over the expressive but sad features as Jori pulled back into her shell and once more became the courteous but reserved woman he recognized from the office.

"So, Doctor, I don't know where you saw me, but I suppose that's why I seem familiar." She picked up their used cups and his empty plate and moved through the patio doors to the kitchen.

"I'll take you to the fair if you promise me that you will try to see these people for who they are. They're kind and good and they'd give you the shirt off their backs. I know a country fair is no big deal to you but for some of them, it's an event that they anxiously wait for. Don't spoil it.''

Her soft, melodic voice was hard with censure, but Chris let it go. He knew her emotions were still whirling and she needed distance. He decided to give her some space.

''When do we leave?'' he asked, bending to tickle the dog lying at his feet.

''I'm going to see my dad this morning so I'll pick you up at one. If you're not ready, I'll go without you.'' The pain and sadness had left her face. She was a woman defending her town.

''And bring a jacket,'' she ordered, walking in front of him to the door. ''It will get very cool before we get home.''

''Yes, ma'am.'' he answered cheekily, saluting irreverently. ''Anything else?''

''Yes,'' Jori returned, her eyes coming to life again. ''Be prepared.''

''I'm always prepared,'' he said, and bent to brush her cheek lightly with his lips. ''Thanks for telling me, Jori. And for what it's worth, I am coming to enjoy Mossbank. And its people.''

She didn't look at him, but kept her dark gaze fixed on her hands. Chris flicked her cheek with one long finger before turning to march down the walk and along the driveway. He whistled cheerily as he sauntered home.

How about that, he had a date. And with the most gorgeous woman this side of the Rockies. Chris chuckled. He guessed he hadn't quite lost his touch. He hoped!

''What's got your face glowing like the sun on a hot July afternoon?'' an elderly lady asked him as he strode past.

Chris stopped and turned, searching his memory for the name.

''I'll tell you, Mrs. Flowerday,'' he confessed, knowing he couldn't keep it quiet any longer, ''I just got myself a ride to that fair we were talking about the other day and it's with my beautiful office nurse.''

"Jordanna agreed to take you? Isn't that wonderful?'' The little old granny beamed from ear to ear. "She needs an outing with a nice handsome man. You are nice, aren't you?'' she asked severely. "I'll not stand idly by while you play with her like that other scoundrel did. I should have smacked him when I had the opportunity.''

"No, ma'am.'' Chris gulped. He stared at her frowning face for a moment and then amended. "I mean, yes, ma'am, I think I'm a nice enough guy.''

"Jordanna's the salt of the earth, she just doesn't believe in herself anymore. She's been banged up and bruised by life. Needs a little patience and some love, that's all.''

Mrs. Flowerday peered up into the sky and Chris allowed himself a grin as he wondered how Jori would feel about being thought of in that way.

"I won't hurt her, ma'am,'' he assured the old lady softly and felt the power of those warm brown eyes focus on him once more. "She's been very kind to me, made me feel right at home.''

Charity Flowerday snorted derisively.

"Don't try to snowball me, young man,'' she chided, hitching up her purse under her arm and starting off down the street. "I heard the two of you going at it in the office.''

"Yes,'' he admitted crestfallen as he walked along beside her. "I'm afraid she is rather peeved at me most of the time. She thinks I don't appreciate her little town enough. I'm not sure why it's so important to her.'' He felt the testing pinch on his biceps and wondered why people always thought little old ladies were weak. He'd have a bruise there from those arthritic fingers.

"Well, you're strong! You can take it,'' Charity sang out over her shoulder as she veered off away from him. "That indignation is a good sign. If Jori didn't speak to you at all, you'd have something to worry about, now wouldn't you?''

As he rubbed his arm all the way home, Chris decided the woman was probably right.

Probably.

"I'm telling you, Hope, he is attracted to her. Very attracted." Charity beamed at her friends. "I was talking to him and he seemed most interested in Jordanna."

"I'm most interested in who you had over to dinner last night, Charity. Why won't you tell us? Is it a secret?"

"A secret? Oh, my!" Faith breathed softly.

"Hope Conroy, you know blamed well that I hate that word. Faith battens on to it as if it's the next thing to heaven and now she won't give me any peace. Honestly!" Charity rolled her eyes, glaring at her best friends.

"Is it a secret man?" Faith whispered, winking at Hope. "Have you got a secret friend, Charity?" She clapped her hands in delight. "I know! It's Frank, isn't it? He's the secret!"

"You see!" Charity glared at Hope angrily, before huffing into her lawn chair. "No, Faith, it isn't Frank. I'd never invite him to dinner."

"Why not?" Faith demanded in an affronted tone. "Arthur says he's a very nice man. They go fishing together all the time."

"Good! Then Arthur can take him out to dinner. I'm not interested!"

"But why not, Charity? He's a perfectly lovely man. So interesting. Harry says…" Hope sank into a thickly padded wicker chair before reaching over to pour out three cups of tea.

"For the fifth time, Hope, I do not care what Harry says!"

Charity's voice rose indignantly. "I have no interest in the local undertaker!"

"I just wanted to know why," Hope murmured soothingly. "There must be something that's made you react so negatively."

"You two," Charity sputtered at last. "Why can't you let me alone?" She sat up and straightened her skirt, shifting her swollen ankles onto a nearby rock. "All right, I'll tell you."

The other two visitors leaned in, as if coconspirators in a plan of the utmost secrecy.

"Frank Bellows never says anything."

"Oh, piffle! He's always talking about his life in Australia and the time he spent in Switzerland," Faith cried indignantly. "You can hardly get a word in edgewise when he starts going on about his daughter in Italy."

Charity felt her mouth flop open in surprise.

"He has a daughter? In Italy? Oh." Her face reddened. "Well, I never knew that. He doesn't say a word to me."

"Have you actually talked to him?" Hope demanded, her face drawn into the severe lines she'd used with her students in the past. "Most times I notice you whisk right past him at church. He'd have to hold you down to talk to you."

"That's because I thought, well, that is…I wondered if maybe he wasn't…" Charity felt her face grow redder by the moment as she searched for the right word. "Wasn't a little…you know?"

"*I* don't know," Faith told them loudly. "What does she mean, Hope?"

"I don't know either, Faith. What do you mean, Charity?" There was a hint of cold steel in Hope's sharp blue eyes.

"I thought he was either deaf or a little bit crazy," Charity blurted out at last. "He always stumbles and stammers whenever he says something. I thought maybe he was handicapped!"

"And so you avoided him because of that? Charity Flowerday, I'm amazed at you!" Hope's forehead was furrowed. "I thought we'd all learned our lesson about judging by appearances long ago." She poured another cup of tea for herself and absently added a cube of sugar. "You've probably made him so nervous, he doesn't know what to say," she expostulated.

"He's probably sick to death of being pressured by you two!" Charity glowered angrily at her friends. "I keep telling you, I don't need a man in my life to be happy. I'm perfectly content the way I am. I enjoy solitude. It gives me time to read and think. I'm managing very well!"

"Oh, Charity," Faith murmured, patting the gnarled old hand tenderly as her eyes filled with tears. "Of course you are. And we didn't mean to upset you." She swiped away the tears with the back of her hand and sniffed in a way that brought a frown to Hope's clear countenance.

"It's just that we don't want you to be left out. We've been so happy lately, now that we've found Arthur and Harry and we're worried about leaving you alone too much."

"Besides," Hope added dourly. "Having a man around can make life interesting. And there's always someone to do things with."

"Right now, all I want is to relax and enjoy the sunshine," Charity told them smartly. "If I want a companion, there are several friends I can ask. Or I'll get a dog. *I do not need a man.*"

"Oh, my." Faith giggled. "I don't think a dog could replace Arthur. Especially when he keeps my feet warm at night."

Charity glanced heavenward and sighed. "I already have a hot water bottle," she muttered darkly.

Chapter Four

"Hi, Dad. How are you today?" Jori leaned over to press a kiss against her father's weathered cheek and breathed in the spicy scent of his aftershave. The memories it brought back coaxed tears from her eyes and she brushed them away. Now wasn't the time to get maudlin.

"'And He said to them, "Why are you troubled and why do doubts arise in your hearts?" Luke 24:38.'" James Jessop inclined his salt-and-pepper head toward his daughter, his eyes intent in their scrutiny. "'Fear not.'" His faded gray eyes studied her intently. "Do I know you?"

"It's Jori, Dad," she murmured softly, clasping his hand in hers. "Do you want to walk in the courtyard? It's nice and warm today."

"All right." Tall and thin, James Jessop ambled to the door, his hand protectively under her elbow. "Mind the step, miss," he murmured.

Jori searched his face, praying that today would be one of his better ones. She needed him; needed to lean on him for a bit.

Her father held out an armchair for her before slouching

down in a lounge next to her and closing his eyes to the bright sunlight.

"I love the feel of the sun," he murmured. "It's like heaven is shining right down on me. When it was sunny, Ruth used to say the windows of heaven were open. I miss Ruth."

Jori smiled at this hint that his memory was still there. Somewhere. "So do I, Dad."

She sat quietly, content to be near him as he dozed in the sunlight. He seemed calmer today and she was thankful for that. Perhaps, at last, her father was really settling in to Sunset.

"Hi, Jori!" Melanie Stewart called out from the doorway. "Your dad's having a good day today. He ate quite a big breakfast." She stopped as soon as James's eyes opened. "Good morning, Mr. Jessop. Had a good nap?"

"I wasn't napping, Melanie." James voice was cooly rational. "I was just resting my eyes. I never sleep during the day. It's a waste of time."

"Of course." Melanie winked at Jori and waved. "I have to get back to work. Have a good visit."

"Jori, dear!" James hugged her tightly. "When did you arrive?"

"Oh, just a few moments ago," she told him. "I just needed to see my dad for a few minutes. How are you?"

"Happy to stare at the beautiful woman my daughter has become," he averred proudly. "And don't frown like that. You are beautiful. Everyone knows it."

"Beauty is only skin deep, Dad. Isn't that what you always used to say?"

"Did I?" James frowned. "Well, I was wrong. I think beauty goes right to the soul in some people and you're one of them, Jori." He hugged her close and then leaned back. "You're not still thinking about that young man, are you?"

"What young man?" Jori pushed the image of Chris's handsomely smiling countenance out of her mind.

"Hmmm. Who makes you blush like that?" James teased, flicking a finger against her cheek. "*I* was talking about that exceptionally dull young man you brought to visit me one time. Travis or something, wasn't it? Who were you thinking about?" His eyes were bright and Jori felt relief that he was still able to connect that much from the past, even if it was terribly hurtful for her.

"It was Trace," she offered quietly. "And no, I wasn't thinking of him at all. We have a new doctor, Dad. I've been working with him for a couple of weeks now."

"Hmmm," James Jessop murmured. "Seems to me I should know that. Who told me? Faith? No, Charity, I think. Somebody told me something about a doctor." The confusion on his dear face was painful to see and Jori patted his hand.

"It doesn't matter. Anyway, his name is Christopher and he's from the big city. He's very famous." Jori wondered why she'd chosen this particular topic.

"Not that famous," a voice murmured from behind them.

Jori whirled around to stare into those bright blue eyes and felt the heat rise in her cheeks at his knowing grin.

"Dad, this is the man I was telling you about, Dr. Christopher Davis. Dr. Davis, this is my father, James Jessop."

"I know him!" James voice was excited. "Plays chess like a pro." He beamed happily up at them.

"Not nearly as well as you, Mr. Jessop." Chris grinned. "I've yet to win a game."

"You see," her father teased, patting Jori's cheek. "I haven't lost all my marbles." He frowned as her face fell. "None of that, my dear. It was a joke. How can you not laugh on such a wonderful day?"

"Oh, Dad," she whispered tearfully. "I love you."

"Come now, dearest." James brushed his hand over her

swath of glistening hair. "I have few enough good days. Let's just enjoy the ones God gives us." His eyes twinkled merrily. "What have you got planned for today?" he asked curiously.

"Actually, Jori's taking me to the fair," Chris said, butting in. "I'd better get moving. She said if I wasn't ready she'd leave me behind." He grinned at the older man. "I think she means it, too."

"Don't pay too much attention to what my daughter says," James advised solemnly. His eyes were serious. "Sometimes she doesn't express her true feelings, but that's because she's been hurt."

Jori could feel Chris's fathomless blue eyes on her, studying her closely. She tried to pretend a nonchalance she didn't feel.

"Oh, Dad." She laughed nervously. "We're not going in to all that old history today, are we?"

But neither her father nor Chris was paying any attention to her. Each studied the other with an intensity that sent little waves of apprehension up her spine. Finally James nodded, as if he'd found what he sought.

"You take care of her," he ordered in a firm no-nonsense voice that Jori hadn't heard since high school. "I don't want my daughter hurt again."

Chris nodded, shaking the other man's hand with a firm grip.

"Don't worry," he murmured. "I won't hurt her." His eyes were speculative as they slipped over Jori's still silent figure, and she felt the old familiar doubts wash over her until his soft words reached her ears. "See you after lunch."

After that, James seemed content to talk sporadically and Jori finally left him in the dining room, ready to sample the barbecue lunch.

"See you tomorrow," she whispered, kissing his cheek. "Take care."

"First Peter 5:7. *'Let Him have all your worries and cares, for He is always thinking about you and watching everything that concerns you,'*" James quoted, smiling at her. "It's a promise, Jori. You can depend on it, you know."

"I know. Thanks, Dad." Jori drove home thinking about those words and trying to apply them to herself. But it made little difference. She still felt the same old apprehensions and qualms assail her. Why didn't she feel the sense of peace that her father did?

"Aren't you there, God?" she prayed at last, as she changed her clothes. "Can't you see how much I need my father right now?" But there was no response from heaven and Jori was left wondering if God cared at all.

"I'm doing this as a favor to him," Jori told herself sternly. "That's all. It's not as if I need a man to complicate my life."

She brought the Jeep to a stop in front of Dr. Dan's house barely two minutes before one. If Chris was ready, they should make good time driving to the fairground. As one of the judges for the children's entries in the exhibits, she liked to arrive early enough to look everything over thoroughly before settling down to reward the best.

It looked as if someone had recently cut the lawn, she mused, glad to see the city doctor was taking good care of their own doctor's home. She wanted everything perfect when Dan and Jessica returned—with their little one, God willing.

When Christopher didn't appear, Jori honked the horn once and then checked the mirror again. Why, she didn't know. What did she care if her hair was mussed or lipstick smeared? Chris Davis's opinion meant absolutely nothing to her, she told herself.

Yeah, right, her heart thumped.

He came strolling out the front door, wearing perfectly creased designer blue jeans and a thin pale blue cotton shirt with a designer logo on the pocket. The blue only enhanced the sapphire sparkle of his eyes.

He looks gorgeous, she decided and then chided her brain for noticing. Dr. Christopher Davis was not her type, Jori reminded herself. Not at all.

Chris tossed his black bag and jacket onto the back seat before folding himself into the front. Then he stared at her curiously.

"Somehow, this isn't what I had pictured you driving," he said, head tilted to one side as he watched her manipulate the steering wheel of her Jeep.

"I didn't know you pictured me doing anything," Jori returned pertly, pulling expertly away from the curb before shifting gears. Her long dark hair whipped behind her in the breeze and she tucked the strands behind her ear.

"Exactly what did you picture me driving, Doc?" The question was only half-teasing, her brown eyes crinkling at the corners.

"Something more sedate," Chris replied and then added, "and stop calling me that. You know my name."

"Yes, sir," Jori replied, tongue in cheek. "Sedate? Thanks a lot. It just so happens that this was a bonus from one of my contracts." She patted the black console lovingly. "I can tell you, it's come in very handy during some of our blizzards. No matter what, Baby and I can always get through."

"Baby?" His blue eyes twinkled with mirth. "You really have a way with names, Jori." His long lean fingers marked off the names. "Flop. Baby. What's next?" His mouth tipped up.

"Makes me wonder about your children's future." His face was wreathed in smiles.

Jori merely turned off the highway onto a gravel road, refusing to answer him. He was quiet for a few minutes and then began questioning her.

"Where is this fair held, anyway?" He searched the waving fields of grain that stretched out around them. "I can't see a thing but this stuff."

"This *stuff* is what pays the bills, Doc. And don't you forget it." Jori's voice was firm with reproof. No one would get away with disparaging her county. When she noticed his wide startled eyes focused on her in surprise, she relented a little.

"We have to weave in and out here for a bit," she told him. "Then you'll see an old barn on one side and a house on the other, just before we cross the river. It's not far after that."

Jori burst out laughing at the look of shock holding Chris's handsome features immobile.

"People come away out here just for a fair?" He sounded confused by the whole thing. Jori could hardly wait for the look on his face when they arrived.

"Oh, a few do." She smirked. There was no way this smug city doctor could understand just what this event meant for the area without having lived here. She didn't want to spoil the effect Jori knew it would have on him.

"This must be the house and barn," Chris noticed, studying the weathered old buildings standing sturdily by. He peered through the window looking for the river. Evidently, the carved landscape gave him a slight clue, but he continued to peer down.

"Where's the water?" he complained more to himself than to her.

Jori pressed her lips tightly together, refusing to answer. As they crested the hill, she watched his blue eyes widen in amazement. There were vehicles parked everywhere. On the sides of the road, in the ditch, beside a row of poplars. Grouped together on any open area of unused field, they numbered in the hundreds.

"Wow," he breathed.

Jori burst out laughing. She couldn't help it.

"Come on," she said, pulling in beside a muddy half-ton.
"I hope you remembered sunscreen," she observed, privately
thinking that his darkly tanned skin was less likely to burn
than her own.

"Yes, ma'am," Chris teased, swinging out of her vehicle.

The shimmering wave of heat hit him flat-out and Jori
watched as he caught his breath.

Chris followed her lithe figure down the narrow trail to
what he presumed was the fair entrance. Jori walked with an
unconscious grace, her long legs bare in the summer sun. He
liked her outfit, he decided.

She wore a denim skirt and matching vest that left slim,
lightly tanned arms bare. Jori had twisted her hair into a
ponytail that flowed down her back like toffee. On her feet
she wore canvas flats that kept out the dust. He suddenly felt
overdressed.

She quickly paid the two elderly gentlemen the fare posted
on a piece of cardboard.

"No charge for the workers, Jordanna," they told her.

Grinning, she threw the money into the box on the tabletop.
"It's a donation then," she called merrily.

Chris felt her hand on his, tugging him along. "Come on,
Doctor," she urged. "I'm late, thanks to you. Don't make it
a habit, okay?"

"Late for what?" he asked. Unfortunately the answer
eluded him as they walked through an arch of maples to a
sight Chris was sure came straight out of the 1800s.

The fairground was set in a huge circular area surrounded
on all but the west side by towering green poplars. To the left
were a few older buildings. One had a sign on it announcing
the Welton School 1958-1977. Beside that stood a long, low
building with the word *Exhibits* across the entrance. A broad
red ribbon prevented anyone from entering.

Directly in front of him was a softball field where Chris noticed a group of people of all ages eagerly cheering on their teams from weathered bleachers placed on the sidelines. He could hear old-time fiddle music coming from the red-and-white-striped tent behind the diamond. And everywhere there was the smell of horses. Sometimes stronger, sometimes fainter, but always there.

Well, he reflected, it wasn't the World's Fair but it was still pretty interesting. Especially the collection of old machinery puffing and grunting across the way. It looked like some type of tractor pull, but then what did he know about farm machinery?

He felt someone yanking on his arm and looked down dazedly. Jori stood there saying something. He shook his head to clear it before looking down at her again.

"What?"

"I have to go to the exhibit hall to judge the children's work. Do you want to come, or would you rather look around?" She was tapping her foot impatiently and Chris made up his mind quickly.

"I'll go with you first. Then maybe I'll look around." He stared at the people milling about the grounds. "Where did they all come from?" he wondered bemusedly.

Jori giggled, and he decided he liked the sound of her laugh.

"From about a thirty-mile radius. Everyone just shows up when they want. Come on," she urged, trying to hurry him.

She pointed out the bathrooms tucked into the far corner of the grounds. Chris had a sneaking suspicion they were outdoor toilets, although he'd never personally had the opportunity to use one before. My, how his narrow life was being enhanced!

"All the ladies' aid groups offer food for sale to raise money for their charities," she told him. "We'll eat later.

They have pies of all kinds here.'' Jori grinned up at him, her white teeth flashing in the hot sun. "You should be able to pig out to your heart's content.''

Chris leered at her playfully, before hugging her shoulders to his big body in a burst of happiness, caught up in the festivities. He did notice that she immediately tugged away from him, and filed that information away for future thought.

Inside the building, it was hot; hotter than outside, he decided. He watched carefully as Jori greeted her friends and then introduced him to those he didn't know. He saw the glimmers of speculation in their eyes and wondered if she was aware of it also.

"I'm going to look around, Jori," he told Jori, who was bent over the sheaf of poems and samples of handwriting submitted for a prize. He touched her arm to gain her attention and noticed that she pulled away immediately but only answered, "Mmm-hmm.''

"I'll catch up with you later,'' he whispered in her ear, deliberately brushing his hand over her back. When she didn't flinch, he moved away, smugly satisfied that she hadn't reacted negatively to his touch. He wondered if Jordanna Jessop would ever thaw out enough to let him hold her the way he wanted to.

Christopher surveyed the room dourly. He gave a cursory glance at the huge cabbages that stood out among the produce displayed, but only because everyone else was. He dutifully smelled the flowers, checked out the ladies' handiwork, the coloring contest and the children's crafts, following the example of those in front.

Then he left, but not before a large woman in a huge straw hat talked him into purchasing tickets for a door prize to be drawn for later in the day.

"What do I win?" he asked innocently.

"A kid," the woman told him, beaming happily.

He had to think twice before he realized she didn't mean one of the human variety. Chris paid for the tickets, sincerely hoping he wouldn't win. There was little room in Dan's back-yard for a goat!

Outside, the baseball game was in full swing and he watched from the edge of the stands for a few minutes before deciding to take a closer look at the old school. It was dim inside, with that stale, dusty odor all schools seem to retain.

The old-fashioned desks were a curiosity and he wedged himself gingerly into one until someone else came in. There were initials carved here and there throughout the building and he grinned as he thought of those lovesick kids. A tar-nished bell stood atop the teacher's desk, waiting to call the next class to order.

Across the top of the blackboard, the alphabet was carefully chalked in. Underneath, someone had drawn a huge heart with an arrow through. *A.J. and D.S.* Chris wondered idly whose initials they were.

At the back of the schoolhouse, an intense game of horse-shoes was being waged between several older men. Chris stood to the side watching until a familiar voice caught his attention.

"Hi, Doc. How's it going?" Aubery Olden stood before him, hand outstretched. As he shook the old man's hand, Chris found himself also checking for other signs. Mr. Olden was one of the few patients Dan had asked Chris to particu-larly watch out for.

"I'm fine, Mr. Olden. It's a gorgeous day for your fair, isn't it?" The old man's color was good, although he was breathing quite heavily.

They bantered back and forth a bit before Aubery offered him some personal advice.

"If you're after Miss Jordanna, Doc, you will have to take your time. She's a lady who has been depending on herself

for so long, she doesn't find it easy to lean on anybody else.''
The old man coughed loudly for a moment and then grinned.
His weathered old face creased with happiness as he spoke.

"But you'll never find a lady more worthy of your love,
Doc. She's a fine one, our Miss Jordanna. Looks after everybody without them even asking.'' He cackled a rasping sound
Chris thought was meant to be a laugh. ''She ain't too hard
on the eyes, either!''

They grinned at each other while Chris's thoughts swirled
round and round. As Aubery explained the game, Chris asked
himself how the man had known his very personal thoughts.
The old gent was cagey in the extreme, but to Chris's certain
knowledge, he and Jori had never been together outside of
the office, at least not in anyone's sight before. Anyway, the
old guy was off the track a bit.

He liked the very gorgeous Miss Jessop, all right. She
floated through his thoughts at the oddest moments. He
wanted to kiss her, just once. But she backed off every time
he even touched her.

Love? Chris wasn't sure he knew what that was. And he
was pretty sure that Jordanna Jessop hadn't the least intention
of allowing him to get anywhere near that close. He'd seen
the flash of interest in her café au lait eyes, of course. But
Jori had told him in too many ways to count that her allegiance was with her townsfolk and in her opinion, he didn't
fit in. With a sigh, Chris acknowledged that she was right. He
was just passing through.

Wandering again, Chris moved over to the children's play
area to watch for a few moments. He considered what it would
be like to come to a fair like this with your own kids. Surely
children these days knew that bigger and better exhibitions
could be found most anywhere. Why would they be content
to come here?

And yet, as Chris watched, they eagerly participated in the

three-legged races and the potato sack races. He watched them follow the one lone clown about the grounds, giggling with delight when Chuckles finally handed them a balloon.

The scene tugged at his subconscious somehow and Chris was deep in thought when long, cool fingers covered his eyes.

"Having fun?" The voice was low and seductive and Chris knew immediately that Mirabel Matthews was behind him. Ducking away, he turned to smile coolly at her.

"Hello, Mrs. Matthews." Chris deliberately addressed her in this manner in an effort to keep their exchange as formal as possible, while praying fervently for Jori's return.

The town's loneliest widow stood clad in the tightest white pants he had ever seen. She wore a top to match in a plunging bikini style that looked vulgarly out of place in the country setting of cotton and denim. Glittering diamonds winked at her ears, deep in her cleavage and on her long-nailed fingers.

"Doctor," she remonstrated, "how can you be so formal at a country fair? Call me Mirabel."

Her arm snaked through his and Chris found there was little he could do to disentangle himself. She was like a boa constrictor, he decided dismally, waiting to squeeze the life out of him. Desperately, he glanced over her shoulder, surreptitiously searching for Jori among those curious folks who ambled past.

"Does this make you long for your own little ones?" she drawled, oblivious to his discomfort.

"What? Uh, no, uh...I don't have any. Little ones, I mean." He sucked in a breath of air and tried to extricate himself. "That is, I was just looking, Mrs. Matthews, while I wait for Jori. That's who I came with."

Could he get any clearer than that? Chris wondered. He glanced away from her black-rimmed eyes with their false lashes, trying to avoid the abundant cleavage she was flaunt-

ing as he lifted the long, slim octopuslike arm from around
his neck and stepped backward.

"Oh, there she is. Sorry, Mrs. Matthews, but we promised
to…" Chris let the sentence die away as he yanked his arm
from her bloodred-tipped manacles and marched over to the
woman who stood across the way, grinning merrily from one
gold-hooped ear to the other.

"Thanks a lot," he muttered, brushing his shirt down. To
his amazement, two of the buttons had come undone. "The
least you could have done was help me get away from that
barracuda." His voice was accusing but he was quite sure Jori
felt no pity.

Instead, her dark eyes beamed up at him.

"Didn't want to interrupt," she said with a giggle.
"Seemed to me that you and Mirabel were getting along famously."

"I need something cool," he rasped. "Where did you get
that?" He pointed to the orange-colored ice she held in her
hand.

"Come on." She tugged on his arm. "I'll show you. After
a run-in with Mirabel, I'm surprised that's all you need."

It *wasn't* all that he needed, not nearly. But Chris decided
that a triple-decker ice cream might just fill his mouth enough
that he wouldn't say anything too stupid. Maybe he'd even
be able to carry on a normal conversation.

Jori found a spot in the covered wooden stands where they
could sit protected from the sun while they watched the young
4-H riders take each horse through its paces. But even in the
shade with a breeze blowing, it was hot.

After they finished their icy treats, the two of them strolled
past the booths housing the different ladies' groups who sold
their wares to hungry visitors.

A surfboard sat on a bed of air, begging adults and kids
alike to try their skills. In the background there was a long,

narrow awning under which any who wished to play bingo could sit in the shade and lose money. It was probably the coolest place on the grounds and Chris wondered for a moment if he could learn to play a game he'd never considered even remotely interesting.

Jori, however, was indefatigable. She dragged him past the air house filled with multicolored balls and insisted on spending precious moments in the hot, hot sun trying to placate the crying child whose mother wouldn't allow yet another turn on a ride that made him dizzy.

"Isn't it great? Hi, Mrs. Flowerday. Wonderful afternoon for the fair, isn't it?" Jori beamed at the elderly woman who sat decked out in red gingham under a striped umbrella clipped to the arm of her plastic chair.

"It's just lovely, dear." The warm brown eyes slid over the two of them, widening appreciatively as Chris guided Jori out of the path of several wild youngsters. "You two have a happy time, now," she directed cheerfully.

"We will." They moved on through the growing numbers, pausing to chat with a hundred different people that Chris was positive he'd never seen around Mossbank and wouldn't remember if they came into the office tomorrow.

He wasn't sure exactly how it happened, but when Jori gleefully coaxed him onto the giant trampolines, he went, jumping and bouncing as she dared him to leap even higher. Which he did—just to prove he could, of course.

Laughing uncontrollably and giggling so hard she lost her footing, Jori fell in a heap of laughter, long legs sprawled across the surface, tangling with his. Chris wondered if his blood temperature, which was already steaming while they untangled themselves, would withstand the rest of the afternoon.

"I think I've had enough of that for a while," he said firmly, pulling her away from the center.

"Okay." She bounded over the side. "But it's so much fun. One of these days I'm going to buy a trampoline just for myself."

Lest she drag him into some other trap, Chris steered her away from the three children's rides to the animal barns.

"This is my least favorite place!" He watched as Jori's nose curled in distaste at the strong smells, but she obediently walked beside him checking the pens of sheep, cows, steers, rabbits and pigs. As they walked, Jori explained the intricacies of judging animals.

"Many of the local people prepare their livestock in order to win a trophy or one of the cash prizes sponsored by the town's businesses. Lots of the contestants are children. Oh, just look at this." She pointed.

Her good-natured laughter burst out again when she read the plaque someone had hung on the end of the barn, donating a cash prize for the biggest *bore* shown in memory of their father.

"I wonder if he was a big *bore,* too," she said, chuckling with glee, brushing Chris's shoulder with her hand as she laughingly drew his attention to the words.

The motion, innocent as it was, spread a trail of fire across his chest. It was the first time she had willingly touched him and he was loath to move. But if he hugged her back, would she push him away?

"This is too rich! A bore, for goodness' sake! Oh, I can't take any more."

"Neither can I," Chris agreed. "I'm too hot." He fanned his hand across his warm cheeks, wishing for a sudden rainstorm.

Suddenly sober and strangely aware of his intense scrutiny, Jori realized that she was hot, too. But she wasn't sure exactly how much was due to the temperature and how much to the man standing next to her. Even with bits of straw sticking out of his mussed blond hair, he looked inordinately handsome.

Chris Davis got to her the way few other men ever had. And that bothered her. A lot. It also raised an immoderate amount of curiosity in her vivid imagination. Jori wondered fleetingly what would happen if he ever broke through the shell of reserve she held tightly around herself.

Here, in the center of the compound, it was hotter than ever. All at once Jori thought of her special hideout.

"I know the perfect place," she told him grinning, the image floating into her mind like a mirage. Without thinking, she grabbed his arm, urging him past the throng of people waiting to register for a school reunion.

"Come on," she begged. "There's nothing really happening till after supper anyhow, and we'll be back by then."

Chris made her stand still long enough to collar two sodas and a neatly wrapped plate of watermelon from a nearby refreshment stand.

Jori tugged on his arm, her expressive eyes sparkling in anticipation. "Hurry," she ordered, matching her strides to his longer one.

"What's the rush?" he asked, feeling the trickle of sweat down his backbone. "We'll both die of heatstroke if you don't slow down."

Jori ignored him and whizzed away for a moment to speak to one of the men at the gate before he felt her slim, firm hand digging into his arm again.

"All right, all right," he grumped. "I'm coming."

Chris knew that the Jeep would be a furnace and while she unlocked and opened the door, he held back. When he thought he was prepared, he looked inside. Jori was already in her seat, feet on the pedals, impatiently ready to put the vehicle in motion.

"Get in." She waved.

Chris leaned back in his seat. He had no idea where they were going, but his beeper hadn't gone off yet so he would play along for a while. Groggily, he let his eyelids fall as he savored the light breeze from the dashboard vent.

Seconds later, a hard pinch on his upper arm brought reality back with a slam. Jori's big brown eyes were peering into his, mere inches away. Her face was tight with stress until he looked at her and then her generous smile cut a swath across her face.

"Sheesh, I thought you were dead for a minute there." Her voice was light and airy as she straightened away.

"Come on, I want to show you something," she said, looking like a cat that had just downed the canary. Chris reluctantly stretched himself out of the vehicle, loath to leave the cool confines as a wave of heat smacked him squarely in the chest.

"Leave the car running, I'll just watch from here," he told her. Jori swung the keys on one finger.

"You'll need these then." She grinned, stepping backward. "And I'm going down there."

Chris looked around curiously. They were in some sort of hollow. There were trees all around, creating a kind of hidden alcove. The road they had followed in was not much more than a dirt track. Directly in front of the Jeep was a pool of water fed by a tiny stream.

Jori disappeared behind a bush. A few moments later she emerged clad in a swimsuit. He was half-afraid to look, but curiosity got the better of him and he stared through the overhanging leaves.

He caught his breath as he watched her long lithe figure stride with ease to the edge of the glistening pool. She wore a black swimsuit that wasn't in the least exotic. He could just make out a thin black strap across her back before she plunged into the clear water with a squeal of delight.

Slowly, feeling like the atmosphere was pressing in on him, Chris walked to the edge of the pool. Jori surfaced near him, her dark hair streaming out behind her, her eyes glittering with suppressed excitement.

"Come on in," she coaxed, splashing some water on him. "It's not very cold, but it sure feels great." She dived under the water gracefully, her shiny red toenails the last to disappear. Seconds later she was standing before him again, her chest filling as she gasped for air.

Chris knew Jordanna Jessop was beautiful. She'd been to exotic places, played with world famous celebrities. And yet as this strong vibrant woman with her mane of walnut hair splashed joyfully in the tiny pool, Chris had the impression that he didn't really know her at all. And it was imperative that he find out what lay behind that tough, glossy facade.

He took off his shoes, pausing to stare at her solemnly.

"I can't go in." He sighed. He dipped his toes into the water and then rolled up his pant legs, eager to immerse more of his overheated frame.

"Why not?" Jori stared at him, head tilted to one side. Her long lashes were spiky with droplets of water and they blinked at him innocently. "You look really hot."

He needed her to tell him that! Chris groaned.

"I haven't got a suit." It should have been obvious, he thought. Jori just smirked.

"There's a suit of my dad's in the back of the Jeep. You're welcome to try it if you like. It's a little old-fashioned, but…" Her voice died away as she stared at him standing on the edge of the river as if rooted to the spot. Her eyes opened wide and he saw a flicker of something in their depths before she blinked and shrugged her indifference.

"Suit yourself," she called over her slim shoulders, then dashed deeper into the water once more, her body flashing in the dappled sunlight, hair gleaming like a seal's coat.

Chris sat there for about thirty seconds before his hand went to his perspiring forehead. In for a penny, in for a pound. He could hardly wait to sink himself into that pond and feel that coolness lap against his skin.

Seconds later Jori heard a huge splash. And then Chris's blond head surfaced next to her. "Took him long enough," she whispered to herself.

She wasn't exactly sure why she'd brought him here. Sympathy, she told herself. She'd felt sorry for him at the fair. He'd been hot and dirty and totally ill at ease.

No one would ever expect Jori Jessop to go pond dipping with a man, but Christopher Davis was one man who intrigued her like no one else had. He also made her more aware of her femininity than she had ever been. She wanted to know why. And yet at the same time, she was afraid; scared to open herself up to his intense scrutiny.

"Well, Doc," she teased, whipping a hand through the water to splash him in the face. "Great, isn't it?"

Chris's eyes had darkened to a deep electrifying blue. He strode through the water toward her with a look in his eye that Jori knew meant trouble. She backed up as far as she could, but he kept advancing until Jori was treading water in the deepest part of their private pool.

"I said not to call me that," he growled. "Now you'll have to pay."

"Go ahead," she egged him on. "Duck me. I like it."

His big warm palms closed over her shoulders. Then he tugged, bringing her against him.

"That's not what I had in mind," he warned with gleeful menace. "The payment is this."

Without any warning, Chris's head bent to hers. His lips were soft yet purposeful. It was a kiss that was full of unasked questions and tentative responses.

When he finally pulled away, Jori could only hang on to

his broad shoulders as she stared up at him. When she finally pushed back, it was to duck her head under the water and swim away from him, as if his kiss meant nothing.

But she couldn't let it go. Something about him, the safe harbor of his arms, made her ask, "Why did you do that? We barely know each other."

Chris shrugged and paddled circles around her.

"I've wanted to kiss you properly for ages," he told her, glittering blue eyes met hers straight on. "You can't deny there's something between us."

He grinned that wide-open easy smile at her and Jori felt her heart turn cartwheels. He looked so cute, so *trustworthy*, standing there soaking wet with that silly smile. She tamped down her inner doubts. After all, she wasn't a model anymore. It wasn't as if someone as famous as Christopher Davis would need to use her.

"You know," he continued, "This country fair thing of yours is hot work." She saw his gaze shift to her mouth. "Why did you bring *me* here, Jori? Do you bring all your dates to this little oasis?"

"I've never brought anyone…" Jori's voice trailed away in embarrassment.

Why couldn't she learn some self-control? she asked herself. With heart sinking, she watched the light of understanding dawn in his eyes before they turned a deep navy.

"Well, I'm scandalized." His laughing voice drew Jori out of her introspection. "The always perfect Miss Jori Jessop gave way to the moment and brought her boss to her own private swimming pool. What would the townsfolk think of their favorite citizen now, indulging in such abandon?"

Jori's face was burning. Deep in her heart there was an ache that wouldn't go away. This was a side of Chris she hadn't seen before. He was funny and teasing and lighthearted. All the things she had thought she wanted in a man. Frankly, he was hard to resist in this mood.

Jori turned away, treading water as she strove to regain control.

"I don't do things for the townspeople," she said sharply. "I came here because it's cool and we can relax and be comfortable." Jori scrambled to assume her severest schoolteacher look. "I didn't plan this as some secret assignation, you know. I was just trying to help you."

She wasn't defending herself, merely stating the facts. It came as a surprise to hear Chris's low voice in her ear.

"I know. But there's cool, and then there's *cool*." He grinned.

There was only one recourse and she took it, concentrating on her swimming.

When she finally stopped, puffing and gasping air into her starved lungs, Chris sat perched at the water's edge on a huge boulder, sunning himself dry. She studiously ignored him as she paddled to the grassy edge and sprawled out on her stomach. The feathery green blades caressed her skin with a delicate touch.

There was no way, Jori decided, that she was pulling on her denim skirt while her swimsuit was still soaking wet. Her dip had left her cool and relaxed and she was loath to break the solitude and peace of the afternoon. Closing her eyes, she pretended to relax in the sun, fully aware of the man across from her as he sat munching watermelon.

"You're self-conscious around me." Chris's soft puzzled voice carried on the still afternoon air. "I don't understand that. I thought models would be used to people watching them in various states of dress."

Chris flopped his long lanky body next to hers on the soft grassy carpet. His arm brushed hers as he found a comfortable position. Immediately her armor went up and something inside whispered, "Be careful."

So we say with confidence "The Lord is my helper; I will not be afraid. What can man do to me?" The old memory verse reverberated through her mind and Jori almost grinned in delight. Talk about timing!

"You're not a client or a customer," she prevaricated. "Anyway, it's different here. This is home. And I haven't modeled for quite a while." Jori twisted her head to look into his smooth velvet eyes, noticing the way the flaxen mop fell carelessly across his forehead.

"I never was very comfortable around men," she admitted, waiting for that wry look of disbelief to cross his face. She wasn't disappointed.

"I'm sure."

"Look, it was just a job. I needed the money and so I modeled. Some of those assignments paid me very well." She stared straight into his face, daring him to interrupt. "So well, in fact, that my dad got most of what he needed to keep him happy." She gulped down a deep breath and pressed on, needing to get it all out.

"I'm not especially proud of some of what I had to wear, but I did a good job for my clients. Anyway, my father got to spend a few more years happily in his own home. That was the point."

Jori took a deep, calming breath before sitting up slowly, dragging her knees to her chest.

"After I took over his affairs, I found out that he had stashed some money away for my education. I wish I'd known. I would have spent more time with him and less working."

"I'm sorry," he murmured. "I have no right to judge."

Jori stared down at her feet. She'd noticed his large, capable hands soothe a fussing child, or stroke a patient's wringing hands. Now they tipped her chin up to meet his compassionate countenance, strong yet gentle under her chin.

"I think your father is very proud of what his daughter did for him," he murmured, his lips very close to hers. "What man would not have been proud to see the world admiring his beautiful daughter?"

"It wasn't exactly the traditional approach to caring for one's parents," she whispered, mesmerized by his compassionate look.

"Unusual circumstances call for unusual solutions," he whispered. "No one's blaming you for being a model, Jori. Least of all me."

He bent his head slowly and pressed his lips to hers then, and it was unlike anything Jori had experienced before. His mouth was soft and gentle.

Finally Chris pulled his lips away, but continued to touch the silky strands of her hair.

And all the while a tiny voice whispered in Jori's ear. "He will never settle here. He's from the city and that is where he will return." She hated that nagging little voice and its cheerless message.

Thing was, she knew it was right.

Christopher Davis was very good at kissing and he could draw a response that echoed through her body to her toes.

But there was no future for them. She was committed to staying in Mossbank, caring for her father. It was what she'd focused on for months now. And hadn't God directed her home?

So how could she have these feelings for this man? He would leave, move on with his life and then she would be alone. Again. Jori jerked out of his embrace, her cheeks burning as she watched his blue eyes darken.

"Why do you always do that?" he asked, allowing her to slip out of his grasp. "Are you afraid of me? I'm not like your fiancé, Jori. I don't care much about what happened in the past, or your money.''

''That's because you have a lot,'' she told him, her glance downcast. ''If you're in this world long enough, you come to realize that there are people who would do anything for money.'' She glared across at him. ''I'm here because I couldn't stand to be around people like that anymore.''

He watched her when she plucked a spear of grass and shredded it with her fingernails. The action only made her seem more nervous.

''Like what?'' he asked softly. When she frowned, he clarified. ''People like what?''

''People who devalue everything that's important. My father taught me to love God and trust him with my life.'' She laughed harshly. ''Believe me, that's not something that you hear much anymore. And I've decided that that was an important heritage. That's why I'm going to stay right here, in this community. This is where I want to live, maybe raise a family, grow old.''

''There are lots of communities like Mossbank in this country,'' he murmured. ''Why limit yourself to here?''

''My dad's here,'' she told him bluntly. ''And I have to be nearby in case he needs me.''

''But he's in the nursing home! He has someone there all the time. Some days he doesn't even recognize you.''

Jori felt the tears well as she swallowed down the lump in her throat with difficulty.

''I know.'' She hiccupped. ''But he has better days and knows who I am. I can't not be there for him.''

''Jori, your father has Alzheimer's. He's not going to get better.'' Chris shrugged. ''I'm no expert in that field, but I do know that these patients don't wake up one morning cured. You're talking about a degenerative disease. Surely, as a nurse, you know what that means.''

"Of course I know," she returned angrily. "But I have no intention of deserting my only remaining family. There's nothing out there—" she waved her hand in front of her "—that I want enough to leave Mossbank. This is where I belong. It's where I have to be."

"Nothing to make you leave," he murmured, so softly Jori barely caught his words. "I wonder."

"We'd better get going," she muttered, jumping to her feet. She had to move, to do something that would avoid that knowing look. Chris's blue eyes were bright with understanding. She avoided them. She didn't want to hear him call her a chicken.

She found her clothes and put on her skirt and vest, then turned to find her shoes. As she moved, Jori caught sight of Chris, just standing there, staring at her.

"Well?" Jori snapped, unable to control the exasperation that flashed through her at the notion that she could easily be swayed from her life's plan by a mere kiss. All it would take was a little more of that gentle compassion and she'd start dreaming about a future that was impossible. "Do you intend to stay here?"

"I'm not giving up on you, Jori." The words were quietly spoken, blond head tilted to one side. "You and I have something special going on, you can't deny it. But just when things start to get interesting, you duck out." His wide mouth tightened. "I'm not going to hurt you, Jori." He smiled, brushing one hand down the length of her almost dry hair. "You can trust me.

"You only hurt yourself if you don't live your *own* life. I don't believe either God or your father intended that."

Jori was shaken by his perceptiveness and she let that fear translate into anger. She attacked him verbally while her palms stayed clenched at her side.

"Big deal. You kissed me. The great Dr. Davis! So what?"

She snickered. "Am I supposed to be grateful for your attention?" She watched his face darken, a dull red suffusing his healthy skin.

"You kissed me back," he taunted. "You felt the same spark that I did, only you won't admit it. Why, Jori? What do you think is going to happen if you admit that you enjoy being with me?"

In three strides he was standing in front of her. "I didn't force you or coerce you to kiss me, Jordanna Jessop, and I'm sure not going to hurt you. I am not your ex-boyfriend."

Her flashing brown eyes met his glittering blue ones. But what she saw in his eyes only made her more uncomfortable.

"You just shut me out," he murmured. "I thought we'd gone beyond that. I don't scare easily, Jori."

Chris turned away after a few moments and retrieved his clothes. Quietly he slipped them on behind a nearby bush without saying another word. There was a pinched tightness around his mouth, but that was the only hint as to his frustration.

He climbed into the Jeep and sat waiting for her without uttering a word. But Jori could feel his condemnation. She took her time getting into the hot stuffy vehicle.

He was right. She wasn't playing fair. And it was because she wasn't sure what was right or proper anymore. Christopher Davis had mixed up her mind and emotions so badly, she couldn't decide if she liked or hated him more, and she was very much afraid it was far too much of the former.

She sighed. Perhaps she had been too abrupt. They were going to have to work together for the next little while and she owed him at least an apology. Her eyes closed for a moment before she gritted her teeth in determination. She would try again.

"I'm sorry about that," she offered. "I really am just a small-town girl. This is my home and I can't pretend to be somebody else." It didn't come out exactly the way she'd intended so Jori tried again.

"I'm not the sort of person who has a fling with a visiting doctor if the opportunity arises. I'm too old-fashioned, I guess." Jori turned to glance at his stern profile. He still looked mad.

"I want all the things you see in this little town—a family, friends and a neighborhood where you can trust your next-door neighbor." She stopped for a minute and then lest he still didn't get it, blurted out, "The bottom line is, I don't sleep around."

"Who asked you to?" His voice was low and disgruntled. "All I recall doing was kissing you." He turned then to stare straight into her eyes. "Maybe *Trace*—" he laid heavy emphasis on the word "—was the kind of person who expected that, but I'm not him. And why do you immediately assume I'm looking for some kind of a fling? I wish you'd stop treating me as if I have some terminal disease that I'll inflict on this town."

"I don't do that," she gasped in an aggrieved tone.

"Yes, you do," he asserted grimly. "Look, Jori, I like you. You're smart and funny and I'd like to get to know you better." He grinned at her suddenly and Jori let out the lungful of air she held.

"I'm perfectly willing to take it slow while we get to know one another. I want to know things about you like your favorite food, what you eat when you pig out, what countries you modeled in, how you got started." Chris reached out and stroked his hand down the long strands of her shiny tresses.

"We'll take it nice and easy. Just don't run away. Trust me, don't be afraid of me." His soft voice soothed her jangled nerves.

The problem was, Jori reflected, she didn't trust anyone who got too close. Not anymore. And especially not after

Trace's desertion. Besides, if he knew the truth about her, Jori wasn't sure Dr. Christopher Davis would want to spend any more effort on getting to know her.

But as she stared into Chris's solemn blue gaze, Jori wondered if perhaps the man upstairs was telling her that it was time to let someone into at least a tiny part of her life.

"Peaches," she told him finally, letting down her guard just the tiniest bit.

Chris looked up from the study he was conducting on her long pink fingernails. "What?" Confusion creased his eyes in perplexity.

"My favorite food—peaches." She smiled at him. "Fresh, ripe and so juicy that it drips down your chin when you bite into it. And I love chocolate."

"Now that wasn't so hard, was it?" his deep voice chided as he smiled at her.

As she sat smiling with him, Jori decided that she wouldn't let herself get too used to him. For her own good. He was a very successful doctor who was just filling in for a friend. When Dan returned, Chris would be gone like the wind. Small towns were not his style; they couldn't be. His work necessitated a city and she had no intention of leaving Mossbank. Perhaps they both needed to remember that.

Jori moved back into her seat and put the Jeep into gear. She drove away from their tiny oasis with resolution. This crazy attraction…no, infatuation…was only temporary. It would pass, she reassured her doubting voice as they drove toward the fairground. It was just temporary.

Chapter Five

"Faith, have you seen Charity? I've been searching for twenty minutes and there's no sign of her anywhere!" Hope's voice echoed the frustration she felt. She grimaced at the dusty marks on her skirt but no amount of brushing would remove them.

Faith swallowed the last of her double fudge bar and swiped one hand across her mouth in the hopes of removing the traces.

"Charity? Oh, she went off with Aubery. They were going to get an ice-cream cone, I think. One of those triple-decker things." Faith's eyes blazed with happiness. "Don't you just love this fair?"

"Aubery Olden? Oh, no! And why are they eating ice cream at this time of the day?" When Faith began to answer, Hope waved her away. "No, never mind. I don't want to know." She puffed out a breath of air in disgust. "And to think I went to all the trouble of arranging for Frank to join us all for supper."

"Frank Bellows?" Faith shook her head. "You know how she feels about him, Hope. Good heavens, we've tried to get the two of them together often enough, but Charity's dead set against the man.''

"I don't understand why. He's a wonderful man and Charity would enjoy him if she'd let herself. She's so stubborn.''

Faith wisely refrained from commenting on others of her acquaintance who possessed the same trait and applied herself instead to dabbing at the chocolate smears on her favorite pink blouse.

"I saw Mirabel earlier,'' she offered as a red herring, smugly happy when Hope's startled glance flew to hers. "She's after our new doctor.''

"Mirabel? But she can't be,'' Hope wailed. "I so wanted Jori to link up with him. She needs someone now that James is in Sunset. She spends far too much time by herself.'' Hope's blond head whirled around as she searched the crowd. "Where do you suppose Mirabel is now?''

Faith nodded at the refreshment tent on the right. "Chatting to your husband,'' she murmured softly. "And she's sitting beside mine!''

"I was just coming over to mention that,'' Charity's voice sputtered from behind them. "Isn't it time you and your husbands had supper? There's the nicest little spot by that hedge over there and I've got a cloth on the table already.''

"Charity, you scared the daylights out of me!'' Hope pressed a hand to her racing heart before frowning down on the older woman. "I wanted to talk to you about supper,'' she said. "I was hoping you'd join us.''

"I might,'' Charity acquiesced.

"Come on, Faith,'' Hope chortled, linking her arm in the other's with a grin. "Let's go rescue Arthur and Harry.''

Ten minutes later they were all seated around the red-painted picnic table, plates of cold cuts and salads in front of them.

"I hope you don't mind," Charity said, buttering her roll carefully. "I've asked Aubery Olden to join us."

"You haven't," Hope gasped, spying the old gent making his way toward them. She glanced over her shoulder. "But I asked Frank Bellows!"

"Oh, piffle!" They all stared at Faith's unhappy face. "I suppose it was a bad idea to invite Howard Steele over, too?"

In the end, the seating arrangements had to be revised. Judge Conroy was most vocal in his distaste at sitting four on a side and finally announced that he was moving to the next table. Hope followed him with a backward glance at Charity, who sat happily amid the three men.

"Why don't you go with them, Faith?" she heard Charity offer. "You and Arthur are squished up there like sardines in a can."

"Why did you move?" Hope whispered angrily as Faith sank onto the seat beside her. "Now we can't hear a word they're saying." She glanced in dismay at the cherubic smile on Charity's round face and sighed. "I just wish you hadn't asked Howard Steele," she muttered in frustration. "He's too young for her." Her face brightened suddenly.

"Ah, hello, Jordanna. Enjoying the fair?"

"It's wonderful," Jori replied, following Hope's glance to the table next door. "Mrs. Flowerday certainly seems to be enjoying herself."

"Yes," Faith grumbled in an unhappy tone as Charity's bright laugh rang out. "She does, doesn't she?"

"I saw you with Dr. Chris," Faith murmured in a low, conspiratorial tone. "You left for a while and I haven't seen him since. Did he have a call?"

Jori felt her heart sink at the curious look in those faded eyes. She pasted on a smile and answered as best she could. "No, Mrs. Johnson. No call. We just left to get out of the heat for a bit. He's around here somewhere." She glanced over her shoulder, as if she were searching for Chris. "I suppose I'd better go find him. We're supposed to have supper together." She waved her hand and moved away before Faith could ask any more questions. "Bye for now."

Chris was deep into a discussion about agricultural practices when Jori found him two hours later. She had deliberately wandered around on her own for a while to give them both some space. After their time at the pond, she needed to regroup, gain perspective.

As she listened to his knowledgeable response on the difficulties with anhydrous ammonia, Jori was forced to smile. It seemed the good doctor knew a lot more about farming than she would have given him credit for. And when he glanced up to grin at her, his sparkling blue eyes negated any progress she might have made in slowing up a racing heartbeat.

"Not a bad looker, is he?" The voice belonged to Amy Grand, Jori's best friend since kindergarten. "You two have something going?" The question was not posed as innocently as Amy's wide green eyes seemed to imply.

"Hi, Amy," Jori greeted her friend. She grinned at Amy's outfit. Blue jeans and T-shirt, again. "We're just friends. I thought a trip to this fair might open his eyes a little."

Amy smirked saucily before she teased, "Seems to me your eyes are wide-open, too, my girl." She swatted Jori lightly. "It's nice to see, for a change. I thought that heart of yours would be frozen forever!"

Jori wished for the hundredth time that her friend's voice was just a trifle less strident. At this rate, the whole town would be speculating about them.

Jori wished an emergency would set off his beeper and relieve her embarrassment. But she'd never backed down from trouble before and she faced Chris bravely now.

"We've got to be going, Amy," she babbled. "Nice seeing you again. Bring Bob over for coffee tomorrow night. Bye."

It wasn't a great exit but it was the best she could do with those glittering navy orbs daring her to ignore him. She tried to make small talk as they moved toward the grill.

"Sorry about that," she murmured. "Amy always says what she thinks."

"Does she always say it so loudly?" he growled. Jori could hear the dismay in his voice.

"Amy didn't mean anything." Jori frowned. "After all, you are new to the area and very good-looking, so…" Realizing what she'd said, Jori slapped a hand over her mouth.

She stopped at the end of the lineup, afraid to meet his gaze, fumbling with her keys. A choking sound made her look up finally. Chris stood behind her trying not to laugh out loud.

"What is so funny?" Jori demanded, hands on her hips.

"You are." He gasped the words out between gulps of laughter. "And thanks for the compliment. I think."

Jori watched him for a few moments and then decided she had gotten off lightly. At least he wasn't mad.

They ate their meal surrounded by a swarm of young people who chatted madly back and forth. There was no need for conversation and not much opportunity if they'd wanted one.

After supper the 4-H youth presented a special routine with their horses marching in formation around the dusty track. Jori sat on the crowded bench with her leg brushing Chris's and tried to concentrate on the patterns that had taken hours of practice to perfect.

"What happens next?" he asked.

Jori tried to control the flutter of nervous awareness that noticed the cowlick on the left side of his head and the way his eyes crinkled at the corners when he smiled.

"There's a talent show now," she whispered back. "Local people who are competing for some of those prizes." She indicated a booth across the way. "The kids have really entered this year because there's a CD player there."

"Are you singing, Jori?" Mrs. Hansen leaned across Chris to ask the question in a voice loud enough to cause several heads to turn.

"No. But I'm supposed to be one of the judges." Jori glanced up at Chris. "I have to move down there." She pointed to where several adults stood around a table placed about twenty feet back from the stage.

"You can come if you want, there are extra chairs. Or you can stay here and I'll meet you after." She waited for him to decide.

"I'll go," he said, inclining his head to the left. "I think I'm a little out of place here." Jori followed his gaze and smirked at the dearth of seniors that had congregated around them on the stands.

"That's one of the best things about a country fair. Everybody fits in," she whispered back.

"I'm judging the singing. You can help if you want. Or leave. It's up to you." She moved down a step.

Her face grew warm as his blue eyes studied her.

He grinned, tightening his hold on her fingers. "I always go home with the woman I came with."

"Well, come on then," she said at last, thrown off by the fatuous grin on his handsome face. "They're ready to start."

"I should tell you that I don't know a thing about singing."

"As a matter of fact, you're tone-deaf," Jori added kindly. She grinned and shook her head at his offended look. "I heard you singing to yourself at the office one day. Totally off-key."

"If my voice is so offensive—" he began indignantly, but Jori just grinned and shushed him.

"The first number is about to come on," she explained.

"You'll like it. Just relax and enjoy it. The *guest judge* is allowed."

Four minutes later, Jori knew he was enjoying himself by the way he clapped for the preschool performers. As the tiny sister and brother tucked their fiddles under their arms and took a bow, Chris cheered enthusiastically. Apparently, the crowd agreed for everyone was on their feet.

Once the group had settled down, the next number came on and gave a rousing version of an intricate square dance number that involved full ruffled skirts with stiff crinolines. There was a fourteen-year-old comedian who poked fun at everyone, a ten-year-old piano whiz and two guitar players who harmonized in a Wild West medley that had every toe in the place tapping out the beat.

"These people are all from around here?" Chris leaned over to ask after the fifth entry. When she nodded, he shook his blond head. "There's a lot of hidden talent in Mossbank."

"Didn't I tell you that?" Jori admonished with a reproving grin. Her eyes widened as a young girl with a cropped haircut and tight blue jeans came onto the stage carrying a set of drums. "I was afraid of this," she whispered.

"What's wrong?" Chris stared at her curiously.

Jori grinned and shook her head. "Wait," she commanded with a grin. "Just wait."

There was a two-second interval between the time the announcement was made and the cacophony of thumping, thudding, clanging noise began. Several times Jori glanced over her shoulder, studying the stupefied look on Chris's face before turning back to her notepad and jotting down something in tiny scribbles.

When the silence finally came, it was deafening. The entire assembled throng sat dazed and paralyzed with shock. Jori nudged Chris in the arm and started clapping loudly. Seconds later others joined in until there was a resounding clamor from all around them. The girl calmly picked up her drums and carried them off the stage, her head held high.

"What is the best thing you can think of to say about that performance, guest judge?" Jori hid her smile as she watched his shocked features rearrange themselves in their normal structure.

Chris's eyes were glazed and unfocused as they stared down at her. Finally his mouth opened and whispered something she had to lean closer to hear.

"That it's over!"

Jori nodded and pretended she was writing something, carefully aware of the scrutiny of the townsfolk.

"Just keep that to yourself," she advised softly. "Another small-town rule is that nobody must be offended by these proceedings. Nobody."

"You mean, 'If I can't say something nice, don't say anything at all'?" Those blue eyes were sparkling and clear as they reprimanded her. "I learned that lesson from my nanny a long time ago," he chided her in an aggrieved tone. "It's just as true in the big city, you know, Jordanna."

A young band was announced then and as they crooned a famous country song about young love, Chris's arm slid along the back of her chair. No doubt it was an innocent move. She just happened to be sitting there, next to him. He didn't mean anything by it. Perhaps he just needed to stretch, Jori told herself. But either way, it felt nice to have that strong arm behind her, sort of protecting her.

It was a strange thought. As if she needed protecting, Jori derided her subconscious. She certainly didn't want him to think she couldn't manage alone! But when his arm stayed there through the next three numbers, Jori couldn't ignore the cared-for feeling it transmitted to her weary heart.

It must be nice to have someone to lean on, she thought,

staring at the young woman who was arranging her micro-phone. Somebody to take over the load once in a while.

Reality intruded. Of course, it wasn't likely that any man would want to take on a woman who was tied to this town. Never mind someone with all the doubts and fears she had.

No, Jori decided. She wasn't the type of woman Chris Davis would normally be interested in. She just happened to be here now. Chris was sure of himself and his path through life. He would never understand the misgivings that gripped her each day when she considered her future.

"This one is really good," Chris murmured in her ear, drawing her out of her self-examination. "She gets my vote."

The young woman with the guitar strummed quietly as she sang, her voice building to a crescendo as she told of her love for a young man who had left to find his fortune, and rejected her because she wouldn't go with him. The words were ach-ingly poignant and Jori couldn't help glancing at Chris, as-sessing his reaction to the song.

There was thunderous applause when the young woman finished. She bowed and then quietly left the stage with many in the audience still clapping.

"She was good, wasn't she?" Chris's voice was full of enthusiasm. "I'd like to hear her again but with a different song. Something lighter."

"I take it you don't believe in love lost," she teased, only half joking.

His eyes were bright and clear as he stared into hers; his voice firm and direct. "I believe that love is a rare and valu-able gift that God gives to humans," he murmured, his hand squeezing her shoulder. "If you find it, and many don't, you need to do everything in your power to nurture it, keep it growing. Nothing should be allowed to come between two people who love each other. Nothing."

Jori tore her gaze away from his only because someone on

the other side was saying something to her and she didn't understand what it was. As if in a trance, she agreed with the other judges that the young woman was indeed the best performer and deserved the CD player. They went through the list of contestants and awarded a prize to each of them, including the raucous drum player.

"You're giving a prize for that...that noise?" Chris demanded in a shocked whisper but his eyes were twinkling in the dusk. "You always play fair, don't you, Jori?"

"I try." She smiled. "There are enough prizes, so why not? It might encourage some future musician." There was more she wanted to say but he hugged her against his big wide chest then and the words got stuck in her throat.

"You're a very special woman, J.J." His lips brushed across her forehead before he set her free and Jori could only hope that it was dark enough that no one in the audience would see.

"J.J.?" She stared up at him in confusion.

"It's my new nickname for you." He grinned. "Makes our friendship more...personal, don't you think?"

Jori wondered if things weren't quite personal enough between them, but he gave her no opportunity to comment, wheeling away to speak to one of the youth gathered nearby. Reluctantly, Jori turned away to converse with the other judges, pushing back the longing his words engendered. How close did he want to be?

After the awards were given out, Chris insisted on another piece of pie and Jori gladly accepted the cup of coffee he purchased for her. Many of the younger children had been taken home now and the grounds were quieter as a senior's group played softly onstage. Here and there a few couples swayed to and fro to the old dance tunes of a bygone era.

"I've got to go back to restaurant eating," Chris murmured, licking his lips appreciatively. He patted his flat stomach with a grin. "I didn't eat nearly as much then." He noted the tiny shiver Jori tried to repress. "Are you cold?"

"A little," she admitted ruefully. "I have my sweater in the Jeep but I'm too lazy to go and get it."

"Do you want to leave?"

"We can't go yet!" She stared at him appalled. "The fireworks will be starting soon."

Chris grinned, flicking a finger against the tip of her nose. "Well, we certainly can't miss *that*," he agreed, a roguish look in his eye.

Jori grinned in reproof.

"Stop making fun of me," she ordered. "I happen to like all these small-town traditions. And nothing, *nothing*," she reiterated firmly, "can compare with *these* particular fireworks."

"Nothing?" Chris teased in a slow and easy tone. "Hmmm. That sounds like a challenge. I never could resist a challenge."

She waited, but when nothing more was forthcoming, Jori got up, tossing her cup into a nearby garbage can. "I guess I'd better get my sweater," she murmured. "I'm getting really cold."

They meandered back to the Jeep, meeting people coming and going along the dimly lit path. Chris obligingly pulled on his jacket when she handed it to him and waited with his back turned while Jori slipped into her jeans beneath her skirt, then she removed her skirt. When she'd pulled on her sweater she sighed.

"Mmm, that's better. I was freezing."

"Why didn't you say so?" Chris murmured, inclining his head. He wrapped his arms around her. "I would have warmed you up."

"Oh." There were a thousand things she wanted to say and nothing at all that seemed appropriate, so Jori simply stood there, his arms around her waist, holding still as his mouth lowered to hers.

His gentle kiss made Jori forget all about the country fair and all the people who might see them together like this. His arms were big and solid, yet gentle as they cradled her, and Jori couldn't move. It felt somehow right to be here with him in the dimness of this rustic setting. When he lifted his head, she blinked several times.

"Do you see stars?" she asked in bewilderment. "Blue and red ones with little tails?"

Chris laughed and moved behind her, turning Jori so that she faced the open field. His arms stayed linked around her waist and she relaxed against him when he murmured in her ear.

"Thanks for the compliment, but I think the real fireworks have begun." His lips brushed her hair gently before his chin rested on the top of her head. "And according to a certain nurse I know, they're pretty spectacular."

They watched in silence as the series of explosions rang across the countryside. One after the other, the small puffs of smoke disappeared as yet another blaze of dazzling, glittering bursts lit up the darkening sky. Jori heard his sigh of appreciation as the grand finale, a glistening, wildly colorful waterfall sprayed its sparkling glory across the thin wires that had been rigged earlier.

She hated to leave the comfort of his arms, but streams of people were flowing out from the fairground and Jori could just imagine the speculation if they found her in the arms of the new doctor.

"And that, Dr. Christopher Davis, is the Silven Stream Fair. It's time to call it a night." She eased away from him and dug in her pocket for her keys.

"Yes, I guess it is. Thank you, Jori. I enjoyed it very much. All of it." His eyes were strangely incandescent in the shad-

ows. The gleam in them made Jori nervous. After unlocking
the door of the Jeep, she climbed in, conscious of his hand
under her arm. When Chris finally got in, Jori couldn't look
at him. Instead she drove carefully back over the winding
road, ignoring his sudden silence, thinking.

As an instructive experience for a man used to the city, this
day had been an unqualified success. But, it seemed that she
had learned a few home truths herself. And one of them bothered her. A lot.

She really liked Chris Davis.

"It was nice of you to take me today, Jori," he murmured
when they arrived at his home. "I guess I can see why some
people want to live here. It must get awfully boring, though.
Good thing the city's not too far away."

It wasn't the best thing he could have said and Jori felt that
irritating flick of dismay at his cavalier words.

"They stay here because their families, friends and neighbors are here and because they can stop and smell the roses
without driving for an hour," she muttered, trying to suppress
her frustration.

"But it's so isolated. You have to drive for ages before you
can dine out properly. It feels like another world!"

"I suppose you mean because we don't expedite people
here like you did in Boston." She emphasized the city sulkily.
"In and out without even knowing your patient's name. Well,
Doctor, in Mossbank, the guy you malign today is the guy
you'll have to do business with tomorrow. You won't find the
chilly impersonality of the city here." She tried to stop them,
but the bitter words flowed out anyway.

"I suppose that's what you liked most about your work in
Boston. You did your thing in the operating room, your patients were gone from your life and you didn't have to think
about them anymore."

"Jori, I didn't mean to imply…"

"Yes, you did," she sputtered. "You meant that you feel stuck here. Well, it's true in a way. You can't just change things by shifting a case to someone else. There's no way to opt out if you don't like Mrs. Newsom's test results. You've got to treat her tomorrow and the day after that until she dies of some horrible disease that no one can cure."

Jori stared at him, trying to remember all the good things about him, but the pain of his words would not abate.

"You can't run away here, Chris. You have to sit and patiently wait until that mom is ready to give birth and whether or not you're ready has nothing to do with it. When she needs you, you'd better be there." She stared at the road and forced herself to speak calmly when all she wanted to do was cry. For what, she wasn't sure.

"If you stay in the rat race long enough, you never take the time to listen, really listen to what your best friend or your sick patient or God is telling you. You scurry away, pretending this or that is more important. And it's not. Nothing is more important than God's voice and lots of times he uses the people in your life to speak."

She barely heard his chilly answer.

"Maybe. But I think hiding out is exactly what you're doing. And sometimes you have to get away from the people in your life in order to carry on." He lunged out of her Jeep and slammed the door before walking around to her side of the vehicle. "Thanks for the day, Jordanna. Good night."

And then he was gone, leaving her to wonder about his words and the obvious pain behind them. He was hurting, although he tried to hide it behind a mask of self-sufficiency. And Jori felt totally unable to cope with it.

"Father, you know what this is about, I don't. Please draw near to Chris tonight. And let him see that you are able to deal with it all, you never grow weary or faint. And please, God, if this thing between us isn't your will, let me know. I'm so mixed up!''

Chris wasn't sure exactly how it happened.

After all, he hadn't really attended a church regularly in years. Except for the odd wedding and funeral. And certainly never one like this. The churches he had known had always seemed such cold, grim places; and once he'd started working, well, shifts being what they were, going to church had been the last thing he'd thought of.

He tried to ignore the voice in his head that snorted he was only here today because of a woman. And yet, here he sat, dressed in a suit and tie, on a polished oak bench, waiting for the service to begin.

It was her fault, of course. Jori Jessop had invited him rather casually one day last week and he'd brushed off the invitation with as much politeness as he could. Not his scene, he'd told her brusquely when the truth was, he didn't want to get any more involved with these people. But when old man Olden had told him Jordanna was singing this morning, Chris had experienced a rapid change of heart.

"Sweet as a bird, Jori is. Sings like one, too. Gonna hear her this Sunday," the old fellow had teased, clearly trying his hand at matchmaking.

"What does she sing?" Chris asked the question before thinking.

But Aubery Olden was nobody's fool and he knew when a fish was on the line. Chris felt like one of those suckers he'd seen the kids catch in the river and he waited impatiently while the old man reeled him in.

"Oh, most 'bout anything she takes a fancy to. Soul, blues, gospel. Jori tries 'em all out sooner or later." As he'd buttoned his shirt the old man's eyes twinkled up into Chris's.

"Church starts at eleven," he'd said softly.

He'd been greeted enthusiastically when he entered, Chris mused. He had also been amazed by the grip of some of the elderly parishioners, particularly Frank Bellows. A surgeon's hands were his most important tool, Chris reflected, flexing his hands carefully and deciding nothing was broken.

"We're glad to have you here with us today," the man had said, a warm smile tilting his straight lips. Frank had the soft empathetic voice one expected of an undertaker and Chris knew he'd be good at comforting the bereaved.

Frank showed him to a seat, and for lack of knowing any different, Chris had taken his place, idly watching the assortment of families that filled the rows in front and beside.

When a drooling toddler crawled under the pew in front of him to gnaw on his shoelaces, Chris picked him up easily. The child was a friendly one and grinned happily as he dribbled over Chris's navy blazer. One lone tooth stood out proudly and the little boy used it effectively when his temporary caregiver foolishly allowed the child to play with his thumb.

The frazzled mother rushed up moments later and smiled her gratitude as she ushered the rest of her children into the bench.

"Thank you so much, Doctor," she whispered. "He just gets away from me so fast these days."

"He's certainly a mover," Chris agreed, noting that the rest of her brood looked happily excited to be at the small church. He felt a pang of envy when the father took his place at the end of the pew beside his wife, completing the family unit.

To the left a group of young adults gathered, chattering madly over the worship music of the organ. He saw no signs of wealth on any of them and yet they smiled and talked freely, obviously content with their world. They belonged here and they knew it.

Even the elderly ladies behind him were discussing something with great animation. He was astounded to hear his name moments later.

"That's Christopher Davis, the new doctor." He recognized the birdlike tones of Mrs. Flowerday.

"Filling in for Dr. Dan and Jessica, isn't he?"

"And working with Jori. Now, wouldn't that be a match made in heaven!"

They twittered and talked among themselves as Chris wriggled uncomfortably at their matchmaking. He disliked being the topic of conversation. He also felt guilty sitting in this holy place and scheming to get another date with the lovely Jori.

Plans for marriage were the last thing on his mind these days, especially since he knew Jori intended to stick it out in good old Mossbank! Anyway, permanent entanglements weren't his style. Not at all.

Chris was flipping through the worn red hymnal when someone slid into the seat beside him. Jori. He felt his heartbeat quicken as his lips twitched involuntarily, unable to stop smiling.

"Good morning," he greeted her, tamping down the rise of excitement he felt.

Jori stared at him for several seconds before replying. He could tell she was surprised. He felt sort of shocked himself. Today Jori Jessop looked like a model. Her waist-length hair was loose and free, cascading down her back like walnut silk washed sparkling clean. She wore a slim fitted suit in some reddish color that gave a lovely glow to her cheeks.

The jacket had short sleeves, baring her slim arms to the summer heat. Tapered in, it ended in a point just below her waist. The straight skirt had a small slit in the front where it stopped demurely just below her knees. She wore gold hoops in her earlobes and a tiny gold locket that dipped into the

V-neck of her jacket. The total effect was one of ultra-French chic and totally suited her slim tall figure.

Her big dark eyes, fringed by those incredible lashes, shone brightly back at him. "Good morning, yourself. And welcome here."

Chris was conscious of a peace and serenity that pervaded the service that followed. Even the squall of a baby in the back, or the muffled whisperings of two fidgeting youths up front didn't disturb him as he joined in singing the old familiar hymns.

When Jori was introduced, he watched as she moved with that smooth long-legged grace to the front. A taped background provided her accompaniment, but Chris didn't notice it much as he listened to her voice soaring through the stillness of the morning. He watched, totally rapt, as she poured emotion and feeling into her words, drawing the congregation along with her. And when she was finished, he was tempted to clap.

"That was beautiful," he whispered when she sat down once more. Jori merely smiled at him and brushed a strand of hair off her face.

It was then he noticed her hand was shaking. Gently, he covered it with his, squeezing her fingers just a little. And there it lay during the entire sermon. Somehow it made him feel a part of her group. As if, at last, he belonged.

The sermon was short but pertinent; a well-placed talk that described the benefits of belonging to the family of God. As he bowed his head and repeated the prayer's simple words, Chris felt a tingle of electricity in his heart. In this, at least, he belonged, he told himself. He was a part of the family of God.

After the benediction, everyone surged toward the doors, pausing to greet friends and extend invitations. Chris followed, amazed by the warm welcome everyone gave him. He'd never been in a church where everyone was so friendly.

"How's your wife, Jason?" That was Frank Bellows, softly questioning the young man who stood holding a squalling two-year-old boy and the hand of a frightened-looking blond girl.

"She's feeling down today, Frank. That chemo's really taking it out of her." The voice was discouraged and Chris knew why. Tracy Forbes was undergoing one of the strongest treatments available. It was no wonder she was ill.

"You got your spraying done, Jason?"

Chris could see the undertaker's white hand on Jason's shoulder, sharing his sorrow.

"No. I haven't had time. It's Tracy that's important now."

"Course it is, son. Of course it is. Still, you've got to look after that fine crop of yours. I haven't anything on for tomorrow. Do you think the kids would like to go for a boat ride?"

Jason Forbes's face turned up in a smile for the first time that Chris had seen. Relief washed across his young face as he grinned happily. "I know they'd like it, wouldn't you, kids?"

Forbes's two-year-old son's face turned up in a happy smile as he stared at the older man. "Fishin'?" he asked hopefully. "Jody fish?"

"Sure you can fish, Jody. You and Casey both." Frank glanced up at their father. "I'll pick them up around nine, then?"

"It's not going to be too much for you, is it, Frank? It's been mighty hot and you know what Dr. Dan said about getting too much sun." Jason peered down at the pale white skin. "You don't want to get heatstroke."

"Don't worry so much, Jason. I've been taking care of

myself for a good long time now. Besides—" Frank beamed "—I might just enlist myself some help."

Chris saw the undertaker's eyes move to where Charity Flowerday stood talking to a tall portly gentleman. Frank's eyes were soft and full of an emotion Chris was loath to identify.

"If she isn't busy with Adam, that is." Frank's voice had dropped to a whisper but Chris heard the dismay in his voice.

"Well then, thank you very much," Jason agreed, pumping his white hand. "Tracy'd be glad of the rest."

"No problem at all. Say, Doc, I'd like to speak to you for a moment, too."

Chris stood where he was, waiting for Frank to approach.

"I was wondering if you might like to go out for dinner one evening?" Frank asked, half-apologetically. "I often eat on my own and it's nice to have someone to talk to."

Chris swiveled his head, trying to keep up with Jori's progress. "I'd like that, Frank. Can I call you?"

"Sure." Frank's gaze narrowed as he watched Chris. "She's beautiful, isn't she?"

"Who?" Chris asked, and then flushed at the look of understanding on the other man's face. "Yes, she is. Unfortunately, she's also as quick as lightning and not too fond of doctors from the city."

Frank laughed and Chris saw his eyes move to Charity once more.

"Yes, I'm familiar with the situation," he agreed. "Somehow they get one picture lodged in their minds and that's all they can see, whether it's reality or not." He turned back to Chris with an uncertain smile. "Maybe we ought to do something about that."

"Yeah. Maybe. Got any ideas?" He watched the older man curiously, noting the sparkle that lit up his grey eyes.

"Not yet. But I'm thinking on it."

"Let me know what you come up with." Chris grinned, shaking his hand. "I'd like to see if it works." Meanwhile, he intended to try some ideas of his own.

Chris waited until Jori was finished speaking to the couple behind them. Then he leaned his head closer to hers, and asked, "Will you have lunch with me, Jori?"

He figured he had given her less opportunity to resist with a crowd of observers around them. He watched as she stared at him, head tipped to one side. When she spoke, it was hesitantly.

"Well, I was going to go for a picnic. You could join me for that, if you like."

"That would be great," Chris replied, thinking about the last time they'd enjoyed nature together.

"There's just one thing you might not like," Jori told him.

"Nonsense." He brushed off her hesitation. "It's perfect weather for a picnic. I'll pick up something and then stop off at your house right after I change. We can choose our spot after that. Okay?"

"Chris, I really don't think…" Jori stared at him, her eyes dark with apprehension.

Someone interrupted them and she was tugged away from him in the sudden movement of people. He mouthed the word *later* at her and she nodded, although her forehead was creased in a frown.

An hour later when he arrived at Jori's, Chris found out the reason for her frown. Not only weren't they to be alone, but she planned to bike there. As in bicycle, a two-wheeled vehicle that one pedaled.

"This is Billy Smith. He's in my Sunday school class and today he memorized all the verses for July. So we're going for a picnic." She glanced at Chris's immaculate clothes. "It's okay, you know. If you don't want to bike, we can drive." Her voice was kindly patronizing and Christopher Davis wanted nothing more than to strut his stuff, especially since that freckle-faced kid was ripping off wheelies around him. If he had to prove himself on a bicycle, so be it.

"Hi, Billy. Congratulations." He glanced down at Jori's superior look. "No way, lady. Then you'll be on about my age. If you want to bike, we'll bike." He surveyed the old green model with dismay. "Although, I must confess, I haven't been on a bicycle in twenty or more years, and this one looks like it hasn't been ridden in two decades."

Gingerly, Chris planted himself on the seat and lifted one leg to the pedal. Jori rode around him.

"Come on, Doc," she cheered, giggling merrily. Even Billy joined in, chortling with glee as Chris wobbled and teetered three feet down the drive.

He caught on to the thing, finally. But there was a good chance the tires wouldn't hold him for long and he reminded himself to fall on the grass and not the gravel. Wobbling crazily, he followed her down a rough track of unpaved road behind her house.

As they pedaled along, Billy started singing at the top of his lungs and Jori chimed in. It was clear they were enjoying the day. Chris began to appreciate the benefits of cycling himself, watching Jori ahead of him.

Seconds later he was flat on his back in a patch of weeds alongside the trail. Jori stood over him giggling, her hand outstretched.

"Come on, I'll help you up." Her laughter rang out in the clear afternoon air as the wind whipped the pigtails of hair she had tied up with yellow ribbons. "What happened, Doc?"

Chris took her hand, deciding it was time for a little retribution, especially since Billy had motored on ahead—far ahead. Tugging slightly, Chris was gratified Jori's graceful body landed on the ground beside him. He turned so that he was lying beside her in the weeds.

"I told you not to call me that." He kept his voice low and menacing. "Now you'll have to pay the price."

Jori was still giggling but she stared up at him as she asked carefully, "And what is the price?"

"This," he murmured and gave her startled mouth a gentle kiss.

"There are certain advantages to bike riding," he told her.

Jori's dark chocolate eyes opened wide. "Such as?" Her voice was innocence personified.

Chris shook his head. "This," he replied, kissing one of her eyelids closed. "And this," he added, kissing her cheek. Before he could kiss her lips again, his stomach grumbled.

Jori jumped slightly at the low rumbling. "What's that? Thunder?" She peered around his shoulder, searching the clouds. "It doesn't look like rain."

Chris sat up, brushing his hands through his hair. Shame-faced, he met her eyes bashfully.

Jori stared at him for a moment before she burst out in a new fit of giggles. Gathering herself, she stood gracefully, brushing down her clothes.

"What are you doing lying around here, dallying?" she demanded, hands on her curvy hips. "Let's move, Doc... man." She had changed the latter only after glancing sideways at him.

"You'd better watch your mouth, miss," Chris advised her. "That's what got us off the track in the first place."

Jori looked at him, frowning, lips pursed. "I don't think it was my mouth you were staring at," she lectured him sternly.

He let her get away with it, standing carefully. Gingerly, Chris mounted the bike once more, intent on keeping his eyes on the road ahead.

"Lead on, Macduff," he urged as his stomach emitted a louder plea for sustenance. Jori, he noticed, suffered no problems from their tumble in the grass. In fact she looked even more beautiful with that flush of pink high on her cheekbones. Her usually candid eyes avoided his as she waited at the side of the road.

"Are you okay, Chris?" He forced himself to look up at her.

"Yeah. But parts of me are more okay than others, if you know what I mean." He patted his hip gently.

Giggling, she rode off, pedaling furiously down the road as if monsters pursued her. Chris heaved a huge sigh and placed his feet on the pedals. He wondered tiredly how far their destination was. Jordanna Jessop and this bucolic country scene wore him out faster than Boston and its eight operating rooms ever had.

In a sunny glade just over the hillside, they found Billy flopped on the ground, chewing a blade of grass.

"You guys sure must be outa shape," he muttered, red faced. "I been here for ages."

"We're older," Chris told him coolly. "We don't like to hurry through life."

Jori raised her eyebrows but said nothing as she spread out their lunch and they hungrily dug in.

"This is a terrible way to eat." Jori laughed as she popped another bite of the fried chicken into her mouth. "Way too much fat." Chris watched her lick her fingers. "But I could force myself to like it."

Billy jumped to his feet. "I'm going fishing. I'll see you later," he said, and took off on his bike.

Chris shook his head when she tentatively offered him the remaining coleslaw and then smirked when she ate what was left. Billy had long since bolted his food and dashed off to check out the trickling brook, so even the last of their shared chocolate bar was hers.

"I don't believe your appetite, J.J. How do you stay so slim?"

"Good genes." She beamed, sprawling on the blanket they had so carefully placed on the ground. "I am stuffed." One long slim hand patted her tummy in satisfaction. Her dark eyes turned toward him, studying his as he sat cross-legged, watching her.

"Actually, I walk a lot. I guess that takes care of most of it. When I was modeling, though, I had to watch every little bite." She sat up and grimaced. "Every ounce counts, we used to say. I decided I'd never eat cottage cheese again."

"Didn't you like modeling?" Chris asked.

"I hated it," she told him starkly. "It's all smoke and mirrors. All anyone cares about is what you look like on the outside," she whispered, playing with the twisted fringe on the blanket. "There are a lot of really bad people in that business but no one sees or cares because on the outside everything looks so perfectly lovely. After a while you start to believe in the hype and you forget who you really are."

Chris watched the sadness swamp her beautiful face. She was lost in past memories. Painful ones, by the look of it.

"What about your fiancé?" he asked softly, not really wanting to know.

"I thought he was special," she told him softly. Her voice ached with sadness. "He turned out to want the same from me that everyone else did. He only wanted what he could see on the surface—the money, the fame. He didn't care about me as a person and because I believed in the lie, I forgot who I was." Jori's eyes met his.

"I let myself trust in those illusory things. I became the person in those pictures. When things altered and my reputation was smeared, I felt as naked as those pictures. As if the real me was exposed and I wasn't anything like the person I'd pretended to be. Trace turned into someone I didn't even know. And then he ran."

Chris could only sit and wait for the calm beauty of the afternoon to wash away the grief he'd just witnessed.

And while he waited, he experienced a feeling of guilt. He had been doing the same thing, he realized. From the start he'd judged Jori by what she looked like. Reality had proven less simple to define. In a few short weeks he had seen that she was gentle and yet fiercely loyal to her priorities, energetic and confident of her future, independent but also curiously attached to this town and its people.

But most of all, Chris thought he could see insecurity beneath all that confidence. She didn't want him to, of that he was sure. But every so often, when she thought no one noticed, Jordanna Jessop the confident, give-as-good-as-you-got woman turned into Jori, the small-town girl. It was a complicated picture.

"Sorry," she murmured after several minutes, clear skin flushed. "Sometimes I get maudlin. You have my permission to give me a swift kick in the keister." Her wide mouth stretched in a grin. "My Granny Grey used to say that."

Chris watched her dark head tip to one side as she studied him. He knew the questions were coming and he dreaded them. How could she possibly understand him when she'd grown up protected in this small, closely knit community.

"How did you get into medicine?" Her coffee-colored eyes sparkled at him. "Did you decide when you were five that your lifelong ambition was to be a doctor, and then scrimped and saved to make it so?" Jori stared at him as if expecting her fairy-tale dream to come true. How little she knew.

"Hardly," Chris snorted, wondering just how much of reality Jori had sampled. In spite of her worldwide exposure and life in the jaded world of modeling, she projected a childish naïveté that Chris had never really appreciated.

Until now.

"I don't think you're really all that interested in my child-hood," he muttered, trying to think of another subject.

"Really, I am." Jori rushed to reassure him, wide eyes sparkling. "Tell me."

Chris stared. She was serious. He'd thought to escape with a smart remark or two but she sat there peering at him, waiting for his answer. He sighed and straightened his shoulders with determination.

"In my family, the eldest son was expected to be a doctor. I grew up knowing that I would become something in medicine. End of story." He'd deliberately cut it short—by about twenty years.

Jori wasn't satisfied. He hadn't expected her to be.

"How large of a family?" Why were her eyes so big and shiny?

"Four children—three girls, one boy." There, perhaps that would satisfy her.

"What did your parents do?"

Apparently not. Sighing he let her have the information.

"My father is a professor of biological sciences at McGill. My mother's a chemist. My sister Anne is with a research institute in Boston, Joan is still working on her physics degree and Jayne has just finished her residency in orthopedics. Should we go?"

"Wow."

It was clearly the only descriptive phrase she could think of. He grimaced. At least it was different from the "That's nice," that women usually offered.

"You must be so proud of them all." Jori's sunny tones brought him back to earth. He scowled.

"Why? I didn't have anything to do with their successes." He was curious about this woman, Chris admitted. She had a strangely odd outlook on life.

"No, but I mean, it must be great to share so much knowledge in one family. Christmastime must be a riot at your house.''

Chris figured he might as well let her have it all. No sense sparing her sensibilities. Somehow, he doubted she'd ever understand.

''My family doesn't celebrate Christmas, or any of the other religious holidays.'' His tone was cool and controlled. ''We never have.''

He knew what she was thinking. What a bunch of cold fish. And Jori was right, they were. He'd always felt the same way about his family. But that didn't mean he liked other people thinking the same thing.

Jori, on the other hand, probably always celebrated Christmas. He could picture her singing the carols, joyously abandoned as she decorated house and yard. He knew she would always have a tree and stockings no matter where she was. Chris was pretty sure Flop would be decorated with a big red bow in honor of the season.

Jori Jessop was everything he wasn't—and a lot of things he wanted. Chris was beginning to realize just what he was missing in his life: a family that was close and involved in each other's lives. People who yelled and hollered at one another and then forgave and forgot. He wanted to be part of a couple who shared everything—a bathroom and a bed, and children whose futures were not planned out years ahead of time. Parents who celebrated each child's arrival for the miracle it was instead of mapping out careers for their progeny.

Chris thought back on the thousands of operations he'd performed over the years. As always, the Martins came to mind. A couple so bedraggled and quiet, they'd been ignored by almost everyone in the hospital. He'd only seen them because he was checking on a postop gall bladder and Mrs. Martin had passed out in the hallway right in front of him.

It was Christmas Eve, he recalled. Mrs. Martin had been in

labor for a number of hours due to the old-fashioned beliefs of a doctor who should have known better. By the time Chris saw her, the woman and child were both in distress.

The cesarean began routinely until she'd begun to hemorrhage. He'd pulled out all the stops to save her. And finally succeeded. Mr. Martin had been overjoyed to see his wife and child alive and relatively healthy. Tears had flowed down his cheeks as he thanked Chris. And when Chris had stopped in to check on the woman Christmas day, they'd invited him to join their celebrations. They had nothing. But they had such love, such joy. They were a family.

"Chris?" The delicate hand was softly tugging at his arm. Chris realized Jori had spoken to him several times.

"What?" His voice came out gruffly and she shrank back. He raked his hand through his hair in frustration, organizing his mind. "Sorry. Did you say something?"

Brown eyes studied him searchingly for several moments. Finally she gave up when he refused to permit her entrance to the dark secrets whirling around inside his head.

"I just wondered if you wanted to leave now."

Chris knew he'd hurt her by refusing to disclose everything. She could probably guess most of it by now anyway. Years of hiding his little-boy wants for a family like the Martins kept him from sharing his pain, however, and he stood immediately.

"Ready when you are." He grinned, forcing a light tone into his voice. Come on, Davis, get with it, he told himself. Get the mask back in place.

She was a good sport, Chris would give her that. She gathered their picnic without a word and stuffed it carelessly into the huge straw bag she carried on the front of her bike. She mounted the old two-wheeler and waited for him.

When he was beside her, she put her hand on his arm, stopping him from going any farther. Her sympathetic eyes met and held his. One hand reached up to push the hair off his forehead.

"If you ever need someone to talk to, someone to listen," she told him quietly, "I'm here." Then Jori called out to Billy and pedaled away down the lane while he stood staring after her.

Chapter Six

"Hi, Dad. How are you?" Jori tugged the thickly padded leather chair a little nearer her father's recliner and patted his hand. "Enjoying the sun?"

James Jessop stared at her, bleary eyed. "Jori?"

She grinned happily, pleased at this evidence that her daily visits were paying off. Her father seemed to recognize her more and more frequently.

"Yes, it's me, Dad. I brought you some pie. Fresh peach." She held out the plate and slipped the plastic wrap off. "Fosters are having their auction today. Do you want to go?"

"Reginald Foster died?" Her father stared at her with disbelief and Jori rushed to correct the error.

"No, Dad. He's moving, remember? Wanted to be nearer Barbra and her girls. In Minneapolis," she added when he continued to stare at her. Maybe it wouldn't be a good idea to remove him from the security of Sunset just yet, Jori considered.

"Oh." James continued to frown for several more minutes before taking the fork Jori offered and cutting off a piece of the pie. "It's good," he said after another mouthful.

"Thanks. I know it's your favorite so I made a couple of them. You let me know and I'll bring some more."

"Apple's my favorite," he told her firmly, pushing the empty plate away. "Always has been. *'A word fitly spoke is like apples of gold in settings of silver.'*"

"But you always said…" Jori stopped, refusing to be drawn. It would only confuse him more.

"Had your snack, have you, James?" Charity Flowerday patted the graying head with a gentle hand. "What was it today?"

But James seemed not to see her. He merely stood and wandered over to the blooming fuchsia plant nearby.

"Oh, dear," Charity murmured, peering down at Jori. "Did I say something wrong? I didn't mean to interrupt, you know."

"Of course you didn't." Jori sighed. "He's just a little confused today."

"Well, we all have those days!" Charity fluffed out the white pleated skirt of her summer dress. "For instance, I thought today was Friday and that I'd meet a friend here."

"It's Thursday," Jori smiled. "And aren't Dad and I friends?"

"Yes, of course, dear." Charity blushed, veering her eyes away from Jori's curious ones. "It's just that I meant a gentleman friend. It's so hard to get any privacy and I thought if we met here we could talk without Faith and Hope butting in."

Jori stared as the elderly woman shuffled her orthopedic shoes back and forth.

"Oh, don't misunderstand me. I love those two girls. We've been through so much together. But I need a little time and space on my own. Without their meddling."

"But you said you were meeting someone," Jori reminded her, frowning. "A man."

If anything, Charity Flowerday's face grew even redder. Her warm brown eyes were shuttered and she looked away from Jori's enquiring gaze.

"I just said that," she admitted at last, her mouth drooping. "I'm so tired of people trying to match me up with someone. Peter was a wonderful husband, but he's gone now and I've accepted that. I don't want anyone else in my life. Not like that. I have more than enough on my plate with Melanie and Mitch expecting." She glanced furtively over her shoulder and then relaxed a little farther into the chair back.

"I know it was silly but I thought if everyone believed I was interested in some mystery man, well…" She blushed again. "You know. They'd leave me alone."

"Yes," Jori whispered softly. "I know. But why didn't you just tell Faith and Hope the truth? I'm sure they'd understand."

Charity snorted. "Have you ever tried to get those two to stop once they've made up their minds?" She shook her head gloomily. "It only makes them determined to fix me up. I don't want that." Her voice was firm.

"It would serve you right if I told them." Jori grinned. "After all the matchmaking stunts you three have pulled on everyone else, it seems only fair."

"I can see how you'd think that," Charity murmured, glancing up warily. "But you're young and beautiful. You have your whole future ahead of you. You should have a husband and children." She stopped, staring off through the windows to the fountain spraying in the courtyard.

"That's all in the past for me. I shared some of the best years of my life with Peter and I wouldn't change that for anything, but that part of my life is over."

"You must have loved him very much," Jori breathed, gazing at the sweet face. "I can understand how it must seem that no one can take his place."

"No one can ever take another person's place," Charity agreed archly. "Each of us has our own personal part in the lives of those around us. I didn't mean that. I meant that I can't start reliving my life now. It's too late." She lifted her twisted hands toward Jori. "Besides, who'd want a worn-out crotchety old woman like me?"

"You're a beautiful woman, Mrs. Flowerday." Jori tried to keep the tears out of her voice. "You've given so much of your time and energy and love to this community. Why, no one even notices your hands, except to comment on how much you do with them!"

"I notice them." Charity's voice was so low Jori had to lean nearer. "I look at them every day and feel embarrassed to see how bent and misshapen they've become. And look at my feet." She held out her legs covered in the thick support hose.

"I was once voted the girl with the shapeliest legs, did you know that?"

Jori shook her head.

"No one does anymore. They've all forgotten that I used to be young and beautiful."

Jori was stunned by the admission and couldn't think of anything to say that wouldn't make the woman feel as if she were trying to compensate. She was desperately searching for the right words when, from behind them, James's voice boomed out.

"Man looks on the outward appearance, but God looks on the heart." He stared down at them vacantly, his eyes unfocused.

"Thank you, James." Charity smiled, patting the hand that sat on the back of her chair. "I've told myself that a hundred times, but somehow it just isn't the same."

She stood slowly and straightened, gathering up her purse with brisk birdlike movements that belied the wrinkle of tension on her forehead. "I'm getting maudlin," she said self-deprecatingly. "I'd better go home."

"You could come with us." The soft smooth tones came from behind them and Jori whirled around to see who was there.

Chris Davis stood grinning beside the smaller, more compact frame of Frank Bellows.

"We're going golfing," Chris announced. "Frank's going to teach me the finer points of the game. Want to come along, you two?"

Jori noted the look of longing in the older man's eyes as they moved over Charity's still figure. What could be better to prove to Charity that she was still a desirable woman than to spend the day with two attractive men? The added bonus of time spent in Chris's company couldn't hurt her either, could it?

"We were just saying we needed some fresh air," Jori murmured, linking her arm in Charity's. "I'm going to take Dad to the auction sale this afternoon, but we could go for a round or two until then. You did say you were free Charity," she reminded the older woman.

"Oh, but, I've never been golfing," Charity blustered, a spot of color on each cheek. "It's a long way around the course, isn't it?" She looked doubtfully at them all.

"Yes, it is rather," Frank agreed quietly. "That's why I always take my cart. Don't get so tired then."

Jori recognized the olive branch for what it was—an attempt to make Charity's physical limitation less obvious and realized that Frank really did want to spend time with Charity, whether she knew it or not.

"That would be great, Frank." Jori grinned. "When shall we go?"

"Why, right away!" Frank stared at Charity, obviously a little stunned by his good luck. "May I?" He held out his arm for Charity and that bemused lady slipped hers through it and walked down the hallway without a backward glance.

"Way to go," Chris cheered in Jori's ear. "He's been trying to get a date with her for ages."

"He has?" Jori stared. "How do you know?"

"He told me. Right after he noticed I was trying to get your attention." Chris slipped her arm through his and encouraged her down the hall. "I guess the Lord's looking out for both of us today."

"Oh." It was all she could think of and as she spotted James sipping his coffee and staring out the window, Jori pulled away. "I have to say goodbye to my dad. I'll be back in a minute."

But if James knew she was there, he gave no sign. His eyes were busy watching the flurry of hummingbirds sipping the red nectar from a bottle on the other side of the glass and he didn't respond to either her hug or kiss.

"Everything okay?" Chris's voice was soft with concern as he waited for her down the hall.

"I guess so. I just can't get used to him not noticing me. It's like he's there one minute and gone the next."

"It is the nature of the disease," Chris reminded her. His voice dropped. "And it probably won't get any better."

"I know." She sighed. "I know. Come on. Charity and Frank are probably waiting for us."

The morning passed in an abundance of laughter as Jori and Charity proved they neither knew nor cared about the difference between chipping and putting. Frank's patience was unending but even he shook his head when Jori whacked a ball off the green and far into the trees and shrubs beyond.

"Why don't we just leave it and you can start at the next hole?" Frank offered in his usual quiet tones. "There are wild roses in there and stinging nettles. You'll be a mess."

"No," Jori refused, determined to give the two seniors a

few moments together. "I'm not wimping out. You and Charity go on ahead. She's much more adept at this game than I. Doc, you'd better come along. In case I need some medical treatment." Jori opened her eyes wide as she stared at Chris, daring him to back out when she had it all planned.

"Oh! Yeah. Sure." He followed behind her and then squeaked out a protest. "Ow! Jori, put that club down off your shoulder. I have a feeling I'm the one who's going to need the medical help."

Jori turned back just once and that was to wink at Frank Bellows as he stood transfixed on the green.

"Go ahead," she called cheerfully. "We'll catch up."

Frank smiled and nodded and she knew he'd gotten the message.

"Jori, how could you possibly have hit that ball away back here? You must have more strength than I thought."

"More brains, too." She dug around in the undergrowth of ferns and shrubs. "Couldn't you see he wanted to be alone with her? And Frank is exactly what Charity needs right now. Ouch!" She rubbed the sore spot on her brow and found his eyes just inches from her own.

"You sure have a hard head," she muttered, unable to tear her gaze away from his. "I think my skull is cracked."

She stared at the flopped-over lock of hair lying across his forehead, feeling his arms slip around her waist as he leaned a little closer, blue eyes sparkling.

"Can I kiss it and make it better?"

His kiss was like coming home, Jori decided hazily. His arms were like soft clouds of welcome closing around her. There was no threat; she didn't feel pressured as she had with Trace. She felt safe and secure and more alive than she had in weeks. And when at last his mouth moved to her neck she felt cherished.

"What kind of medical treatment was that?" she protested halfheartedly, drawing away as the heat rose in her cheeks.

"It's a specialty of mine," he replied slowly. "I've been doing a bit of research into it lately. What do you think? Is it effective?"

"That depends on what you're trying to cure." Jori chuckled.

"I take my profession very seriously, I'll have you know," he began indignantly. "If I can help relieve the pain and suffering of the masses, I'm going to try."

Jori snorted, appreciating his attempt at humor. Things *had* gotten a little too intense.

"Yeah, right. And the side benefits don't hurt too much either, do they?"

He looked affronted as he picked up the ball and guided her out of the brush.

"Are you implying that I'm somehow in this predicament because of the side benefits? My dear woman, you wound me deeply." He tried to brush the patch of burrs off his pant leg and grimaced when they refused to budge. When Jori burst out laughing, he frowned even harder. "I suppose you think this is funny?"

"I don't know what you mean," she sputtered, walking beside him with a smug air. "I merely came along for a lovely game of golf, out in the fresh air." Her eyes widened when he grasped the club out of her hand with a loud burst of laughter. "What?"

"We're going that way, remember?" He pointed down the fairway in the opposite direction.

"Oh." She peered across the elegant lawns. "Of course," she muttered as if she knew exactly what she was doing.

"Of course," he repeated seriously. But there was an impish glint in those innocent baby blues.

They finally found Charity and Frank on the restaurant

patio sipping glasses of iced tea. The two were deep into some heated discussion that stopped short when Jori approached the table. Charity's eyes widened.

"Oh, my word! Jori, dear. Are you all right?" She brushed gently at the twigs and dried leaves caught in Jori's untidy hair. "What happened? Did you have a nice game, dear?"

Jori was about to explain when Chris flopped down beside her, his teeth flashing in the bright sunlight.

"She had a lousy game. She's the worst player I've ever seen," he muttered in frustration. One hand brushed the lock of gleaming blond hair off his forehead. The gesture was totally ineffectual. "I've had easier eighteen-hour days in the operating room," he declared, motioning for a waitress.

"You're the one who insisted on chopping away at that ball." She leaned back in her chair and puffed the bangs off her forehead. "It's really quite a silly game," she announced. "Chasing a stupid little ball around in a circle. I much prefer swimming or baseball."

"You only say that because you don't understand it," Chris counseled. "There is a sequence, a pattern, that you have to follow. You can't just go batting balls around the course willy-nilly. I'm sure some of those you hit belonged to other players."

"Oh, well. They can always find another one. There are hundreds of them in the bush." Jori thought he seemed inordinately worried. She shrugged indifferently.

"Is that where you were, dear?" Charity's voice sounded choked. "You seem to have gotten quite dirty."

"It's filthy out there," Jori told her seriously. "And Chris kept making me change sticks. They're all backward anyway."

"They're not backward," Chris protested vigorously. "How was I supposed to know you're left-handed?"

"Oh, my." Frank sighed. "If I'd only known. I have a set

in my garage that has been there for ages. Ever since my daughter left home. She was left-handed.''

Jori swallowed her mouthful of tea, shaking her head in disgust. "I don't understand why you need a set,'' she argued. "One stick works as well as the next to bat with.''

"Oh, so that's what you were doing,'' Chris groaned, shaking his head in disgust. "Batting!''

"He did that the whole time,'' Jori told the other two self-righteously. "And then when I got a home run, he was all stuffy and rude.''

"A home run?'' Charity inquired, a tiny smile flickering at the edge of her mouth.

"She means a hole in one,'' Chris explained, raising his eyebrows at Jori. "Although if you were batting all morning, I suppose technically it was a home rum.''

"I got it on the fifth hole, too,'' Jori exclaimed, ignoring his sour tone. "One of the guys there told me that he's never seen it done before.''

"The fifth?'' Frank frowned. "But that's a really tough one. How in the world did you do it?''

"Don't ask,'' Chris ordered but Jori ignored him and launched into her personal technique, slapping at the dust on her shorts as she did.

"And so the thing just flew down the hole. I didn't realize someone else was making the shot and when I jumped up and down like that, I guess I distracted him. He sure was cranky.'' She ignored Chris's snort of disgust and glanced at her watch. "Good grief, I've got to get home and change if I'm going to that auction.''

"I was thinking of going myself,'' Frank murmured. He glanced at Charity and then clearly took his courage in both hands. "Would you like to go, too, Charity? We could have a little lunch here before we head over there.''

To Jori's surprise, the older woman readily agreed. "I'd

love some lunch. They have the loveliest deep-fried shrimp here. You know, all that exercise has made me quite hungry!''

Jori took a quick second look, but when it seemed that Charity was indeed serious about staying, she got up from her chair and shuffled toward the door. ''Thanks for the game. See you at the auction.''

''Now that went pretty well, I thought.'' Chris's fingers on her back propelled her forward.

''What?'' She peered up at him curiously.

''Those two.'' He jerked his head to one side, indicating the senior couple now busily engaged in a discussion. ''I knew if he could only get her to sit down and talk, she'd like him. Frank's one of the most interesting men I know.''

Jori strode down the street beside him. ''I hope that Charity thinks so, too. She's really lonely right now and Frank might be just what she needs.''

''A single man, you mean,'' he derided.

''Nope. Somebody to talk to. She won't come out and say it, but I think Charity is really feeling left out now that Faith and Hope are busy with their husbands. Apparently now they've even started trying to find someone for her and Charity feels that no man would want to be seen with her because of her arthritis.''

Chris had one comment and he made it just under his breath. Even so, Jori heard him.

''Women!''

''Well, thanks for walking me home,'' she said when they reached her front gate. ''I've got to go and change before I pick up Dad.''

''I'll wait.''

''You're going, too?'' She peered at him through the tangle of hair that had blown across her face. ''Why?''

''Because I've never been to an auction before,'' he blurted out, eyes daring her to comment. ''Why are you going?''

"I'm not really fond of auction sales," she told him, opening the front door and inviting him to sit down with a sweep of her hand. "Especially when it's the Fosters'."

She watched him sprawl in her father's recliner and grinned. Chris Davis overshot the thing by a good foot, his legs dangling out beyond the chair.

"What's so terrible about an auction sale—besides all the junk, I mean?" Chris watched her face close up.

"Auction sales are awful because they always mean we've lost another member of the community. Either through death or because they've moved. And I don't want Mossbank to change," she told him passionately. Her face colored and she glanced away, self-consciously twirling the ends of her hair.

"Reginald Foster saved my life," she told him shortly. "Once when I was ten and then again later when I came home. I hate to think of him moving away from Mossbank. He's been a part of my life for so long." Jolting herself out of her thoughts, Jori turned and started up the stairs. "I'll just be a couple of minutes."

Chris stared at her disappearing figure, wondering at her curious words. This Foster man had saved her life? How?

Jori didn't bring up the subject again and Chris couldn't think of a way to introduce it into the conversation so he let it lapse while they drove to the nursing home. James Jessop was dressed and ready to go.

"Don't understand why Reg thinks he has to leave," he grumbled, fastening his seat belt. "He's the only fellow I know who can fix a piece of furniture so it stays fixed."

"I'm going to miss him, too, Dad," Jori murmured. Chris saw the glint of a tear at the corner of her eye but wisely refrained from commenting on it.

They wandered through the various items set out for auction, pausing now and then as James exclaimed over some tool or another.

"Don't you just love Reg's house?" Jori stared up at the stone walls with the creeping ivy. "It's so solid. It always makes me think of God's love—safe, secure. You can trust it to hold up."

"It doesn't need a bit of work, either," James announced prosaically. "The windows have been replaced. And the doors are all new and solid." He slapped a brick planter with one hand and grinned. "It's as strong as a rock." He turned to Chris. "Jori used to play out there on that lawn. Reg's wife, Gena, would bring her tea for her dolls and they'd pick lilacs and daisies and bring home beautiful bouquets."

"Yes." Jori smiled at her dad. "I love this flower garden. I lugged home all the flowers I could to brighten up the house when Mom was sick. We never had enough room for all these hedges and stuff."

As she trailed past the honeysuckle, Chris watched her delicate nose thin while she breathed in the scent. Seconds later she was bent over a huge yellow rose, cradling it tenderly between her palms.

"And the roses. Aren't they fantastic? I can never get enough roses."

James winked at Chris. "There was a time when she thought dandelions were just fine." The older man chuckled "It was a lot cheaper to buy those by the tons, I can tell you."

"It does look a lot like a family home," Chris murmured, running his hand over the redwood picnic table and chairs as he remembered his own childhood home. Stiff and formal, it hadn't beckoned like this one did.

"If you close your eyes, you can almost hear the kids rolling in the grass," Jori whispered, her thoughts meshing with his. "Up there in that maple is the most wonderful tree house. Or it used to be. We slept out here on those hot summer nights. I can still hear the crickets."

"It's the kind of home that needs a family," James interrupted, bringing them back to the present. "No wonder Reg wants to move—he must be lonely without Gena."

"Yes, I miss her every day, James. But time goes on and I want to be near my grandchildren." The two old friends slapped each other on the back, laughing and teasing as if time stood still.

"Come on inside," Reg invited. "I've just made some blackberry tea."

As they went inside, Chris watched Jori's bright eyes move to and fro as if searching for something. Moments later he found out what it was.

"Mags is gone, sweetie," Reg murmured softly, his hand brushing over the soft waterfall of Jori's hair. "She was a terrific dog but she just couldn't take the cold winters anymore, I guess."

"Oh." Chris saw the tears form in her eyes. "I guess it all changes, doesn't it?" she whispered to Reg.

"Yes, everything does," he admitted sadly. Then his face lit up with a huge grin. "Even you," he teased, tweaking her nose. "I can't even see the scar."

"What scar?" Chris took his place at the wrought iron table on the patio and accepted the cup of tea he was passed. Reg and James sat peering at Jori, lost in memories of long ago. "Did you hurt yourself or something?"

"Or something," she admitted breathlessly, jumping up from the table. "I'm going to go look around, Dad. You guys can talk about male stuff." With a grin and a toss of her glossy head, she was through the door.

Chris glanced from one man to the other, trying to assess the situation.

"She's never forgotten what you did for her, Reg." James Jessop's voice was filled with something Chris couldn't define. "I doubt if she ever will. I think she's finding it hard to see you go."

"It was a long time ago, James. I did what anyone would have done. It was nothing."

"It was everything," the older man corrected, leaning forward earnestly. "It was her life, her future."

Reg smiled. "Let's talk about happier times."

As they began to rag each other about the biggest trout ever caught, Chris excused himself and went outside. There was something here he didn't understand. And he thought he needed to if he was to comprehend what made Jordanna Jessop so determined to stay in this little town.

"Do you collect china?" His voice was dryly sardonic as he watched her finger the mismatched teacups and saucers. "Is that why you're so determined to stay here forevermore?"

"I never said forevermore," she muttered, flushing at his intense scrutiny. "And I do owe these people a huge debt. They saved my life."

"How?" Finally he would hear the truth behind her reasons for wanting to bury herself in this little town of nobodies.

"Oh, it was a long time ago. When I was little." When he didn't look away she sighed and continued. "I was ten and my friend and I were playing on her farm. There was a stack of newly cut hay and we would jump off the barn roof and into that stack." Her eyes closed, long lashes dark on her fair skin.

"I can still smell the perfume of that fresh hay," she murmured. "Even after all these years."

Chris stood, waiting for her to continue.

"I was a tomboy, kind of a daredevil, I guess. I went a little farther up the roof each time. The last time I went as far as I could and took a flying leap into the haystack. Unfortunately, I missed the hay."

He sucked in his breath at the thought and clinically searched her limbs for some damage he hadn't previously noted.

"What happened?"

"Oh, I guess I bounced off some bales and onto the edge of the cultivator that was nearby. Apparently I cut my head open. I woke up four days later in Minneapolis with my head shaved. Boy, was I mad."

Chris sighed in relief. A few stitches, that was all. Nothing serious.

"They told me that when I hit my head, I'd injured something in my brain that required immediate surgery. The doctor who could operate happened to be in Minneapolis at a convention. He agreed to stay there if they'd fly me in immediately." She shrugged. "He operated and I was fine. End of story."

"I don't think so." Chris drew his eyebrows together. "You haven't said anything about what makes you so indebted to the people of Mossbank."

She was silent for a long time before she replied.

"Reg set up a fund and got everybody to chip in to pay for the surgery and my hospital stay," she told him. "Reg even donated his own blood. My dad was out of work and my mother was sick and we didn't have any insurance left and he was so helpful." Her slim arms squeezed tightly around herself in a defensive gesture learned long ago.

"That's certainly the mark of a good friend," he murmured quietly.

"They did the same thing when my mother died. For months these friends—" her arm waved to the groups of people now browsing the sale area "—made sure that we had a hot meal every night. They cleaned house, washed my clothes and helped me with my homework until my dad could get back on his feet." Her eyes sparkled and shimmered at him, the depths of her feelings obvious.

"I owe them. A lot. It's a debt I can never repay but I intend to try."

The auction was beginning and everyone was moving toward that area. Chris decided to let her go for now. He'd find out more later, he told himself. A lot more.

Chapter Seven

It was one of those days—those crazy mixed-up days when everything happened at the same time. Jori pushed the damp wispy tendrils that had worked free of her topknot off her overheated face and decided to go with the flow. What else was there to do?

First the air conditioner had given out.

"Stands to reason," she muttered to herself, checking the stack of files laid ready for afternoon clinic. "It is the hottest day of the year, after all."

Grimacing, she plucked the sticky nylon uniform from her stomach. It had to be the nylon one, because her washer had died last night in the middle of a load, leaving black grease spots spattered over everything. Nestled at the bottom was, naturally, her coolest cotton outfit.

Then, of course, there was the chicken pox epidemic. Jori vowed every kid in town had it, and all at the same time. And of course, every mother wanted her child checked when the poor little things only wanted to be home, with as little as possible touching their very itchy skin.

Which, for some reason, made her think of Chris. The prob-

lem was that his itches were buried deep inside and he wasn't
letting anyone scratch them, least of all her. With a brisk
shake of her head, Jori dislodged the fanciful thought and
forced herself to concentrate on matters at hand, checking to
make sure the kits were ready.

"Let's see, we've got a throat culture, remove a couple of
sutures, at least two physicals." Jori checked the list again.

"Talking to yourself."

"Aaagh," Jori jumped, pressing her hand to her throat.
"Don't do that," she remonstrated with the grinning blond
giant behind her. "I'm getting older daily and my heart isn't
what it was."

Doc Davis just grinned. "It's not actually my specialty,"
he murmured, lifting one eyebrow. "But I can perform certain
resuscitation techniques if you want." The sun caught the
blond stubble on his determined chin as he leaned a little
nearer.

Jori's cheeks flushed a bright pink at the suggestive note
in his voice.

"Doctor!" She checked to be sure no one had heard him.
Thankfully, Glenda was busy arranging her own afternoon
and so paid little attention to them.

Chris burst out laughing at her concern. "I didn't realize
you were so circumspect. I'll be more careful in the future."

"What future?" Jori kept her head bent, concentrating on
the files. That way he wouldn't see the longing in her eyes
for the future they would never have.

But he wouldn't let her get away with it. One strong finger
tipped up her chin so her dark gaze met his laughing blue
ones. He traced the curve of her chin for a moment, his eyes
brimming with mirth.

"Oh, I just meant I'll plan it better so next time I'll be able
to catch you in a consultation room, or something," he told

her, his eyes flashing. Oddly, his skin had flushed a deep red and Jori forced herself to look away.

"Quit flirting, Doctor." Her voice was primly correct. "We have patients to see." Jori snapped the files upright against the counter.

She turned to collect the first appointment of the day, but Chris's hand on her arm stopped any progress she might have made. Jori's round eyes flew to his in surprise. Chris's face was stern with reproof, although his blue velvet eyes caressed her with a sparkle.

"I've warned you several times, J.J. My name is Chris."

"Yes, Doc…I mean Chris." She shook her head and strode away while Chris's chuckles followed her down the hall. You couldn't win with the man.

It was appropriate that chaos chose that precise moment to arrive. He was three and well used to speaking his mind; today was no different. His name was Jonathan Grand and he was Jori's godchild.

"Happy bird-day, Auntie Jori," he crowed, alerting the whole waiting room to her milestone. "How old are you?" He chirped the little chorus to the snickers of the roomful of grinning patients.

"Thank you, darling." Jori accepted his hug with aplomb. "I'm twenty-eight, sweetie." She ruffled his brown curls before returning him to his mother with raised brows. "I will get you for this," she promised, teeth clenched in a grim smile.

Amy Grand dangled one jean-clad leg for Jonathan to bounce on.

"I know." She grinned. "That's why I came bearing gifts." With a wide smile, she handed Jori an envelope. "I know you've been wanting to do this for ages, so go for it. Happy birthday!"

Inside were two tickets for a riverboat cruise down the

beautiful Missouri River just outside of Bismarck, including a sumptuous dinner for two onboard. Jori stared at her friend, eyes glistening, deeply touched by Amy's thoughtfulness.

"Thank you, Amy. I really appreciate this." They hugged to the benevolent smiles of the rest of the room. Then Jori quirked an eyebrow at her friend. "Two tickets?"

Blunt as usual, Amy blurted out, "For you and Dr. Chris, of course."

Jori figured she might have carried it off if she hadn't turned just then to find said doctor beaming at her over the gray filing cabinets. He nodded, grinning like a Cheshire cat.

Jori turned her back on him. Drat Amy! She had been wanting to ride that cruise for ages, but she wasn't thrilled about having her date chosen for her. Maybe...she smiled at Amy kindly.

"Well, thank you for thinking of him, but actually Friday is Dr. Davis's night on call, so I doubt very much that he could..."

"Yes, he can." Chris cut in, beaming fatuously. "It's all arranged. He switched shifts just for your birthday."

Jori groaned inwardly. There was no way out, it seemed, not in front of this crowd. She smiled shakily at the room in general, muttered another thank-you and went back to work.

He was getting too close, and she knew it. She also knew there was no possible future for them together. He would leave Mossbank. And she couldn't. Closing her eyes in frustration, Jori counted to ten. It didn't help.

Neither did the beautiful flowers Granny Jones brought from her garden, or the delicious peach pie Zelda Adams had baked. And it was downright difficult to look at another praline cheesecake from Emma Simms.

But when Aubery Olden arrived with one of the beautiful wooden bowls he had so lovingly created from a burl of cherry tree, Jori was forced to relinquish her bad humor. They were kind and generous people, her friends. How could they know she was highly attracted to someone who would leave in a few weeks? Someone she would probably never see again.

"You're something less than thrilled with this arrangement, right?" Chris's low tones brought her abruptly out of her meandering.

They had been driving for twenty minutes and, other than the perfunctory greetings and a thank-you for the iris bouquet, she had purposely said nothing to him as the miles passed.

"Oh, sorry. I guess I was just thinking," Jori hedged nervously. She plucked at the skirt of her turquoise dress self-consciously.

A lot of thought had gone into her choice of clothes for tonight. Jori had wanted to look special since it was Friday night and the boat would be packed with people celebrating. A tiny voice in her head called her a liar. Sighing, she accepted the fact that she had wanted to knock the socks off of one smugly superior substitute doctor.

And Jori was pretty sure this turquoise chiffon thing did it. He had gulped when his eyes took in her figure swathed in the garment with a cinched waist and matching belt. Yards of filmy sheer fabric billowed out in a full knee-length skirt.

"Have you heard anything from Dan?" His deep voice carried softly above the Bach concerto playing in the background.

Jori turned to look at him, shifting comfortably in the T-bird's low-slung bucket seats. A tendril of hair had escaped her tumbling topknot of curls and she pushed it behind her ear.

"Yes, Jessica sent me a card. Apparently, she's been checked in. If she doesn't deliver within the next few days, they'll do a cesarean. I don't think the baby is doing that well.''

Surprisingly, her voice was normal and Jori relaxed a little deeper into the seat. She prayed daily for her friends and she just had to believe that God wouldn't let them down when it came to the crunch.

"Dan phoned yesterday to ask me if I could stay longer. Apparently a heart repair on the baby is imminent, although I'm not sure Jess realizes that yet." He glanced at her sideways but Jori faced straight ahead, dreading the question she knew she had to ask.

"And can you?"

Chris turned his dark head to stare at her. "What?" he asked, lost for a moment.

"Can you stay longer?" Jori didn't like asking it, but she had to know. In some ways, it would be easier if he left soon. But her heart soared with happiness when he answered.

"Yes, I can stay as long as I'm needed. My time is my own right now." His tone wasn't welcoming but Jori asked anyway.

"Why did you leave Boston when you were doing so well?"

Chris had known the question was coming. He'd expected it because Jori wasn't the type to ignore significant details like that. She'd want to know everything. But he still didn't have his answer ready. And he knew she'd keep at him until he did. He heaved a sigh of capitulation, searching for the right words.

"Aside from helping out Dan, I guess I had my fill of medicine there. It was a huge hospital and the rotations were fairly spread out, but I felt I needed something different. Something more connected to other people. For now."

There—he had spilled his guts. Let her make what she

wanted of it. Knowing Jori, he would bet a tidy sum that she would sense the effort it had cost him to open up.

True to form, she nodded understandingly. "Community, sense of belonging. I think everyone feels it sooner or later." They stopped and parked the car. She linked her arm with his as they stepped onto the waiting boat.

"Well, Doc, here we are." She grinned up at him before moving away to survey the sumptuous dining room with its elegant furnishings.

He tugged her arm gently. "Let's go for a stroll around this tug."

The evening was a balmy one with the sun just setting. Stars twinkled here and there while the lights of the city began to glimmer around them. The gentle motion of the boat was calming and Jori found she was enjoying herself.

In the background, a band began to play old movie tunes. Without much thought they moved into each other's arms and began to sway gently to the music.

"I love this song," Jori murmured as the group segued into "Moon River." She sang along with them for a few bars.

"You have a beautiful voice, J.J. I enjoyed hearing you sing." Chris whispered, the words gently grazing her ear. "And this dress—I don't know if *awesome* quite describes you tonight." He spun her around.

Jori giggled.

"Yeah, I know what you mean." She laughed, leaning back to study him. "You are quite a picture yourself. Especially in that suit." Her dark head tipped back as she studied him. "Yep, sure beats the lab coat."

And that was no lie. His blond good looks were certainly accentuated by the black suit and crisp white shirt Chris wore so comfortably. It was the perfect foil for the blue striped tie that matched the exact azure color of his eyes.

He bowed to thank her just as the maître d' announced

dinner. While they waited for directions to their table, Jori
glanced around once more. There were a lot of men in the
room but she seriously doubted that one of them could hold
a candle to Chris. And when her heart repeated that silly little
pitter-patter as his arm moved around her waist, Jori made
her decision.

She'd enjoy tonight because she doubted there would be
another one. Chris would be gone from her life soon and it
wasn't likely that she would ever see him again.

Once she made that decision, it was easy to enjoy, even
savor, every moment of their time together. They both chose
the chef's special for the evening and while they waited, Chris
told silly jokes.

"Why didn't the chicken cross the road?"

Jori groaned but he insisted she guess.

"Because she didn't want to get to the other side."

Chris's mouth stretched in a wide grin. "Wrong."

She sat waiting, but Chris just grinned at her. Jori sighed.
He was like a big kid himself.

"Okay, I'll bite. Why didn't the chicken cross the road?"
Jori just knew she would regret this.

"Because there was a stop sign." His blue eyes twinkled.
"Guess who told me that?"

"Jennifer," Jori guessed, naming a young lady who was a
glutton for joke books.

"Tommy Banks." Chris chortled just remembering the
young boy. "And when I asked him what his favorite book
was, he told me he really enjoyed *Parents* magazine because
then he could keep up with what the adults had planned."

Jori giggled at the picture Chris painted of the freckled little
boy whose precocious attitude she had experienced more than
once.

They had barely set their salad forks down when the ribs
arrived, redolent with oregano, garlic and lemon juice. The

baby potatoes were cooked to perfection and the broccoli spears steamed a bright fresh green. They were both hungry and tucked into the delicious meal with relish. When she could eat no more, Jori leaned back in her chair, replete with the fine meal they had enjoyed.

"This is so wonderful." She sighed, gazing out the windows as the sun colored everything in a rosy glow. "I'm going to have to thank Amy appropriately for this wonderful gesture." She glanced at Chris suddenly.

"And you, too." She blushed. "It was really kind of you to rearrange your schedule this way."

"This is good, but I think your roast beef dinner was better." He rendered his verdict with a haughty tilt of his arched brow. Then he spoiled it by grinning. "And you are very welcome."

During the meal they chatted about Mossbank and its people. Jori was surprised to hear how much Chris had learned about each of his patients in the short time he had been in the town.

"By the way," she asked slyly, "what did you do with the rest of your cheesecakes. Did you really freeze them all?" Actually the problem had been bothering her for days.

Jori giggled as he groaned in dismay. But when a flush of red coursed over his face, she became concerned. She would not have her friends hurt by his insensitive attitude.

"Oh, no!" she moaned, anticipating the worst. "What did you do? Tell me."

His blue eyes met hers, tiny points of light twinkling deep within.

"I wanted to save something for Dan and Jessica. So, I cut one piece from each one and froze it with the appropriate name attached. Then I phoned that kids camp out at Minotka Beach." He grinned. "When I explained my situation to them, they agreed to take the rest off my hands." He held his hands palm up. "*Et, voilà!* It's gone!"

Jori breathed a sigh of relief. Then a thought crossed her mind. "How long ago was this?" she demanded.

Chris stared at her strangely. "Last week. Why?"

"I wondered why we had so many indigestion cases from them." She teased him, beaming with mirth. "Marta, the director, forgot to tell me about the cheesecake."

Jori burst out laughing at the look of chagrin on his face. It was clear that the good doctor had not connected the arrival of his dubious gift with the stomach cramps and other assorted maladies experienced by several of the campers.

Holding up his hand, Chris licked his forefinger and made a number one in the air.

"One for you," he conceded in a grumpy voice that only made Jori's grin widen.

She sipped her coffee while they waited for the dessert cart. The room seemed very quiet all at once, but perhaps the band was taking a break.

When the familiar notes of "Happy Birthday" were played, however, Jori sat straight in her chair. He wouldn't...he couldn't...could he?

It appeared that he had!

Two waiters carried out a huge cake decorated with fat pink roses. As they moved, the two men sang to the cheerful clapping of the other diners.

Happy Birthday, Jori lay scripted in delicate pink lettering across the glistening white icing. Around the edge glowed a ring of pink-striped candles. Jori would have covered her face but Chris reached out to grasp her hand just then, holding it on top of the table for all the world to see.

The song ended as the cake arrived beside their table. Jori was thankful when the band resumed their musical selections.

Her cheeks felt as though they were on fire, but she kept her chin up and met Chris's glance head-on.

"I wish you a very happy birthday, Jori," he said quietly, and then pressed a delicate kiss to the inside of her wrist before allowing her hand to move away.

"Thank you," she murmured, unable to get anything else out. The whole week had been a chain of one surprise after another, but this took the cake, Jori mused. Then laughed. Hah, a pun!

Chris looked at her uncertainly, his eyes narrowed in speculation.

"She overdid it, didn't she?" His voice was quietly sympathetic. Jori stared at him.

"You mean Amy arranged for this?" She motioned toward the monstrous cake. When he nodded, she groaned and laid her forehead on her palm. "I should have known."

"Yes, you should have," Chris's low tones were reproving. "Not my style at all." He stuck out a finger and dipped it into the fluffy white frosting before popping it into his mouth. "Mmm, not bad, though," he told her, grinning.

"What do you mean, not your style?" Jori strove to keep her voice down. "This is exactly like something you would do, Christopher Davis." She had been sure of that once, but now Jori reconsidered.

"Uh-uh. I'm much more subtle."

Jori searched his face. "Yes, you and a steamroller," she mocked. He sat staring at her, perplexed by her attitude. It was clear that the idea had never crossed his mind and Jori felt guilty. "What is your style, then?" she asked, half-afraid of his answer.

His forefinger beckoned her closer. She leaned across to hear his conspiratorial whisper. "I'll show you later."

Dumbfounded, Jori sat wide-eyed and staring until Chris asked for some cake. She cut him a huge piece and a smaller one for herself, going through the motions automatically while she found herself wondering about "later."

They moved outside and Jori sipped her coffee, loath to break into the charming stillness that had fallen. When Chris moved, Jori jerked out of her dreamworld to find him facing her on the narrow bench.

"This is for you," he told her, holding out a beautifully wrapped parcel held together with a tiny bit of silver ribbon. "A very happy birthday, Jori," he offered.

"You didn't need to do this," she murmured, accepting it. "You've done more than enough tonight." Her dark eyes searched his wide blue ones for answers, but got lost studying the tiny smile that turned up the corner of his mouth.

Oh so slowly, Jori slid off the ribbon and the pretty iridescent paper. Inside, a slim black box nestled in white tissue. Holding her breath, Jori slipped off the lid to find a delicate gold chain with a tiny boat attached snuggled into a puff of white cotton. A card read, "To Jori on her twenty-eighth. Chris."

"It's beautiful," she breathed, lifting the tiny weight in her palm. "So delicate and fine. Thank you very much." As she lifted her head, Jori found Chris's eyes much nearer than she expected. She pressed a kiss to his cheek, mere inches from his mouth.

"You're welcome," he murmured before turning his head to meet her lips with his own. It was a questioning kiss. Slowly, tentatively his lips touched hers as if evaluating her response while he waited for her answer.

When she returned his caress, he drew her closer. Jori raised her arms and wrapped them around his neck, happy to oblige his unspoken request.

"Is he the one, Lord?" she prayed silently.

"Jori?" His hands slowed then stopped their delicate caress. His lips pressed softly against the side of her mouth before he pulled gently back, his big hands cupping her face as he stared into her eyes.

"I think we had better go dance," he muttered, closing his gleaming blue eyes for a moment. They popped open a second later when Jori tugged on his hand.

In her palm she held the tiny necklace.

"First, would you put this on for me?" she asked quietly, turning around.

As Chris fumbled with the clasp, Jori drew the wispy tendrils of hair off her neck to give him free access. It seemed to take forever, but finally he turned her around, strong fingers pressing into her waist.

In a trance Jori moved into his arms and allowed him to lead her effortlessly onto the polished dance floor that occupied the upper deck. She swayed to the dreamy music, lost in the feel of his arms around her. She was falling for him. Hard. And the landing, when he left, would be more painful than anything she'd yet endured.

This was wonderful, Chris decided, breathing in her fragrance. Jori Jessop was like quicksilver—strong and supple, gorgeous and ethereal.

But Jori was not his type, he acknowledged grimly in another part of his mind. She was a small-town girl who liked it that way. Her life revolved around her community and she wasn't the type to turn her back on it all for a thirty-six-year-old doctor who had little to offer in terms of stability and even less when it came to family, home and hearth.

Frustrated, Chris glared at his watch. Suddenly he wished the boat would dock so they could get home before he did something really stupid—like tell her his feelings.

Just then Chris felt Jori burrow closer against him and, ignoring his better judgment, he wrapped his arms more tightly around her.

Best make hay while the sun shines, he smiled, thinking of

Aubery Olden. The old coot had a lot of sense under all that grime. Perhaps he should listen up. Chris dropped his chin on the top of Jori's piled-up hair. As the faint whisper of her perfume drifted to his nostrils he decided to have another talk with the old fellow. Possibly, Chris considered, he could learn a little something.

"The band is shutting down." Jori's voice was husky, dreamlike. Chris understood that feeling completely.

"I think we have time for a last cup of coffee before we leave this boat." He grasped her hand in his and tugged her over to a table.

Jori sat across from him, staring off into space. "I love this place," she murmured, looking back over her shoulder to the twinkling lights of Bismarck at night.

"Do you come here often?" Chris asked, trying for a neutral subject.

She tipped her head to one side. It was one of her mannerisms that Chris had noticed early on. When she was thinking of something pleasant from the past, Jori always rested her head on one shoulder and closed her eyes. He waited and sure enough, three seconds later her hand came up to twiddle with a tendril of hair. He grinned knowingly.

"My dad used to bring me to Bismarck each Christmas," she reminisced, a tender smile curving her lips. "We always went to the top floor of Enderby's because they had a huge display of animated Christmas scenes."

Her voice was dreamy with the memories. She blinked her eyes, peering absentmindedly into the night.

"I would plan ahead for weeks, waiting to see the tree displays and hear the carolers that strolled through the store, dressed in English outfits straight from Dickens. And boy, could they sing."

Jori turned toward him eagerly, intent on explaining the

wonders she'd seen. Chris found himself fascinated by the animation that flew across her expressive face.

"It was totally dark up there, with tiny fairy lights hanging all around. Each scene had its own lighting." Her eyes opened wide as she remembered.

"There was always a pond with ice-skaters," she explained. "And Santa and the reindeer, of course." Her long fingers formed a tent as she thought. "Oh, and Frosty usually walked around, handing out candy canes." Her voice was breathless with delight.

"There was a beautiful Nativity scene with the animals all around it." There was a tiny break in her voice, but Jori recovered immediately, continuing her account. "I especially remember the horse and cutters with kids crammed inside, so happy. The sleighs and toboggans slid down little snow hills and there was always the sound of children laughing."

Chris shared her silence for a few minutes and thought how much he had missed. Jori had such wonderful memories, he mused. It would be something for her to pass on to her own children.

She was speaking again, her voice whispery soft with a tinge of sadness. "I loved the family scene. You know, where everyone gathers round the tree as they open their gifts. I always wished there were more people to share our tree with. Dad and I could have used a family."

Her round dark eyes sparkled with tears. Surprised and touched by the loneliness that threaded through her voice, Chris reached out and covered her hand with his. They sat quietly together for a few moments before he broke the silence.

"Do you still go there to see all that?" He liked to think of her now, wandering through the displays, as enchanted as any child there.

"They don't go to that extent with their decorations anymore. But I still think the window displays are fabulous. And on New Year's Eve I go to *The Nutcracker* ballet."

"Oh." His one word spoke volumes and Jori's ready laugh bubbled out.

"I know what you're thinking, but *The Nutcracker* is a very special ballet. Dad and I used to go. We would get all dressed up in our very best, go out for a special dinner and then to the theater. I never fell asleep even though it lasted until well after eleven. And each year Dad would give me a nutcracker doll to remember the year." She grinned. "I have quite a collection now."

"You have some lovely memories, Jori," he told her, half-envious.

'Yes, I do." Her voice wobbled a little, but Chris noticed she recovered quickly. "What sorts of things did your family do together?" she asked politely. "It must have been nice to have sisters." He heard the wistful note in her voice and almost laughed.

"I'm not sure you would have enjoyed it," he told her grimly. "My parents are academics. They tried to do a fair bit of entertaining at Christmas so they could work without interruption through the rest of the year." He grimaced, recalling those stiff occasions.

"There were a lot of very formal, very boring dinners where the discussions were usually scientific." Man, he was getting maudlin, Chris decided. He turned his sardonic grin toward Jori.

"Perhaps that's where I began to learn about surgery," he said with just a tinge of bitterness. "Heaven knows I certainly had enough time to dissect anything that crossed my plate."

It must be the dark, Chris decided. Here he was spilling his guts about the worst times of his life to a woman who had experienced the best. This is not the way to end a romantic evening, Davis, he told himself sourly. Unfortunately, he couldn't think of anything else to say.

After a few minutes Jori changed the subject.

"You know, there's a wonderful folk festival near here. It's held in a park and they have some famous names performing at all different times. It's very informal but it's fun. You should go on your day off."

She turned to smile at him and Chris felt an ache in his heart. He couldn't deny it any longer. As he drove down the highway, he acknowledged the truth. He wanted to love and be loved by this woman. He wanted to raise a family with her and grow old together without feeling as if he'd failed someone. He wanted all the dull boring routine things he'd scorned for so long.

But most of all he wanted Jori Jessop by his side for the rest of his days.

The idea was so overwhelming that Chris struggled to concentrate on the last bit of road ahead. He flicked a quick glance at Jori and smiled. She had fallen asleep. Her dark head snuggled against the seat, she had one hand tucked under her cheek. Beauty and innocence, he mused, staring.

"We're home," Chris whispered, his breath blowing the tiny curls away from her face. The night air wafted in the open door and she unconsciously shivered at the chill.

"Jori," he called a little louder, pressing his hand against her shoulder. No response. Shaking his head, Chris lifted her lax body into his arms, carrying her up the walk to the front door. Flop rushed forward to greet them.

"Down, boy," Chris told him quietly. "The lady is sleeping. Let's not wake her."

She was a soft, gentle weight in his arms. If only… Chris held her tightly against his chest.

He opened the front door and let himself in, shaking his head at the unlocked door. Carefully he eased his way through the darkened house, climbing the stairs to her bedroom. A night-light was burning, barely illuminating the frilly white mound of pillows.

Carefully, gently, he laid her on them, sliding her arms slowly from his neck. Chris watched as she shifted her hips to turn sideways, snuggling into the soft cushions. Her hands moved together to fold prayerlike beneath her cheek as she sighed once before resuming that slow, even breathing. Dark and spidery, her lashes fanned out against her soft cheek.

Slowly, knowing he would regret it later, Chris bent and placed a soft, featherlight kiss against her lips. They were soft as velvet against his.

"Happy birthday, Jori," he murmured, watching to see if she wakened. When she didn't, he straightened and with a last look, turned and left the room.

But as he slowly drove home, Chris knew that the image would not be removed. It was pointless to pretend. Jordanna Jessop was the one woman who could cool this burning discontent in his soul and help him move into the future with confidence. Perhaps with her at his side, he could overcome the regrets of his bleak past and the worries that yawned gapingly in the future.

But he had to remind himself that Jordanna Jessop was not a part of his future. She couldn't be. They were worlds apart.

Chapter Eight

"**H**ope Conroy, I will not entertain that nosy group in my home one more time." Charity glared at the two women standing on her doorstep. "They poked through my china, discussed my 'strange' furniture and felt duty-bound to comment on my choice of flowers. I am not impressed!"

Hope swept in through the door, dodging the older woman with an agility newly found on a tennis court.

"You say that every time they come over, Charity. But the ladies' society has to have somewhere to meet and you know you love to watch them quilt." She sat down on the sofa with a whoosh of relief, swiping one hand across her forehead. "Why don't you tell the truth? What you're really mad about is all the questions they asked about your men friends."

Charity flicked the switch on the air conditioner one notch higher, trying to hide her flushed cheeks.

"So I've had a few friends over for a meal. So what? I'm certainly old enough to entertain whomever I like." Her gnarled hands reluctantly poured out two more cups of tea. It was evident to the other two that she was reluctant to say more.

"A few? There were five men over here on Friday night," Faith gasped, peering across at her friend's flower-festooned buffet. "I suppose those are from your suitors?" Her eyes gaped at the surfeit of roses. "Who brought the yellow ones? I love yellow roses!"

"I don't remember," Charity muttered, flushing an even darker red. "They come as a group and they go as a group; as if they're attached at the hip." A sigh whispered out through her lips as she lifted her aching feet to the leather stool. "It's very trying."

"Trying? How can it be trying to have half a dozen men fawning over you?" Hope shook her head in disgust. "You'd think you'd be happy to have so much attention."

"I do enjoy their company." Charity sounded embarrassed by the admission. "They're all very nice men. But I'm not as young as I once was and sometimes I really enjoy just being alone."

"So? Rest when they're not around. What's the problem?" Hope peered across the dim room, noting the still-closed blinds. At that precise moment the doorbell rang and Hope saw the tiredness that crept over her friend's usually smiling countenance as she shifted awkwardly to her feet.

"The problem, my dear," Charity muttered irritably as she limped toward the door, "is that they're always around. Hello, Harold."

"Oh, Charity!"

"Yes, it's me. I live here, remember?" Charity fidgeted from one foot to the other, glancing over her shoulder to check if her friends were listening. They were. "Did you want something, Harold?" She had to ask it for Harold had apparently forgotten whatever it was he wanted to say.

"Oh. Yes, I did. That is, I was wondering if you're free for dinner tonight. I remembered you had that leftover beef and I thought maybe we could go for a drive after, down by the river. You know, cast a line?"

"I'm sorry, Harold. I'm having some guests over. Two young friends of mine. They're bringing dinner with them so, I'm sorry, but you can understand that I couldn't possibly invite you. If it was me who was making the meal, you know I'd be happy to have you stay."

"No, no! I understand, believe me." Harold shuffled uncomfortably on the doorstep, his straw hat in his hands. "I'll find something at the diner. It's just that I was looking forward to your wonderful cooking." The hangdog look on his face tugged on Charity's tender heart, but she stood firm.

"Perhaps another time," she suggested quietly.

Harold sniffed miserably, nodded and shuffled off down the driveway. It was all Charity could do not to slam the door.

"Of all the nerve," she stormed, flopping into her chair.

"He was just asking you out," Hope murmured consolingly as she handed her the teacup. "Don't get so flustered."

"He was asking to come for dinner," Charity snorted, slapping her hand on her thigh as the phone rang. "And that'll be another one, looking for a free meal or an open ear to listen to another of those long-winded stories about the good old days. Although I'm hanged if I can remember what was so all-fired good about them!" She glared at the phone malevolently.

"I am not answering that thing."

"But, Charity," Faith blurted, her eyes huge, "that's your gift. You've always listened to other people when they tell their troubles. And then you make them feel better. That's your ministry."

"Not anymore." Her voice was firm. "I'm finished listening to other people. They never take my advice anyhow. From now on I'm going to be quiet and listen to myself. And God," she added as an afterthought.

"She's tired," Hope whispered to Faith. "She just needs to rest. I'll get that," she offered when the phone began its shrill peal once more.

Charity leaned back and closed her eyes, shaking her head in despair. How had it come to this? she asked herself. All she'd wanted was a little attention, someone to notice that she wasn't dead yet. And now she had six, count 'em, *six*, suitors all looking for a free meal.

"It was Aubery," Hope told her. "I said you were too tired to see anyone." She grimaced as the phone started again. "I'll deal with this one, too. This place is like a zoo!"

"There's the doorbell!" Faith jumped to her feet. "I'll send whoever it is away, shall I, Charity?" She sounded eager to dispatch whoever was holding the doorbell down.

"Yes, please," Charity called over the noise, shaking her head as she heard Faith's voice reprimanding her visitors. Curious to know who was there, she hid around the corner where she had a good view of her entry.

"Get your shoulder off that doorbell, Hank Dobbins," Faith ordered. "Do you think the whole world is deaf?"

"Eh?" Hank frowned as he stared at her. "Where's Charity? I brung some bread for supper." He thrust a loaf of semi-flattened white bread at Faith, trying to edge past her. "You say something?"

"Turn your hearing aid on," Faith bellowed, glaring at him and pointing to his ear. "I don't know why you bought the thing when it's always turned off!"

"So's I could avoid all the caterwauling you women like to do," Hank told her frankly. "And stop yelling. It's turned on."

"Good. And I don't caterwaul so you can just listen to what I have to say, Hank Dobbins, and don't go trying to ignore me."

Faith didn't budge, standing squarely in the door frame.

Short of physically moving her, Charity couldn't see how Hank could get in. She smiled at the scene.

"I didn't come to see you," the old gent informed her with some asperity. "I come to see Charity. To have dinner with her."

"Charity asked me to tell you that she's busy tonight. And tomorrow night." Faith handed back the bread. "So you'd better get on home and butter a slice of this for supper."

"It's that sneaky Tim Carruthers, isn't it?" The old man fumed. "I mighta known he'd try to budge in and get another free meal. Well, he can jest think again! Tim Carruthers, you git out here!" His voice rose as he called out a challenge.

"I am out here, Hank," an amused voice announced behind his back. "If you'd get some batteries for that hearing aid, you'd have heard me coming up the path."

"I got lots of batteries, an' I can hear just fine!" Hank wheeled around and held up his fists. "I'm the one who should be havin' dinner with Miz Flowerday t'night," he announced clearly. "You had yer turn t'other night. So git outta here."

"Tonight's my turn, you silly old coot! You were here last night." Tim shook his head in disgust. "Go home and eat the supper Esther Sue left."

"My daughter's a real fine cook but Esther Sue hasn't got a patch on Miz Charity." Hank licked his lips in anticipation.

"I'm afraid you'll both have to go home," Faith announced firmly. "Charity has other plans for this evening."

"No, she doesn't." Tim edged his way past Hank and stepped up beside Faith. "I made a deal with Aubery for tonight. Cost me plenty, too."

"Are you telling me that you paid someone to stay away so that you could have dinner with Charity tonight?" Faith stared. "But that's ridiculous!"

"I just promised him I wouldn't come to the box social on

Friday so he could dance with Myrtle Bigelow. And he gets half of my potato crop. I planted way too much anyhow."

Inside the house, Charity shook her head at Hope's furious gasp of outrage. She placed one finger across her lips and they both listened to Faith's disgusted response.

"Piffle!"

"Eh?" That was Hank, fiddling with his hearing aid again. "What did you say, woman?"

"I said *piffle!* On the lot of you. Now get going and leave Charity alone for a while!" She turned to go inside but Tim Carruthers was standing there. "Well?"

"But what about dinner? I've been waiting all day to taste one of her special dishes. It wouldn't be fair to make me..."

"Charity is having dinner with someone else tonight. Now away you go—the both of you!" Faith whirled inside and slammed the door behind her in a snort of disgust.

"That's wood swearing," Hope reminded her, glancing at the solid oak door. "It's just as bad as actually saying the words."

"Maybe. But it's a lot better than knocking those two gray heads together! Honestly!" She stormed into the living room and began gathering up the tea things. "Now what?" She shot the pealing telephone a most venomous look. "Who's left, for Pete's sake?"

"It's Jordanna," Hope interrupted. "She wants to know if this is a good time."

"Yes, it is." Charity sank back into her chair with a sigh of relief and closed her eyes. They opened a moment later. "That leaves Frank Bellows," she told Faith wearily. "Let's hope he's busy with the church board tonight." Her ears picked up Hope's soft voice.

"She's really tired, Jori. The phone's been ringing off the hook and the doorbell's been going nonstop. Can you see if

Dr. Chris would come? It mightn't hurt for him to have a look at her. You say he's on the way? Oh, thank you, dear. Bye.''

"I don't need a doctor, Hope Conroy." Charity's tone was not friendly. "I need some breathing space."

"Which you will get. I'm sure Jori and the doctor can help you. It's obvious something has to be done." She grasped her purse as the doorbell rang again. "If that's another male suitor of yours, I'm going to set him straight."

"Well, I am a male," Chris said laughing. "And I can always use some good advice. What's the problem, ladies?"

And the three seniors launched into Charity's predicament, one interrupting the other until the whole story was laid out.

"I can't imagine what I can do," he told them. "But I'll give it some thought. Okay?"

"Is what okay?" Jori stood in the doorway frowning. "Do any of you know that there are two red-faced men arguing outside the gate? What is going on around here?"

The fearsome threesome launched into new explanations.

"I don't know just what it is that I could do," Chris told them. "I mean, I'm new here and so far I've stepped on more than my share of toes. I take it that you don't want anyone's feelings hurt too badly?" He glanced from one to the other of them, pulling out his cell phone as it rang.

"Hello? Oh, hi, Frank. Fishing? Tonight? Hmmm." He glanced at each of the curious faces around him and then smiled a wide grin of excitement.

"Fishing's a great idea. In fact, we were just leaving for the park. Want to meet us there?" He ignored Hope's rolling eyes, Faith's "piffle" of disgust and Charity's slumped shoulders to linger on Jori's frowning countenance and the bag from Hamburger Haven that lay on the floor at her feet.

"Good. We've got dinner so don't worry. J.J., Mrs. Flowerday and me. We need to talk to you about something, too, Frank. About this little plan I've got. Okay." He clicked the phone closed and smiled at the group, his teeth flashing in that tanned face.

"All right now, ladies. It's all set. Charity will have dinner on the lake with Frank and I. We can all relax and talk this situation over. Are you ready?"

They bustled about, gathering a jacket for Charity, a thermos of coffee and three more cups. In the midst of it all, Jori sidled over to the doctor.

"I don't know what you've got planned," she said. "But it better not hurt my friends."

"Trust me," he whispered, his lips brushing her cheek.

She stood back, hands on her hips and glared at him fiercely, except Chris could see the little tick at the corner of her mouth and knew she wasn't mad at all.

"At this point, I haven't got much for alternatives," she grumbled before holding open the door. "You'd better pray this works."

"Oh, I am," he murmured, more to himself. "I'm praying that it works in more ways than one."

Out in the boat in the middle of the lake, life seemed to slow into a wonderfully calm pattern that was completely free of problems and difficulties. Jori watched as Chris turned into the wind, his chiseled face outlined in the waning sun as he explained his plan.

"So if Charity and Frank pretend to be dating and are seen going out together, the others will give up. All her dinners will be promised to Frank and they won't have a chance." His eyes watched the older couple as he whispered to Jori, "I think it just might work. And she needs a break. She looks very tired. The arthritis pain saps her energy, I think."

"I really am sorry about all this, Charity," Frank apologized, his hand tenderly squeezing hers. "We had no right to run you ragged like that. And we should have taken you out instead of making you cook all the time. It's no wonder you're feeling a bit exhausted.'' His eyes crinkled at the corners. ''Although no one would know it to look at you. You look as young as you did twenty-five years ago.''

''Why, thank you, Frank!'' Charity preened a bit before glancing at the others. ''But aging doesn't really give up, no matter how hard you fight it. This Charity is nothing like the one you knew so long ago.''

''Of course she is!'' He sounded amazed, Jori decided, eyeing the two with a tender glance. ''Why, you look exactly as you did then! I remember how those big brown eyes flashed when I corrected that child picking sweet peas in your backyard and howling at the moon. What was his name?''

''Evan Schultz,'' Charity breathed, a smile tipping up the corners of her lips. ''And he was trying his darndest to get into the kids' choir at church.''

''Yes, but he had the words wrong. I can still hear him. 'Gee the baloney's good'—that's what he sang,'' Frank told Chris, winking at him and Jori as he held Charity's hand on his knee.

''What was the song?'' Chris looked puzzled at the strange words. ''I don't remember a church song about baloney. Or any kind of meat.'' He turned the wheel and slowed the engine just a bit.

''It wasn't about meat. The words were 'G, double O, D, good!' It was about God and his faithfulness to his children.'' Charity's laughter rang out over the water. ''And Evan couldn't carry a tune in a bucket! That's why I didn't want Frank to hurt his feelings. I knew the child wouldn't get the part.''

''I wasn't going to hurt his feelings!'' Frank pasted on an affronted look but it couldn't hide the glint of merriment in his kindly gray eyes. ''I was going to offer to buy him a trumpet if he'd stop making that infernal noise!'' He smirked at Charity.

"But no, you had to assure him he was doing fine and that he just needed to practice! Agh! Thank goodness he took up sports not long after."

Charity giggled like a schoolgirl. Jori was amazed at the change in her. Her eyes sparkled in her flushed face. Her shoulders were thrown back and she giggled happily, leaving her hand wrapped in Frank's.

"She still looks after all the kids in the neighborhood." Frank's voice was soft and admiring. "There's never a kid who can't go to Mrs. Flowerday and find some good advice and a slice of double-chocolate cake to make them feel better."

"You should talk!" Charity grinned. "Who offered to take his boat up to that juvenile camp and tow water-skiers around for three weeks last summer, Franklin Bellows? And then got conned into teaching a class on archery?"

"Okay." he held up a hand. "We're both guilty! But I was trying to make the point that you haven't changed. You're still determined to see God's goodness in people, no matter what."

Jori met Chris's gaze with her own and they both turned away, pretending they weren't listening.

"But I have changed, Frank. This arthritis has crippled me up so badly, I look ugly." She held out her knotted fingers for him to see their twisted disfigurement.

"You look beautiful," he whispered, brushing a strand of gleaming silver off her forehead. "Your skin is as smooth and velvety as an eighteen-year-old's and your nose has the same tip-tilted, smart-aleck angle it's always had." He'd smiled benignly when she blushed.

"And you haven't lost that same lovely glow I saw twenty years ago. That comes from inside, Charity. Not from your hands. From your heart. That's why everyone wants to be around you."

Jori let the wind ripple through her hair as it flew around wildly, her fingers curling in Chris's as they watched Charity and Frank have this special time together. She was so engrossed in Frank's words and the wealth of love in them, that she almost missed Chris's excited whisper.

"What?"

"It's working! She's beginning to see Frank in a new and different light. Thank the Lord! He's been crazy about her for ages." He grinned with delight.

"You mean, you've been matchmaking?" Aghast, Jori could only stare. "Of all the people in this town, you, Christopher Davis, should know how chancy that can be."

"Only if it's done for the wrong reasons and with the wrong people. In this case, I think God means for them to be together."

She stared at him.

"You don't have any fears, any worries?" She shook her head. "I admire you, Doc. You don't have any inhibitions. You just jump in and grab whatever it is you want out of life."

"Yeah, sometimes I do. And I hope you remember that," he whispered in her ear, his arm slipping around her waist. "Some things are worth jumping in after."

And for once, Jordanna felt jealous of a little elderly woman who could cause that glint of loving admiration in her old friend's eye. Jori had been so sure that her ex-fiancé was the man for her, would share those same kind of moments with her.

Instead, he'd publicly exposed her to the world's ridicule by breaking off their engagement and taking off with her best friend. Now she so badly wanted to trust again.

But as Chris's blazing blue eyes searched deep into the depths of hers and she remembered the touch of his mouth, Jori wished, for once, that she could believe that someone could love her again. Part of her wanted so badly to be that one special person to someone else; to have them near, to share hopes and dreams with. To raise a family. And part of her was scared to death to open up to that kind of hurt and rejection.

Maybe it was better to just stay free and clear of it, after all. At least you never got hurt.

You never really live, either, a tiny voice whispered.

The scent of lilacs and lavender was thick in the big airy bathroom as Jori laid back even farther into the deep claw-footed tub. It was the old-fashioned kind that let you put in enough water to really sink into and relax. And boy did she need to relax, Jori thought, grinning.

She had spent the entire day whirling through house and garden, trying to forget the effect a tall, blond doctor had on her nervous system. Consequently, not a weed could be found in the flower beds, vegetable garden, along the walk or within the confines of her rather large yard. Jori had mowed the grass even though ten-year-old Bobby Moore was paid to do it for her. In fact, he had been there only two days before.

The house had been put through a rigorous spit-and-polish regime, from top to bottom. Not a speckle of dust marred the gleaming surfaces in any room. She scrubbed the old kitchen floor to within an inch of its worn life and then waxed and buffed it to a shine that hurt the eyes.

And the worst of it was, it was still only three o'clock in the afternoon!

Jori played with a mound of bubbles and considered what the remainder of the day's entertainment should be. An image of Chris grinning from ear to ear flew into her mind. She shoved it away resolutely. Banishing all thoughts of him from her mind, Jori leaned back once more and closed her eyes.

Unfortunately, he would not leave. And neither would the problem of his presence.

"All right," she mumbled to herself in frustration. "Let's discuss this rationally." She straightened up and glared at the faucet of the tub. "Would a perfectly wonderful doctor who makes pots of money cutting people open and sewing them up, who is inundated with adulation from masses of people telling him he's the best thing since fudge brownies, have any desire to remain in a one-horse country town like Mossbank when his self-imposed sabbatical is over?" Jori snapped the bubbles with her fingers. "Of course not!"

It wasn't a very satisfactory answer and so she tried to reason it out again.

"No doubt he lives in some elegant condo with a pool, weight room and a bevy of drooling nurses for neighbors."

No, she frowned. It was worse to think this way. Jori turned the water on with her toes. "Well, what makes you think he'd hang around Mossbank, then?"

Answer: he wouldn't. Not for any longer than it took Dan and Jessica to get back home and into the groove.

"And you can't leave. You know you can't. Even if he asked you." She squeezed her eyes closed and remembered.

"I'll repay you every dime, every dollar that you've scraped together to send me to school," she'd promised Reg and the men with him tearfully. "I won't renege. You can count on that."

Reg had told her to pay the debt out after her court case had been resolved.

"The town won't hold it against you if you get on with your life somewhere else," he'd insisted. "We never expected you to stay this long."

"I promised seven years," she reminded him. "And anyway, I wouldn't dream of leaving. This is my home now."

Chris's searching blue eyes swam into focus and she could hear his words as clearly as the radio playing in the bedroom.

"Trust me," he'd said.

"I could trust him, I think," she said to herself, trying to wash away the sensation of those arms holding her so gently. "But there's no future in this relationship so just stop thinking about weddings and babies and all that stuff. It's not for you!"

Luckily, the motion picture running across her brain in vivid Technicolor ended there, due to the loud peal of the telephone. Water slopped over the side of the tub as Jori rose hastily grabbing a towel to wrap around her wet body. She scurried into the bedroom to lift the receiver just as the caller hung up.

"Shoot!" Jori tugged on an old chenille housecoat before mopping up the trail of puddles marking her newly polished floors. That job was barely complete when the doorbell rang.

"What is this?" she grouched. "Grand Central Station?"

She yanked the door open to find Chris standing on her front step. The look on his face would have been comical if Jori had been in a mood to appreciate it.

"Oh, uh, s-sorry," he stammered, staring at the gaping V her robe exposed. His eyes flew to her face. Confusion clouded his eyes. "Were you sleeping?"

"Don't be ridiculous," Jori said, horrified that he had to see her in such disarray. "It's three o'clock in the afternoon." She motioned him into the hallway. "I would prefer that the entire town didn't witness me in this ratty old thing," she told him.

Chris seemed amused by her bad temper, which only made it worse. She clenched her teeth at his grin when he spied the ragged bandanna that held up her hair.

"I can go away and come back some other time," he told her softly, watching her face closely.

Jori sighed. She should have gone along with the senior

bus trip to Minot and spent her day in the craft store, she told herself tiredly. Perhaps then she would have avoided all tall blond male humans, she muttered inwardly. And dogs, she was forced to add at the sight of Flop's huge brown woebegone eyes peering through the screen door.

"I was in the tub when the phone rang," she explained carefully, as he sat in the huge armchair across from her. She curled her legs carefully under her, making sure they remained covered. "Whomever it was had just hung up when you rang the bell." She shoved the wet stringy hair off her face. "I must look a mess."

Chris sat there staring at her until the color rose in her cheeks.

"Well, don't just sit there staring at me! I look terrible."

"No," he murmured softly, "you just look like a little girl getting ready for bed."

Silence yawned between them like a great gaping hole, but Jori couldn't think of a thing to say. His gaze held hers, solemn and probing. She couldn't look away so she stared back, mesmerized by what she saw in the blue depths of his eyes.

The shrill ring of the phone finally broke the spell. Jori picked up the receiver slowly, dazedly.

"Hello, Jori. How was the birthday cruise with the handsome doctor?" Amy's voice bubbled enthusiastically over the line.

It was a little disconcerting to discuss her date with the man in question sitting across from her. Jori decided to skirt the issue.

"Hi, Amy." She cleared the huskiness from her throat and continued brightly. "Thank you very much, I had a lovely time."

Chris coughed just then and she glanced at him from under her lids. He was grinning hugely.

"What you can remember of it, at least," he teased, blue eyes dancing.

"Who's that?" Amy demanded. "I heard a voice."

"I have a guest right now, Amy." Jori frowned at Chris as she spoke. "Can I call you back later?"

"Well, actually, old pal…" Jori knew there was something coming when her friend began that con.

"What do you need, Amy?" She sighed, staring at her carpet. This was turning out to be a strange day.

"Uh, well, it's about Jonathan."

Jori tried to think of something to say but Amy was rushing on.

"I need a sitter for tonight. We're going out for dinner." It came out in a rush of breath. Amy's voice was so hopeful that Jori's soft heart caved like mush. "Mom's taking Brit, but she's too old to take on him, too."

Jori could quite understand. Little Jonathan was a terror and he would be no end of trouble but it was the least she could do for her friend, she pointed out to herself.

"Dinner? Wow! Must be some occasion. What's up?" Jori demanded, knowing her friend seldom splurged on anything for herself.

There was a pregnant pause and then Amy's tearful voice came across the line.

"I passed."

Jori shrieked with joy. She grinned, happily including Chris in the pleasure of the moment.

"Way to go, kid!" She cheerfully congratulated her friend. "Do I call you Madam Certified Public Accountant now?"

They laughed and talked and arranged, and the entire time Jori sat there, uncomfortably aware of the handsome doctor seated on her sofa, unashamedly listening.

A thought suddenly occurred and Jori asked her friend anxiously, "Have you got something special to wear?" There was a murmured response before Jori hooted, "No way. You're not wearing *that*." She stared at Chris searchingly for a moment then nodded as if that settled everything.

"Look, you and I have enough time to scoot over to Mirabel's and get something really special for tonight. It's my treat." When the voice on the other end of the line started speaking, Jori's voice became louder.

"This is my treat and you are not doing me out of the fun. You've come through for me enough times, Amy."

Apparently she had gotten her way, Chris mused, smiling at the grin of satisfaction tipping those full lips. Then he sat upright at the mention of his name.

"Look, Dr. Davis is here. He can watch Jonathan while you and I go shopping. You would like that, wouldn't you?" She pretended to ask Chris, then ignored his wildly gesticulating hands and shaking head. Jori put her hand over the mouthpiece when he told her no, but after a moment she kept right on talking to her friend as if he weren't there.

"He'd love to do this for you on your special day," she said sweetly, glaring fiercely at Chris.

His shoulders slumped. How did she do it? he wondered. She was always conning him into something. And what did he know about little kids? Nothing, that's what! Sure, he could give them a physical, check them over for health problems, or sew them up very neatly. But he doubted that would be much fun for this Jonathan kid.

"What time are you leaving?" He heard Jori arranging everything as if he had agreed wholeheartedly. Chris got up and walked toward the kitchen. He needed a drink of something to keep his hands busy. Otherwise he'd throttle her.

When he returned, Jori had slipped into white slacks and a blue-and-white-striped sweater. She was dialing a number.

"Just a minute, Jori," he demanded. "I can't look after a…"

She help up her hand as someone answered.

"This is Jordanna Jessop. I'd like to speak to Alex, please."

He tried again.

"Jordanna, I *cannot*..."

"Shhh... Hi, Alex, this is Jordanna."

Chris wondered at the sudden animation that lit up her glowing brown eyes. A huge grin curved her mouth.

"Great! Listen, Alex, I need a favor. A friend of mine has a very special celebration tonight. I want that window table that overlooks the river, a bouquet of fresh flowers and anything they order charged to me." She listened for a few minutes.

"Good. Oh, and Alex, when they're finished can you get a cab for them." Jori's face was dancing with glee as she gave him the names. "They're going to the Palace but they don't know it. Can you do it? Thank you, you are a sweetie! Okay, bye."

Chris let her enjoy the moment and then tried again.

"Jori, I need to talk to you. There is no way..."

Once more she held up her hand and began dialing.

Well, if Jordanna Jessop thought she could bulldoze him into this she had another thought coming. He would darn well wait her out.

"Mrs. Rivers, this is Jori. I need you to pack a bag for Amy and Bob. I've got it all arranged, but I don't want them to know. You're keeping Brit, right? Okay. Well, Jonathan will stay here."

Chris thought she'd never get off the phone, but when Jori finally hung up, he breathed a sigh of relief. Now, perhaps, they could clear this up.

Then the doorbell rang.

"Blast it anyway!" He clenched his teeth in vexation.

Jori's wide eyes stared at him.

"You can't say that around Jonathan," she instructed. "He repeats everything he hears. And for goodness' sake, don't give him chocolate." She opened the front door. "Hi, Amy. All set?"

Everything was happening too fast. Chris felt like a passenger on one of those roller coasters at the amusement park. Everything rushed past and he couldn't quite get a grasp on reality.

Jori's friend Amy was speaking to him. Chris tried to pay attention to her, but tiny hands were pulling on his pants, diverting his attention. He hung on to his waistband with one hand, and pulled the sticky hands away with the other.

"He doesn't need to be fed. And don't give him any chocolate." The woman studied him dubiously and Chris straightened his backbone under the survey. "Jonathan will tell you if he needs to use the potty," she said. Her eyes moved uncertainly over the now stained gray slacks.

"Are you sure you want to do this?" Her question was full of doubt and Chris was about to assure her that he certainly did not when Jori broke in.

"Of course he does, don't you, Chris? We had a lovely time on that cruise and this is our way of thanking you. And, after all, it is *just* Jonathan. Her mom's watching Brittany." Jori's eyes were black hard stones now, daring him to refuse.

When he smiled grimly, the two women moved toward the door, giggling excitedly. Neither one paid him any attention. Jonathan headed straight for the china cabinet.

Chris recognized defeat. He would be graceful, he decided. So magnanimously helpful that Jori would not be able to find fault with him. And then he'd leave. He was pretty sure the kid was here for the evening, so he wouldn't be. It was that simple.

Except it wasn't simple at all, he observed an hour later, staggering under the impact of a three-year-old ball of lead against his midsection. Jonathan laughed uproariously. And launched himself at Chris again.

Chris, however, was not a slow learner and he moved. Too quickly, as it happened. The child banged his head against the edge of Jori's solid oak coffee table and let out a wail designed to bring the cops.

It probably only took a few minutes, but when the racket was finally over, Chris concluded surgery was infinitely less tiring than comforting a crying child who was seriously hurting. He decided to take the boy outside. The dog, that was it!

Chris was pleased with himself. Jonathan could play with Flop. Kids like dogs. Dogs like kids. They'd have a great time.

Except that Flop had apparently met little Jonathan before. The cocker spaniel took one look at the three-year-old and barked. Then he sped as fast as his stumpy little legs would carry him, to the thick growth of trees and bushes behind the house.

"Dog," Jonathan said, pointing. "Me go." As he started after the frightened animal, Chris decided diversionary tactics were needed.

He couldn't very well let the tyke get lost in the woods, Chris knew, but he didn't want a recurrence of that bloodcurdling screeching, either. Chris searched the yard for something, anything! When his frustrated glance returned to little Johnny, the kid was in the garden carefully picking the flowers off Jori's pea plants.

"Flowers," he told Chris, grinning his toothy smile. "Pitty flowers."

"Yeah, kid," Chris agreed morosely. "It's a pity, all right." Sighing, he bent to take the little boy's hand. "Come on, Jonathan. Let's go see cars. Okay?"

The round cherub face twisted in sorrow first. The fat little hands dropped the crushed white blossoms on the ground sadly.

But the word *car* seemed to have some significance. The shiny black button eyes sparkled at his baby-sitter in delight.

"Car, Car," he sang in a cheerful tone. "Wide in car."

Too late, Chris realized what the word *car* meant to this three-year-old. As they walked out the gate, Chris looked to see if Amy's car, with a *baby seat,* was by the curb.

Unfortunately, only his vintage black T-bird, restored and refurbished at an exorbitant sum, sat there. Jonathan seemed delighted. He patted the gleaming rear fender lovingly, and crowed, "Pitty car. Wide in car wif man." Fat little hands imprinted themselves on a wax job Chris had painstakingly completed only this morning. He groaned as the child leaned closer to press a slurpy kiss on his shiny chrome bumper.

"Jon wuv car," he told Chris, smiling happily.

They stood in the hot sun for ages while Chris tried to persuade the little boy to walk down the street for a look at the red sports car parked nearby. But the kid wasn't buying. Jonathan clung to the door handle, persistently saying the same thing over and over, his happy face dropping a little more each time.

"Jon go car wide. Dis car."

Chris picked him up, thinking he'd carry the tiny boy inside, but a wail of distress soon stopped him. Several ladies were entering the house across the street and they turned to peer down their noses at him, heads shaking disapprovingly, obviously concerned by his inability to placate the boy. He set the kid down. Immediately, Jonathan ran back to the T-bird.

"She will pay," Chris promised himself grimly, jaw throbbing as he gritted his teeth once more. "I will make her pay for every single moment of this very long afternoon." He opened the door, resignation in the slump of his shoulders.

"Okay, kid. We're just going to sit in the car, now. Just sit."

The boy scooted across the driver's side and nestled into the passenger's seat. Jonathan was very familiar with what happened next, Chris realized, his heart sinking into his shoes. With great dexterity the kid fastened the seat belt around himself like a pro. His dark eyes shone with excitement.

"Wedy," he chirped.

"Well, I'm not." Chris felt like a grumpy old man, talking to an innocent child like that. But he had reason. Darned good reason to be cranky, he figured.

This was not the manner in which he had planned on spending his afternoon. Not at all! Fleeting thoughts of a picnic, at the beach, in the sun, with Jori, ran rampant through his head. Chris turned to face the little boy. Time for a reality check, oh, great doctor, he chided himself in disgust. Scenario's changed!

"Jonathan. We can't go for a car ride today because I don't have a special seat for you." The kid stared at him, beaming that silly smile. Chris tried again.

"In Mommy's car you have a special seat, don't you, Jonathan?"

The child blinked. "Car wide?" he asked innocently.

"No, Jonathan. No car ride." Chris tried to yell above the kid's bawling. "I haven't got a car seat for you."

The child had well-developed lungs for his age, Chris decided, cringing at the shrill bellows. Surely Jori would hear him downtown and get back here, pronto.

When several minutes had passed without any signs of the relief team, Chris took matters into his own hands.

"Okay, kid. You win," he hollered. "We're going, we're going."

The slow motion of the car finally penetrated and Jonathan's crying ceased abruptly. Chris kept it on a sedate fifteen miles per hour and prayed no one would notice he was plodding down the street at a snail's pace, in a racy black Thunderbird whose engine had not been designed for creeping, with a kid next to him who was not belted in according to government specification. Of course, they'd have to be able to see Jonathan first, Chris reasoned, glancing down. This way they'd think he was out by himself. Cruising, no doubt.

"Better and better," he grumbled in revulsion. "Now they'll really be talking!"

Jonathan's happy face beamed satisfaction as he jabbered away.

"Go wide car. Jon like car. Nice car. Pitty." He turned his solemn eyes on Chris, and ordered, "Sing."

Chris ignored him, hoping the child would forget. Fat chance!

"Sing," Jonathan ordered insistently. "Sing."

Chris turned on the radio. There was no way he was going down the street singing. He already had the windows open because he thought air-conditioning would give the kid a chill. Anyway, he couldn't imagine what tune they could possibly share.

As luck would have it, an old country-and-western song was playing. Chris smiled grimly. He'd always suspected that God had a sense of humor, and "coward of the county" described his present condition perfectly.

Jonathan appeared quite happy with the song, though. He crowed away, off-key, as they turned the corner. Chris braked slowly in front of Jori's, noting there was still no sign of Amy's car. He groaned inwardly, but determined not to show it.

"Okay, Jonathan. All finished. Let's go inside, okay," he wheedled.

"Car wide, more." Jonathan was getting angry. Chris could

see the little hands curling into angry fists. "Car wide," he shouted.

"Do you want to drive, too?" Chris inquired sourly, raking his hands through his hair.

That was a mistake.

Faster than lightning, the child had released the latch on his belt and landed with a thud on Chris's lap.

"Jon dwive," he agreed cheerfully.

"Uh, I don't think…" The little face scrunched up and Chris caved in. "All right!"

And so Jonathan drove. Chris turned the key and the motor purred quietly while his prize car sat in one place and the kid happily turned the wheel left and right to the accompaniment of *Brrrm* and *Rooom*.

Chris let himself relax for a moment, wondering if he'd need to replace his front tires after this grueling workout. His blue eyes narrowed in thought. And he would send the bill to Jori Jessop, he decided. It was the least she could do after setting him up like this.

Still, he considered, if it got him any further beneath that protective shell she always threw up against him, Chris decided it was worth it. He was definitely interested in the woman, he acknowledged.

And so, as Jonathan drove his car, Chris sat thinking about Jori. And while a low voice on the radio crooned about her dream lover, Chris fantasized about his relationship with his office nurse. He thought of her laughing eyes, that solemn glint they got in them when she spoke of her past, the way she opened up, just a bit, and then hid her thoughts and feelings.

"Why me, Lord?" The question stemmed from his need to know why he'd been presented with a woman who met every one of the traits he'd deemed desirable in a partner for life and yet seemed totally unobtainable. "Why *me*, Lord?"

Suddenly Chris felt the insistent tug on his arm. And the warm wetness soaking through his pants.

He asked the question again, but with totally different intent.

"I haffa go potty," Jonathan advised him solemnly.

"I think you're just a bit late, pal." Chris grimaced sourly as he stepped gingerly out of the car. His brow furrowed when he surveyed the boy's dirty smeared face.

Great! The kid had snitched a chocolate bar Chris had left in the cup holder. Now they were both covered with the gooey brown stuff but Chris wore more of it than Jonathan.

Chris wondered, What next? just as his eyes caught a glimpse of the dark wet patch creating a highly *visible* circle on the front of his slacks. He shook his head darkly.

"I concede defeat," Chris informed anyone who was listening. "I have no pride left," he muttered in frustration. "None."

Oh, she'd pay, all right! Big-time!

After a trip to the bathroom and a change of clothes which Chris finally found in Jonathan's blue-striped diaper bag tucked discreetly behind the front door, they sat together on the sofa to read one of the books that had been secreted inside said bag. Chris wished he'd noticed it sooner. There were enough toys in there to amuse ten kids.

A few minutes later they were back in the bathroom removing all traces of a regurgitated chocolate bar that should never have been eaten. Fortunately for Jori's sofa, most of it had landed in Chris's lap.

As he surveyed his new pants ruefully, Chris wished he had his own diaper bag. There was a peculiar odor in the air and he was pretty sure he was the source. He dabbed at the expensive fabric as best he could while swallowing thoughts of retribution.

"Vengeance is the Lord's," he quoted self-righteously.

Soon Jonathan's rumpled dark head rested tiredly against his chest as Chris read about Peter Rabbit. No wonder the kid was so smart if he heard this stuff all the time. Beatrix Potter was not one to mince words, Chris decided.

Halfway through the little book, he realized Jonathan had fallen asleep. The child's tiny hand lay on top of his own as the boy snored gently, his chubby body pressed comfortably against Chris.

This is what it would be like to have a son. The words sounded in his brain with a clarity that made his eyes widen. *Here's a demanding little person who depends on you to make his world all right. Someone who needs you to bandage sore knees, read bedtime stories and take for a car ride. Someone who needs you to be there to tuck him in at night.*

Chris had never thought of himself as a father. Never wanted the responsibility. But somehow it seemed perfectly natural to cuddle little Jonathan's body as he lay sleeping. And a feeling of intense longing coursed through him even as the sadness brought reality.

"I'm not the father type," he told that resonant voice. "I haven't got a clue how to raise children except that it wouldn't be the way my parents raised us." Thoughts of happy excited voices debating across the table made him smile. "Mealtimes are fun times," he murmured. "That's the first rule I'd make. And everyone laughs."

A picture of Jori holding a baby in the rocking chair across the room flew into his mind. She should have a family. She was full of warmth and giving and caring. Jori would know the right words to say. She would have the understanding a child would need in this world.

But why did he want it to be his child? He wasn't the type to settle down in a place like Mossbank. He couldn't; he accepted that inevitability as the sun rises each morning. His whole professional career was about maximizing the medical care that he'd been taught to provide. His whole life had been about fulfilling his parents' dreams. And unless there was exponential growth in the future of the little town, he wasn't looking at hanging around. Was he?

In the back of his mind, Chris listened tiredly as his mother's voice droned on.

"You can be the best surgeon in the world, Christopher. People will come from miles to be operated on by you. Your fees will entitle you to the best of everything. You can advance in your field as far as you're willing to go, be among the top brains in the world. You can have it all."

But did he want it all?

Jori pushed open her front door to the same quiet peacefulness that always reigned in her home. How long would she have to wait to hear the sounds of children laughing as they slid down the bannister or swung in the backyard? Would she ever have a child of her own?

Now, however, a tiny frisson of fear coursed through her veins. It was so silent. Where were they?

Stop it, she told herself sternly. Nothing bad has happened. And if it had, Chris would be well equipped to handle an emergency.

All the same, Jori breathed a sigh of relief when she came upon the two of them lying on her sofa, snoring in unison. Flop raised his nose from his comfy position on top of Chris's feet and Jori had to smile at the picture they made. Wistfully, she wondered how Chris's own child would look.

Would his son have that flaxen blond hair and those sun-bleached eyebrows? Would his eyes sparkle with the same navy blueness when he was amused? Would he be as tall and broad as his father?

The pain that shuddered through her as Jori contemplated

these and a host of other questions forced her to realize just how deeply she was falling for him.

She wanted to be the mother of his son. Jori calmly accepted her own desires, painfully realizing that it would never happen. Chris would never be happy living in a small town like Mossbank. And why would he?

But while he was here, Jori decided, she would enjoy his company whenever possible. Nothing could come of it, and she would learn to live with that, but she wasn't going to regret that she had grown to love this man.

"Chris." She shook his shoulder gently. When those wide blue eyes popped open, Jori wasn't prepared for the feelings that struck her heart. It took a minute for her to regain her poise.

"You're back," Chris murmured, brushing his hair from his forehead. His eyes darkened as he remembered. "You owe me one," he told her. "More than one."

Jori giggled. She put her hands on her hips, and taunted, "Like what?"

"Supper, for one," he informed her. His blue eyes glinted in the sun.

"One meal for you and Jonathan coming right up," she promised, moving toward the kitchen. She turned in the doorway, tossing a saucy look over her shoulder. "Anything else, your majesty?"

"Yes," he told her. His voice lowered to a whisper. "But I'll tell you later."

It was a promise that Jori rolled through her mind a dozen times as she readied the steaks for grilling. When Chris strolled into the kitchen sometime later, she smiled at the mussed blond hair, dirty wrinkled shirt and stained pants.

"You can shower and change before supper if you want," she told him, eyeing his discolored pants with mirth. "Did you have an accident?"

She kept her tones mildly questioning, which was difficult, because inside Jori was aching to laugh. When his blue eyes glared at her, she moved over to pat his cheek.

"Poor baby," she consoled him. "Did you have a bad day?"

Jori was surprised when his long arms reached out to pull her into his arms. She was even more surprised when his lips touched hers.

"Yes," he answered. "I have had a *very* bad day, but it's getting better."

She wrapped her arms around his neck, still holding the salt shaker in one hand. Her senses were caught on a curious smell. Her nose twitched as she stared up at him.

"Chris?"

"What?" His blue eyes looked at her curiously.

"What is that smell?" she asked, wrinkling her nose in distaste. To her surprise, he backed away immediately. Her hands fell to her sides as she stood staring at him. A flush of red suffused his strong cheekbones. Jori watched the sheepish look cover his face.

Just then, little Jonathan walked into the room. He was mussed and sleepy eyed, clutching his teddy in one grubby hand. As she bent to pick him up, Jori caught the same scent on his clothes. Eyes wide, she turned to stare at Chris.

"It's him, not me!" Chris's voice was defensive. "He stole a chocolate bar, got sick on me and forgot to tell me about going to the bathroom until it was too late." He looked mortally offended, plucking the expensive material away from his thighs. "Unfortunately, he was sitting on me at the time."

It was jumbled, but she got the drift. And she couldn't help herself. Laughter burst from her like a wave in a tidal pool, filling the room with its sound. She laughed until tears ran down her cheeks and then laughed some more. Her stomach ached and quivered with laughter until finally Jori sobered up enough to see the light of battle in his eyes.

"I told you, no chocolate," she reminded him, stifling her glee.

Chris did not look placated. In fact he looked...rumpled, she decided grinning.

"I'm sorry," she bubbled, "but it's just the thought of someone, anyone, let alone a child, ruining the great Dr. Chris Davis's p-p-pants..." Fresh gales of laughter shook her narrow shoulders as she tried to control her mirth.

Chris marched over to stand in front of her. "It is not funny," he complained. "These were my best pants." He stood watching her set the little boy in his high chair. "In fact, they *were* brand-new."

Jori began feeding the child as he spoke. She was ignoring him, Chris realized. It bugged him.

"Jori," he complained, turning her chin to meet his eyes.

"Yes," she answered, staring at him for a minute before popping another spoonful of food into Jonathan's open mouth. "What did you say?"

"I said, I had plans for tonight. And they didn't include him." His thumb jerked toward the three-year-old safely ensconced in the chair, huge eyes watching them curiously.

"Perhaps next time," Jori advised him, "you should ask me before you make any plans for me." She fixed him with her best office nurse look. "Now, go get changed while I feed Jon. We'll eat when he's asleep."

"Jon not sleepy," the little boy told her seriously. "Jon play wif toys."

"You will be, sweetie. You're going to eat your dinner and after you've had your bath, you are going to bed."

Jori watched from the corner of her eye as Chris lingered in her kitchen for a few minutes, before he strode, muttering, out the back door.

Contrary to his assertions, Jonathan did go to bed and finally to sleep after his dinner and bath, although not without protest.

"Jon not sleepy. No bed."

She had been calm but firm and finally the little tyke had settled down enough to close his eyes and drift off. Jori went downstairs a few moments later, to find Chris had returned and was seated at her kitchen table.

"Whew," she told him seriously. "I was afraid there for a minute that he wouldn't go to sleep and then he would start bawling." She eyed Chris piteously. "You have no idea how loud he is when he starts crying."

Chris surged to his feet. "Yes, I do. I have a very good idea of just how many decibels he reaches with those lungs. When I return to Boston, I am going to have my hearing checked. And I'm sending the bill to you."

"Poor baby!" Jori grinned saucily before she pointed to the array on her counter. "I have seasoned T-bones waiting for grilling. There are new potatoes, fresh green beans, a salad and garlic bread." She smirked. "Will that cover my debt to you?"

"Not nearly! But it is a good start."

And so the evening progressed with neither able to stop the little touches and telling glances they each threw when the other wasn't looking. It could have been a very relaxing evening, except for little Jonathan's peculiar timing. And not once but several times!

Chris had finally gone home, grumbling all the while. But not before he had made Jori wish he was staying. For good.

Chapter Nine

"I wish to speak with Dr. Christopher Davis, Nurse. Fetch him immediately, please." The tall, elegantly dressed woman on the other side of the desk gave Jori a thorough once-over as she impatiently tapped her fingers.

Jori raised her eyebrows at the woman's supercilious tone. Indeed. She wondered where the woman had come from. Her white linen suit was immaculate on a day when the dust was blowing freely across the prairies. Ash blond hair was pulled severely back off her tense face and coiled into some complicated knot at the back. Her face was a study in patrician features with its long aquiline nose, highly defined cheekbones and intense blue eyes. At the moment her full lips were stretched in a thin line across her perfectly made-up face as she waited for Jori to obey.

"Your name, madam?"

"Dr. Charlotte Davis." The smoothly arrogant tones gave the information haughtily. "I am Dr. Davis's mother."

Jori felt the world shift and tilt and wondered why she hadn't expected this. This woman was here to make sure Chris returned to the city.

Somehow she struggled past all that and remembered that Chris would be tied up for some time counseling the young girl in his office on the merits of abstaining from sex. There was no way she was going to interrupt that.

"If you would have a seat, Dr. Davis, I'm sure Chris will see you as soon as he is free." Jori waved her hand toward a waiting room already jammed with patients before glancing down to the appointment book dismissively.

She had pulled a few more patient files from the bulging cabinets before Jori noticed that the woman had not left. She raised her eyebrow questioningly.

"Was there something else, Dr. Davis?"

"I don't think you understand." Her tone was mildly condescending. Jori bristled at the supercilious words.

"I believe I understand perfectly," she insisted quietly. "But perhaps you don't understand that this is a clinic. These patients have made appointments and they are waiting to see the doctor." Her eyes seared around the room before coming to rest on the aristocratic woman standing at the desk. Jori relented only a bit.

"Dr. Davis is attending a patient right now," she told his mother, keeping her voice low. "When he is free, I'll tell him you are here." Her voice was firm. "Now, please be seated."

Dr. Davis sat. Her back was ramrod straight as she perched on the edge of the worn chair as if fearful it would contaminate her.

Twenty minutes later, Jori eased into Chris's office. She watched him as he pored over the next patient's file. After a moment his blond head tipped up, blue eyes crinkling. "What?" he asked.

"Um, well, you see..." Jori didn't know exactly why she felt the woman's presence was going to disrupt Chris's concentration on his needy patients, but the niggling feeling of impending doom was there. She tried to tell him quickly.

"Your mother is in the waiting room, Doctor. She wants to see you."

The wide grin that had stretched his mouth fell away as he stared at her. His face froze, a chilly look in those gorgeous eyes.

"My mother is here? J.J., she couldn't be. She's working on a top secret project right now." He smiled absurdly. "You must have misunderstood."

"She said her name was Charlotte Davis." She watched the light of recognition dawn. "Ah, I see you believe me now."

He frowned fiercely. "But surely she hasn't come way out here? My father must be working overtime if he's had to recruit her. And I can just imagine what she wants."

Jori stared at him. He said the words to himself, obviously turning it all over in his mind. "But what does she want?"

The comment wasn't directed at her but Jori answered anyway. "I'm sure I don't know. She certainly didn't bother to explain it to me. After all, I'm just the office nurse." Jori shrugged, her eyes carefully studying him. "Shall I show her in here?"

He seemed to pull himself together suddenly, drawing his shoulders up with an inner strength. His eyes were cold as ice when he looked at her, his mouth a thin, straight line.

"No." The word was sharp. "I have a room full of patients. She's the one who always says work comes first." Chris gathered the file together and tapped it against his desk, aligning the papers inside. When he looked at her, Jori could feel the tension crackling around the room.

"You may tell Dr. Davis that I will see her at five." And with that stark statement, Chris left the office to see his next patient as if nothing had happened.

Jori was stunned.

Shrugging, she went to deliver Chris's message, knowing

Dr. Charlotte Davis would not be pleased. And she wasn't, but not for the reasons Jori had presumed.

"But, I'm afraid you don't understand, Miss…" The words trailed away as the woman stared down her nose.

"Jessop, Nurse Jordanna Jessop," Jori told her, disliking the woman's patronizing tone.

"Very well, Miss Jessop. Apparently what Christopher doesn't understand is that I have very little time at my disposal right now and it is imperative that I see him at once." She issued the edict disdainfully, obviously expecting Jori to race off immediately.

"I'm sorry. Chris did ask me to tell you that he could see you here in the office at five, if you wish." Jori knew that every ear and eye in the waiting room was focused on them. She tried to control the anger raging inside her as the woman addressed her once more.

"*Dr. Davis,* you mean, don't you, Nurse?" It was a very thinly veiled hint which Jori chose to ignore, turning back to her work at the desk.

She was conscious of the woman leaving moments later, but she kept her head bent, filling out the lab forms for one of Chris's most worrisome cancer patients. Just the same, her mind whirled with questions. And with fury.

How dare that woman treat her like some peon!

It was a busy day with a number of drop-ins. Jori flew about, hoping to get the last few letters and notes sent out in the weekend mail. Mondays always presented enough problems. Leftovers from the previous Friday threw everything out of sync.

When Chris's mother returned at five, she ushered the woman into one of the consulting rooms and then crossed the hall to tell Chris. She found him seated, staring vacantly out the tiny window at the sheets of rain that were now falling.

"She's here." It wasn't a question.

Jori nodded. "Room six. Do you want me to arrange dinner for you both?" she asked in a rush, feeling sorry for that lost look on his face.

His blue eyes swiveled over to assess her intently. "I doubt very much if she's staying," he told her without expression. A crooked smile tugged at the corner of his mouth. "But I will be happy to come over for dinner after I do rounds," he teased halfheartedly.

Jori smiled at him, letting him know she knew what he was doing. "Fine," she murmured. "I'm cooking liver. Feel free to bring your mother."

Chris's tongue stuck out at her. "Yuk, that's gross. I hate liver. And Charlotte isn't exactly your typical motherly type." He glared at her. "You might have noticed that for yourself, J.J. I don't think a nice cozy dinner at your place is going to make her ease off."

"Well, what does she want?"

"That's what I'm going to find out." He got up and came around the desk, taking her hands in his.

Jori knew it was stupid and she told herself a thousand times that she was being a fool. She even whispered a prayer that God would make her immune to Chris's laughing good looks. But when Dr. Christopher Davis looked at her like that, she totally lost it, wanting only to wrap her arms around him and keep him away from the woman on the other side of the door.

Chris kissed her nose.

"Now, can't you please make something I like?" he begged piteously, sounding very much like a bratty little boy.

Jori giggled at his downcast expression. "You're a doctor—you should know that liver is very healthy," she lectured.

"It's also full of cholesterol and I can't afford to pile up on that.'' The light bantering had partially restored his natural effervescence.

Jori gave in gracefully. "Okay. I'll make something else.'' She blew out a long-suffering sigh. "I think doctors are very spoiled,'' she noted for his benefit.

"Not all of them, Miss Jessop. Most are far too busy to play silly games.'' The voice was cool and very controlled. Dr. Davis had apparently given up waiting for Chris and decided to find him for herself. She stood in the doorway glaring at them both.

"I don't think anyone is playing games here, Charlotte. Least of all J.J. and I.'' Chris's voice was tight with barely concealed anger. His eyes bored into the other woman, who had the grace to flush. "The question is, what are you doing here? And why now? What's so urgent?''

"You are my son, Christopher. Don't you think I should be concerned about you?'' Her voice had lightened considerably, Jori noticed, and she now wore a most beguiling smile.

"It's just unusual, that's all. You were never that concerned about me when I was in Boston. I would hardly think you'd have time to even think about me with your new project.'' Chris turned to wink at Jori, who immediately felt her heart beat a little faster.

"Yes, well, I do wish your staff had not forgotten me in the room like that,'' the older woman complained. "I've been sitting there for seventeen minutes. I have to be back at the airport as soon as possible. I'm doing an important experiment tomorrow afternoon.'' She glared at Jori. "Nurses never understand how important a doctor's time is.''

Jori blushed and turned to leave. The woman was a stickler for punctuality, she decided grimly. Seventeen minutes indeed.

"Excuse me,'' she asked the older woman, hoping to leave unscathed.

"Certainly," Dr. Davis moved deliberately in front of Jori. Her ice-cold eyes fixed on Jori's and she gave her orders. "Christopher and I have a lot to discuss. Please see that we are not disturbed."

Jori said nothing. She refused to start an argument with the woman. She wasn't one to be ordered about but there was nothing to be gained by indulging in a power struggle. For once she put a clamp on her lips, moving past silently to go about her usual routine, locking the office doors when the last patient had finally finished dressing. She left at last, tugging her light poplin jacket around her shoulders.

The heavens chose that precise moment to open again and by the time Jori reached her home, she was soaked to the skin from top to bottom. Even Flop refused to do more than wag his tail and bark a little greeting, standing well back so his golden coat absorbed none of the droplets her coat scattered across the braided rug.

"Fair-weather friend," she grumbled at him. He woofed in agreement and went to lie on the hearth rug.

Jori showered quickly before tugging on a fleece jogging suit in a periwinkle shade that she loved. Her hair twisted easily into an intricate coil of interlocking braids and she pinned the ends under so that the effect was one of neatness. Any remnant of makeup had long since washed away and Jori didn't bother to refresh it.

Minutes later she was in front of the freezer, surveying the possibilities for supper. Nothing but hamburger would thaw properly in the short time she had left, so Jori opted for lasagna with the oven-ready noodles. Before long she had it baking in the oven, a small loaf of garlic bread ready to heat and freshly grated coleslaw to accompany everything.

"I don't know what this is about, Father," she murmured, setting the table, "but work it out to your will." She placed the last item on the table and then quickly shut her eyes once more.

"Only, please, please, if he isn't the one for me, make him leave before I get in too deep. I don't know if I can deal with another heartbreak." Embarrassed by the admission, Jori acknowledged inwardly that Dr. Christopher Davis now had in his hands the power to hurt her very badly. And after today, she doubted he had any intention of staying in Mossbank.

The ringing doorbell startled her out of her thoughts. As she yanked open the door, teasing words flew out of her mouth.

"Well, Dr. Davis, it's about time. If you must beg supper the least you could…" Dead silence greeted her.

Charlotte Davis stood on the doorstep with Chris's tall figure behind. Neither one looked particularly pleased to be there.

"Jori, I hope you don't mind, but Charlotte said she would join us." His blue eyes begged her indulgence.

As Jori stared at him, she noticed tiny lines of strain radiating from his eyes and around his pursed lips. His shoulders drooped dejectedly. Chris's whole manner was rigidly tense, as if his plans had been rearranged and there was nothing he could do about it. She was about to answer when Dr. Davis broke in.

"Don't be ridiculous, Chris. Of course your little nurse doesn't mind feeding another person." And without batting an eyelash, the woman pushed her way past Jori into the hallway, slipping off her coat as she entered.

Jori straightened her spine. When dealing with rudeness, she decided, one had to face it head-on.

"Oh, please, Dr. Davis, do come in," she invited softly. "And please take off your coat. My home is yours."

The woman had the grace to flush a dull red. Jori picked up the navy trench coat slung over her father's antique oak table and dabbed up the droplets. She opened the closet and stuffed the coat onto a hanger as she spoke. Her voice mellowed considerably when she spoke to Chris.

"Come on, Doc. Hang your coat up, then we'll eat. Your mother is more than welcome to share our feast." She arched an eyebrow at his relieved look. "Does she like liver?"

When his startled gaze met her limpid brown one, Jori could have crowed with laughter. His mouth dropped in surprise before it turned down in a reprimand. But to his credit, Chris said not a word.

Charlotte, however, had already made her way into the living room and was trying to retain her stiff-backed pose in an overstuffed chair that had been Jori's dad's favorite. Worn and tired, its springs no longer firm, it finally engulfed the slim form in a most unladylike way.

"Excuse me a moment," Jori muttered, trying to stifle the bubble of laughter in her throat. All that pompous stuffiness fell around the woman like ashes as she struggled to liberate her rigidly elegant self from the enveloping folds. "I'll be right back."

In the kitchen Jori gave way to the guffaws of laughter that could only be silenced inside the pantry's thick walls where no one could hear. She was surprised to find Chris pushing his way in moments later.

"Thank you," he breathed pressing a kiss to her forehead.

"You're welcome," Jori answered automatically. Her dark eyebrows flew upward. "For what?"

"For not taking Charlotte up on the gauntlet she tossed at your feet." His blue eyes swept in quick assessment over her. "I like your hair better when it's free," he told her softly, brushing his hand over the coil around her head. "But either way, you're still gorgeous."

"Supper," she murmured at last. "I have to get your supper."

Reluctantly, Chris eased away from her. "You always make all calm and rational thoughts leave my mind," he told her. "I just have to get near you and my mind turns to mush."

"Pretty good stuff, that mush." She chuckled. Her finger pointed to the table. "Dinner's almost ready," she said. "You'd better set another place."

When they finally sat down to dinner, Charlotte Davis looked more severe than ever, watching Chris as he enjoyed the noodles with a gusto that was somehow satisfying to Jori.

"Do you usually eat in the kitchen?" Dr. Davis asked, glancing around. "I suppose one must fit in with the local farm customs."

"Well, yes, there is that," Jori agreed, tamping down her anger. "But generally speaking, I find the kitchen to be more homey."

"What in heaven possessed you to come to this backwater town?" the woman demanded of her son, totally ignoring her hostess.

"I came to help out a friend." Jori listened as Chris quickly told her about Dan and Jessica and their baby. "It's not permanent, Mother," he told her placatingly.

Jori felt her heart drop. She had always known it, of course, but when Chris said it out loud, those words were so much more destructive. She struggled to retain her aplomb as the woman turned toward her.

"Have you always lived here, Miss Jessop?" It wasn't really a question, it was a demand, but Jori forced herself to answer civilly.

"Please, call me Jori," she invited, smiling. "No, not always. I returned a few years ago."

"How can you stand living in such primitive conditions?" The words cut deeply into Jori's pride.

"It's a small town, yes," Jori agreed, "but the city is only a bit away." Her defiant chin went up as she told the woman,

"I love it here. I know just about everyone and they know me. We're rather like a large extended family." Jori kept her words crisp and devoid of emotion.

"But my dear, surely you don't intend to stay here, to raise children in this, this Mossbank place? Anyplace less suitable I simply can't imagine. Don't you want them to know the world they will be living in?"

The scorn was evident in her tone and Jori could feel Chris shuffling in his chair. She made a fist under the table and smiled serenely, facing his mother.

"I don't have any children yet," she said firmly. "But if I did, this is exactly where I'd want to raise them. Many of the people who live in rural farming areas are not sophisticated. But they are good people who work hard and care for one another. If the world had more people like them, perhaps there wouldn't be so many problems."

Jori took a sip of her water. But it was clear that Chris's mother was not finished.

"But my dear," she advised in a patronizing tone. "You miss out on so much of the finer things in life here in the—" she stopped at the warning glance from Chris, but went blithely on seconds later "—in this area."

"People always think that anyone who lives in a small town is limited," Jori countered. "But everything is a trade-off, isn't it?" Her hand pointed to the table. "You probably have access to some wonderful wines, but we have pure water from wells that are uncontaminated. And while you can go to the theater or the opera whenever you choose, we *rural* folks can watch a beautiful sunset without obstructions, or listen to the birds twittering in wild areas behind our homes."

Jori stopped to draw a deep breath. Her fuming brown eyes fell on Chris, who was sitting with his face glued to his plate. She thought his shoulders were shaking. She kicked him. Jori was sick of being laughed at by Chris Davis and his mother.

"Just because I live in this area, doesn't mean I'm not interested in what's happening in other parts of the world. I just choose not to live there anymore. More lasagna?"

At the negative shake of Dr. Davis's perfectly groomed head, Jori swept up the empty plates and returned to the table with slices of angel food cake smothered in garden fresh raspberries and thick whipped farm cream. Those distributed, she returned with the coffeepot and poured some for everyone, before plunking the pot angrily onto a cork mat.

The remainder of their meal was silent except for Chris's attempts at lightening the atmosphere. He tried repeatedly to engage his mother in conversation with only limited success. Dr. Davis described the current social scene he was missing out on. She went into long detailed descriptions of her projects that had Jori's eyes glazing over. Charlotte even namedropped once or twice about local debutantes who had missed him. And through it all, Chris merely sat silent, shifting uncomfortably in his seat.

Jori was disgusted with the haughty woman who sat across from her. At the same time, she remembered her father remonstrating that a guest was still a guest, no matter how ignorant.

Finally, amid the tense, strained mood of the evening, Dr. Davis and her son finished their dessert. Jori could hardly wait to draw a deep relaxing breath and try to ease the strain from her shoulder muscles.

"Please, take your coffee into the living room," she told them both, tired of everything. "You need time to talk and I have a few things to do out here."

"But, Jori, we can't just leave you with all this," Chris protested. He picked up a few dishes and began stacking them in the dishwasher. Jori scooped the remainder from his hands.

"Thank you, but I think it would be best if you and your

mother talked in the other room," she said firmly, refusing to give way.

Dark blue eyes searched hers for a long moment. Finally Chris nodded in agreement. He escorted his mother out, but stopped in the doorway.

"It was a delicious meal, Jori. Thank you very much." His big hand brushed over the coil of hair around her head. "I'm sorry Mother upset you."

Once he had gone Jori took out her frustrations on her dishes, leaving two chipped plates and one broken cup. She couldn't help it after the remarks she heard coming from the other room.

"Your training is wasted here," Dr. Davis informed her son. "A GP could serve this community just as well with a third of the training and much less expense than you've caused us."

"Mother, you don't understand. Mossbank gives me back so much."

She'd cut him off, obviously furious.

"Mossbank." She spat the word out. "What is there in this backwater town that has you so impressed? It looks nothing like heaven to me. More like the back forty with those dreadful roads." Jori had grinned but kept her ear near the door. "You'll lose your position, Christopher. They won't hold on forever and then everything you've gained will be lost."

"What 'everything,' Mother?" he'd asked quietly, his voice dull.

"The money, the prestige, the importance of your work. The opportunity to advance—make a name for yourself. Maybe even teach someday. That was always your dream, as I recall." Jori heard the squeak of her father's chair. "Don't you care about those things anymore? Don't you want to be a contributor to society where it matters?"

Jori had wanted to yell that it mattered here in Mossbank.

To a whole town and the surrounding community, Chris Davis, M.D. mattered a lot. And to her he mattered more than anyone she'd ever known. But of course, it was none of her business and she highly doubted that he would thank her for interfering.

"Can you imagine what people are saying?" Dr. Davis's voice was low and filled with disgust. "Our son, a surgeon just beginning to make a name for himself, suddenly abandons his life's work to move out here—Nowhereville!" Her voice lowered and Jori had to strain to hear the next part.

"If it's that girl that has you so entranced, there are hundreds of them in Boston that are far better educated and much more suited as your escort."

"How can you say that after Jori invited you here, opened her home and fed you a wonderful meal?"

"Fine, she can cook. So what?" Charlotte Davis had an edge to her voice that brooked no discussion. "The kind of woman you need has to be able to host a dinner for the medical society. She has to be able to hold her own among the rich and elite of Boston, to encourage them to support your rise through the ranks." The contempt was evident in her voice. "That little office nurse would be totally out of her depth."

There was more—a lot more, Jori figured. But she just couldn't listen anymore. She could see all her hopes and dreams driving out of town and her heart sank. Disgusted with herself for eavesdropping, she pulled on an old anorak hanging on the back door, slipped on a pair of duck shoes and went for a walk.

Outside, the cool moist evening air caressed her hot cheeks, dissipating some of the irritation nagging at her. Jori talked to Flop as they walked down the sidewalk. She tried to sort out the variety of emotions that whirled through her mind.

"She's really a piece of work, isn't she, boy? All that

haughty posturing. She's certainly pouring on the guilt to try to talk him into going back to the high, muck-a-muck life in the city." She frowned. "I don't want him to go," she told the dog. "I want him to stay here." Flop woofed his agreement.

They walked across the small park that stood kitty-corner to Jori's property. She had played there many times as a child. Cried there, too, when her mother had died, when she had scraped her knees, and when, at eight years old, Douglas Morris had kissed her on the lips. A tiny grin whisked across her lips as she remembered those times.

Flop ran off to investigate the wonders of the park grass, so Jori sank onto the old rope swing and pushed herself back and forth. At last Jori admitted to herself what she had known for weeks.

She was in love with Chris. The knowledge had hung there, suspended in her unconscious until she could deny it no more. It wasn't just his good looks or his handsome physique. It had more to do with the sad, mischievous little boy that hid behind those deep blue eyes, waiting to be freed whenever propriety got lost.

It had a lot to do with the way Chris's big strong arms made her feel secure and the way his very nearness comforted her.

Jori admitted that her love also had a lot to do with the effort he had made to fit in with the community. Chris was a good sport. He had tried hard to get to know his patients and their life-style while clearly acknowledging his deficits in the area of agriculture.

Finally, Jori conceded the impossibility of that love. Chris would return, sooner or later, to his big-city hospital and his wealthy friends. He would resume the cold, impersonal medical practice he'd had before. It was inevitable.

And he should, she told herself vehemently. It was what he

loved to do, the reason he had spent years in training and then working in residencies that offered little in monetary recompense and a lot in stress and worry.

Abruptly, the reason for Chris's choice in the field of medicine dawned on Jori. She had heard only a little of his childhood, but it was enough to leave Jori with the impression of a cold, sterile atmosphere. Chris was a person who liked to touch people—a handshake, a pat on the shoulder, ruffling a child's hair. He was always touching her—brushing a hand over her hair, or pressing his long finger against her chin. Jori could only imagine the impact such a frigid childhood would have on a man as sensitive as he.

But Chris had risen above it. In his own way, he had eventually let himself come to care for the people of Mossbank. And in such an atmosphere, he seemed not to need the immunity a large city hospital would have given. For so long Chris had taken care of others while he ignored his own needs. He'd found this place where he could relax, be himself, be accepted. But Jori wondered if his newfound peace would last in the impersonality of the city hospital.

Jori stared at the sodden grass beneath her feet. "I know how much he loves his work." The words came heavily but she said them, nonetheless.

"I know that he's not mine. He never was. He's committed to his life and I to mine here in Mossbank. So, Lord," she sighed heavily, "what am I going to do? I still want to be part of a happy loving family. I want to have children and enjoy them while I'm still young. Do you have another plan for me?

"I love him, God. I never thought it would happen again, but it has. And it's all so hopeless." The heaving sobs finally ebbed away, leaving her drained and lifeless. "What am I going to do now?"

"What's a pretty girl like you doing out on an awful night like this?" The voice was low and filled with laughter.

Jori wheeled around to stare up into a face she barely recalled from high school.

"David? David Andrews?" Jori whispered at the tall lanky man in front of her. "What in the world are you doing back in Mossbank?"

"I could ask the same of you." He grinned, bending to grasp both of her hands in his. "Last I heard you had made it. Big-time."

"I live here now," she told him quietly. "What about you? You were doing something political, as I recall. And married, too!"

His craggy face fell.

"Yes, I was but we split up about three years ago. Marilee wanted to stay on and move up the fast track but I got downsized and decided to change directions. I'm setting up an office in town and I'm going to practice here. Nothing earth-shattering. Just small-town basic law."

They chatted for several moments before the clouds opened again.

"I'd better get back home. Davey's with a sitter but I don't like to leave him too long. He's my five-year-old son," David explained. "And the pride and joy of my life. Hey, maybe we can go for coffee or lunch sometime."

"I'd like that," Jori murmured, thinking of the woman who had left little Davey with his father. It didn't seem fair somehow. She wanted a child to love and take care of so badly and other women abandoned theirs.

"Good. How about lunch tomorrow?" David's face crinkled in a huge grin. "No sense wasting time."

Jori agreed with a smile, and they arranged a time and place. As she whistled to Flop and headed for home, Jori considered this new turn of events. Maybe this was what God had in mind for her. No doubt Chris with his fathomless blue eyes and big grinning smile was meant for someone else and God had sent David along for her to be with.

"I can be the best darn stepmother going!" A few seconds later she was giggling merrily. She'd only just met David again and suddenly she was a stepmother? "Come on, Flop. The rain's seeped into my brain."

Thankfully, Chris and his mother seemed to have left, and although Jori supposed she should have felt guilty for abandoning them, she relished the opportunity to sink into the hot, bubbling bathwater and soak away her frustrations.

For her, there was no future outside of Mossbank. There couldn't be. If there was one lesson she had learned, it was that she belonged right here. The people who cared about her were here and she couldn't abandon them. She would stay and pay off her debt to them, and lead whatever life God gave her.

"I'll learn how to be satisfied with that," she told herself. "Just like Paul says in the New Testament—I have learned to be content in whatever state I'm in." It wasn't a cheering thought but Jori knew there was nothing else to do.

"Not unless a minor miracle comes along," she whispered to Flop. The phone rang as she was emptying the tub.

"Miss Jessop? This is Lara Mandon. I'm sorry to call you so late, but I knew you'd want to know our decision immediately."

"Yes, I do." Jori crossed her fingers as the woman from the agency cleared her voice. "Am I going to be allowed to adopt?"

"I'm sorry, but no. The board feels that with the shortage of babies and the surplus of couples willing to adopt them, it would be remiss of us to put you on our list. I hope you understand."

"No," Jori said trying to keep the bitterness from her

voice. "I don't understand at all. I'm more than willing to give a child a home and you're telling me that I can't. That you don't want to let me have a baby."

"There are several other avenues open to you, Miss Jessop. You could try fostering for the state, although they generally prefer two-parent families. Or perhaps some medical intervention...artificial insemination, maybe?"

"I don't think so, but thanks anyway, Miss Mandon. It was good of you to call."

As she replaced the phone, Jori steeled herself against the tears. Her dream of a family had turned to ashes.

Stoically she stood and began straightening the room, pretending that life went on when she felt dead inside. The phone rang again and Jori picked it up listlessly. It was Jessica.

"Hi, Jori. We have a daughter, Liza Jean!"

Jori swallowed her pain and congratulated her friend before demanding all the particulars.

"Well, she was born early this morning. She weighs five pounds, two ounces." There was a long pause and Jori knew something not quite as wonderful would follow. Finally Jessica's tearful voice told her the rest.

"They are going to operate in the morning, Jori. Her heart is defective. The doctors are going to try to repair it right away. Dan and I are sitting here, just waiting." Her friend's soft, tearful voice faded away.

"Jessica, little Liza is going to be fine. You have to believe that. I'll be praying and so will the rest of the town." Jori made her voice firm and convincing. "You and Dan just rest and know that we'll all be here, waiting for you three to come home."

They chatted for a few moments more until Jessica turned the phone over to Dan.

"How's my best nurse?" Jori thought he sounded tired, deflated.

"Oh, I'm just fine, Dr. Gordon, sir. Congratulations, I hear you are a father. Poor little girl to end up with a bossy fellow like you." The banter continued for several moments. Jori hid her own feelings as she fought depression off. Gradually it seeped away as Dan teased her.

"How's my stand-in doing?" he demanded. "I hope he's taken advantage of the good advice I gave him."

"What advice?" Jori asked absentmindedly, pulling a brush through her long hair.

"About you, of course. I told him my nurse was ready for love and he would fill the bill nicely."

Jori groaned, blushing furiously. The words lined up in her head, ready to blast out at him when she heard Jessica's voice in the background.

"Stop lying, Dan. You only said Jori would keep him in line."

Jori breathed a sigh of thanks that she hadn't made a fool of herself. Still, Daniel Gordon, GP, had one coming. In a moment the answer came to her.

"It's okay, Dan. When you get home you will be far too busy changing diapers and eating Emma Simms's cheese-cakes. I'm sure you won't have time to worry about my love life." She grinned, satisfied, as she heard his groan in the background. She added the last bit of bait. "Chris's been fill-ing your freezer with them for weeks."

"Jori, that's not fair. You know the woman can't bake..."

Jori cut him off midstream, smiling at Jessica's chuckles in the background.

"I have to go now, Dan. I have a hot date to plan and it's *not* with a doctor. Kiss Liza and Jess for me and thanks for phoning."

"Jori?" Dan's voice was soft and consoling. "I know how much you want your own child and that this must hurt you.

But if God can look after Liza's medical problems, he can give you the desires of your heart.''

"I know.'' Jori choked down the emotion that gripped her. "It's just that I'm having a little trouble on the when part.'' She straightened her backbone and tried for a light tone. "I'll be fine. You guys take care of each other and the baby. I love you, bye.''

Happiness and sadness vied for uppermost position in her mind as she thought of the tiny baby that hung on to life so precariously. Another family looking toward the future with hope, she mused sadly. And she was still out in the cold.

"Stop feeling sorry for yourself and get on the phone,'' she ordered angrily.

Her mind breathed a prayer for the baby as she phoned Faith, Hope and Charity who would organize the members of the local ladies' group into a prayer chain. She had to believe that there would be a baby shower when the Gordons returned.

As she dialed, a question whisked across Jori's mind, leaving her shaken and wondering. Would she ever have a new little baby to hold and cuddle and call her own? Or a husband to share those wonderful moments with?

Chapter Ten

Dr. Chris Davis was not looking forward to leaving Mossbank even given the cool, wet weather that had hampered the
farmers this past week. The fact that it had also put a blight
on his mother's now extended visit had something to do with
that.

Not that she had been thrilled to be there anyway, for he
knew she'd only stayed longer to insist he give up this work.
And with the constant rain, there was little opportunity for
him to point out the obvious natural beauties of the area. Not
that she was interested.

Charlotte Davis was not accustomed to studying nature in
the raw. She spent most of her time in her pristine, climate-
controlled lab. Her trip west had been of necessity not for
pleasure, she'd told him shortly. A duty she felt compelled to
attend to.

"I did not come to this remote community to see the local
sights. Your father and I agreed that one of us had to try to
bring you to your senses." Her glance through the shabby
hotel window had been disparaging. "I came to bring you
back to where you belong."

"Well, I'm not ready to leave. Not just yet. Come on, Mother. It's not that far to the city and you might enjoy it if you got to know the locals."

Her straight, severe mouth had curled at that and Chris had known there was nothing to be gained by pursuing the matter. She would fulfill her *mission,* as she termed it, and then return to the work she considered more important than anything: research. Within minutes of entering the lab, Chris knew she would lose herself in the current project and forget about him until something or someone else reminded her of her motherly duty.

He didn't mind. Not anymore, he corrected himself. There had been a time when he had craved his parents' attention, some show of affection; had wished his mother knew how to bake cookies or hold birthday parties; that his father would come out to play catch once in a while.

But somehow, Chris acknowledged sadly, the impossibility of achieving that dream had finally been accepted internally. His parents were not like that. They could not show outward signs of affection with the spontaneity and uninhibited ease he had longed for. To compensate for the shortfall, they strove for excellence in their professional fields and taught him to search for it himself. It was just that work wasn't enough anymore.

Of course they loved him. Chris knew that. Both his parents were concerned about his career. He grimaced as he remembered his mother's caustically cynical remarks regarding Chris's current situation.

"I can't believe you're going to throw it all away," she'd muttered. "And for what? There are lots of women who are just as pretty as your office nurse. And a lot more cosmopolitan in their outlook, I can tell you."

"Mother, Jordanna Jessop was a world-famous, top-notch model. She is hardly small-town stuff!"

"Then why is she hiding herself in the boonies dispensing peace and goodwill? And if you two are so thick, why is she going out to lunch with that young man?" his mother had countered. "She doesn't want you, Christopher. If she did and you decided to go back to Boston, I guarantee she'd follow. Don't sacrifice yourself here."

Chris didn't bother to explain that Jordanna couldn't and wouldn't leave the tiny community. Nor did he want to hear about some new man in her life. The bottom line was that Charlotte wanted him back in Boston. Now. She could not understand his growing affinity with his patients, let alone the unexpected pleasure he derived treating people who had become known entities. How did he expect her to understand someone like Jori? Charlotte couldn't even understand why he had consented to staying here for so long.

"You belong at the General, or somewhere like it," she had told him, mapping his future out in her usual organized style. "There is little call for your specialized skills here. You're wasting your talents."

That, it seemed, was the end of that.

"Mother, these are people with needs every bit as great as those I treated in the city. And if I screw up, or prescribe something that doesn't work, they come back and tell me. It's face-to-face here, personal. There are no huge bureaucratic paper trails to follow up."

Chris made no attempt to tell her that he had been enjoying himself. He knew her opinion very well. This wasn't *important* medicine. Not like the major surgeries he had performed within the hallowed confines of the major hospitals. To Charlotte, these were the little people, and as such, far removed from her milieu.

And in a way, Chris brooded, she was right. He had trained long and hard in order to be qualified to perform the specialized surgeries he had done. And he had enjoyed the work at first. He'd been proud of the success he'd become and the prestige he'd gained. But gradually, his life had become impersonal and cold.

In Mossbank, impersonal would never happen. Oh, some moved out and new folks arrived, but by and large, the majority of people were stable to the area. The baby you delivered last week would be back in periodically for the next eighteen years or so and you could monitor his progress as you stitched and casted and advised.

Chris liked that component of medicine more than anything. That sense of continuity was new and intriguing. And while he occasionally missed the high-tech, fast-paced operating room equipment, he relished the familiarity and friendliness with which his patients treated their doctor. He liked the way Jori treated him even better.

He loved her!

The realization hit him squarely in the stomach, driving away his breath. Chris didn't know why he was surprised. He'd been entranced by her ever since Dan had introduced them. She had only to stare at him with those melting chocolate-colored eyes, or tip her wide, generous lips into a smile and he could feel his knees buckle.

Jori was saucy and beautiful and bright. She glowed with a zest for living that refused to be dimmed by anyone. Her joy in life was as fresh and unspoiled as a child's. She bounded forward, embracing each day with her brisk, no-nonsense attitude that dared him to rain on her parade. And she refused to back down where her principles were concerned.

One of her most steadfast principles was to remain right here in Mossbank. Chris thought he had accepted her decision to bury herself here. Now, suddenly, he realized the personal implication her decision would have on him. Dan and Jessica would come back and he would leave. Alone.

It would be extremely difficult to build a surgical practice here and the travel involved in commuting to a city center didn't bear thinking about. Besides, there wasn't any teaching facility near by.

"It's all right, Mother. You can go back and tell Father I'll be returning to the fold. I've been offered a teaching position in the East. I start as soon as Dan and Jessica get back."

It was amazing how quickly his mother had left after that. In less than half an hour she had packed her rental car, called the airline and taken off out of town like a cat chased by a dog.

"Nice seeing you, Mother," Chris muttered to himself as he strode back to the clinic. "Don't worry about me. I'll be fine."

Now he noticed Jori coming from the opposite direction. She was laughing and smiling at a tall skinny guy by her side. Every so often she leaned down and ruffled the hair of a little boy plodding along beside them, and Chris felt a fist of jealousy clench the muscles of his stomach. That should be him she was with, their child she spoke to. She waved at Chris then walked into the clinic.

But it can't be, Lord. I understand that. I can't ask her to leave everything she holds dear. He slowed up his pace, enjoying the ruffle of wind across his skin. *Her father's getting worse; day by day, week by week, he forgets a little more, and I can't, I won't ask her to abandon him. Maybe in the future...* The thought died away. There was no future. Not for the two of them. They would soon be separated by thousands of miles.

He sat on the park bench, lost in his thoughts, until an urgent voice broke through his musings. "Chris, you've got to come right away. There's been an accident!"

He jolted to his feet, a surge of adrenalin racing through his bloodstream.

"It's Jonathan," he heard Jori gasp as she raced beside him to the clinic.

The little boy was whimpering as his mother held him, one hand pressing a spotless white tea towel against his scalp. His eyes were half-open, and Chris recognized the drowsiness of his patient.

"Hi, Jonathan," he called out cheerfully, patting the boy's little hand. Carefully he peeled back the towel, wincing mentally at the gash that yawned open on the child's scalp. He replaced the towel and spoke sharply, hoping to rouse Jonathan enough to keep him awake.

"Jonathan, do you want to go for a car ride?" The child blinked slowly, his huge eyes regarding Christopher solemnly. "Keep him awake," he ordered Jori. "I don't want him nodding off just yet." He turned to Amy Grand, scratching notes on his pad as he spoke. "Did he fall?"

"Yes. About eight feet," she whispered, brushing her hand over the child's small body. "I was working in a flower bed and I'd left a shovel there. That's how he cut his head." Tears flowed down her white cheeks. "Bob's in the field so I piled both kids in the car and drove like crazy." She swatted away the tears and stared at Chris. "He's going to be okay, isn't he?"

"I'll know more after I've had a better look." She tried to stand and he pressed her down. "No, stay there. I want to move him as little as possible. Jori, bring a cart, will you?" He specified what he wanted on it and then left her to get it while he checked Jonathan's pupil reaction.

"You know that I'm a doctor, don't you, Jonathan?" The boy nodded imperceptibly, his eyes drooping. "And I want to help make you all better?" Again the child's head nodded. "Okay then. But I need you to help me out. And the first thing you have to do is stay awake."

"Too tired," Jonathan slurred.

"No, son. You can do it. You're strong." Carefully, Chris lifted away the towel and dabbed gently at the wound on the child's scalp, carefully removing the dried blood and dirt. As he took the swabs from Jori, Chris noticed that her hand was shaking. He checked swiftly, surprised to see how white she'd become.

"I'm fine," she told him grimly. "Go ahead."

One searching look was all he could afford but it told him that Jordanna Jessop would stay the course. He turned back to his patient, all senses on alert.

The injury was a jagged cut from below Jonathan's ear to the back part of his head. There was some swelling, but Chris could not tell much beyond that.

"I want pictures," he instructed Jordanna. "And I'd like them before I suture him. Can you phone the hospital and tell them it's a rush?" She nodded and hurried away while Chris sat down to explain to Jonathan and his mother.

"At the hospital they have this machine that can take pictures of the inside of your head, Jonathan."

"Why?" The question was drowsy, and Chris sat the boy up more solidly in Amy's arms, checking the pulse as he did.

"The pictures tell me whether this is just a plain ordinary cut from a shovel or if you bumped your brain. I want to make sure your brain didn't get hurt."

"What if it did?" Jonathan demanded. "Do you have to cut it out? Auntie Jori said you're a cutting kind of doctoh."

"Sometimes I do that," Chris grinned. "But usually I don't take out brains. Sometimes I sew people up so their insides can't fall out. I think that's what we'll have to do with you."

"Will it hurt?" Jonathan's voice was small and he bit on his lip bravely.

"The pictures won't hurt. But yes, when I sew you up it will hurt. A little bit. But it won't take long and then you'll be good as new. Will that be okay?" He waited while the child thought it over, head tilted to one side as Jonathan considered.

"Can Brit come, too?"

"No." Chris shook his head. "She's too small. Anyway, hospitals are really for people who need help. Did she fall, too?"

Jonathan giggled; it was muffled and short, to be sure, but it was a giggle.

"Brit didn't fall! She don't walk." His eyes were wide-open now as he grinned at his sister.

"What's wrong with her?" Chris pretended amazement. "Does she need her legs fixed?"

"A 'course not!" Jonathan sounded astonished. "Don't you know babies gotta learn to walk?"

"I'll have to study up," Chris promised gravely, lifting the child carefully from his mother's arms. "Shall we go now?"

He waited for Amy's nod of approval and then glanced back at Jori, assessing her state of mind with a clinical glance.

"Maybe Auntie Jori could hold you while your mommy holds Brit and I drive the car."

"Jon dwive?" The little boy's eyes twinkled up at him and Chris felt a stab of something deep within his heart at the trust he glimpsed there.

"Not today, pal," Chris said with a laugh, helping them into his car. "But when Jon's head is all better, I'll take him for a drive. Okay, buddy?"

Jon agreed happily, leaning against Jori's shoulder with a sigh and Chris let his eyes slide up to meet her brown ones, conscious of the woman in the back seat.

"Children suit you," he murmured, shifting into gear. "You should have lots of them." Mine, he whispered mentally and then stopped in disbelief as he saw the huge tears roll down her cheeks. "J.J.?"

"Drive," she whispered, staring straight ahead. "Just drive."

* * *

"Jordanna Jessop has a new boyfriend." Faith Johnson smiled triumphantly as she imparted this latest bit of news. When she noticed the skeptical looks on her friends' faces she frowned. "His name is David Andrews, he has a little boy called Davey and he used to live here, so there."

"The only Andrews I knew other than Clarence, was a family that had a shoe store in town. As I recall, their kids would have been much younger than Jordanna." Charity frowned.

"No, dear. That was Anderson. Andrews was the fellow at the seed plant, where they crush canola to make margarine." Hope smiled gently. "They moved when David graduated. He was such an intelligent boy—very good in the debate club, I recall."

"But why would Jori be going out with him? I'm sure she's in love with Dr. Chris." Charity glared accusingly at the other two. "Have you two been matchmaking?"

Faith grinned cheerfully.

"Only for you," she blurted out. "And that didn't seem to work out very well. Not now that you and Frank Bellows are together all the time."

"We're not together *all* the time," Charity muttered, face flushed a dark red. "And anyway, it was just for pretend—at first."

"What?" Hope stared. "Charity Flowerday, what have you been up to?"

With as little detail as possible, Charity tried to explain how it came about that she and the local undertaker spent a goodly portion of each day together.

"He's been very kind," she asserted. "I don't know what I would have done without him."

"You're in love with him!" Faith's faded eyes twinkled

merrily. "At last!" She clapped her hands together. "I thought it would never happen."

"Hush, Faith!" Hope caught the glimmer of anger in Charity's brown focus. "Don't tease her. If and when Charity has something to say, I'm sure she'll tell us."

"I *have* something to say," Charity admitted softly. "Frank and I have decided to get married."

"I knew it!" Faith hugged and kissed her friend gleefully. "I just knew you were in love with him."

"I didn't. I thought you said you couldn't stand the man." Hope's perplexed face mirrored her confusion. "As I recall, you said he was boring."

"Well, as we got to know one another, we found we had a lot in common. But I thought we were going to decide about Jori and Dr. Chris?"

"Just one more thing," Faith begged, her face glowing. "When's the wedding?"

"We're having a very small one," Charity cautioned. "Close friends and family, but that's all. At my age you don't have a big celebration."

"Why not? It's a big occasion." Hope frowned.

"I'm not the kind of woman who looks good in satin and lace and I don't intend to wear it, Hope Conroy. I want something plain and simple but it will have to be soon because we want Dr. Chris there. After all, he was the reason we got together and he'll be leaving as soon as Dan and Jessica get back."

"But he can't leave without Jordanna." Hope's usually calm voice was raised. "I thought for sure they'd come to some arrangement, figure out some plan. Anyway, I wanted them to stay here."

"No, he's definitely going back...alone." Charity's voice was filled with sadness. "Dr. Chris has been offered a prestigious post in a teaching hospital. He says he's wanted it for a long time."

They sat, the three of them, pondering the situation.

"You say Jori's going out with someone new, Faith?" Charity frowned, scratching her nose.

"David Andrews," Hope murmured. A gentle smile tipped up the corners of her mouth. "He had quite a crush on Flossie Gerbrandt, if I recall. The two of them spent the last two years of school as steadies. I always thought she'd marry him."

"He did get married. But he's divorced now," Faith imparted knowledgeably.

"Is he? How nice." Faith and Hope stared at the strange sentiment coming from their friend's smiling lips. "I do believe I'd like to have some people over for dinner," she whispered with a wicked tilt of her eyebrows. "Flossie's already asked to help me with the wedding. What better time to discuss it than tonight! Now let's see…" She thumbed through the church directory, shifting her trifocals a little lower on her nose. "Ah, yes, here it is. New members—Andrews."

"She's doing it again," Faith whispered to Hope. "She's going to try and get them together."

"I know. And while she's busy with that, you and I need to plan a shower for her and Frank. I think a nice couples affair would be a rather pleasant shower."

"Piffle! She's already got her cupboards full," Faith exclaimed. "What in the world would we give them?"

"I think," Hope elaborated slowly, "we might consider a money tree with the funds to go toward a trip to that mineral springs. Remember? It's that spa that's supposed to be so helpful for arthritis. Frank has bad knees, you know. He'd enjoy it, too."

And they whispered and giggled merrily until Charity put down the phone. Her eyes studied them suspiciously.

"What have you two been talking about?"

"The future," Hope told her, jabbing an elbow in Faith's side as that woman started to speak. "And we think it might be a good idea if we have Dr. Chris over for dinner. In fact, we could make it a farewell evening. We've a lot to be grateful for."

Chapter Eleven

Jori knew she was in rough shape. It had been two weeks since little Jonathan's injury but she still couldn't erase the memory of Chris's wonderful skill as he'd soothed the boy. But hearing him say the same thing that was in her heart had made it so much worse. She would be good with kids, darn it! And she wanted to share them with Chris!

Christopher Davis was wonderful with children. He would make a wonderful father. But they wouldn't be her children; they couldn't be. He would leave and then she'd be all alone again.

She couldn't stop the awful message from whirling around in her brain regardless of how hard she drove herself. Alone. Alone.

"I declare, Jordanna Jessop, you look as skinny as a rail!" Jori heard Charity's voice as she got out of her car and walked toward her house. "What are you doing to yourself, child? Is your father worse?"

"A little." She pasted a smile on her lips. "But why are we talking about me? It's the day before your wedding—how are *you* doing? You're glowing!"

"I feel like that, too," Charity admitted. "Once I gave up all my fears and inhibitions and explained to Frank why I was so hesitant to get married again, well, the burden just lifted." She giggled. "Isn't it silly? I thought Frank had stayed away from me because I was all crippled up with this arthritis and now he tells me that he's been in love with me for years. He was just too shy to make the first move." She blushed. "Thank goodness for Dr. Chris."

"Yes, thank goodness," Jori agreed doubtfully.

"How are the two of you getting on now, dear? I know you were beginning to feel something for him. Hasn't it worked out?"

"No." Jori frowned. "It hasn't. He's leaving, you see. And my place is here, in Mossbank. I've always known that."

"Is that why you began going out with David Andrews?" Charity asked waspishly. "You feel Chris is unattainable?"

"Something like that." There was no point in prevaricating, Jori decided. Charity was her friend. It was time to tell her the truth. "I want a home of my own, Charity. I want a family that I can share my life with. But I just can't let myself rely on someone and then have them abandon me."

"And you think Chris Davis would do this?" Charity demanded with a frown.

"He's leaving, Charity. As soon as Dan gets back. And I can't." She straightened her shoulders defensively. "Besides, David is kind and funny. We share things from the past."

"I think he's simply comfortable," Charity muttered, glaring at her knotted fingers. "You're settling for less, Jori. And what's more, you're selling God short."

"I don't think we should continue this," Jori murmured, not wanting to hurt the older woman.

"Yes, we should. And I'll tell you why. David is a nice man. *And*," she paused expectantly, "he has a son. A cute little child that tugs on your heart strings, whose very look begs for some mothering.'' She waited for a moment. ''But David Andrews is a man, not a little boy. And he deserves a woman who can share his *life* not just his child. Someone like Flossie.''

''Flossie? Oh, but she's...''

''Been out with him several times,'' Charity confirmed with a nod of her white head. ''And he's been to dinner at her house. I think he really cares for her, or he could. If you'd let him.''

''But I haven't...'' Jori's voice died away at the intent look in Charity's discerning eyes.

''God has something special in mind for you, Jordanna. Something that He's planned since before you were conceived. And if you'll only let Him work in your life, you'll find more happiness than all the manipulation you can manage on your own.'' Charity wrapped one thin arm around Jori's shoulders and hugged her close.

''But you can't walk in fear, Jori. You can't duck out and take the easy way. You have to learn the lesson before you get the prize. Maybe it's time you stopped trying to control events and let God direct you the way He wants.'' Her voice dropped to a soft whisper. ''God has something He wants to teach you, my dear. Something so wonderful, you can't imagine. And when that day comes, today's trials will seem like nothing.''

''You sound like Dad,'' Jori murmured, glancing down at the gnarled old hands that held hers so lovingly. ''He quoted Psalms 30:5 today. *'Weeping may endure for the night, but joy comes in the morning.'*''

''James may have lost bits and pieces of his past but he has kept his wonderful memories of the scriptures.'' Charity smiled. ''And it's true, dear. You may not believe it now but take it from an old lady who's been through the valley. Cling to this—*'You will show me the path of life; Your presence is fullness of joy; At your right hand are pleasures forever-more.'''* Charity moved back a step, her face shining with happiness.

"Let Him show you the path to a full life, Jori."

The wedding of Charity Flowerday and Frank Bellows took place in the local church. It was a brief affair with the bride's best friends escorting her down the aisle, one on each arm. Charity had decided on a lovely cream woolen suit and she carried a small sheaf of deep pink roses.

"I, Charity, take you, Frank, to be my lawful wedded husband. To have and to hold, in sickness or in health, from this day forward, forever more."

The words rang through the tiny sanctuary with a sureness and clarity that brought tears to Jori's eyes. Frank's face was beaming with delight as he leaned down and pressed a hearty kiss against his new wife's lips in a way that made his devotion and great love that evident to the entire congregation.

Christopher had managed to seat himself beside Jori and now his fingers entwined with hers as his blue eyes noted the moisture on her cheeks.

"It's pretty special when it's someone like those two, isn't it?" he whispered softly. "But then," he added, staring at her, "I guess marriage is meant to be pretty special."

There was nothing she could say to that, so Jori contented herself with clapping as the happy couple strolled down the aisle, beaming as they accepted their friends' congratulations. She'd tried to keep him out of her life just as she'd wanted him out of her heart.

"Are you going to use all that confetti?" Chris whispered in her ear. Jori put half of it into his open hands and then eased her way to the front of the crowd surrounding the bride and groom on the cold, windswept sidewalk.

"Best wishes, Charity, and you, too, Frank. I know you'll

be very happy together.'' Hugging the older woman, Jori felt the constriction in her throat and hung on for an extra moment.

"You will be, too, my dear," Charity whispered. "Just keep trusting."

Jori stepped back and raised her arms, sprinkling the multicolored dots of paper over the white heads of her friends.

Just like God's blessings, Jori remembered from some wedding long past.

"All right, everyone!" Faith stood at the top of the steps clapping her hands to gain everyone's attention. "Don't stand around freezing. We have a lovely meal at the senior's hall. It's warm in there and you can visit all you like."

As a group, the townsfolk quickly moved to their cars to drive the short trip to the hall. Jori hugged her coat around her more snugly to shield out the wind and headed for her Jeep.

"Can I tag along?" Christopher stood beside her, his collar up around his ears. "I'd walk but it's too c-cold."

"That's North Dakota for you," Jori agreed, ordering her pulse to slow down. It didn't mean anything; he just needed a ride. "And this is only October!"

"You look very beautiful," he murmured when she pulled to a stop. "Red is certainly your color. Vibrant and full of life."

"Er, thank you," Jori murmured, unable to tear her gaze from his. "You look very nice, too."

"Jori," he whispered as she moved to open the door. His blue eyes were deep and intent as they studied her.

"Yes?" She tried to look away and found she couldn't. There was something so compelling in his eyes. Something that riveted her attention on him and denied her attempt to look away.

"I'll be leaving soon, J.J." he murmured. "Dan's on his way back and then I've got to go."

"I know. And I can't tell you how much we in Mossbank appreciate this time you've given to us. I've enjoyed working with you, too." Deliberately, Jori kept the conversation on the same businesslike footing she'd used for weeks now. "But I think we'd better go in now. They'll be starting soon." She slid out of her seat and grabbed her purse before slamming the door and moving to the front of the vehicle. Her evasive tactics didn't work.

Chris caught up with her at the front door of the hall, his fingers closing about her elbow. His face was tight and controlled, his lips clamped together. Those vivid blue eyes were cool as they stared at her, but she caught the glint of understanding in his voice.

"We are going to talk, Jordanna. Maybe not here. Maybe not now. But before I leave, I intend to say what I have to say. And you will listen. It's too important to ignore." And then he leaned down and pressed a kiss against her surprised lips before yanking the door open. "After you, ladies."

Jori turned in time to see Faith and Hope sweep through the entry, their grins wide and understanding. With a grimace in Chris's direction, Jori tilted her head and walked through the door, somehow staving off her fury at his temerity.

Still, she mused, hanging her coat on top of another one in the cramped entry, he had kissed her as if he meant it. At least she had that to hold on to.

The reception was unlike anything the people of Mossbank had seen at a wedding before. Tables of food were scattered here and there throughout the hall inviting the guests to snack whenever they wished. There were plenty of chairs for anyone who wished to sit. No stack of presents waited to be opened. The bride and groom had requested no gifts in their invitation in the local newspaper. That didn't stop Harry Conroy and

Arthur Johnson from collecting donations from anyone who cared to contribute and it didn't mean that there weren't a stack of cards and a few gag items displayed around the hall.

"The wedding cake is a train?" Chris sounded amazed as he stared at the seven-car confection that sat upon licorice tracks.

Jori grinned at him, catching the sense of fun that prevailed. "Yes, and I understand that it's all edible. Melanie said her mother insisted on it." As they stood staring, a group of small children ventured near, eyes wide as they stared at the masterpiece. Jonathan Grand was among them and it was he who reached out and stole a mint from the caboose.

"He looks good, doesn't he?" Chris murmured. "No aftereffects from his slight concussion, thank the Lord."

"They all look good," Jori told him sincerely. "Thanks to you. You've done a fine job here. I don't know how we could ever thank you."

"I don't need thanks," Chris told her gruffly. "I've gained more from being here than I could ever give. I'll be sorry to leave."

Jori was about to turn away when a sudden scuffling at the entry drew her attention.

"Hey!" A voice she knew and loved called out laughingly. "Can't a couple leave for a few weeks without you folks carrying on like this?"

Dr. Daniel Gordon, M.D., stood grinning in the doorway, his arm around the waist of his happy wife who carried a tiny baby in her arms.

As the rest of the crowd rushed forward to greet the prodigal and his family, Jori turned around, her eyes on Chris's bemused face.

"You knew, didn't you?" She felt her heart drop to her feet. If Dan was home, Chris wouldn't be staying long. There wasn't any point.

"Yes, I knew," he admitted softly. "But you anticipated that from the beginning, didn't you, Jori? My coming to Mossbank was only ever a temporary thing."

As the words stabbed through her heart, shattering all her dreams, Jori turned away, fumbling toward the ladies' room at the back.

No matter how much she'd hoped, how much she'd dreamed, the result was still the same. Chris was leaving.

Why? she begged, staring into the mirror. *Why couldn't he stay here?*

But there was no answer from heaven and other ladies were clustering into the bathroom now. Gathering composure like a cloak around her, Jordanna walked out of the room and toward the entrance. She would trust God with this; at least she would try.

"It's so good to have you guys home," she lied easily. "And this is Liza! Hello, sweetheart." She ignored the pain in her heart and accepted the bundle of softly scented sleeping baby from her friend. "She's a darling, Jess. Just a darling."

Over the heads of the crowd, Jori's eyes locked with Chris's. She saw the need darken their depths and the way his eyes squeezed shut, as if to ward off the pain. Without a word he turned and walked through the door, completely forgetting his coat.

Chapter Twelve

Jori expected the days to drag, but in fact, she was kept busy as the three doctors spent the week catching up. Dr. Green wasn't affected by the transition much, except that he and Dan had grown close over the years, often covering for each other on a special weekend or holiday. The same connection had sprung up between Chris and Dr. Green, and Jori had noticed how frequently Chris had taken over some of the older man's workload. Now that was to be transferred back to Dan which meant checking and rechecking the files to make sure Dan saw the updates of those patients he'd been worried about.

If that wasn't enough to keep Jori hopping, there was a lot of after-hours community planning and organizing going on to welcome the new baby and shower Liza and her mother with an abundance of baby things.

"I'm so glad we had that house cleaned from top to bottom before they arrived," Charity rambled happily over the phone to Jori. "Jessica can have a bit of a rest. Speaking of that, it's my shift with the wee one soon, not that she needs monitoring. Her heart is better than ever. I'd better go." She stopped for a moment and then in a softer tone asked, "How are you doing, dear?"

"I'm praying a lot, Charity. That's all I can do now." Jori carried her dishes to the sink, dragging the phone cord behind her shoulder.

"My dear, that's the very best thing! When you can't see a way through, you have to pray and ask God to open one up."

They had just finished their conversation when the doorbell rang. It was Chris. A tired, pale Chris who stood on the doorstep shuffling from one foot to the other.

"Hi. Can I come in?"

Silently, she opened the door wider.

"I'm leaving tomorrow," he said bleakly.

Jori walked through to the living room dazedly and sank into the nearest chair, telling herself to breathe normally. The time had finally come, as she'd known it would. But now was not the time to be weak and give in to the tears that threatened to spill out at the thought of losing him.

"I'm sorry you have to go," she offered in a friendly but distant tone, her throat clogged. "We've enjoyed having you here."

"I've learned so much from you, Jori. I'm in love with you and I've been trying to tell you for days. But you've been so busy pushing me away, and there's been so much to do with Dan's return, that I let it go. I was afraid to hope, afraid to dream we even had a future."

His face clouded over, his eyes dark with the seriousness of his words. "But now I'm leaving and I've got to know for sure. Do you love me or do I have a bad case of wishful thinking?"

She stared at him. "Love? You really love me?"

He nodded.

"I love you. I've known it for ages. And I think you love

me. I think we could have something wonderful together—if you'd give it a chance. Couldn't you come with me?'' The whispered words were soft and full of agony. "We could get married right away.''

"Chris, I have a contract with this town that I won't renege on. My father is here and he needs the routine of seeing *me,* his one familiar face, every day.'' She sighed miserably, knowing that wasn't the only reason as the ugly thought of fear outside of this protected oasis gripped her. She could deal with life here.

Grimly she continued. "Besides, I love this town. I've always wanted to raise a family here. I want to savor each moment of my days with people I like and respect. I guess that's the way God made me. This is the place He keeps bringing me back to.''

She stood before him and spoke the words as she watched his face tighten with that mask he so often hid behind.

"I've never pretended that I'm the big-city, sophisticated type. That's not me. I'm small-town, old-fashioned.'' She drew in a deep breath and continued in a whoosh of excuses.

"Besides all that, I don't think I could live your kind of life. The reason I know that is because for a period of my life, I pretended that I fit in, that I had something in common with people I neither knew nor cared about. And I paid the price for it.'' Jori cleared the tears from her voice and appealed to Chris to understand. "But even if I *could* get past all that and leave my past behind, I still am not free to move.''

"Jori, I can't live here. I'm a surgeon. Boston is where I live, where I work.''

"I know,'' she agreed sadly.

He peered up at her in disbelief, a pained smile tugging at his lips. "It's ironic really. I've always thought I was the type who couldn't be part of a family. But now, here, these past few weeks with you, I'm beginning to believe you and I could

have the one thing that's always been beyond my reach—
love, Jori. Real love. The kind that builds families.''

Jori stood staring at him, silently begging God for help.

"Say something. Doesn't it mean anything, that I want you
to come with me? That I love you. Or are you too afraid?''
he demanded, eyes widening in his intensity. "Too scared to
leave your safe, cozy little town and take a chance on life in
the real world?'' He was angry now.

"You'd better decide, Jori. Are you willing to throw away
everything we could have together just because you're
afraid?''

"I can't leave here, Chris. Not now, anyway.'' She hated
saying it, but there was no other way out, no matter how badly
she wanted one. "I'm sorry. I've prayed and prayed but I just
don't see a solution. We each have our own paths to travel.''

"But I'm in love with you! I want us to have a future. But
not if you can't meet me at least halfway.'' His hands fell to
his sides. "I can deal with a lot of things, Jori. But I can't
handle that. You're the only one who can find enough strength
to let go of the past and embrace the future. I can't do it for
you.''

Jori felt his words hit her like nails. She was trying! But
he was asking her to give up everything!

"But Mossbank is my home,'' she muttered. "These are
my friends. I'm…''

"Safe here,'' he concluded for her flatly. "You don't have
to extend yourself one bit more than you want to. You can
sit and wallow in the past as long as you want and no one
will force you to see that life is passing by without you.'' His
face was white as he gazed down at her.

"We could be there for one another to support and encourage when we needed it,'' he continued. "We could move
ahead with our lives, be somebodies, go somewhere.'' His

voice dropped. "We could have it all. But you have to let go of the past, of the fear that I'll hurt you like he did."

She was shaking, Jori realized. His words and the pictures they'd painted made her long for such a life. But it was impossible. She couldn't give up her father, her town, her friends. Her security, a tiny voice whispered.

"What about my dad? And what do you give up?" she demanded at last, unable to stem the doubts and fears. "Even supposing I could get out of this contract and didn't have to worry about my father, you're still doing your parents' bidding. You're following their plan for your life. What is it that you want, Chris?"

He stood staring down at her for several long minutes. "You," he whispered finally. "And you know your father's not a problem. We can take him with us. But you won't even consider it."

"I'm sorry," she said. "So sorry. But this isn't God's time for us to be together."

"There's a way," he said fiercely, drawing her into his arms. "There is some way for us to be together. I just have to find it. And I will."

Then his lips were on hers and Jori could do nothing but savor his kiss, his tender touch. For tomorrow it would all be gone and she would be alone again.

"You'll move on," she whispered brokenly, trying to hold back the sobs that raged inside. "You'll be a wonderful teacher and your students will take what you know and pass it on to the world." She straightened and pulled away from him, watching his hands fall to his side.

"Go and do the work God's given you, Chris. You'll find someone who isn't afraid to give back your love and you'll be very happy." It hurt to say those words, but Jori knew there was no choice. She had to set him free; make him see that they both had to go on with their lives. Separately.

"I've already found her," he said stubbornly. "The woman I love is you. You just won't accept it."

"I wish I could." It was a prayer from the heart. "But I have to do what I think is right, even if it hurts. And my place is in Mossbank. We both know that you can't run a teaching hospital from here." She swallowed painfully. "Go and live your life, Chris. Be happy."

His fingers had brushed across her cheek, but he shook his head adamantly.

"We will be together," he insisted. "God didn't send me here, introduce me to a wonderful woman who is everything I've ever dreamed of, and let me see what my life could be like with her, just to snatch it all away. I'm going to believe that He has more planned for us." He brushed a quick hard kiss on her lips and then strode to the door.

Standing there, framed in her doorway, his blond head gleaming in the sunshine, Jori heard his low voice clearly across the expanse of the room.

"I'll be back, Jordanna Jessop. Somehow, some way, I'll be back. And we will be together. You just have to trust in that. And wait for me."

And with one last look, he left, leaving a finality and silence behind that tore at her heart. Alone. Again.

It hurt, but she had expected that, Jori told herself. And she had to get on with her life. And try to staunch the flow of pain that haunted her at what she'd given up.

"Medical clinic," she answered the phone several weeks later. A long drawn-out pause greeted her words.

Finally a cool, crisp voice inquired, "Is this Jordanna Jessop?"

"Dr. Davis." Her heart sank at the sound of Chris's mother's voice. "How are you?"

"I'm fine, thank you. I'm calling to extend my gratitude

for your hospitality. I neglected to do that and Christopher has remonstrated with me several times.''

"You're welcome," Jori told her, pain clutching at her heart. "H-how is he?"

"Christopher is very well, thank you. He has settled into a term position while another surgeon is on leave. It's just temporary, of course, but I can't tell you how happy they were to have him back."

"Oh." Jori couldn't think of anything else to say.

"He is very pleased to be back with his friends and is quite involved in several new projects." It was obvious that Chris's mother couldn't quite conceal the pride at her son's accomplishments.

"At the present he is negotiating with a team from another hospital to improve the surgical technology currently available there. In Australia, I believe. It's a lucrative position, and his father and I are hoping he will accept it. We're both very grateful for the kindness you extended toward our son."

Jori smiled sadly. Kindness, was that all they had shared? She could read clearly between the lines. Christopher Davis had moved far beyond her reach. He'd clearly put Mossbank and her behind him. Don't expect him back, his mother was saying. He doesn't belong there.

Unable to bear the pain of memory, Jori cut the call short, thanking the woman for her duty call and promising she would look them up if she ever traveled east.

Time dragged on. Months passed. Thanksgiving came and went.

"Good gracious," Glenda exclaimed one frosty December day. "Do you realize there are only tens days till Christmas? I've been putting off my Christmas shopping long enough."

"Maybe it's time for you to get away, Jori, even for a weekend," Dan gently advised her later that afternoon, noting the dark circles under her eyes. "You didn't take holidays this year, Jori. You need a break. Go and enjoy yourself for a change. Take Friday off.''

Jori nodded her agreement. She took the day off and drove to the city to do some shopping, hoping to drown herself in the business of the holiday. But the busy mothers directing children through lines to see Santa ate at her like acid, and she turned away, unwilling to watch it any longer.

Listlessly, she drove to the old stone church her father had loved and sank into the worn pew as the famous choir began its yearly rendition of Handel's *Messiah*. The joyous message of peace and mercy swelled out, filling the arched building and resounding back to those in the audience. As one, they surged to their feet to the resounding ''Hallelujah'' chorus.

The wonderful old songs of joy filled her heart as she sang with all the others gathered for the festive celebration. Although there was no one she knew in the crowd, Jori felt her frozen heart melt with the joy of the season. And when several people wished her a merry Christmas, she cheerily did the same.

It wasn't strange or unusual. No one was unfriendly. In fact, she decided, gazing around, there was the same sense of community here that she'd always found in the church at Mossbank. She watched as the little old lady in front of her wrapped her arm through the elderly gentleman beside her. They exchanged a tender smile that tugged at Jori's heartstrings.

Was this what Chris had meant? she asked herself. That wherever they went, they would have each other. That other people and places could be home as long as Chris was there?

When she finally left, Jori carried away a sense of peace tucked within. She drove through the streets, gazing at the gaily decorated homes as a new emotion gripped her. It wasn't fear. It was longing; aching covetousness for a home with Chris and their family.

You'd have to move, her mind whispered.

"You wouldn't be moving away. These people will still be our friends. You'd be moving on *to* something."

Jori felt the aloneness close in on her when she steered back onto the highway. Tears coursed down her cheeks as the pain tore through her lonely heart. She had thrown away the best thing in her life. Tossed Chris away as if his love didn't matter.

"No more," she sobbed to herself in the darkened vehicle. "I can't live in the past anymore. Help me, Lord," she pleaded.

Perfect love casts out all fear. She heard the words through a fog of misery. Her father had said them many times; times when she had been so confused, afraid to venture out into the unknown. *Nothing is as bad as knowing you could have changed things and didn't.*

Her father had been right on the money. If she really and truly loved Chris and wanted to be with him, fear could have no part in it. She had to let him know that place or conditions didn't matter. She loved him; that's all that counted.

The next day she sat at home, wrapping the gift she had purchased for Chris. Jori brushed a finger over the leather-bound volume, a first issue of a Robert Louis Stevenson classic. Dated in the late 1800s, Jori had found it in a dingy bookstore. She remembered Chris's whispered admission from what seemed long ago.

"We never got to read fairy tales when I was a child," he had told her once.

She wanted to remind him to take the time. She wanted him to read them to his own son. She wanted to share those moments, to watch as he took the time his own parents never had. And when he did, Jori wanted to be there.

She wavered back and forth all day, but finally made her decision.

"Dan, it's Jori. I need to ask you something." She waited a few moments and then blurted out her request. "Can I have next week off?"

"What? Why?" he demanded brusquely.

"There's something I need to do," she told him. "Someone I have to see." She waited, tensing as the silence stretched tautly between them.

"I'm sorry, Jori. Glenda has already asked for extra time off. Erma Stant will fill in for a bit but I can't really spare you. How about the week after New Year's? Would that suit you?"

"Are you sure?"

"I'm sorry, Jori. I just can't do it. Where were you going, anyway?"

"I'm not sure. Boston, I think. Maybe Australia." She refused to say any more and thankfully Dan didn't question her any further. "I guess I'll just have to work something else out," she muttered, deflated now that she had finally made the decision to go.

"See you tomorrow," he replied. Jori frowned at the sound of it. Why did he have to sound so darn happy about it?

She sat in her lonely living room, thinking everything out. The house was terribly quiet, the fire flickering softly in the fireplace and Flop snoring at her feet when the telephone rang. She picked it up absently, wondering who could be calling now.

"J.J.?" His voice sounded so dear, Jori's throat clogged up with joy. "Jori, are you there?"

"Y-y-yes," she whispered. "I'm here, Chris."

She heard his sigh, a whoosh of breath over the telephone line.

"How are you?" she asked softly, aching to hear the sound of his voice. "Where are you?"

"In New York. I'm at a conference. I'm presenting a paper." His words were clipped and short. "Jori, I don't want to talk about work. I want to talk about you. I need to know something, J.J."

His voice dropped to a whisper and she just caught the hint of unsureness in it. "I love you, Jori. It's not a temporary thing. It's not going to go away. You're buried deep in my heart." His voice stabbed pricks of pain at her heart while a swelling gladness filled her eyes with tears.

"I keep seeing your face when I go to work, your smile when my patient makes it. I went to church the other day and someone sang. They weren't half as good as you."

"I miss you, too," she whispered, half afraid to say so but overwhelmingly glad that she had when she heard his shout of joy.

"That's what I was waiting for," he bellowed.

"Chris? Are you okay?" She studied the receiver worriedly, wondering if everything was going as well as his mother had said.

"Tell me the truth, J.J. Do you love me?"

Jori could see his face in her mind's eye—his eyes sparkling with mischief, his mouth tilted up, his hair mussed, giving him that little boy look that tugged at her heartstrings.

"We've been all through this," she began.

"No, we haven't. I know all the problems. Believe me, I know!" Chris groaned, but there was a tingle of excitement in his tone that caused shivers to race up and down her arm. "Just answer the question, okay, sweetheart?"

"But..."

"Please?"

She couldn't deny that soft, cajoling dear voice any longer. On a sob of relief, she told him what was in her heart.

"Yes! I love you so much that I cry myself to sleep at night. And then I dream of you, and when I wake up I'm lonelier than ever."

There was a long space of silence before he rushed into speech. "J.J., if I can find a way for us to be together, will you marry me?"

The question stunned her and she stared at the black instrument for a moment, wondering if she had made it up in her mind.

"Jordanna? Will you?" The sureness had dropped away now. She could hear the apprehension filling that smooth low tone.

"But, Chris, how?"

"Jordanna, I've been searching for you my whole life and I'm not going to accept that God dangled you in front of me, just to show me what I was missing. No, there's got to be a way. But I have to know that you feel the same way."

"Yes, Chris," she whispered, brushing tears away and straightening her shoulders. He was worth it, she told herself. Chris wasn't Trace; he wouldn't leave her in the lurch. "I love you," she told him plainly. "I would gladly marry you tomorrow if we could get something worked out." Silence dragged out between them until she heard the hiss of his breath against her ear. "I was coming to Boston to tell you that."

"I wish I was there." His voice was soft. "I'd hold you in my arms and never let you go."

Jori got lost in that vision and found herself abruptly jerked back to reality when his disgruntled voice chided her. "Jordanna! Are you listening?"

"Um, yes, I'm here." Her voice was dreamy. She tried to pay attention to what he was saying.

"Then listen. This is going to work out for us. I'm not letting you go. There's a way for us to have our dreams and I'm going to find it, so you'd better be ready, lady. Because when I do figure it all out, I'm coming for you and we're going to be married faster than you can say, 'Dr. and Mrs. Christopher Davis.'''

Jori tried to interrupt but he wouldn't let her.

"Never mind how or when. I don't know that yet." His voice was filled with jubilation. "But I'm going to knock on heaven's door until I get my answer. You get your wedding dress ordered and do whatever else needs doing, because when I come for you, I'm not waiting one day longer than necessary. It might take me days or weeks or months, but we are going to be together, Jordanna Jessop. And don't you forget it."

Jori heard his words through a fog in her mind as happiness washed everything else away. She couldn't have misunderstood him; there was no doubt in Chris's voice.

"I'm giving it over to God, J.J. And you do the same. We can come through this."

"I know we can," she whispered, taking the first tiny step of faith toward him. "And when I get this contract finished, I'll live wherever you want, Chris. I can come back and visit with Dad and Mossbank will always be here." She swallowed hard, ignoring the warning voices in her head, trusting in the love that filled her heart. "I want to marry you, Dr. Davis. As soon as you can work it out."

"Thank you." His voice was barely audible above the clapping sound she could hear in the background, but the joy and relief in it couldn't be mistaken.

"Oh, no! It's my turn. I have to give my speech now! How am I going to talk about suctioning and sutures when all I can think about is you?" he complained with a laugh.

"You can do it," she told him, a sureness ringing through her voice. "You can give the best speech ever. Because when it's over, your mind will be free to start tackling our problem. I'll be thinking about you, Chris. And wishing you were here with me. Goodbye, my love.'' And gently, carefully, she hung up the phone.

"I will not be afraid," she whispered to herself with resolution. "I will trust in the Lord for His perfect timing and I will wait."

As she turned away, Jori caught a glimpse of herself in the mirror and tried to imagine what she'd look like in a wedding dress and veil.

"Please, God," she prayed softly, "let it be soon."

Chapter Thirteen

Jordanna Jessop was ready. She had her wedding dress; it hung in her father's bedroom, covered by a sheet, waiting for "that" day. She'd been given bridal showers by three local groups and the gifts sat in the basement, waiting for their new home. She'd chosen her bridesmaid, flowers, even the invitations. But although she had spoken to Chris almost every night on the phone, by March she still had no bridegroom and no wedding date.

"He'll be here, dearie." Faith breezed into the office with a smile. "The Lord works in mysterious ways, His wonders to perform."

"Uh, thank you." Jori stared at the woman assessingly. There was something different about her today. A light, she decided. Some inner joy that made her glow beautifully.

"You seem especially happy today, Mrs. Johnson. Is something special happening?"

"Just the spring," Hope Conroy interrupted, stepping into the waiting room with careful regard for the mud on her feet. "She always gets like this in the spring."

"In the spring a young girl's fancy turns to love," Faith misquoted, winking at Jori.

"Did you want to see Dr. Green or Dr. Dan today?" Jori decided to focus on her job. These days it was all that kept her sane.

"Oh, we're waiting for Charity," Faith informed her with a grin. "Then we're all going in together."

"Together? The three of you?" When Hope nodded her agreement, Jori shrugged and made a notation on the book before taking another stack of files from Dan's basket. By the time she returned, the three ladies had disappeared.

It was a relatively slow day so Jori began typing out the forms that lay waiting and tried not to think of Chris's phone call last night. He'd seemed distant, preoccupied. And when she'd pressed him about his location, he'd been vague.

"I'm hopping around a lot," he'd said. "Trying to get things organized. I'm hoping I can be with you soon."

Soon. It was an old line, and frankly Jori was growing tired of it. She'd managed to get through Christmas by spending time with her dad and having a long phone conversation with Chris. He'd spent all of January traveling with a group of medical men in Australia, which seemed hardly fair considering the winter she'd suffered through in Mossbank.

In February, Chris had suddenly decided to update himself on some medical thing that was happening in England and so she hadn't been able to write to him there, either. He wasn't going to be in one place, he said. Moving around a lot.

There had been flowers, lots of them, for Valentine's Day. And a monstrous box of Parisian chocolates that Jori dared not eat in case he came back and she didn't fit her dress. He'd even sent her a necklace, which was wonderful, and she'd thanked him for it. But she would rather have had him.

"If you'd tell me where you'll be, I could arrange to take

my holidays there," she had murmured sadly. "At least we could be together for a while. I miss you."

"Oh, Jori! You know I want to be there more than anything. And I will be. I think things are finally beginning to move forward."

But when she'd pressed him on how forward, he'd changed the subject.

"Just be patient. I am coming. Probably sooner than you expect."

"It couldn't be soon enough for me," she told him, stifling the sobs that tried to break through her iron control. "We can go anywhere, Chris. As soon as I'm finished here in September, I intend to find you. And you're not putting me off."

"I wouldn't dream of it!" He'd sounded amused, and Jori had petulantly said goodbye, wondering if he'd changed his mind about wanting her. It was the end of March, for goodness' sake, and nothing, to her knowledge, had changed.

"You can go home early today, Jori," Dan offered, emerging from a consulting room with a grin. "And I'm officially giving you next week off. You need a break."

"No, I don't," Jori protested, frustrated by everyone's good intent. She was alone, she wanted to be with Chris and she needed to keep busy. "I'll want extra time off when Chris comes, so I need to pile up the hours now."

"Well, you're piling up too many hours," Dan informed her sternly. "I know all about the extra shifts you've been putting in at the nursing home. But they won't be calling you this weekend. I've told them that you're to be off for a week." He smiled sadly. "Look at you, kiddo. You're skin and bones. Go home, have a bubble bath and order in some Chinese food. Relax and get some color back into those cheeks. And that's an order. Now, get out of here."

"Yes, sir, Doctor," she muttered gloomily, and shut down the computer dutifully.

"No, leave the filing. I want you to go home and relax. Understand? Liza can't use a baby-sitter who's burned out, you know."

"I'm going, I'm going," Jori muttered, grabbing her purse and heading out the door. "Boy, you've gotten really bossy lately. Must be fatherhood."

"You'll know all about it some day," Dan told her seriously. "Now, get going. And remember, go straight home."

"Yeah, okay." But as she headed down the street, Jori changed her mind and headed for the nursing home to see her father. Maybe he, at least, was having a good day.

James wasn't in his room so she checked in at the nursing station.

"I'm looking for my father," she said clearly. "James Jessop. Can you tell me where he is?"

"He was with the doctor a moment ago. In the television room, I think." The harried nurse turned away to remonstrate with a candy striper who had just knocked some medications on the floor.

"Okay, thanks." Jori strode down the hall, pleased to see her father standing by the window. "Hi, Dad!" She stood on tiptoe and pressed a kiss to his cheek. "What have you been up to?"

"I haven't been up to anything. I don't know why you say that." James looked in a bad humor and Jori took a deep breath for patience.

"I just meant, what have you been doing. The nurse said the doctor was here." She frowned. "I didn't see Dr. Green leave."

"Doctor? What doctor? Do you see any doctor? I was talking to a young fellow—what was his name?" He frowned, slapping his forehead with one hand. "Drat this memory."

"It's all right," she murmured hastily, and then stopped as James walked down the hall. "Where are you going?"

"It's supper time," he told her absently. "They always eat so early in this place. I get hungry at night." He kept going, walking down the hall, muttering to himself.

With a shrug and a deprecatory smile, Jori left the residence and moved toward home. It was a bad day when not even James wanted to talk to her!

She was almost through her front gate when a shrill, persistent voice stopped her.

"Jordanna!" Charity Bellows stood on the front steps of Hope Conroy's house, her face flushed and arms waving.

"Oh, good. I caught you." She scurried over and moments later had her hand on Jori's arm. "I've goofed, I'm afraid. Or rather, Faith has. She thought today was her turn to cook and she's made the most wonderful supper for my birthday."

"Oh, happy birthday," Jori said in confusion.

"Well, thank you, dear. But you see, the thing is, Frank is taking us all out for dinner and we have this food just waiting to be eaten. Might I bring some of it over for you? You've been working so hard lately and I'm sure you could use a good, hot meal."

"That would be very nice. Thank you, Charity."

"Oh, it's my pleasure, dear." She patted Jori's shoulder tenderly. "I know how awful it's been for you. All this dreadful waiting. It's a little bit like in the Bible, isn't it?"

"I'm sorry. I don't know what you mean." Jori frowned, trying to organize her thoughts.

"Yes, you do." Charity chuckled. "Where it talks about Jesus as the bridegroom coming back for us, his bride, and says that we don't know the day or the hour, but we must be ready at any time. That's just like you and Dr. Davis. It's so romantic."

"Isn't it, though?" Jori muttered dourly. "I'd appreciate anything you want to bring over, Charity. And thank you for thinking of me. I'm going to have a long soak in the tub, so just feel free to walk in and leave whatever you want in the kitchen. And thank you. Thanks a lot.''

"You're welcome. I know it's hard," she whispered. "Please don't give up on him. Not yet." Then she turned and walked back to Hope's house.

"I won't," Jori murmured a long time later, drying herself off. "But it's getting so hard to keep believing. Help me, Father."

Jori pulled on a pale peach velour suit that was supposed to be part of her trousseau and started down the stairs, thinking of her dinner. Halfway down, the scent of flowers caught her nostrils and she glanced around, amazed to see huge vases of lilacs and lilies and pansies and daisies scattered around the room. And there, standing in the middle, holding the biggest bouquet of long-stemmed red roses was Christopher Davis.

"Hello, J.J."

She stared at that dear face, soaking in every detail of it, from his blazing blue eyes to his dazzling white smile.

"Don't you remember who I am?" he asked quizzically.

With a shriek of delight, Jori bounded down the stairs and across the room, throwing herself into his arms and hanging on for dear life. She sighed with delight as Chris's strong arms tightened around her and his mouth closed firmly over hers.

"I can't wait anymore," he breathed before his lips touched hers.

Jori knew exactly what he meant. She kissed him back with all the longing she had kept bottled inside for the past months.

"I love you, Jordanna Jessop," he said, his big hands tightening around her tenderly. "I've missed you so much." One hand slipped through the silken length of her hair as he kissed her again and again.

Jori stroked her fingers over his golden head and tanned

face. Nothing seemed real, but if this was a dream, Jori was determined to enjoy it and let time stand still.

"Chris," she murmured, staring into his sleepy blue gaze. "Where did all these flowers come from?"

"I brought them. For you." Chris stared straight into her eyes as he spoke. One hand pressed a small package into her hand.

"So is this."

Jori stared at the package nestled in her hands and carefully opened the black velvet box. Glittering brightly, a wide gold band waited inside. It was a perfect match for the engagement ring Chris had sent her for Christmas.

Chris pulled it free and held it up for her to see. His blue eyes stared solemnly into hers. "I'm not waiting any longer, J.J.," he said firmly. "I want us to get married. Right away. I love you," he told her steadily. "Please, say you'll marry me?"

"I—I..."

"Do you love me, Jori?"

Jori nodded. "Oh, yes. I love you more than anything, Christopher Davis. More than I thought I could ever love anyone."

He grinned that silly grin she had come to love.

"Then, darling Jori, does it really matter where we live as long as we're together? Isn't that the important thing?"

"Yes, darling," she told him firmly. "It doesn't matter where we live as long as we are together."

And as she wrapped her arms around his neck and returned his embrace, Jori vowed that she would never let anything come between them again.

As she pressed closer to him, she heard the crackle of papers against her ear.

"What *is* that?" she demanded curiously, thrusting her fingers into his jacket pocket. An envelope with Dan's office letterhead lay there and Jori stared at it curiously.

"Oh, that," Chris murmured, tightening his arms around her. "Well, that envelope contains our future, my love." He had a smug, self-satisfied look on his face that Jori didn't understand.

"Go ahead, read it, my darling," he urged, as he sat down on the sofa. "Read it."

Jori pulled out the single sheet of letterhead and attempted to decipher the legalese covering it. She could make out Chris's name at the top, the word *partner,* and Dan's signature below. Hope billowed in her like a sail catching a morning breeze.

"Chris?" she whispered, half afraid to believe.

He puffed out his chest before swinging her up in his arms and dancing around the room.

"You are looking at the newest partner of the Community Health Clinic located in Mossbank, North Dakota," he told her triumphantly. "I'm buying out Dr. Green's interest."

"But I thought…your mother said…Dr. Green is…" Jori stumbled over all the questions running through her mind. She was afraid to believe her fantasy had come true.

"Yes," he muttered, "my mother." He tipped her chin, blue eyes meeting her soft brown ones. "My mother was wrong about a lot of things. But especially about Mossbank and my future. It's here, with you."

His kiss made Jori forget the questions that seemed so important. Nothing was more significant than the fact that Chris was here, holding her. She did allow one tiny doubt to surface.

"Are you sure this is what you should do?" Jori peered at him anxiously.

"Sweetheart, I've spent years doing what was expected of me. My parents wanted me to go to medical school. I went. They wanted me to choose a specialty. I did. They wanted me to work in Boston and I did that, too, hoping it would satisfy that need I had inside for their love, their approval. But while I was here, I realized that my parents' dreams aren't mine. They never were.''

He kissed her nose and leaned back tiredly.

''I was wrong to let them superimpose their belief system on mine. I thought going back and teaching was what I wanted, but it was just another case of accepting other people's opinions over my own instinct.'' He glanced down tenderly, his hands closing around hers as one finger played with the brilliant solitaire on her left hand.

''By December, I realized that what I wanted was you and what I had right here. But I didn't know how to get it. Those months I spent here were the most satisfying medical moments I've experienced in a long time. I felt like I mattered and I knew that I wanted to keep you in my life. I just didn't know how God was going to work it all out. Now I know. And, yes, I'm sure.

''So, what do you say about marrying me tomorrow?'' he offered.

''I just happen to have a week off,'' she murmured. ''Thanks to Dan.'' She eyed Chris severely, a gleam of suspicion lighting the brown depths.

''Wait a minute,'' she demanded. ''Do you mean to tell me Dan was in on this?'' She was furious at the agony she had been through while her boss had known all along. Her fiancé nodded.

''You mean I sat here, alone, wishing, when he knew all along...'' Jori slapped at his shoulder in frustration.

''Don't be angry at Dan,'' he pleaded with her. ''It took me a while to realize what I had left behind.'' His hands tightened around her, hugging her close. ''When I did, I wanted to tell you myself. And then, of course, the ladies helped, too.''

"What ladies?" she asked.

"Faith, Hope and Charity, of course. They remembered Dr. Green talking about retiring and when they questioned him, found that he hadn't because he'd never been able to find anyone to move here. He didn't want the townsfolk to suffer." Chris beamed at her. "When I phoned him and made an offer, he jumped at it like a trout after bait. Seems his wife wants him to travel and he's pretty keen on the idea himself."

"The Lord works in mysterious ways," Jori murmured, trying to understand it all, but losing the battle when Chris hugged her close.

"Amen," he murmured into her ear.

"Something's burning," she murmured at last, and whisked out of his arms to retrieve a smoking loaf of garlic bread from out of the oven. Fortunately, only the paper had been singed.

As she turned, Jori caught sight of a small hand-painted card on the counter.

"Chris, come and look at this," she called, and found him right behind her, his arms slipping around her waist.

"*They that wait upon the Lord shall renew their faith. Teach me Lord to wait.*' We think you've waited long enough."

"It's signed Faith and Arthur Johnson, Hope and Harry Conroy, Charity and Frank Bellows."

"Angels of mercy," Chris agreed.

Epilogue

Jori panted through the tail end of the contraction and flopped back against her pillows tiredly.

"That's it," she huffed. "I can't do any more."

"Jordanna Jessop Davis! You've been bugging me about babies for as long as I can remember. And now that you're finally going to get your own, you're wimping out? I don't believe it." Daniel Gordon's stern look flashed above the white surgical mask. "Quitter!"

"Dan!" Chris's blue eyes were hard and cold. "Leave her alone. If she wants to stop—"

"Are you nuts?" Jori snorted at her husband in disgust. "There's no way I'm stopping this. Ooooh! Here comes another one." She grabbed his hand in her viselike grip and leaned forward, pushing with all her might.

"Push!" Dan ordered.

"I am pushing," she hissed through gritted teeth.

"Here comes another one. Push."

And so, summoning the last ounce of her strength from someplace deep within, Jori pushed with all her might.

"Congratulations! The Davis family now includes a son."

Ignoring the squalling cry, Dan lifted the red-faced infant and placed him on his mother's chest. "Well done, Jori."

"A son, Chris! We have a son." Jori beamed up at her husband, towering above them. "He looks a lot like you."

"A boy." Christopher studied the baby, noting the perfect fingers and toes and the thatch of flaxen blond hair. He touched the tiny face carefully before patting his wife's shoulder awkwardly. His eyes were dazed as he gaped stupidly at Dan. "I'm a father."

"Yeah, pal, I know." Dan slapped him on the back, grinning like crazy. "Don't you have somebody to talk to now?" At Chris's puzzled look, he jerked a thumb toward the hallway. "Three nosy old ladies and a grandfather."

"Oh, James. Right." Chris leaned down and kissed his tired wife on the lips. "I'm going to tell your father, Jori. I'll be right back."

"Give her a bit of time to rest and get cleaned up," Dan advised softly. "You can stop by later."

It wasn't much later when Chris returned to his wife's hospital room. She was sleeping but woke immediately, glancing at the bouquet in his hands.

"Oh. Thank you," she murmured as she took the flowers from him.

"You don't like them?"

"Of course I like them. They're beautiful," she whispered, accepting his kiss. She hung on when he would have moved away. "I just somehow thought you'd bring roses."

"Roses?" He sounded scandalized. "You can have roses any day of the week, my darling. These are chrysanthe*mums* for a mom—the mother of my son!" He stood proudly before her, his eyes glowing with love.

A beautiful smile lit up Jori's face as she laid the bouquet of flowers on the side of the bed and wrapped both arms around his neck, tugging his mouth nearer hers.

"Quite right, my dear husband. After all, how often does one get to be a mother?"

"I don't know." He grinned, brushing his lips against hers while his fingers tangled in her hair. "But I'm willing to discuss it again whenever you wish."

Faith, Hope and Charity stood for a moment in front of the nursery, gazing at the lone occupant who slept happily unaware.

"This was by far the hardest case of all," Faith murmured, making silly faces into the glass.

"It took some special doing," Hope agreed, allowing her mouth to curve in a tiny cooing noise.

"That's the truth," Charity whispered, pointing toward the baby. "Sent right from heaven." She glanced at the two elderly ladies making foolish, nonsensical gestures at the sleeping child. "But for once I agree wholeheartedly with James."

"What did he say?" Faith demanded, knocking gently on the glass.

"Love bears all things, believes all things, hopes all things, endures all things. Love never fails." Charity quoted the verse with a smile and threaded her arms through each of the other's.

"Come on girls, let's go home. We've done our job here."

And they toddled off into the night, content with all life offered.

* * * * *

Dear Reader,

Isn't it hard to wait? I'm one of those people who shake Christmas gifts as soon as they arrive, trying to figure out what's inside. I detest long lines and delays in traffic because I want to get on with things. And I simply cannot understand people who dillydally, dithering between one choice or another. For me, the choice is quickly made. Did I mention I often make the *wrong* choice?

Perhaps that's why I empathize with Jori. She's so sure she's made the right decision. She's got things organized, her life is going along as it should, and she's ready for the next step—a baby. The trouble is, God seems to see things differently. And when God says "wait," no matter how hard we try to get around it, we have to wait until finally, His perfect will becomes clear to us mere mortals.

The Bible says that those who wait on God will renew their strength. And it further asks God to "teach" us to wait. You know, that's my prayer, too. But I hope He hurries!

I wish you persistent patience in knowing His will.

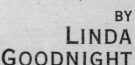

A SEASON FOR GRACE

BY

LINDA GOODNIGHT

THE BROTHERS' BOND

**Separated as children...
reunited as men.**

Police officer and former
foster child Collin Grace
wasn't fond of social
workers, even pretty ones
like Mia Carano. But Mia
knew he was the perfect
mentor for a runaway in
her care—and she wouldn't
stop until she unearthed
the caring man under
Collin's gruff exterior.

Steeple
Hill®

*Available December 2006,
wherever you buy books.*

Love Inspired®

LOVE WALKED IN

BY

MERRILLEE WHREN

Getting close to new
neighbor Clay Reynolds
was not a consideration
for single mom
Beth Carlson. She had
no time for romance.
Clay was good to her
son—and to her—but
she could never give her
heart to a motorcycle-
riding man again.
Or could she?

*Available December 2006,
wherever you buy books.*

Steeple
Hill®

REQUEST YOUR FREE BOOKS!

2 FREE INSPIRATIONAL NOVELS
PLUS 2
FREE
MYSTERY GIFTS

Love Inspired.

YES! Please send me 2 FREE Love Inspired® novels and my 2 FREE mystery gifts. After receiving them, if I don't wish to receive any more books, I can return the shipping statement marked "cancel." If I don't cancel, I will receive 4 brand-new novels every month and be billed just $3.99 per book in the U.S., or $4.74 per book in Canada, plus 25¢ shipping and handling per book and applicable taxes, if any*. That's a savings of at least 20% off the cover price! I understand that accepting the 2 free books and gifts places me under no obligation to buy anything. I can always return a shipment and cancel at any time. Even if I never buy another book from Steeple Hill, the two free books and gifts are mine to keep forever.

113 IDN EF26   313 IDN EF27

Name	(PLEASE PRINT)
Address	Apt.
City	State/Prov.	Zip/Postal Code

Signature (if under 18, a parent or guardian must sign)

Order online at www.LoveInspiredBooks.com

Or mail to Steeple Hill Reader Service™:

IN U.S.A.	IN CANADA
P.O. Box 1867	P.O. Box 609
Buffalo, NY	Fort Erie, Ontario
14240-1867	L2A 5X3

Not valid to current Love Inspired subscribers.

Want to try two free books from another series?
Call 1-800-873-8635 or visit www.morefreebooks.com

* Terms and prices subject to change without notice. NY residents add applicable sales tax. Canadian residents will be charged applicable provincial taxes and GST. This offer is limited to one order per household. All orders subject to approval. Credit or debit balances in a customer's account(s) may be offset by any other outstanding balance owed by or to the customer. Please allow 4 to 6 weeks for delivery.

LIREG06

Love Inspired.
CLASSICS

TITLES AVAILABLE NEXT MONTH

Don't miss these stories in December

AN ANGEL FOR DRY CREEK
AND
A GENTLEMAN FOR DRY CREEK
by Janet Tronstad

Two couples find love
in the snowy Montana town of Dry Creek.

HER KIND OF HERO
AND
SECOND TIME AROUND
by Carol Steward

Under the Colorado sun,
two women find the men of their dreams.